AVENGING
ANGEL

DON'T MISS

The Fallen

ANGEL BETRAYED

ANGEL IN CHAINS

ANGEL OF DARKNESS

NEVER CRY WOLF

IMMORTAL DANGER

MIDNIGHT'S MASTER

MIDNIGHT SINS

And read more from Cynthia Eden in these collections!

HOWL FOR IT

THE NAUGHTY LIST

BELONG TO THE NIGHT

WHEN HE WAS BAD

EVERLASTING BAD BOYS

CYNTHIA EDEN

KENSINGTON PUBLISHING CORP.
www.kensingtonbooks.com

BRAVA BOOKS are published by

Kensington Publishing Corp.
119 West 40th Street
New York, NY 10018

All Kensington titles, imprints, and distributed lines are available at special quantity discounts for bulk purchases for sales promotions, premiums, fund-raising, educational, or institutional use.

Special book excerpts or customized printings can also be created to fit specific needs. For details, write or phone the office of the Kensington special sales manager: Kensington Publishing Corp., 119 West 40th Street, New York, NY 10018, attn: Special Sales Department; phone: 1-800-221-2647.

ISBN-13: 978-0-7582-6765-8
ISBN-10: 0-7582-6765-7

First Kensington Trade Paperback Printing: June 2013

10 9 8 7 6 5 4 3 2

Printed in the United States of America

First Electronic Edition: June 2013

ISBN-13: 978-0-7582-8949-0
ISBN-10: 0-7582-8949-9

Prologue

Marna awoke to pain. Her eyelids flew open as a white-hot fire sent bolts of agony throbbing through her whole body. The fire burned the hottest near her shoulder blades. *Burned.*

She screamed as loud as she could and she jerked, trying to rise and get away from that agony—only to find that she couldn't move.

They'd strapped her onto some kind of table. She was lying facedown, held almost completely immobile by the bonds.

"Easy . . ." A man's slow, drawling voice came from beside her. She saw faded jeans. Tanned hands. Then he bent and brushed back her hair. "You're gonna be all right."

Marna stared into his face—strong, fierce, dangerous—and knew he was lying. A tear leaked from the corner of her eye. She knew his face. Knew him—and knew that he wasn't a man at all. Not really.

Monster.

A beast lived beneath his skin. One that was just dying to break out.

Another stab of pain hit her back, and she flinched at the fresh burn. The monster's face tightened, and he said, "Don't worry. He's almost finished sewing your wounds closed."

Sewing you . . .

She swallowed back the scream. Someone was sewing up her back. Mending flesh that had been sliced open.

Nausea hit her. Fear and fury had her shaking. "My . . . wings . . ." She barely managed to get the words out because her throat was so dry. Parched. Probably from all her screams. But she had to ask about her wings. They were the only things that mattered.

Marna was an angel, and an angel without wings . . .

Hello, hell.

An angel without wings could never return to heaven.

Memories rushed through her mind. She'd had her wings hours before. She'd been doing her duty. Just following orders, until another monster had attacked. Until a bastard had sliced her wings right from her flesh and left her to die in the rotting vegetation of a Louisiana swamp.

The man before her—*no, remember, he's a monster, too, you've seen the panther beneath his skin*—brushed his fingers over her cheek and wiped away her tears. "I'm sorry, but there was nothing we could do."

She bit her lip to hold back any more cries.

A muscle flexed along the hard line of his jaw. "He—he sliced them all the way off. Fuck, he cut into your *bones.*"

There would be no going home for her.

Her eyes closed as hope died. She didn't speak. Couldn't.

Another poke in her back. More fiery pain. She knew what that pain was now. A needle. Thread. Going in and out of her body. Sewing up the gaping holes that had been left behind.

My wings are gone.

For centuries, she'd been an angel. Her job had been to ferry the souls of humans from this world to the next.

She'd never known fear. Anger. Pain.

Those were all human emotions. Angels were far from human. She'd never known—

Not until her wings had been cut away by a panther shifter who feared no one and nothing.

Without the wings, the magic that had kept her immune from human feelings was gone. Wiped away. The emotions hit her now, slamming into her with the force of a speeding train.

Fear.

Rage.

"All done." Another male voice. Had to be the guy with the needle. She opened her eyes, but didn't look his way. She didn't want to see him or see her own blood staining his hands. Marna had turned her head so that her eyes met the monster's green stare.

Such a pity. A monster shouldn't have a face like his. He shouldn't have such deep eyes, eyes that made it look as if he actually cared what happened to her.

"You're gonna be all right," her monster told her. Hadn't he said that before?

Marna managed to slowly shake her head. No, she'd never be all right again.

Then the monster leaned close to her. His breath feathered over her cheek as he promised, "I'll kill him for you."

She wasn't supposed to care about revenge. She hadn't been a punishment angel. Vengeance *shouldn't* have been her calling.

It shouldn't . . .

But she wanted to give pain for pain. Her life was gone, ripped away by a panther shifter's claws. And now another shifter stood in front of her—and offered to destroy for her.

Vengeance *would* come. She'd make sure of it. After all, there wasn't anything else waiting for her now. Not heaven. Not hell. She was *in* hell for an angel.

There was only . . .

Vengeance.

* * *

The delicate angel had broken.

Did she even realize that tears slid down her cheeks? Tanner Chance kept guard by her side. His hand was on her arm, stroking her.

He couldn't seem to stop touching her.

They'd found her body in the swamp. At first, he'd thought that she was already dead.

So much blood.

Then she'd moved, and he'd realized just what his sick freak of a brother had done.

Sliced the wings right off an angel.

Her lashes lifted and her eyes, the palest blue he'd ever seen, locked right on him.

No, those eyes seemed to see right *through* him. Tanner cleared his throat. He was a cop. He'd spent too many years seeing blank expressions like that on the faces of victims.

"You . . . you're safe now." He'd keep her safe. "You just need to rest."

She didn't speak. He didn't know what else he was supposed to say to her. He never knew what to say to the victims. He just knew how to make the bastards who hurt them pay.

He was very good at delivering justice. But this time . . .

An angel.

She had to hate him. She knew who he was. Knew that his brother was the fucked-up asshole who'd tortured her. Tanner cleared his throat and had to say, "I'm not like him."

Her eyes never left his.

And he was still touching her. Her skin was the softest he'd ever felt. The smoothest. Her flesh was golden and perfect.

Or, it had been, until claws had ripped into her back and torn that flesh wide open.

Her breath exhaled softly. "When I'm stronger . . ."

Tanner leaned closer because he could barely hear her words. "What is it? What do you need?" *Anything.* He'd do—

"When I'm stronger, you should . . . stay away from me."

He glanced at her small hands. They'd had to bind her wrists when they strapped her down. Not to hurt her, but to keep the little blond angel from hurting *them.*

The angel before him—*Marna*—she wasn't some sweet and gentle guardian angel.

She was an angel of death. One who could, and *had,* killed with just a touch.

He could touch her all that he wanted. That was the way the game worked with angels. But the instant her hand touched him . . .

Dead.

If she wanted him dead, all she had to do was touch him, and she could send him straight to hell.

She smiled at him. The smile made her seem even lovelier, and then the angel said, "When I'm stronger, when I'm free . . . get as far away from me as you can." The faintest of pauses, then, "Because I'll have my vengeance."

She didn't look so broken anymore.

"Remember . . . to run, shifter."

He didn't move, and he damn well kept touching her. "I'm not the running kind." Not anymore. The scared kid he'd been had died long ago. Now he fought any bastard who came his way, and he made sure to win his battles.

His angel kept her cold smile and told him, "Wait and see. . . . You will be. . . ."

Chapter One

Two months later

A girl knew when she was being stalked.

Marna didn't glance over her shoulder as she made her way through the bar. What would have been the point? She felt his eyes on her. *Knew* he was there.

Sometimes, it seemed that he was always there.

Bodies brushed against her as she wound through the crowd. Marna didn't recoil as she'd done when she first lost her wings. She'd grown used to the touches over the last few weeks.

Music blasted out in a steady beat from the speakers that hung near the ceiling. The place was packed, filled with men and women drunk on a powerful combination of alcohol and lust. The too-loud club shouldn't have been her kind of place.

It was.

She made it to the bar and lightly tapped her fingers against the glass counter. Then she let her gaze lift to the mirror that waited behind that bar.

In that shining surface, she saw him perfectly.

Tall, strong, with wide shoulders and muscled arms, her watcher easily cleared a path through the dancers. Maybe it was the harsh intensity of his face that made folks step back.

The man stalking so purposefully toward her wasn't handsome, not really. His features were too hard, too stark.

But . . .

But there was something about the high arch of his cheeks, the square cut of his jaw and the sensual curve of his lips. With that thick mass of dark hair that skimmed his shoulders, Marna supposed that some human women might find him attractive. Even sexy. Humans always seemed to think the dangerous ones were sexy.

Good thing she wasn't human.

His eyes, dark green and burning with a quiet fury, were on hers in that mirror. She almost smiled at him. Instead, she lifted her drink and sipped it lightly.

What did the big, bad shifter want now? She'd tried to play it nice. She'd told him to stay away. She'd given the guy fair warning, but . . .

"What in the hell have you done?"

Tanner Chance closed in on her. His voice had been pitched low, so that only she could hear him, and the guy's body curved around hers.

He didn't touch her, not yet, but only a few inches separated them.

She turned her head and felt the whisper of his breath on her cheek. For some reason, Marna shivered.

"You didn't have to do it," he gritted and, oh, yes, that was most definitely fury burning in his gaze. He'd better be careful. Too much fury wasn't good for the beast that he carried inside. "You could have just lived your life. Could have just gone on—"

A laugh slipped from her, but the sound was bitter. "What life?" Her life had been clawed away from her. There was no heaven for her, not anymore. Just hell on earth. Feelings, emotions, needs—they seemed to constantly swamp her now, and they were driving her *crazy.*

No one had warned her about the hungers . . . for food, drink . . . pleasure.

Men.

Without the magic from her wings, every human need and emotion slammed into her, and each day, Marna felt she was losing a bit more of herself.

And I used to wonder what it would be like to be human.

What she wouldn't give to be ignorant again. To just . . . *not know.*

He leaned in closer to her. Still not touching, but every part of her was hyper aware of him.

"Others know what you did," Tanner said.

Marna blinked, lost. "Uh, good?" Because she didn't know. Had no clue what the guy was rambling about now. But . . . he smelled good. Not like the others in that place. He didn't reek of stale beer or too much cheap cologne. He smelled—

"They know you killed those men."

Whoa. Back up. She hadn't killed anyone.

His eyes narrowed, the faint lines tightening on his face. "You left their bodies in the alley. What did you think would happen? That no one would find out what you were doing?"

Another laugh came from her as she turned away. "I have no idea what you're—"

His fingers closed around her shoulder.

Marna stilled. "You know better." He did. The guy had a pretty thorough knowledge of angels, so he understood just how dangerous her kind could be. She'd gone out of her way to warn Tanner off. Seeing him reminded her too much of what she'd lost. Because of—

"Why am I still breathing?" His other hand rose and pulled her off the bar stool and up against him. "If you want me dead, then why am I still standing?"

His body was so hot and hard against hers. Her heartbeat

kicked faster in her chest. She had to tilt her head back to look up at him because the guy was really just huge. His hands seemed to burn right through her clothes, their weight a heavy touch that made her feel strangely restless.

His gaze searched hers. *"Why?"*

She brought her hands up between them. Placed her palms right over his chest, smiled and—

"We got a problem here?" the bartender demanded as he slapped his hands down on the counter.

Tanner didn't turn his way. "Mind your own business."

Didn't he sound all tough and deadly? Didn't he look that way, too? In his faded jeans, in that black T-shirt that pulled across his muscled chest, with his dark hair mussed and that jaw clenched . . . he looked like he could kick the ass of any fool dumb enough to get in his way.

Marna wasn't a fool.

She also wasn't weak.

She spared a glance for the bartender. About six-three, way over two hundred pounds, and sporting fists that would probably make most men tremble in fear. "I'm okay." She had this.

The bartender's eyes narrowed and clearly showed his doubt. "You sure, honey? 'Cause I can—"

Tanner swore and stepped away from her. *Ah, giving up already?* But then he shoved his hand inside his back pocket and yanked out some kind of wallet. He flashed his ID and snarled, "Police, asshole. Now step the hell back."

Right. He was playing the police card? Figured he'd stoop that low.

Her lips twisted as she started to walk away.

"You're not leaving me, Marna." There was no missing the anger beneath his words.

So what? She had her own share of anger. "Watch me." Yes, she'd actually taunted the big, bad shifter. Marna marched away. She kept her head up and her back straight. She'd just clear her own way through the crowd.

Tanner grabbed her arm after she'd taken about five steps. "Not gonna happen, baby."

Wait . . . *baby?*

She glanced at him and saw that the guy had pulled out a pair of handcuffs. Her jaw dropped.

"I tried to do this the easy way, but you didn't want that." He snapped one cuff around her wrist before she could even blink. "So I guess we'll go for the drama."

He spun her around and locked both cuffs behind her back. Marna was aware of the avid stares and not-so-quiet whispers that focused on her.

"You're comin' with me," Tanner told her, his faint Southern accent deepening a bit, "because there is no way I'm letting you out of my sight now."

She yanked at the cuffs. She should have been able to snap the things in two with hardly any effort.

Only . . . no snap.

He pushed her forward. The crowd backed up. "Thanks to a voodoo priestess I know off Bourbon Street, I was able to add a little something extra to those cuffs." Tanner's words were pitched low. "They can keep level-ten demons locked up, so I figured they'd keep you held tight, too."

This wasn't happening. She yanked against the cuffs again. No give.

Tanner had promised that he'd never hurt her. He'd seemed . . . good, despite his sadistic freak of a now-dead brother. She'd been willing to let Tanner keep living.

Only now he was cuffing her?

Fury churned in her gut. "You aren't doing this to me."

He leaned in close to her, close enough for her to see the dark gold flecks in his eyes. "I've got two dead bodies that I can trace back to you. Trust me, I *am* doing this."

Two dead bodies? Marna shook her head. She hadn't killed anyone.

Though that certainly hadn't been for lack of trying.

I can't kill anymore. No one knew that secret shame yet.

But the shifter wasn't giving her time to respond. More cops were spilling through the doorway, guys in uniform this time, and they were all closing in on her. Great. Obviously, she was having another one of her lucky days.

"It shouldn't have been this way," Tanner told her, and anger was heating his voice again. An anger that seemed to match her own. "Fuck, *too many know.* Don't you understand? There's nothing I can do."

She was surrounded. Men and women in blue were staring at her with narrowed eyes while Tanner started spilling some lines about her needing an attorney and having the right to stay silent.

And she did stay silent. While Tanner led her outside. While he pushed her into the back of a patrol car. And even while the vehicle raced down the road.

Silent, but the fury within her continued to build.

An angel in hell.

Tanner's jaw clenched as he led Marna through the busy New Orleans police station. As always, she looked delicate, vulnerable—deceptively so. The woman barely skimmed the top of his shoulders. Her frame was small, slender, but Marna did have some curves he'd admired far too many times.

Not now.

Now wasn't the time for admiring. Now was the time for figuring out how the hell he was supposed to save that curvy ass of hers.

A few of the cops stepped back when Tanner and Marna approached them. He could tell by the look in their eyes that they thought a mistake must have been made. No way were they looking at the face of a killer.

A killer shouldn't have an angel's face.

A killer damn well shouldn't *be* an angel.

He glanced down at her, sparing her a brief glance as he led them back to the interrogation room. Her eyes were wide, a pale blue that had haunted his dreams too often. Her cheeks were high, and her chin the slightest bit pointed. Her nose, small and straight, was currently held in the air. Though his angel wasn't talking, she sure was pissed. He could see the fury in the set of her jaw and in the tightness of her lips.

Her lips.

He didn't even know how many fantasies he'd had about her lips. Should an angel truly have lips that looked like they had been made just for sin?

Jonathan Pardue, his new partner, whistled as he headed toward them. "*This* is the woman who killed those men?"

Marna stiffened. "I didn't—"

Tanner's hold on her tightened. He needed to get her away from all the eyes and ears as fast as he could. If so many cops hadn't already been aware of the situation, he would have been able to protect her longer.

But, no, the lady just had to start making her kills public. Shit. She should *know* better. Most paranormals at least *tried* to keep their kills in the dark.

"You know what they say. . . ." Tanner murmured as he plastered a tight smile on his face. He'd been working with Jonathan less than a month. Not nearly long enough to trust the guy with all the secrets he carried. "Appearances can bite you in the ass." Because if you were fool enough to think a pretty face belonged to an innocent woman, you deserved to get your ass bitten.

Jonathan laughed and opened the door to the interrogation room. His brown eyes lingered a bit too long on Marna.

Tanner felt the beast that he carried begin to stir inside of him. *Back off.*

"I can help you with this one," Jonathan said as he tried to follow them into the room. "I'll be glad to—"

"Get us some coffee," Tanner told him as he steered Marna toward the small table. "Then we'll all settle down and find out just why this lady thought it would be fun to kill."

Tanner saw her shoulders tense.

Jonathan headed out, grumbling about having to fetch shit, but Tanner was just glad the guy was gone. He forced Marna to sit in the wobbly chair—the thing always wobbled and irritated the suspects, a nice bonus, usually. Then he leaned in close and put his mouth right at her ear.

And he had to fight back the impulse to lick. To taste.

She's a killer.

But then, so was he.

"I know that you wanted your revenge." His breath feathered over her ear, and Tanner was close enough to see the small shiver that shook her. "But, dammit, baby, you should have been more careful." His voice was whisper-soft. "You left two eyewitnesses in that alley." Eyewitnesses that had provided perfect, matching descriptions of her.

Because of those witnesses, everyone in the station knew about her. An APB had been put out instantly, and Tanner had known that he had to act. He hadn't been willing to trust anyone else to bring her in.

Hell, Marna might have just decided to *kill* anyone else who'd gone after her.

He'd had to move, fast, and get her under his control.

Her head turned, and her eyes met his. "I don't know what you're talking about, shifter." Her voice was as low as his. The room was monitored, and knowing the guys in the station, Tanner had no doubt that other folks were in the next room, watching them through the two-way mirror that lined the left wall.

But while they could watch, those guys wouldn't be able to hear anything that was said. Tanner had taken the liberty of disconnecting the audio system *before* going after Marna.

Yeah, he knew how to plan ahead. Some days.

"My brother and his asshole packmates hurt you." *Hurt,* such a tame word for the hell they'd put her through. His brother Brandt had cut the wings right from Marna's back and left her to die in the dirt. Brandt's packmates hadn't done a thing to save her. They'd been too busy following Brandt like the fools they were. She'd suffered so much because of the events of that night.

Wanting a little payback, yeah, he could understand that, but . . . "Did you have to kill them in front of witnesses? I told you that I'd make sure they weren't threats to you any longer." Brandt was already dead, courtesy of a fallen angel named Azrael, the most powerful being that Tanner had ever seen. After their battle, there'd literally been nothing left of Brandt.

Nothing, except the remains of his pack.

So Marna had decided she wanted her vengeance, and she'd gone after them. But killing them so blatantly? Hell, didn't the woman realize she had to be careful in a world full of humans? Murdering bastards had to be stopped, damn straight, but they didn't have to be taken out by her hand.

He exhaled slowly and kept his body between her and that two-way mirror. He could be her shield, or try to be anyway. "My boss wants you locked up." He jerked a hand through his hair. "And what do you think will happen to you in jail?"

She smiled then, and the sight iced his blood. "Nothing."

Right. His back teeth clenched. What did she have to be

afraid of? It was the poor assholes who'd be locked up with her —*they* were the ones who needed to fear.

Someone like her could never see the inside of a jail. He had to make sure things didn't go any farther.

But with those witnesses and the story already spreading to the media, he didn't have a whole lot of options.

Except . . .

"You made this too public. Shit, Marna, you're backing me against the wall here." He was supposed to uphold the law, but he wasn't human. Far from it. He knew the score.

Supernaturals can't always follow the rules. Jails sure as shit couldn't hold the most powerful threats out there.

He had to get the rest of the cops off his back. Off *her.*

"I didn't do anything." Her voice was still soft, but more anger cracked through the words. "I don't know who your witnesses *think* they saw, but it wasn't me."

At her words, he blinked, stunned.

Tanner remembered the very first lesson he'd learned about her kind. *Angels can't lie.*

Even angels who'd fallen were still bound to tell the truth. Sure, they could twist facts to suit them—they were real good at twisting—but they couldn't tell a straight-out lie.

He caught her shoulders and pulled her even closer to him. Her hands were still bound behind her back, and her chin notched up as she faced him.

"Two members of Brandt's pack are dead. Their bodies were found in an alley, without so much as a scratch on them." No scratches, but there'd been plenty of terror to see on the frozen faces of Michael LaRue and Beau Stokes.

While there might be plenty of paranormals lurking in the shadows of New Orleans, there weren't very many who could kill with a touch.

Even fewer who looked like *her.*

He thought her face paled as she stared at him, but Marna told him flatly, "I swear to you, it wasn't me."

Then someone sure wanted him to think it had been.

Footsteps tapped outside. Jonathan, hurrying back. Tanner leaned forward and unlocked her cuffs. Her breath sighed out as her hands were freed. "Thank you." The words whispered from her.

Her scent, fresh flowers, teased his nose. "Don't be thanking me yet." Because they weren't even close to being out of this mess.

But he owed her, and he couldn't just leave her to twist in the wind.

Innocent or not.

"Trust me." That was all he had time to say. The door swung open, and Jonathan came sauntering back in, with two cups of coffee cradled in the elbow of one arm.

Marna didn't respond to Tanner's words, but that wasn't particularly surprising. Trust? From her? Like that would happen any time soon. His angel wasn't the trusting sort.

Since her fall, hell, he wasn't even sure what she'd become.

Dangerous.

With a light touch on her shoulder, Tanner pushed her down into the wooden chair once more. They'd have to play the interrogation game, for a while.

"Here you go, ma'am," Jonathan said as he slid a Styrofoam cup toward her. Marna didn't take the drink. He shrugged and took a seat on the opposite side of the table. Sipping his own drink, Jonathan reached for a manila file that had been waiting on the table. "You don't look like the killing type."

The asshole hadn't brought him any coffee. Jonathan offered him a smug smile, one that vanished as the human flipped open the file and stared back down at the crime scene photos. "I just don't know how you did it."

Marna glanced down at the photos. Because he was watching so closely, Tanner saw the faint widening of her eyes.

Surprise.

"No physical signs of attack. No internal injuries," Jonathan rattled off the death details. "Their hearts simply . . . stopped."

Marna shrugged. "Then maybe those men had heart attacks."

Jonathan put his cup down on the table. "They were both in their prime, barely mid-thirties. Two guys like that, what? They just both magically had heart attacks? Is that what you want me to believe?"

"A lot of things magically happen in this city," Marna murmured.

Tanner stalked around the table. Didn't sit. Just crossed his arms over his chest, leaned against the two-way mirror, and stared at her. She didn't look nervous. No nervous twitches or gestures. Too calm. Too cool.

"Bullshit." Jonathan leaned toward her. "A lot of things happen because there are just some twisted fucks on the streets." He glanced down at the crime scene photos and then back at her. "I've seen kills like this before. It *looks* like nothing happened to them, but when we get the tox screen back, are we gonna see something different? 'Cause I'm bettin' we will."

Because Tanner didn't want to interrogate Marna, he let the human keep going with his questions. The guy was blundering in the dark, so Tanner wasn't particularly worried about him stumbling onto the truth.

Unless Marna decided to overshare. She'd better not.

"I'm bettin' that you took a needle and shoved it into those poor bastards." Jonathan's fingertips tapped on the photos. "You jammed 'em up with something, some drug, and killed them, and just because the ME can't find the injection site yet doesn't mean—"

"It doesn't mean that she won't," Tanner broke in, saying

the words he knew he was *supposed* to say. He had to at least act like he was after her, for those uniforms and brass who were watching. "She'll find the evidence, and it will be the final nail in your coffin, baby."

A faint furrow appeared between Marna's pale brows. Tanner's hands fisted. Hell, had he just called her baby again? He'd have to watch that.

"There will be nowhere for you to go," Tanner continued as he tried to force his body to relax. The beast inside wanted *out*. "Your face will be splashed across every paper in the area. Broadcast on every TV. People will find out just *exactly* what you are." Because of those witnesses. The ones who'd already been too eager to share with reporters. For the right price, everyone would talk in this town.

Marna's hands lifted and flattened on the table. Her head inclined toward the photos. Death hadn't been kind to the shifters. No wounds were on their bodies, but their faces were frozen in masks of terror. "Those men . . ." She spoke slowly. "They deserved what they got."

He really wanted to put his hand over the woman's mouth.

Jonathan rocked forward, way too eager. "So you admit that you killed them?"

"I admit . . ." Her gaze lingered on the photos and then rose slowly. Not to look at Jonathan, but to lock on Tanner. "I admit that they were murdering bastards who enjoyed hurting other people. They were due some punishment."

She was *not* helping the situation.

Jonathan nodded his head. "And you were just the one to punish them, weren't you?"

Did her lips tremble? Her shoulders hunched. In that moment, she looked even more vulnerable than usual. What the hell? Was she playing some game with them?

Jonathan's hand slapped on the table. *"Weren't you?"*

She jumped. *No game.* Marna was afraid.

"Listen, you—" Jonathan began.

E-fucking-nough. Tanner's hand closed around the guy's shoulder as he surged forward. "Ease up." His hard grip said *now.*

Jonathan whirled to face him. Both of the guy's brows were up. "Come again?"

Screw this. "We're taking a break." Because he wasn't sure what would happen if Jonathan kept badgering Marna. A big reveal to the human about all the paranormal creatures running through the city wasn't an option.

The legs of Jonathan's chair groaned as he shoved away from the table. The guy stalked out of the room, not glancing back. Oh, yeah, he was pissed. Whatever.

Tanner leaned across the table. He only had an instant to make Marna understand the plan he'd just pulled out of his ass. "When I come back . . ." He barely breathed the words. "Come at me."

She blinked.

"Come at me," he told her again, "or that guy's gonna try to lock you in a cage tonight."

Then he turned and headed after Jonathan.

The interrogation room door had barely closed before his partner was in his face. "What the hell was that about?" Jonathan demanded, voice rising. "First off, I'm not your errand boy!"

Tanner waited, one brow rising. There'd be more coming. Any time somebody started with a "first" there was always—

"And second, yeah, she's fuckable, but don't let your dick lead you to screw up this case! That woman in there—"

A crash sounded from the interrogation room. Tanner stiffened. *Showtime.*

Jonathan tried to shove him out of the way so he could

head back inside. Right. Like that was gonna happen. Tanner shoved back and the guy went tumbling to the floor. Then Tanner threw open the door to that interrogation room.

Marna had tossed the table against the wall. The chairs lay scattered on the ground, and she'd ripped one of the table legs out, and driven it right through the two-way mirror.

Should have been impossible. Those mirrors weren't made to shatter, but she'd managed to break through it.

Probably because the lady was using some of that amped-up angel strength of hers, and if he didn't watch it, she'd be fleeing right out through that second room—now that she'd made herself a little escape path—and racing head-on into a bullpen full of cops.

"Marna . . ."

She spun back around with the table leg held up, club-like, in her clenched hands.

"Guess she's stronger than she looks," Jonathan said from behind him.

Couldn't that guy ever get off his back?

In the next instant, Marna charged at them. Proving that she was, indeed, much stronger than she appeared. Because Tanner knew he had to make this look good, he rolled to the ground when the table leg swiped out at him.

Her next hit connected with Jonathan, and the guy finally shut up because she knocked him all the way back into the two-way mirror.

But Jonathan had fast reflexes, for a human, and in the next instant, he had his gun out and aimed right at Marna.

"No!" Tanner bellowed as he lunged toward the other cop.

Too late.

Jonathan fired and the bullet slammed into Marna's chest.

Fuck. Fuck. Fuck. This wasn't his plan. Not even damn

close. Rage exploded within Tanner, and he drove his fist into Jonathan's face. This time, when the cop went down, he was unconscious.

"Don't ever hurt her again," Tanner snarled, hands still fisted. His claws were coming out, and they were tearing into the flesh of his palms as he kept his hands fisted.

"T-Tanner?"

He stilled. She'd never said his name before. He'd wanted her to, but this way, with pain and fear darkening the word? *Hell, no.*

In an instant, he was by her side. The bullet wound wouldn't kill her. *It wouldn't kill her.*

He had to keep repeating that mantra to himself because his hands were shaking as he lowered her to the floor.

Angels were tough. They could heal from just about anything.

But her blood was on his hands.

Marna pushed against him. "I-I can—"

Tanner shook his head and forced her to the floor. Other cops were coming toward them. He could hear the rush of their pounding footsteps. This wasn't his plan, but he could make it work. They had to make it work. "He shot you in the heart."

Her eyes widened.

"*That's* the story we're telling." Because if they played this scene right, he'd be able to save her angel ass. "And, baby, a shot to the heart will kill a human. It will put an end to the killer who took out those two men in the alley."

Understanding filled her blue eyes.

He put his hands over her chest, the better to cover the wound and make it look like he was fighting to save her. *"Get an ambulance!"* Tanner yelled. *"Our suspect is down!"*

Then he brought his lips close to her ear. "You have to die, baby." This was their perfect opportunity to get her free. Because if she wasn't the killer, then someone very powerful was setting her up. Someone who wanted her face splashed all across the media.

Someone who'd *taken* her face to commit the murders. *Another supernatural.*

Marna gave the slightest of nods. His breath expelled in a rush.

Trust. It had to start somewhere. For both of them. Good thing that, unlike angels, shifters could lie. He'd spent most of his life lying.

He stared down at her. Behind him, Jonathan was groaning and trying to rise. He'd deal with that trigger-happy SOB later. For now . . . *"She's bleeding out!"*

Other cops raced into the room, but they wouldn't be able to help her. He'd make sure of that.

Slowly, her eyes began to fall and her breathing slowed. Damn, that woman was a pretty fine actress.

You have to die, baby.

It looked like she was going to do just that.

Chapter Two

Just how long did she have to stay in the morgue? The place reeked of antiseptic and bleach, and Marna was tired of the icy feel of her own skin.

She'd been wheeled down at least thirty minutes ago. Right after she'd been pronounced dead.

A door creaked open. Footsteps thudded toward her. "Marna?"

No mistaking that deep voice. She shoved the sheet aside and leapt off the table. Her clothes—what was left of them—were covered in dried blood.

Tanner's green gaze swept over her. "You're looking good, for a dead woman."

The doctor who'd been so eager to declare her dead stood behind him. The not-so-good doctor glanced nervously over his shoulder and said, "You need to get her out of here, fast."

She recognized that guy. Like she'd ever be able to forget him or Tanner.

Tall, dark, with a face too much like Tanner's . . . because he was Tanner's brother. *Cody.* That was his name. Only Cody wasn't a shifter. This guy was a demon doctor. One who'd been ready to lie with no hesitation. Unlike angels, demons always excelled at lying. Maybe because they spent their whole lives hiding what they really were from the rest of the world.

"I wasn't planning on staying around." She'd spent more than her share of time with the dead. As an angel of death, the dead had been all she'd known for far too long.

This place, with the empty shells of bodies and the carefully covered scent of decay, it made her remember too many things. Things she wished she could forget.

Cody's gaze darted back to her. She could see right through the glamour that the guy was trying to use. Demons used glamour all the time—it was how they kept their true selves secret from the humans.

A demon's real eyes were pitch black. But this guy . . . when humans saw him, they looked into eyes as green as Tanner's.

A lie.

Once upon a time, this doctor had saved her life. When Tanner had found her broken and bloody in the swamp, Cody had been there with him. The demon had been the one to patch her up.

He'd been scared of her then, too.

Cody glanced away from her. "What are you going to do with her?" he asked Tanner.

"*She's* going to get herself out of here," Marna said. Enough. She'd been in a morgue, for goodness sake. *A morgue.* Time to ditch this place, and the shifter who kept staring at her way too intently. Like he was starving and she was the best meal option in sight.

Marna headed for the door, but found her path blocked by said shifter.

Tanner shook his head and said, "You're a dead woman. Cops are staked out at the entrance to the hospital. Don't you think they'll notice when you just go waltzing out?"

Did she look stupid? Maybe she was still new to being

earthbound, but she'd been around for centuries. Marna knew more than this guy could ever guess. "There's more than one way out of this place." She could blend. "I can grab a pair of scrubs and put on a face mask. No one will recognize me. I'll blend in with the staff and walk away. You won't see me again."

"I just risked my job for you. There's no way I'm just going to let you waltz away from me now." Tanner crossed his arms over his chest. "With all the evidence in this case, the department had you dead to rights."

Why did he keep up with the *dead* bit?

"Those witnesses described every single detail about you." Tanner's gaze glittered. "They said you walked right by them. That you were less than five feet away. Being so close, there'd be no mistaking you."

"I *didn't* do it."

"I know."

His words had her floundering. Well, if he thought she was innocent, then why—

"Why the hell do you think I did all this?" He waved his hand to indicate the icy morgue. "I had to get you out of that station because, baby, you are being set up."

She was sure happy to hear he realized that fact. "Stop calling me baby," she muttered.

A faint line appeared between his brows. "An angel can't go to jail, so I had to take you out of the equation."

"Consider me out," she said.

Cody edged toward the door.

"Out doesn't mean you're clear." Tanner was like a brick wall in her path, big, strong, and totally blocking her exit. "It means you don't have to worry about cops and reporters trying to dog you, but we sure as hell need to find out who is setting you up."

She knew that. But she also knew . . . "The only enemies I have are in your brother's panther pack."

"Then you've got some dead enemies." This bit came from Cody.

But Tanner shook his head. "No, being *what* you are, trust me, there are plenty of paranormals in this city who'd want to take you out."

Marna swallowed. Angel blood was a rare commodity in the paranormal underworld. Vamps would love to drain her. Witches would try to steal her power, but . . . setting her up for murder? How would that help any of the supernaturals?

"Until we find out what's happening, you're staying with me," Tanner told her as he took a step toward her.

Wait—what? Becoming this guy's 24-7 buddy was not part of her plan. Getting out of the city ASAP? Yes, that was more her agenda. "No, I'm—"

"You're on someone's list, angel. To either be taken down . . ."

By getting tossed to the cops? When had she made an enemy who wanted—

"Or taken out."

Marna straightened her shoulders. She hated feeling helpless. Another new concept for her. She should have been more than able to protect herself, but since losing her wings, she'd suffered a serious power shortage. Did Tanner know the truth? Did he realize what had happened to her?

Angels of death could kill with a touch. Even the Fallen could kill. But she . . .

She'd lost the touch. She'd tried to get it back. Oh, jeez, but she'd tried. She *had* gone after those men in the panther pack. Marna had tracked and hunted Michael LaRue and Beau Stokes. She'd tried to send those two straight to hell.

Not in that alley. That attack truly hadn't been her. She'd gone after the shifters weeks before.

But her touch hadn't worked on them. She *couldn't* kill.

She might as well be . . . human.

Emotions and needs battered her all the time. They clawed at her, threatening to rip her apart. She just wanted it all to stop.

Wanted to go back to her old life.

Not going to happen. Stop mourning, move the fuck on. Not her words. The words of another Fallen in the city, Sammael. He wasn't exactly the comforting type. When he'd come to see her just days before, he hadn't wasted time with false sympathy. *This is your life now. Adjust or die.*

Cody opened a closet and pulled out some green scrubs. She was rather surprised that he hadn't already snuck out. He lifted the scrubs and said, "You'll need these."

She took the scrubs. Fine. She'd go with the shifter cop . . . for now. At the first chance she had, Marna would slip away. It was past time to leave this city. She'd go somewhere new—preferably some place that wasn't soaked in blood. There, she'd be able to start over.

"Won't someone notice," she asked the question that had to be obvious, "when my body disappears?"

But Tanner just laughed. "This is New Orleans. Do you know how many bodies disappear from morgues here every day?"

And what? Cops just turned blind eyes?

So much madness. This city wasn't for her. This *life* wasn't for her.

Maybe it was time for a new life.

But first, she had to get away.

"They saw you die. You'll have a death certificate on file," Tanner continued. "For now, that's all we need."

Because the city was used to such madness. *No body, no worries.*

Swallowing, Marna turned away to pull on the scrubs, and she began to plan her escape.

★ ★ ★

From the shadows, he stared up at the hospital. The stark walls were bathed in the flashing lights of nearby ambulances. *She* was inside.

Dead?

Not her.

His hands were shoved deep in his pockets. No one glanced his way, certainly not the handful of cops who milled around the entranceway.

They all bought the story that was circulating among the ranks. A killer . . . taken out by one of their own.

According to the PD grapevine, the lady had gotten violent and attacked two officers. Only she'd been the one to end up on a stretcher as she was rushed to St. Mary's.

Word had trickled down thirty minutes before that their suspect had died on the operating room table. Cops sure liked to gossip with anyone and everyone.

Tanner Chance hadn't come out yet. Chance had rushed to the hospital with Marna and stood guard over her like some protective giant. Despite the news of her death, he still hadn't shown his face.

When he'd first rushed to the hospital, the cop's fingers had been covered in her blood. Fitting, since Tanner Chance and his brothers had always shown such a taste for violence.

He turned away from the scene. Chance wouldn't be coming out that front exit. The cop wasn't exactly new to this game. It didn't matter, though. Chance wasn't going to stop him.

Slowly, carefully, he made his way toward the small employee entrance on the far left of the building. An entrance that had stairs that led up to the general floors of the hospital, as well as a stairwell that snaked down to the morgue.

As he approached, he finally caught sight of Chance. Climbing into a black SUV, with a small figure beside him.

A figure who'd tried to shove her blond hair under one of those white, cloth caps that doctors wore in operating rooms.

The vehicle's engine growled to life and it shot out of the lot before he could even take a few steps toward them.

Escape.

Laughter slipped from him. Oh, this was going to be good.

Just how long would it be before Chance's taste for violence showed itself again? Just how long did the lost angel have before the shifter turned on her?

Not long at all.

Pretty soon, Marna would be exactly where he wanted her, and Chance would be the one growing ice cold in a morgue. Only the shifter wouldn't be playing some kind of possum like Marna had obviously been doing.

He'd be on his way to hell.

Streaks of dawn's light were sliding across the sky when Tanner opened the door to his home for Marna. She hadn't spoken much during the ride over, but once they got inside, he had a feeling the fireworks would be erupting.

He could practically feel the lady's rage.

And her kind wasn't exactly supposed to *feel* much.

The door clicked closed behind them. She walked around the foyer—okay, what would one day be the foyer. Right then, the house was a piece of crap. He knew it. The antebellum had barely survived the last storm, and the ex-owners had been more than ready to dump the place into his hands.

So, yeah, it looked like hell, but if he kept working on the place, one day, it would be something fancy.

Something he could be proud of. Tanner hadn't exactly been proud of a lot of things in his life.

Not his murdering bastard of a father.

Not his sadistic shifter brother, Brandt.

And he'd sure not been proud of himself. Not with all the blood on his hands. Tanner glanced down at his hands. The skin was a dark tan, smooth, but he knew the blood was still there. Some things just couldn't be washed away.

"I suppose you want me to thank you," Marna said, her words drawing his gaze back to her.

She stood at the edge of the would-be foyer, her hands on her hips, eyeing him like he was some kind of disgusting bug that had crawled across her path.

So what else was new? She'd been looking at him that way ever since he found her. Ever since she realized just exactly who—*what*—he was.

Never good enough for her.

But, hell, who would be good enough? Maybe another angel, one of those lily-white jerks who knew nothing of sin.

And as for thanking him . . . "I did keep your sweet ass out of a jail cell." He'd gotten her clear, permanently. No one would be looking for a dead woman.

Not that anyone *should* go looking for her. But just in case, he had friends at the hospital, folks who knew the paranormal score and who owed him favors. They'd make a paperwork trail to show that she was truly dead, and those hospital connections had even set a plan in motion to cremate one Marna Smith.

He'd only been half bullshitting when he said bodies disappeared from the morgue. In this case, she wouldn't totally vanish—her ashes would be left behind as proof of her death. And with the ashes and death certificate on file, that would be the end of the story.

It wasn't the first time he'd made a body disappear. Wouldn't be the last either.

"You're also the one who led the cops right to me at that club." Marna wasn't relenting. The lady knew how to hold on to her anger. Kinda sexy the way her cheeks flushed and her eyes glittered. But then, he thought most things about her were sexy. "If you'd just stayed away, then—"

He pounced. No other word. Sometimes, the panther inside liked to jump after his prey. In an instant, he was across the room and caging her against the wall with his arms. Tanner made sure that he didn't touch her, not yet.

Soon.

Her scent slid around him. He realized he was already rock hard, but then that wasn't a real surprise. His body had only one response to seeing her: *Time to fuck.* He got hard just being in the same room with her.

But the lust would have to wait. *Not for long though.* He was getting damn near insane from wanting her. Tanner cleared his throat, the better not to growl, as he said, "We got a tip that you were in that club. An APB had been put out for you by the PD. If I hadn't come in to get you . . ." He bent his head and more of her scent—fucking flowers—teased his nose.

A guy could get drunk off Marna's scent. Temptation had never smelled so sweet.

He sucked in a breath and tasted her. "If it hadn't been me, it would have been one hell of a lot rougher. The boys in blue who came after you wouldn't have played nearly as nicely as I did."

Her lips were parted, revealing the edge of her white teeth. "Bullshit."

He blinked. Not exactly what he'd expected to hear coming from an angel's mouth. Looked like Marna was picking up some dirty habits.

He'd like to teach her a few more.

"You were afraid," she charged. "You thought I'd kill any other cops who came after me."

He was being careful not to touch her, but Marna lifted her hand and placed it right over his heart. She had to feel the frantic beat, but he couldn't help it. Being so close to her had his body tensing.

And his cock hardening even more.

Want her.

Even though he knew just how lethal she could be.

"You know what angels like me can do." Marna's voice had a husky edge. Her eyes stared up at his, and he could see the challenge plain on her face. "Are you afraid of me now?"

Fear wasn't exactly what he felt. If she just moved her hand down a ways, she'd be able to tell that. "No."

Some of the challenge faded from her gaze.

He lifted his right hand and caught her chin, tilting her head back. Now it was his turn. "But I know you're terrified of me."

Then he did what he'd been dying to do for the last two months.

Tanner took her mouth. Her lips were still parted, so he thrust his tongue inside. She gasped and he took her breath, kissing her harder. Deeper.

Her lips were so damn soft. And her taste . . .

The sweetest temptation.

Like strawberries. Fresh strawberries. And . . . champagne. The fancy stuff that he hardly ever bought. Delicious. Good enough to make him feel a little drunk.

Want more.

She'd frozen in his arms. Not kissing him back. Not shoving him away. Not responding. Screw that. He pushed her back against the wall and licked her lips. The woman had fire inside of her. He'd find it.

Marna trembled against him. With that small movement, her lips parted even more. A growl broke from his throat, and Tanner let the kiss deepen. Let her taste the hunger and lust that he could barely keep in check around her.

Then her tongue licked against his mouth.

Yes.

Her hand rose from his chest and curled around his shoulder. Instead of pushing him away, she pulled him closer.

Kissed him harder.

Deeper.

Their bodies pressed together. No way could she miss the heavy cock thrusting against her, and the feel of her tight, pebbled nipples against his chest had Tanner desperate to strip her, and taste her—everywhere.

He'd been wrong. She didn't fear him, she—

Marna pushed him away. Because the lady packed one hell of a lot of strength in that slender body, he flew back about five feet.

They stared at each other. Her lips were red and swollen from his mouth. Her breath heaved out, and a flush stained her cheeks. "Why . . ." She cleared her throat and tried again because that one word had been a gasp, "Why did you do that?"

Did she really need to ask? *Because I want you*. But he said, "Because it was time you realized a few truths about me."

She licked her lips. Fuck. His back teeth clenched. Could she still taste him? He could still taste her.

Want. More.

He'd be having more.

Her gaze darted to the door behind him. He could all but read her thoughts, but, *sorry, angel.* She wasn't getting away from him that easily.

"I want you," he told her. The words were heavy, hard, and they seemed to sink into the thick silence that had grown in the small room.

Her hands clenched into fists.

Tanner raised a brow and tried to look like the lust wasn't ripping him apart. "Based on the way you kissed me back, I'd say you want me, too."

Her chin lifted a good two inches into the air. "Lust is for humans. It just makes them weak. It makes them—"

"Horny."

Her flush got even deeper. She was cute when her face was all pink.

She also needed to realize something important. *Not in heaven any longer.* "You're with humans now. Humans, shifters, demons—you're walking right with all of us." There was no holding herself apart anymore. "So it's time you started dealing with the changes in you."

Changes . . . emotions. Needs.

He could help her satisfy a few needs. *Or every need.* If he got her in bed, they wouldn't be crawling out any time soon. He'd make sure of that.

They'd get to the bed part, later. Now that he knew she wanted him—

"I don't . . ." She stopped. Cleared her throat. She wasn't saying she didn't want him. Tanner *knew* she couldn't say it.

Angels and their no-lie rules. He rather liked those particular rules. Made things easier for him.

The whole deadliest-beings-on-earth bit? He could do without that part.

"I don't want to be here with you," she said instead, and he knew those words were the truth. She wanted to escape him and head out in the city on her own.

"Tough." It was. She'd have to deal with the situation—and him. He'd been treating her with kid gloves for the last few months. Watching over her. Being afraid to get too close.

No longer.

Someone was playing a deadly game with her, and he wasn't about to sit back and do nothing.

"Until we find out who is setting you up, you've got yourself a shifter shadow." Thanks to the heavy punch he'd tossed at Jonathan—and the not-so-little matter of Marna's shooting—he was on administrative leave from the PD for a few days. That leave would give him plenty of time to keep an eye on her and do some detective work in the city.

He'd hit the places human cops would never think to look, and he *would* find out what the hell was happening.

"Someone knows what you are—exactly what you can do—and they want you labeled as a killer."

She pushed back her hair. "I am a killer."

Maybe. But in this case, in the murders of Michael and Beau, she was innocent.

Her hand fell back to her side and her shoulders seemed to slump.

He wanted to keep pushing her, but he knew now wasn't the time. "Go upstairs," he told her because she'd been up all night. Up, shot, left in a morgue to play dead.

Hell of a first date.

Not that he'd tell her that he counted the night as their first but . . .

At least he'd gotten a kiss.

Tanner rolled his shoulders and heaved out a rough breath. "At the top of the stairs, take the first room on the right." His room. He'd crash on the couch. He could play the gentleman, for a little while at least. "Get some rest, then we'll start tracking the bastard who set this plan in motion."

Her sigh was soft, and a little lost. But she headed toward the staircase.

In silence, he watched her climb the stairs. She didn't want to be trapped with him, but for now, there was no choice.

You want her trapped with you.

The dark voice came from deep within him. Marna didn't know it, but he'd been finding reasons to seek her out over the last eight weeks. Just to check on her. She'd had such a rough time. He needed to make sure she was okay. At least that was what he'd told himself.

At first.

But the truth was that he'd just wanted to see her.

His gaze followed the curve of her ass. She'd kissed him back. Some folks said angels had ice water in their veins, but she was different.

Marna was at the top of the stairs now. She glanced back down at him.

Tanner tensed. *Invite me up.* Oh, what he wouldn't give to hear her say . . .

"Stay away from me, shifter. Don't even think about coming into this room."

So much for the hot, hard sex he'd been dreaming of. Tanner gave her a little salute. "As long as you promise not to run, I'll be a good boy and stay down here."

Who the fuck was he kidding? He'd never been good.

Marna turned away and walked into his room. She hadn't offered him that promise.

Because she couldn't lie.

Hell. It looked like the day would wind up being even longer than the night.

He'd have to stay on watch and make sure that if his angel tried to flee, then he'd be right there to catch her.

Chapter Three

Marna carefully opened the wooden door. She'd slept for hours—far longer than she'd intended. When she'd first crept into the bedroom, she'd known that immediate escape wasn't a possibility. Tanner would have been on guard. So she'd planned to bide her time and wait a bit before slipping away.

She'd climbed into bed—*his* bed. There had been no mistaking the rich, masculine scent that clung to the soft sheets. She'd eased beneath the covers and just closed her eyes for a few moments.

She'd dreamed of Tanner. Hot, too vivid dreams of his naked flesh and his strong hands stroking her body. Kissing him back had been a dangerous mistake. Those kisses had just made the ache in her grow stronger.

It was an ache for something she couldn't have.

The house was silent as she tiptoed to the top of the stairs. The banister gleamed, the wood shining. The walls upstairs were an old, faded brown, but the staircase was in perfect condition.

As if someone had recently spent a lot of time restoring it.

It looked like her shifter had a hobby.

Her fingers slid down the top of the banister, rubbing lightly against the smooth wood.

Still no sound from below. She could try creeping down

there and slipping out the front door, but Marna figured that plan was too risky. Why get too close to Tanner? Better to stay as far from him as possible.

She headed back into his bedroom and locked the door behind her. The fading light trickling through the window told her that late afternoon was already coming close. Time to get out of there while she still could.

Marna opened the window and glanced below. The fall from this height would hurt, no doubt, but the pain would probably be no worse than that of a bullet. She'd managed to survive yesterday. She'd survive this, too.

Her hand rubbed over the now-healed wound. Good thing even fallen angels could recover quickly from most of their injuries. Otherwise, she still would have been in that morgue.

I'm not ready to die. How many humans had told her that same thing over the centuries?

Just as she was leaning forward, a knock sounded on the bedroom door. Then, Tanner's strong voice called out, "You don't want to do that."

Her fingers curved around the window ledge, but she glanced toward the bedroom door.

"You're just gonna get bruised and banged up, and I'll have you—" He kicked in the door, breaking the flimsy lock easily. Then Tanner stalked inside as if he owned the place. Oh, yes, he did. "I'll have you," he said again, eyes glinting, "before you can even run more than a few feet."

Her heart slammed into her chest and fear had her tensing, but Marna tried to play it cool. She lifted an eyebrow and asked, "Who said anything about running?" *Jumping, maybe.*

His lips quirked.

"The next time you want in," she told him, turning her back to the window so that she faced him fully, "maybe you should give a girl a chance to answer your knock. You know, *before* you go all macho crazy and break down the door."

A real smile flashed across his face. Wow. She hadn't realized . . . the shifter was actually handsome.

He had a dimple in his left cheek.

Then his smile faded. "I heard you open the window."

Shifter senses. She'd forgotten how strong they could be. Marna shrugged and tried to look innocent. For an angel, that shouldn't have been such a hard task. "It's hot in here."

Tanner shook his head and exhaled on a low sigh. "You're so careful with your answers."

She'd had to learn to be.

"But I know this game." He headed toward her, eliminating those few precious feet that separated them.

She didn't back up. Showing fear wasn't an option. Besides, there wasn't any place for her to go now. Not unless she decided to hop out that window. "I'm not playing a game with you."

His gaze swept over her. "Don't you understand? For now, you need me."

That grated, and she said, "I don't need anyone."

One dark brow rose. "We'll see about that." His gaze slipped to her hair. For a moment, his eyes seemed to soften. "Damn but you are pretty."

What?

He lifted his hand as if to touch her.

Marna flinched.

He stilled. His gaze found hers once more.

She took a breath and tried to shove aside the memory that had exploded in her mind. "Your . . . claws . . ."

His claws had come out. Maybe they'd been out from the moment he kicked in that door, but she hadn't noticed them until he'd lifted his hand. Now, she couldn't seem to notice anything else.

His claws were long, curving, wicked sharp. Sharp enough to slice away her life.

Tanner took a step back. "I . . ." He shook his head. Dropped his hand. Hid both of his hands behind his back. "When I broke through the door, the adrenaline pushed part of the change. The claws were like a reflex."

His words barely penetrated. She was remembering another shifter. When Brandt had attacked her, his claws had looked just like Tanner's.

She hated the sight of a shifter's claws.

He slid back a few more steps.

She took a few more breaths.

Her gaze fell to the floor and, behind him, she saw drops of blood. Falling from his hands. Tanner had fisted his hands, and his claws must have cut right through the skin. "Tanner . . ."

His head lifted. "It's okay." After a moment's hesitation, he raised his hands. She could see the small slices in the flesh of his palms. "They're gone."

His claws were gone. The shifter had his control back.

Marna rolled her shoulders, and the scars on her back seemed to burn.

His eyes weren't meeting hers. "We need to get you some fresh clothes and—"

A loud crash sounded from downstairs. Tanner whirled and raced out of the room.

At first, Marna didn't move at all. Then she heard the roar of *"Shifter!"*

It was a familiar roar.

Another crash seemed to shake the house. Goose bumps rose on her arms.

As an angel, Marna had always been taught to fear one being above all others. To fear the ancient angel who had fallen after he left a trail of bodies in a vicious rampage.

To fear the being known as Sammael.

A being she was pretty sure had just broken into Tanner's house. That had been *his* roar. Once you heard Sammael's voice, you never forgot it. At least, angels didn't. Angels learned early to remember the things that were the most dangerous to them.

Marna glanced toward the window. Now would be the perfect time to make her escape. Tanner would be busy—probably fighting for his life against Sammael—and she would be free.

She just had to leave the shifter and make her escape.

One of the deadliest paranormals in the city grabbed Tanner by the throat and threw him across the room. "I heard about what you did, shifter."

Sammael—Sam to his enemies and the maybe two friends the guy had in town—marched toward Tanner. The guy was an ancient angel, a freaking bringer of hell on earth, and it just figured that he'd be the one who'd busted into Tanner's house.

When Sam tried to take a jab at him, Tanner swiped out at the guy and had the pleasure of seeing blood streak down Sam's chest. Sam might be a badass, but Tanner knew the guy's weak spots. Sam wouldn't be taking him down.

When Sam leapt back, Tanner raised his claws, preparing for another round. "Just what the hell did you hear?" Tanner asked.

"You *killed* an angel." Sam's voice was lethally soft.

Huh. Looked like word on the paranormal streets had spread fast. But, technically, he hadn't been the one to take that shot at Marna. The gossips could have at least gotten that part right. The death charge belonged to the detective who'd wound up with a broken nose. Tanner figured that had been a great way to break in a new partner. By breaking his face.

Sam closed in on him. "You're going to *suffer* for what you've done."

Perfect. Now he had to worry about Sam going ballistic on him. And Sam ballistic? *Not good.*

The Fallen reached for him again. Tanner deflected the blow and plowed his fist into Sam's stomach. Sam didn't even grunt at the impact, but Tanner's hand felt as if it had slammed into a brick wall.

Maybe he should have used his claws with that punch. This time, he'd—

"Stop!"

Both men turned at Marna's shout. She was halfway down the stairs and her hands held tightly to the banister.

Sam shook his head. "Marna?" Yeah, that was shock in the guy's voice. So much for being all-knowing.

Taking advantage of the Fallen's distracted state, Tanner punched the guy in the jaw.

Sam growled and lunged to attack him.

"I said . . . *stop!*" Marna jumped the rest of the way down the stairs.

Sam stopped fighting Tanner. After a moment's study, he sauntered toward her. "You look good, for a dead girl."

Marna stared up at the Fallen with wide eyes. "Why . . . why are you here?"

"Because he came to get a little vengeance," Tanner said, understanding Sam's rage far better than Marna did. She just didn't have enough experience with emotions. Not yet. He was working on that issue. Soon enough, he'd make sure she understood everything. "One life for another, right, Sam?"

Sam's gaze swept over Marna. The Fallen was probably checking her for injuries. "I was told the cops killed you."

"That's what we needed people to think." Tanner strode to Marna's side. Didn't touch her, but he sure wanted to. "As you can see, she's just fine."

Sam didn't look convinced. "Are you?" he asked Marna.

"I'm still breathing." Her soft answer.

Sam's eyes narrowed, and, after a beat of time, he offered his arm to her. "Come with me."

The hell she would. Tanner fought to pull back his claws and stay calm, for at least a little longer. *Control.* "She's staying with me."

Sam's gaze seemed to see too much as he glanced over at Tanner. "Hmmm . . . like that, is it, shifter?"

Dick. "Someone set her up for murder. Some bastard killed two shifters but pinned the crime on her." It still pissed him off. "You think I'm just gonna let that go?" Then, before Sam could say anything else, Tanner said, "I'm the cop here." Not some renegade angel out for blood vengeance. "I'm gonna do my job. I'll track the bastard."

But Sam still had his hand up. Had the guy even heard a word Tanner had said? With his gaze on Marna, Sam said, "I came as soon as I heard what happened. Our kind should stay together."

Tanner looked at Marna and was surprised to see that she had actually inched away from the Fallen—*and closer to me.*

Tanner figured he must be the lesser evil in the room. Nice change of pace.

"I want to know who's doing this to me." Her shoulders straightened. "I *will* know." Determination roughened her words. "I won't be leaving New Orleans until I figure out what's happening and *why* it's happening."

Well, well. It looked like his angel wasn't going to turn tail and run after all. Maybe he wouldn't have to chain her to his side, either.

Pity.

He realized that Sam didn't appear particularly surprised to hear about the murders. Eyes narrowing in suspicion, Tanner charged, "You knew that those two shifters got taken out."

"Shifter deaths are hardly surprising." Sam shrugged, looking completely careless. "When I heard, I thought she was just getting some payback." His eyes raked Marna. "But that wasn't the way of it?"

"No." Quiet. Firm.

Sam nodded. "Then we'll find out who's doing the killing. I can help you."

Tanner didn't want the Fallen close to Marna, but he knew just how powerful Sam's reach could be. "If you hear anything, you tell me." Sam had missed his whole *I'm-the-cop* bit. Figured.

Sam turned away and began to head back toward the broken door. He hadn't kicked it in the way Tanner had done upstairs; instead, Sam had pulverized the thing. "If you want to hear the supernatural secrets in this town . . ." Sam tossed this back over his shoulder. "Head to Hell."

Hell. Not the home of the devil—though from what Tanner had heard, the dude had long since left that place—but the bar nestled deep in the Quarter. A bar humans instinctively avoided, as if they felt the evil that lurked inside.

A bar he'd be hitting that night.

Sam paused in the doorway and glanced over his shoulder. His gaze locked on Tanner's. "You'd better keep her safe."

Tanner inclined his head even as he choked back his rage. Like he needed this jerk to tell him—

Sam glanced toward Marna. "And if you need me, remember that I'm here. You have an ally in the city."

There was no missing the surprise on Marna's face. "Why? Why would you help me?"

"You fell in the middle of my brother's battle."

Right, because Sam's brother was the Azrael—Az. The dark fallen angel who'd sent Brandt on a fast trip to hell. The night that Marna lost her wings, Brandt had been intending to kill Az. *He'd* been the target. Only when the dust from that battle cleared, Az had gotten away, and Marna had been the one to fall.

No. She hadn't fallen. Tanner knew that. Not really. She'd just never been able to go back home.

Because Brandt had taken her wings with the slice of his claws.

"I owe you," Sam told her, "and I'll make sure my debt is paid."

The wind howled and the Fallen vanished.

In the silence that followed, Tanner was certain of only one thing. He'd be seeing Hell that night.

"Stay close," Tanner told her as they headed past the two bouncers stationed outside of Hell. Demons, Marna knew that from just a glance. The guys looked at her and immediately stepped back.

Maybe they realized what she was, too.

When they entered the bar, the blasting music hit her first. The darkness came second. It took Marna a moment to be able to see anything, but then her eyes adjusted and she saw the bodies. Couples hidden in corners. Vampires . . . drinking from the prey they'd penned against the walls.

Her hand rose to her throat. She'd heard stories about vampires. Some had drained angels dry because they wanted a taste of power. It seemed that angel blood might be the new delicacy of choice among the undead.

Marna sure didn't want to be on their menu.

She'd be steering clear of the vamps. Marna inched forward and bumped into Tanner's back. He turned around and frowned down at her.

It was crazy, but she wanted to grab on to his arm and hold tight. This place with its darkness and the evil that she could *feel* in the air around her . . . she didn't want to be here.

Marna licked her lips. "H-how are we going to do this?" They were near the bar now, and that was most definitely not your average alcohol in those decanters. She would *not* be drinking tonight. "I mean, we can't just walk up to the first demon we see—" She'd already seen at least ten. "We can't walk up to him and demand information."

Sure, she was new to the whole wing-less scene, but she realized that wasn't the way the paranormal world worked. These guys weren't going to share their secrets out of the goodness of their hearts. From the look of things, goodness was not a key word for any of them.

"Relax." Tanner wrapped his arm around her shoulders and pulled her close. Why did that make her feel better? "I know how to work this crowd."

Okay, so having the cop shifter with her wasn't such a bad thing. She just wished that she didn't—

"You smell good."

A vampire was in her way. Tall, blond. Big fangs. Hungry eyes.

And, for some reason, the guy seemed familiar to her. But Marna couldn't quite place him.

He inhaled and those hungry eyes of his widened with pleasure. "Sweet . . . fresh flowers . . ." He licked his lips. "And fear."

Her heart slammed into her ribs. The vampire couldn't find out what she really was.

Or I'm dead.

"Smells so good . . ." The vampire took a step toward her and lifted his hand. His gaze seemed to burn through her. "I just want a taste. *Just one taste.*"

Tanner grabbed the vamp by the throat and lifted him a good foot into the air. "In a second, you're gonna be tasting my fist as it's shoved down your damn throat."

The vamp was gasping for breath. Vamps had to breathe, just like humans. Their hearts still beat. Their lungs still worked. When a human became a vampire, he only died for a moment, and then was reborn as a bloodsucker. That momentary death was the way the virus spread.

Vampires are mistakes. How many times had she heard that line, coming from the powers-that-be upstairs?

Now the vamp was clawing at Tanner's hand, but the shifter wasn't letting him go.

"She's not on the menu, asshole," Tanner growled. "Remember that." Then he tossed the vamp back against the bar.

There was no missing the fury that tightened the vampire's face. *"Shifter. You think you can tell me—"*

In a flash, Tanner had his claws at the guy's throat. "I was playing nice before, but if you want me to cut your head off—right here, right now—I'll be more than happy to oblige."

Blood trickled down the vamp's throat. Tanner's claws had already sliced through the skin. The vampire wasn't moving now. The whole bar was watching, waiting.

"Off . . . " the vampire said slowly, "the menu." His Adam's apple scraped against Tanner's claws as he managed to whisper the words.

"Good fucking vamp." Tanner stepped back and dropped his claws.

Everyone stopped watching. They went back to blood drinking and making out in their dark corners. She guessed that this crowd liked to see death. If there wasn't a show, they weren't interested in watching.

Marna rubbed her arms. While those in the bar might like the danger, she didn't. She'd seen death for centuries. Wouldn't it be a nice change to finally see something else?

But maybe happiness was something only humans got to experience. Not the cursed. Not the paranormals.

Not me.

The vamp crept away. He tossed a few fast glances over his shoulder.

A shiver shook Marna's body. She could have sworn that she'd seen him before. "You think he's going to stay away?"

"I think if he doesn't, he'll be minus a head." Then Tanner put his arm back around her. She tried not to flinch, but his claws were still out, and she couldn't see a shifter's claws without remembering agony and terror.

Tanner pulled her flush against him. His head lowered and his lips brushed against her ear. "Don't act afraid of me. Don't pull away." The words were barely breathed against her.

Did she feel the lick of his tongue on the shell of her ear?

She shivered again, but Marna wasn't feeling fear right then. Well, she wasn't afraid of him. All the others in the room, yes, they scared her.

"Let them think you're mine," Tanner said, still in that same low whisper. One that she could suddenly imagine in the dark. Would he talk that way if they were alone? His voice low and growling?

Would he sound the same if they were tangled in sheets? Naked?

Stop.

"'Cause if they think you're mine, they'll know to stay the hell away from you."

She turned her head a few inches. Looked up into his blazing eyes. "I can . . . take care of myself."

She was an angel of death. She didn't need him.

Except . . . why won't my touch work? Why couldn't she still kill? Sammael killed at will. Why couldn't she?

"I can smell your fear. Smell it with a shifter's nose that's ten times stronger than a vamp's." He inhaled, like he was sampling her scent. "Fear smells too good to supernaturals. To many of us, that scent is pure temptation."

To the monsters who liked fear and pain. But Tanner wasn't like that, right? Wasn't he the cop? The good guy?

His brother Brandt had been evil, twisted, but Tanner was

supposed to be different. That was what he'd told her, when she first woke after her attack. Over and over, he'd promised he was different.

Lie? Or truth?

Right then, it didn't matter. She needed him. Marna forced her body to soften and slide against his. His arm tightened even more around her.

"Better." His voice was more growl than anything else.

His body seemed so warm and hard against hers. Shifters were usually big, muscled, and they'd been known to be some of the deadliest of the paranormals.

So why was she feeling safe with him?

Tanner led her the last few steps to the bar. "Human clubs . . . paranormal dives. They're all the same." He slapped his right hand down on the counter but kept his left arm firmly around her. "You want information, then you always go to the one source in the place who knows every single thing that happens."

The bartender, a woman with long, curly, red hair and demon-black eyes, strolled toward them. Her eyes widened a little as she looked at Marna and a soundless whistle slipped from her lips. "Don't see too many of your kind."

Her nails—blood-red and wicked sharp—tapped on the bar. Then her gaze slid from Marna to Tanner. The bartender stiffened, but did a good job of keeping any emotion from slipping across her face.

"I'm sure you see all sorts here," Tanner said, voice thickening a bit with a drawl that seemed to come and go as he pleased.

Tricky shifter. Was that slow drawl supposed to make him seem harmless? Nothing could pull off that lie. Maybe it was just supposed to make him seem a little *less* lethal? More good old boy?

"Right now," Tanner continued quietly, "I'm wanting to know if you can give me some information on those . . .

sorts . . . that you might see." He kept his hold on Marna, but he leaned toward the bartender.

The redhead lifted a brow. "Information ain't cheap. You know that, cop."

So she realized who and what Tanner was? Marna didn't know if that was good or bad. But either way, Marna decided she needed to step up her game. She wasn't just going to stand there. "What kind of payment do you want?" Marna demanded. Not that she had any money on her . . .

The woman's dark eyes glanced her way. "The kind that will get me out of this shithole before I turn up dead in a dark alley."

Dead—like the shifters?

"You *know,*" Tanner said.

A little shrug lifted the bartender's shoulders as she grabbed for a glass and began to fill it with a gleaming, gold liquid. "I know two shifters got to meet the devil the other night. Just a few streets away . . ." Her gaze was back on Tanner, but she said, voice whispering now, "And from what I hear, that devil looked a whole lot like the lady you're holding so tight." She shoved the glass toward him.

He didn't drink.

"It wasn't me," Marna said. They weren't going to pay the demon bartender just for telling them a story that was pure bull.

"A lost, blond angel, with shadow wings streaking from her back . . ." The bartender sighed. "Yeah, because there are so many folks like you running around the Quarter."

Shadow wings streaking from her back. Marna stiffened. "I don't have wings." Was that hard, angry voice really hers?

The lady poured another drink. This time, she pushed the glass toward Marna. "Not the real thing. Not anymore." She smirked. "What'd you do to fall?"

Marna leapt up, ready to jump right across that bar. *Nothing. I shouldn't have been forced here. I—*

Tanner pulled her back even as the bartender let out a little gasp and slammed back against the glasses on the wall. "Don't touch me!" the redhead cried out and this time, she didn't keep the blank mask on her face.

Fear.

So someone was finally afraid. *And it isn't me.* Right then, Marna was too angry—too *pissed,* as Sammael would have said—to be afraid. *I didn't fall. I didn't break the rules.*

But she was still in hell.

Pissed. Being angry was much better than being afraid. Fear was for the weak. She didn't want to be weak. "Better watch it," Marna said to the redhead as she shook off Tanner's hold. "I hear the monsters in this place love the scent of fear."

The bartender swallowed as she pried herself off the wall of glasses. She glanced around and flushed when she realized that others had seen her.

Even in Hell, it was hard to miss a scream.

"Meet me out back," she told them, grabbing up another glass and a bottle of gold liquid before turning away. "You can tell me what you'll pay, and maybe I'll tell you what I know."

"There's no *maybe,*" Tanner said.

The redhead kept walking away from them. "Then make the price high enough." She disappeared through a pair of swinging, double doors.

And she left them in Hell.

Cadence LaVert kept a smirk on her face until she entered the back room of Hell. Then she tightened her fist around the glass in her hand, and it shattered.

Sonofabitch.

That angel had almost touched her.

No fucking way. Cadence wasn't ready for death. She'd

screwed up too many times. Nothing good waited for her on the other side.

Before she bit the dust, she had to make some kind of amends.

Maybe for the lover she'd murdered.

But he'd had it coming. Trying to beat her, trying to *hurt* her. Bill hadn't realized just what he'd been dealing with.

Before he'd died, he'd known. She'd made sure of it.

Cadence lifted the bottle to her lips and gulped. She barely felt the burn as the liquid rolled down her throat.

Ten thousand? Would that be enough cash? She knew about the cop shifter. The guy who tried to play good with the humans but who was really just as fucked up as the rest of the supernaturals in New Orleans.

He had some cash, she was sure of it. He could give her the money. She could split town, and the world would keep right on going.

As if she'd never even existed.

A sweet scent teased her nose. Freaking flowers. *That angel.*

"I told you to meet me outside!" Cadence swung around.

No one was there.

Just boxes. A rat scurrying around. Dust.

Her heart was racing. She'd made a mistake. Been in the wrong place, at the wrong time. But when she'd gone to that alley, she'd never known what was going to happen. She'd just needed to make a purchase. Needed to buy a few drugs to get her through the night.

Demons needed drugs. As far as Cadence was concerned, that was a simple fact. She had to use her drugs. Otherwise, she couldn't shut out the voices in her head.

One of those voices had made her kill her father when she was twelve. The voice had told her that daddy wanted to do bad things to her. Such very, very bad things.

She'd stopped him. He hadn't been able to hurt her.

The same voice had told her about Bill's dark side. How he liked to hurt women. To hit until you couldn't move. She'd ignored the voice at first.

But the voice had been right. Her bruises and broken bones had proved its truth soon enough.

The voice was quiet tonight. The drugs were still in her system. The drugs muted all the voices that wanted to whisper to her about the wicked things in the world.

I'm wicked.

She'd gotten the drugs from the alley. Seen the death that waited for those two panther shifters.

I saw what you did. She'd never be able to forget that night.

Now it was time to collect and get out of there. The shifter and his angel should have made it around to the back of Hell by now. She could slip out, make her deal, and get away.

Cadence dropped the bottle. It spilled on the floor, a long, wet stain, and the rat scurried toward it. Cadence grabbed her bag. There'd be no missing this shithole for her.

She yanked open the back door. Slipped out into the night. The air was hot. Always was, down in this freaking pit. Maybe she'd go someplace up north. Someplace where it actually snowed. She'd never seen real snow. Wouldn't that be a kick?

Careful . . .

That whisper came from her own mind. The voice was waking up. Dammit. No. Not now.

Cadence shoved her hand into her bag. She had a few more white pills left. They'd shut up the voice. Buy her more time.

Blood. That horrible whisper again.

She couldn't find the damn pills.

Blood on the dirty bricks. Blood on the ground. Can't scream. Can't—

Her fingers closed around one small pill. She shoved it in her mouth and swallowed. Her hands were shaking, but that wasn't new. When the voice screamed so loud in her mind—or even when it whispered—her hands trembled.

But the pill was in her body now. Her heart rate began to slow. The drug always worked fast. After a moment, the voice fell silent.

It was just her now. Alone in the night.

Cadence sucked in a few quick breaths. Where was the shifter? He'd better show up and get ready to hand over some serious cash. 'Cause if he wanted to hear all the juicy bits that she had to share, he'd need to—

"Hello, Cadence."

She stiffened. Impossible. That voice—it belonged to a dead man. She knew. She'd put Bill in the ground herself. Dug the grave and dumped his sorry ass inside and left him in the middle of the woods.

"Why don't you come here . . . " Bill's voice said from the darkness, "and give me a kiss, baby girl?"

Her blood iced. That *was* Bill's voice. When she turned, she saw him walking from the shadows. Bill. With his balding head, his tattoos, and the slightly crooked smile that had disarmed her from the first moment she met him.

I didn't see the monster. That smile had blinded her.

Bill had been human. She'd thought that meant he was safe. Too late, she'd learned how vicious humans could be.

Bill stalked toward her. Cadence didn't move. She *couldn't* move. "B-Bill?" What the hell? Had he turned vamp on her? That was the only thing that made sense. He must've been a vamp before she buried him. Tricky asshole. And here she'd been feeling all guilty for murdering the guy.

His arms grabbed her and pulled her tight against him. "I've missed you," he said. His hands *hurt*. That was nothing new. His hammy hands always liked to hurt her.

She hadn't missed him.

Then she realized that he didn't smell the same. Not like stale cigarettes and old beer. Not even that musky scent human males always seemed to carry.

She pushed away and stared up at him as terror clawed its way through her.

Run.

The voice in her head was back. Too late.

She didn't see the knife, not at first. But Cadence felt the blade as it sliced through her skin. Sliced so deep that it stole her breath as it cut open her throat.

Blood flew around her, splattering onto the old bricks. Onto the dirt. She tried to scream, but couldn't.

Her voice was gone.

Cadence's body fell to the ground. She was on her stomach, trying to crawl with her last bit of strength.

"Fucking bitch. You aren't telling anybody about me."

Then the knife plunged into her back.

Can't scream.

There'd be no time to make amends. Cadence felt death coming for her.

No time—

Chapter Four

The scent of fresh blood hit him like a punch to the gut when Tanner shoved open the back door of Hell. The beast inside growled in pleasure.

The panther he carried always liked the blood too much.

"Tanner? What's wrong?"

He'd shoved up his arm and blocked Marna's path. He just hadn't wanted her racing into a bloodbath. But she seemed oblivious. How could she miss that scent?

"Stay inside," he told her, pushing her back. He wanted to make sure she was safe while he faced whatever nightmare might be waiting out there.

But she shook her head. "Stay in there with the vamps? I don't think so."

She didn't realize that those bastards could be the least of her troubles. It was just—shit, there *wasn't* any safe place for her.

"Death angel, remember?" she whispered to him.

How could he forget? Marna just looked so fragile, he kept wanting to protect her. When she was probably strong enough to be protecting him.

He let his claws break from his fingertips. Tanner knew that he should always go into a battle with the best possible weapon—and his claws had never let him down before.

He didn't hear anyone else out there. He just smelled blood. Garbage. Stale cigarettes.

Flowers?

What the fuck?

The faint scent wasn't coming from Marna—but from the right. In the shadows.

Tanner edged closer, with Marna on his heels. A few more feet, a turn to the right—

A horrified gasp slipped from Marna. Tanner's jaw locked.

It looked like the bartender wasn't gonna be giving them any info. It looked like she wasn't gonna be doing anything, ever again.

The redhead lay face down on the ground, and with his enhanced vision, Tanner could easily see through the darkness—and see the puddle of blood that surrounded her.

Tanner advanced carefully. His gaze swept the alley. No sign of anyone else, but . . .

Marna rushed by him. She knelt next to the bartender, reaching out to touch her.

"Don't!" Tanner snapped.

Marna glanced back up at him, her eyes huge as her hand hovered in the air above the redhead. "She's still alive."

Knife wounds covered the redhead's back and when he crouched next to her, joining Marna, Tanner winced at the sight of the bartender's gaping throat. Her head was turned to the side, giving him a perfect view of that brutal damage. A desperate rasp escaped from her chest as she fought to breathe.

How the hell was the lady still clinging to life?

The finger of her right hand was trembling. Shaking so hard. And she was dipping it into her own blood. Dipping it and—

Writing?

Tanner stared at the splotches she'd made on the broken cement. He could see an A, an N. Was that C or G?

Angel.

She began to convulse.

"Someone's coming for her," Marna said, voice sad. She stroked back the bartender's hair. "It's okay," she told the other woman. "An angel is almost—"

A woman shouldn't die with that much terror in her eyes. Tanner reached for the bartender, ignored the blood and the growing scent of flowers in the air.

Flowers and fucking angels. You could always smell 'em. No wonder he'd caught that scent mixed with the blood. An angel of death was coming to take the redhead away.

And she didn't want to go. "Go inside!" Tanner snapped out to Marna as he tried to put pressure on the woman's wounds. *So many wounds. Too many.* "Get an ambulance out here! Tell them we need help!"

"Tanner, you know it's—"

Too late.

He turned his head. Met Marna's eyes. Saw the glimmer of tears that she couldn't hide. "She's not dead yet, so it's not too late." He'd fought death before.

Fought, lost.

But still *fought.*

Marna scrambled to her feet and rushed back inside.

That floral scent deepened. The angel was coming, but now, hell, at least he'd gotten Marna away from the scene.

I don't want the angel near her.

A tear leaked from the redhead's eye. "You just have to hold on," he told her. "Just fight a little longer and—"

Her gaze slid to the left. Widened.

Tanner followed her gaze. While he saw nothing, Tanner felt the distinct chill in the air. They weren't alone.

He couldn't see the angel of death walking in that alley, but *she* could, and the redhead was terrified.

Her hands dug into him as she tried to speak. But with

most of her throat gone, there was no way he could understand the grunts and gurgles she made.

More tears fell. Her nails scratched into his skin.

"Stay away from her!" Tanner yelled at the darkness.

Her body was so cold. There was so much blood. Who'd done this to her? Why?

Because of what she knew? What she'd been minutes away from telling them?

Tanner felt the whisper of wind against his skin, and then—

Then she stopped groaning. Stopped crying. Stopped living.

The angel of death had taken her away.

Sonofabitch.

Marna rushed back through the bar. She'd grabbed a waitress and snatched her cell phone to make the nine-one-one call. Telling the dispatcher to come to Hell? Yeah, that had gone over real well. She'd wasted moments arguing with the dispatcher and trying to get her to understand that this wasn't some prank.

A woman was dying.

Marna threw open the door to the back room, hurried forward, and—

Not alone.

"Why would an angel of death . . ." The voice—that freaking voice that she knew belonged to the blond vampire who'd wanted to drink her before—rose from the shadows as he stepped into the light. "Why would someone like you smell so strongly of fear?"

He glided forward in a movement that was way too fast, putting him between her and that back door.

"You need to get out of my way," she told him, heart pounding fast from her frantic race through Hell and from her growing fear. "Someone's dying out there."

"Someone's already dead out there." He inhaled. "That

much blood . . . not even a demon like Cadence could survive an attack like that."

Cadence? Had that been the woman's name? And he already knew that she was dead? But—

In a blink, he was in front of her. Smiling. Flashing those sharp fangs. "Why would you smell like such sweet fear?" he asked again, eyes narrowing. "Unless you had a reason to be afraid." His hand lifted toward her neck. "Do you have a reason, angel?"

"I-I don't want to hurt you."

He laughed darkly at that. "I don't think you can." His tongue slid over the edge of one fang. "If you could, your heart wouldn't be racing so fast right now."

Over the centuries, she'd seen firsthand just what sort of violence vampires could unleash. She'd seen the empty shells left of angels—shells discarded after vampires had drained them dry.

Not me.

She shoved out at him as hard as she could. The vamp flew through the air and slammed into the back door. Marna scrambled a few steps away, and her fingers curled around a knife that had been tossed to the floor. She put her hand behind her back, hiding the weapon.

But then he rose too quickly, pretended to brush himself off, and he said, "Interesting. You're stronger than you look." One blond brow rose. "But is that all you've got?"

No, she had a knife she could drive into his heart. *A knife won't keep a vamp down.* "I—"

His hand was around her throat. *Moved too fast.* He'd leapt toward her and attacked in an instant. "I thought your kind killed when you touched." There was no missing the anger in his voice. "That's what you were supposed to do."

Wait, had this guy *wanted* her to kill him?

Wood shattered as the back door was smashed in. "And you were supposed to stay the *fuck* away from her."

Tanner.

She'd never been so glad to see her panther shifter.

The vampire didn't look away from her. Um, shouldn't he be turning to face the new threat? But he just leaned in closer to her. "I know," he whispered to her. "If you aren't careful, they'll *all* know."

Tanner yanked him away from Marna and raised his claws. "I *warned* you."

The vamp just laughed. "Go ahead. Cut off my head, but then you'll never know who's after your little angel."

"Maybe I won't start by cutting off your head." Tanner flashed his own growing fangs as he lifted his claws. "Maybe I'll have some fun and I'll make you beg to tell me all you know, *before* I cut off your head."

Still no fear from the vamp. "Now is that any way for a cop to act?"

Tanner pushed him against the nearest wall and drove his claws into the guy's shoulder. Marna flinched and glanced away—and she hid her knife.

"Why does the sight of your claws . . . " the vampire asked, voice sly, "make her go so pale?"

Marna looked back at them.

Tanner stiffened and glanced her way. "I—"

The vampire slammed his head into Tanner's, and a powerful punch from the blond had Tanner stumbling back.

"I'll tell you what I know. Tell you every little thing." The vampire's eyes were black now. She knew a vamp's eyes turned to black when they were either having sex or—or—

Killing.

"I'll tell you," the vampire promised, "but there'll be a price for that information."

Tanner put his body in front of hers. "Isn't there always?"

A hard laugh from the vamp. Then he said, "She bleeds for me, and I'll talk."

"*Not* gonna happen." This time, Tanner was the one to drive a punch, one that rammed into the vampire's chest. Marna heard the sickening crunch of bones.

The vamp spat out blood. "Kane. I'm Riley Kane. When you're ready to deal . . ." His eyes found Marna's over Tanner's shoulder. "You come back here, and you ask for me."

Voices rose. Shouts came from out in the bar.

The vamp shook his head and spared her another fast glance. "You called humans . . . to come and help in Hell? How do you really think this will go down?"

Sirens screamed.

Tanner swore. *What? Why was he swearing then?* He'd been the one to *tell* her to get help.

"Better run, cop." Now the vamp was warning them. "Even humans can smell blood in the air." Then Kane whirled and leapt through the shattered remains of the door.

Marna turned back toward the shouts. She had to find a way to help the humans. With all those supernaturals in there, it would be a nightmare for them.

A nightmare that they never expected to see.

"Don't." Tanner caught her arm and pulled her back toward the broken door—and the waiting night. "This place is enchanted. The humans won't get inside the bar. The spell keeps them out."

"But . . . the screams . . ."

"There's always screaming in Hell." They were outside now and moving so fast that Marna had to run to keep up with him. "And the EMTs who are on night-shift duty, trust me, baby, they understand more than you think. Half of them *are* paranormals. They'll find the body, and the right people will know how to handle her." His eyes glittered in the darkness. "I'm not the only paranormal on the force. Not even close."

They'd circled back to the parking lot just a few blocks

away. They jumped in his vehicle and raced from the scene, even as the ambulance roared toward Hell.

They passed the ambulance, and the glowing circle of lights lit up Tanner's SUV.

Then . . .

Silence.

The miles flew past. Marna's heart began to slow to a normal rate, but when she looked down, she realized she had blood on her hands. She swallowed and fisted her fingers. "I-I wish we could have saved her."

Tanner didn't speak.

"It was all for nothing." Anger burned in her. Anger, fear, guilt—why couldn't she have done *something?*

For so long, she'd been the one to greet humans and supernaturals at their moment of passing. She'd never been able to help any of those souls. Her job had been to kill. To take them from this world.

Why couldn't she just save *one* person?

"It wasn't for nothing." Cold. Hard.

Marna peered his way.

"She died right before she could talk to us, and believe me, coincidences like that don't happen."

"But—"

"She died, and she was *terrified* of the angel who came for her." He spared her a fast glance. "What does that tell you?"

She licked her lips. "Everyone . . . I mean, most are scared when they see the angels coming for them." Because humans and those without the blood of celestial beings in them could never see angels, at least not until the moment right before their passing. And who wouldn't be scared then?

"Maybe . . . or maybe she was so scared because she knew what her *killer* was."

Her breath caught, but Marna shook her head. "No, an

angel of death wouldn't kill that way." The attack had been too violent. Too . . . bloody. "All death angels have to do is touch. There's no reason to attack like that unless—"

"Unless you like the feel of slicing into someone's flesh. Unless you want to torture and punish until your victim is left twitching on the ground."

Like the bartender.

"Unless you're one fucked-up angel, and if that's the case, if there's another Fallen in the city, one who's slicing and killing for fun, then, well . . ."

Tanner didn't finish. But he didn't have to. She understood.

If a Fallen was going on a killing spree in New Orleans, then the humans and the supernaturals were all about to face a waking nightmare.

Streaks of blood slid across the sky as the sun rose. Tanner strode toward his bedroom. He hadn't fixed the broken door downstairs, not yet, but he'd cleared away the bedroom door he'd shattered.

Dawn was coming. He'd showered, changed, and, dammit, he couldn't get her out of his mind.

He stood in the doorway, and her scent tried to pull him in. He could hear the light rustle of the sheets. Tanner knew that she was just steps away.

Want.

The panther's growl had him taking another step closer.

"Stay away from me, Tanner."

Marna's words made his hands clench into fists.

"Pretend the door's there," she said, voice drifting to him. "And just walk away."

Screw that. He walked into the room. Tanner heard her gasp.

"I told you to—"

"We have to talk." She was in his bed. The covers were pulled up to her chin—*always so afraid of me*—and her hair was a tangled fall around her face.

"Later." Marna swallowed and lifted her chin higher. Of course, she lifted the covers higher, too. "I want to be alone now. I don't want—"

You.

In two seconds, he was on that bed with her. Marna tried to scramble back. Too late. He grabbed her hand and forced it against his bare chest.

Her breath rasped out, and she tried to jerk away from him. "Stop it!"

"Make me." A cruel taunt, but he had to see what would happen.

Marna's blue eyes widened as she tried to yank her hand away again. He just tightened his hold. Her palm was soft against his chest. Her splayed fingers pressed right over his racing heart.

"Let me go!"

The covers had dropped. She had on a black bra—one he'd raced out and bought for her before they'd gone to Hell. He'd picked up clothes for her, fantasized a bit about her in the silk panties, and—

Her left fist plowed into his face.

He shook his head, barely feeling the sting of that blow, as realization settled heavily in his gut. "You can't do it."

No wonder the vampire had been so close to her.

Her breath rushed out, far too fast, and he could see the frantic race of her pulse at the base of her neck. "Don't push me." Her words were loud, rushed. "I don't want to hurt you!"

"You can't." Certain now. "You can't hurt me." She was touching him. Flesh to flesh.

Her skin was so pale. Her eyes wide. And the scent of her fear was driving him freaking insane. "You can't kill me.

You can't use the Death Touch." Fuck. "Why the hell didn't you tell me? That vamp could have drained you dry!"

But, even as he asked, Tanner knew why she hadn't told him. The lady didn't trust him, not for one single minute.

"I could have handled him," Marna gritted out.

He still held her hand pinned against his chest. "Oh, yeah? How? The way you're handling me right now?"

Then she moved, so fast that he didn't even see the motion of her body. Angels could always move so quickly. Marna just hadn't moved that way in a while, and he'd forgotten . . .

She shoved him back on the bed and straddled him, and Marna shoved a knife against his throat.

Now where the hell had she gotten that little trinket?

The silver began to slice into his flesh.

"I found this back at Hell," she told him, fingers clenched tightly around the hilt of the blade. "I had it when that vamp came at me. I could've used it on him."

"A little knife wouldn't stop him." *Or me.* Silver would hurt like a bitch because the old tale about shifters and silver not mixing so well was true, but she wouldn't have time to do any permanent damage. Permanent like cutting out his heart.

"It would have slowed him down. Vampires get weaker with blood loss. I would have been sure to make him plenty weak."

Strange to hear such bloodthirsty plans come from her lips. He had to remember, the lady was far deadlier than she appeared.

Even if she'd somehow lost the Death Touch.

"When did you know?" Her legs straddled him. Did she feel the swelling cock shoving against her? Probably. Tanner didn't really see how she could miss that. Not like it was a small thing.

The blade dug a bit deeper into his skin. "I went after

those bastard panther shifters, LaRue and Stokes," Marna confessed. "I went after the jerks because I wanted to kill them."

So she had been seeking some vengeance. Tanner tried to keep his body perfectly still beneath her. He had one hell of a view, and other than the stinging pain in his neck, being beneath her was pretty damn pleasurable.

Being *in* her, that would be even better.

A hungry growl slipped from him.

Marna frowned down at him.

Tanner cleared his throat. "What happened?"

Her tongue swiped over her lips. His cock jerked.

"I-I tracked them in the Quarter," she said. "I followed them, for days. I waited, wanting the perfect moment."

To strike.

Definitely a bloodthirsty angel. He'd have to remember that little tidbit about her. Marna sure wasn't all sunshine and light, no matter how she appeared.

"I was going to walk right up to them. Look them straight in the eyes, and watch as their lives drained away."

Cold. Vicious.

He would have done the exact same thing. He liked for his kills to be personal. Those getting payback, well, they needed to see just who was delivering the justice to them.

"They always went to the same place for drinks. I waited until the bar on Bourbon Street was almost empty, and then I went inside."

Tanner heard the echo of pain in her voice. "What did they do to you?"

"Nothing." A laugh, heavy with bitterness, slipped from her. "I marched up to Stokes. Put my hand on his chest and waited for him to look at me with fear in his eyes."

Beau Stokes had always been a sadistic prick. So eager to attack weaker prey. So quick to slice with his claws and laugh when his prey begged for mercy.

"But he didn't even know who I was," Marna whispered. Did she realize she still held the knife to his throat? "He tried to kiss me. Tried to pull me closer to him, like I was another body to screw in that dark bar."

Tanner didn't speak.

"I wanted to kill him. I was trying to. LaRue was coming toward us, laughing, and I wanted them both to die." Her head dipped forward, and the curtain of her hair hid her face.

Tanner lifted his hand and pushed back her hair. He could barely feel the sting of the knife now. "But they didn't die."

Her lashes slowly lifted. "Angels of death—those Fallen and those who still have their wings—all of them can kill with a touch. That's our power. Our one, unbreakable gift. Death."

Death was a gift?

"I ran from the shifters. They were laughing at me while I ran away." Her breath rasped out. "When Brandt took my wings from me, he took away *everything* that I was. I have nothing now. *Nothing.*"

But fury. A rage so dark it had sent her after the panthers—ready to kill and destroy.

"Angels have magic. They can do so much—conjure, stir fire." A bitter laugh came from her. "I can't even make smoke." She shook her head. "So what am I supposed to do now?" Marna asked him and then she blinked, seeming to finally realize that she still had a knife at his throat. Her hand lifted as she took the knife away from his jugular. "Just wait around for a vamp to drain me? Wait for a shifter to slice me and—"

It was his turn to have her flat on her back. Tanner crushed her into the mattress. He didn't have to worry about a Death Touch now. She wasn't going to lose control.

Maybe it was time he did.

"I know what you're gonna do." His mouth was so close

to hers. Less than an inch away. So close he could already taste her.

"Wh-what?"

"Live." It was time that his angel learned what life was really about. Not just pain and fear and rage.

Lust. Need.

Pleasure.

He kissed her.

Chapter Five

Marna wasn't prepared for the lick of fire that seemed to ignite within her body when Tanner kissed her. Part of her knew that she should shove him away, but her hands weren't listening to that part. Instead, her hands were wrapping around his broad shoulders and pulling him closer.

She'd never kissed a man . . . until him. Death angels didn't kiss. They didn't caress.

They only touched to kill.

For her kind, what was the point of touching? Angels didn't yearn. They didn't need. They didn't lust.

At least, they didn't until they fell. Then all of the human emotions and needs slammed into them.

Lust. She was sure lusting right then.

Tanner had been the first man to kiss her, and when she'd felt that initial touch of his lips against hers, she'd wanted more.

"Don't be afraid of me," he whispered against her mouth.

Fear was the last thing she felt right then. Her nipples were so tight they ached, and her body was rubbing against him because she felt so . . . restless.

Aching.

Needing.

"Kiss me back," his rough order.

Her tongue moved against his. Her lips opened wider, and she tasted the shifter.

Her legs were parted, and she could feel the heavy press of his erection against her. Tanner wanted her. Maybe that should have scared her. It didn't. It made her feel . . .

Powerful.

Sexy. She'd never felt sexy before. But Tanner wanted her, so she had to be sexy to him.

His hand flattened over her stomach. The ache between her legs grew sharper, and Marna lifted her hips up against him. His fingers—a little rough, so strong—rose and covered her bra.

She didn't want him touching the bra. Marna wanted his hands on her breasts.

His mouth. What would it feel like if he licked her nipple? Sucked the aching flesh?

Her heart was racing, her body quivering, and she knew this was wrong. She should stop but . . .

Humans enjoyed sex so much. They lied, stole, even killed for their fleeting pleasure.

She'd never tasted pleasure. She knew too much about pain.

I want my taste.

Growing bolder, Marna sucked against his lower lip. Tanner growled. She liked it when he growled. The sound was wild, and that was just the way he made her feel.

Her nails dug into his shoulders.

Then his hand was sliding beneath her bra, and his fingers stroked her tight nipple. The first touch of his hand had her hissing out a breath.

Tanner stilled.

The drumming of Marna's heartbeat echoed in her ears. Tanner lifted his head. She could see the power of his beast reflected in his eyes. His face was harder, sharper, and there was no missing his lust.

For me.

"I want . . ." Were those words really hers? That husky, hungry voice—hers? *Yes.* "I want your mouth on me."

His pupils expanded. "Baby, all you had to do was ask." Then his dark head lowered. His breath rasped over one eager breast and then she felt—

His tongue. Sliding over the nipple. Easing over the peak. Her heels dug into the mattress even as a ragged moan escaped from her.

A hot current seemed to streak from her breast to her sex. She was aching, empty, and her hips tilted up so she could better rub her sex against his cock.

The friction just intensified the ache. Pleasure waited, tempting her, just out of reach.

He sucked her nipple. Scored her flesh with his teeth.

The ache built. Her eyes squeezed shut. She couldn't seem to draw in a deep breath.

Then he began to stroke her other breast. The sensual touch had her jerking beneath him, and she realized that her panties were wet.

"So damn beautiful."

His growled words made her eyes open. She'd never thought about beauty much before. Yet he made her feel beautiful right then.

Feeling beautiful—that just wasn't enough. Her body seemed too hot, her heart raced too fast, and she wanted the pleasure that was so close.

Her hands slid over his chest. Her touch was slower than his had been. Far less certain. But as she touched him, his body stiffened against her, the muscles clenching.

"You should . . . be careful." His words barely sounded human as he gritted them out. "Shifters . . . aren't known for their control."

She was already losing her own control. What did it matter? "I want to know . . ." Marna stopped. She wasn't sure what to say. Pleasure? Sex? Was that what she wanted? Did she just want to know what it felt like?

He wasn't a safe test for her. She should find someone else. Someone *not* a shifter.

Someone who wasn't the brother of the bastard who'd hurt her so badly before.

Tanner isn't like him.

Tanner's hand eased down her body. She expected him to rip away her panties. Weren't shifters supposed to be savage and uncontrolled like that?

But he didn't rip them away. He slowly eased down the silk. Silk *he'd* bought. His mouth kissed its way from her belly button on down to—

Her breath caught in her throat. His fingers were between her legs, parting her to him, and his mouth—*Tanner's mouth*—was on her sensitive flesh. His tongue swiped over her, and her hips jerked as if an electric shock had jolted her.

Again.

She'd whispered the word. But she realized she didn't have to tell him. Tanner was licking her. Kissing her. Tasting her with his tongue even as his finger slid into her body. The pleasure might have been out of her reach before, but right then it was *so* close.

His tongue swiped over her core again. Then his mouth was on her clit and he sucked—

Marna screamed when the climax hit her. An explosion of pleasure shook her whole body. It went on and on, and the room actually seemed to dim around her.

Nothing, *nothing* had ever been like this. So good. So consuming.

So much . . . *pleasure.*

Marna realized her hands were fisted in Tanner's dark hair. Her thighs were trembling, and her breath heaved out. She forced her fingers to unclench. Forced herself to suck in more air for her starving lungs.

Tanner's head lifted. His eyes were shining as he stared at her—and he licked his lips.

Her sex clenched.

"I love the way you taste." His voice was so deep, dark.

She couldn't speak. Had she shouted before? Screamed in pleasure?

Maybe.

"I could eat you up."

Her heart lurched.

His gaze dropped to her sex once more. He swallowed. "Want . . ."

She still wanted him. She'd come, erupted, but . . .

Marna wanted Tanner inside of her.

And he was—he was pulling away? *Why?* This wasn't the way things worked, at least not for humans. "Tanner?"

He rose beside the bed and stood with his back to her. She saw the heavy marks on his skin, marks she hadn't even noticed before. Long, twisting scars that cut deep into his flesh. Scars that curled out from his back, wrapped around his sides and—

He turned to glance back at her.

Her gaze locked on the scars that cut across his stomach. Sunlight shot through the window, so there was no hiding the scars. But then, Tanner wasn't trying to hide the marks.

She was the one who hid her scars.

"That was . . ." His hands were clenched. "You haven't been with a man before, have you?"

Why lie? Oh, right, she *couldn't*. "You're my first."

A shudder worked over him, and his fists whitened. "I could tell. Your response…the way you came for me." His breath rasped out. "Beautiful."

Her thighs were still shaking. And her shifter—he was turning and walking away. "Why? Why are you leaving me?"

His hand lifted and his fingers curled around the door frame. She could see the edge of his claws breaking through the skin of his fingertips. He dug those claws into the wood, and Marna swallowed.

"You aren't ready for what I'll do to you."

Were his words supposed to be a threat? Or a promise?

"First times aren't meant for shifters." He wasn't looking at her. His claws dug deeper into the doorframe. "We're too rough. Too wild." His laugh was bitter. "Especially for an angel."

Marna grabbed for the covers and pulled them around her body. She hadn't known a need for modesty, until she fell. "So what was . . . that?" Him, kissing her, touching her, tasting her?

"It was me being fucking starving for you." His claws had carved deep grooves into the wood. "And realizing how dangerous I can be to you."

She rose from the bed. Marna wrapped the sheet around her and headed toward him. "I don't think you are." When had things changed for her? She could see his claws. His scars.

Doesn't matter.

He was a shifter, and he was the man who'd given her a taste of paradise on earth. Not wild. Not dangerous.

Perfect pleasure.

She leaned forward and brushed her lips over a scar that twisted the flesh of his back.

Her lips had barely skimmed over his flesh when he whirled to face her. *"Don't."*

"I want to." She wanted to kiss and touch more of him. He'd had his chance. Wasn't it hers, now?

"You don't understand." He pushed her back. Took a step away from her as if he needed extra distance. His nostrils flared. "If I take you, there'll be no going back for you. For me."

Marna shook her head. "What does it matter? Humans have sex all the time—"

"I'm not human."

She stared at him.

"Neither are you."

His erection pressed against the front of his jeans. He was that aroused, and still telling her no?

"Panthers," he spoke slowly, "we're territorial. When something is ours, it's *ours.* Nothing, no one, takes what belongs to us." He took another step away from her. "We're vicious, deadly, and the worst nightmares most folks have ever seen."

Marna didn't know what to say. It was true that the only nightmare she'd had since being on earth had been about panthers. Their claws and bloodlust. But now . . .

"For your first time, you don't want that."

She wanted him.

"If I have much more of you . . ." His eyes burned. His fangs elongated. His face—he was *changing.* Shifting. "I won't ever let you go."

He whirled away from her then. Marna chased after him. He was shifting before her eyes. His bones snapped, his body contorted, and he hit the landing below with a thud.

"Tanner!"

His head turned, and he stared back up at her. "Don't . . . watch." Gravel-rough.

But she couldn't look away. Fur burst along his skin, perfect, black fur that lined his body. His eyes glowed, growing brighter, *brighter,* and the man that he'd been vanished as the beast took his place.

The panther was huge. Muscled, lethal. She'd never seen a more powerful killing machine. When he opened his mouth and roared, his razor-sharp teeth glinted. His claws, sharp enough to rip a man to shreds, flashed as he threw up his front legs.

How much of the man still remained inside of the beast? Marna crept slowly down the stairs, the end of the sheet trailing behind her like a bride's wedding dress.

Her hand slid down the wooden banister.

He roared again.

Her panther was very, very angry.

But he wasn't attacking her. Wasn't even trying to come close. Instead, as she neared the bottom of the steps, he spun away and lunged toward the back of the house.

"Tanner, wait!" She rushed after him, but the panther leapt through a picture window. Glass shattered, raining down, and the panther hurtled toward the woods that waited just behind the old house.

He didn't look back.

She didn't call out to him again.

He was an idiot. Tanner ran through the woods until his beast had settled down. Until the wild hunger for Marna eased. Until he could breathe without tasting her.

Fucking. Idiot.

He shifted back into the form of a man and his hands dug into the earth. He'd had her beneath him. Been ready to thrust deep into her silken core, and he'd stopped.

Pulling back hadn't been the panther's plan. The beast had snarled and fought him, desperate for more of Marna. He'd never had a shift come on him so suddenly.

The panther didn't like being denied what was his.

And the beast definitely thought of Marna that way.

Mine.

He'd tried to warn her. Once he'd realized—*her first, her only*—he'd tried to let her know the danger that faced her. Tanner wasn't the sharing sort, and if he had that silken body, no one else would get near her.

Was she ready for the full force of his lust? The dark needs that he had? Could an angel even begin to understand what he'd want from her?

Tanner rose to his feet and began to stalk back through the

woods. He owned over fifteen acres here. Plenty of room for the panther to run without worrying about prying eyes.

He'd been gentle before. Did she realize the battle he'd fought? He'd shown her only the softest of touches. Given her only a glimpse of what could be.

All the while, the panther had clawed and fought inside of him. *Take. Take.*

The beast recognized Marna for what she was. Oh, it wasn't some predestined, our-souls-are-meant-as-one bullshit. He didn't believe in that crap.

It was chemical. Physical. The panther scenting a female that could be a genetic match for him. A female strong enough to carry his offspring.

An angel and a shifter? Insane. The last blend like that had ended up producing his fucked-up brother Brandt.

But . . .

He wanted Marna. He ached for her. He dreamed of her at night.

He hungered for her.

Mate.

If he took her, the panther would claim her as a mate. Then there'd be no turning back, not for either of them.

He reached the shed he'd built in the middle of his property and found the backup clothes he kept when he needed to run. He yanked up the jeans and jerked on the shirt, covering his scars.

She'd actually kissed a scar on his back. He'd carried the wounds for so long. He didn't think about them much anymore.

His father had been a sadistic bastard.

I won't be like him.

Tanner left the shed. He'd taken just a few steps when the scent hit him. Then he realized just what a fatal mistake he'd made.

No, no. He broke into a run as he raced back for the main house.

There was no mistaking the scent in the air—male, human, *familiar.* This was the last thing he needed. With Marna alone there . . .

Fucking disastrous.

His legs burned as he raced faster, faster—

He could see the house.

And he could see the human who was climbing into his broken window.

What. The. Hell.

"Jonathan!" His voice rang out, sending birds scattering from the nearby trees.

His partner froze, then glanced slowly back over his shoulder. Jonathan's eyes were narrowed, and he had his gun in his hand.

Tanner hoped the guy didn't get trigger happy again this time. Tanner lifted his hands, showing he was unarmed. "Easy there, partner."

Jonathan lowered his weapon. "You've had a break-in."

No. A breakout. The guy should have noticed that the glass had fallen the wrong way. Shoddy investigative work. "No." Tanner offered him a slightly embarrassed grin. "Just a little accident." He hoped the man hadn't called for backup. Talk about having to deal with a pain in his ass.

"Your front door . . . it looked damaged, too." Jonathan had lowered the gun, but he hadn't holstered the weapon. Interesting. "That's why I came around back."

Tanner shrugged. "I'm doing some home repairs." He put his hands on his hips. "Sometimes, they don't go as well as I'd like." He couldn't hear anything from inside the house. Good. As long as Marna stayed quiet, they were golden.

But if his angel decided to come out . . .

I don't want to hurt him.

Too bad he'd spent his life doing things that he didn't really want to do.

Jonathan gave a low laugh. "Yeah, man, I guess they don't." Finally, *finally,* the guy holstered his weapon. "Look, I came by 'cause we need to talk." His partner folded his arms over his chest. "I know you think I overreacted—"

Overreacted? The dude needed to try again. "You shot her." That fact still pissed him off. Tanner kept his hands down. The better not to punch the jerk again. Breaking in a new partner sucked. Especially when the guy was human, and Tanner had to constantly watch his step with the fellow.

"She was a suspected killer," Jonathan defended himself. "Coming at me with a weapon—"

"A table leg." The anger broke through his voice. "She had a table leg, not a gun. We could have taken her down without lethal force."

"Maybe." Jonathan's shoulders straightened. "If she'd been human."

Oh, the fuck, no. The guy *knew?* With an effort, Tanner kept his face blank.

"Since she wasn't human, since I'd dealt with her kind before, I knew we'd both be safer if I took the shot." Jonathan rubbed his jaw. "I figured the punch and a mild concussion were worth saving our asses."

You didn't save us. Tanner kept his voice mild, yanking back the anger now. "Uh, partner, I think you might have hit your head harder than anyone thought when you fell. Have you, um, been talking to the department shrink about the non-humans out there?"

Jonathan's lips tightened. "Her body vanished from the morgue. The doctor who was treating her? He's vanished, too."

No, Cody had just headed back to his home in the swamp. He'd done his job and gone back to his life.

"They just misplaced her," Tanner said, and he strode toward the front of the house. Time to get this guy off his property. "Bodies don't just vanish. They put the wrong toe tag on her. She'll turn up." A story he'd used before. And eventually, "Marna Smith's" remains would turn up. The ashes they were gonna use for her should be ready any day.

Only, Jonathan didn't seem to be buying his story. "Why are you pretending? I *know* about you." The guy was following him. Good.

Tanner just kept walking. It figured he'd get partnered up with the one human cop who thought he knew the score in New Orleans. Keeping his voice bland, Tanner said, "You know I'm a cop, big deal. That's pretty obvious to all the uniforms at the precinct."

"I know you're a shifter."

Tanner laughed and tossed a glance over his shoulder. "A what? Man, you're crazy."

"Why do you think I asked to be partnered with you? *I. Know.*"

They were at the front of the house now. Tanner pointed toward the street and the waiting black truck. "I think you need to go home and have yourself a real, nice long sleep. When you wake up"—he offered a smile, one he knew held a hard edge—"I bet the monsters will be all gone."

Jonathan didn't move. Sighing, Tanner looked at him, and he found the human staring up at the second floor of the house. At the open window.

"Time for you to leave," Tanner gritted. He'd about exhausted his quota of friendliness for the month.

Jonathan continued to look up at that window. Fine. Tanner would give the guy some help. Tanner slapped his hand down on Jonathan's shoulder. "This way." He pushed him toward the truck.

Jonathan's lips thinned, but he didn't fight, not anymore. He climbed into the truck. Cranked the engine, then asked,

"Don't you want me to tell you . . . how I know about you?"

"Since you're spouting bullshit, I don't really—"

"I saw you shift. Two years ago, way back on the Highland case."

Tanner remembered that case. Like he'd ever forget it. The husband had flipped out on his wife. Trapped her and the kids inside the house. Set the whole place on fire around them. The flames had been so high that the cops at the scene hadn't been able to get inside the home. The fire trucks had been too far away, and they'd all been afraid that Thomas Highland would kill his family before help could arrive.

So Tanner hadn't waited for help. He'd gone behind the house. Shifted, and jumped right over those flames. He'd thought no one had seen him. He'd been so careful.

Not careful enough.

"You did a pretty good job of setting the scene. The wife and kids were hysterical, and with all the smoke, they didn't really even know what they saw," Jonathan said as his fingers drummed on the steering wheel. "And you sliced the perp's throat wide open."

Claws were good for that task.

"Then you put the guy's knife in his hand, to make sure it looked like he'd offed himself."

Tanner just shook his head. "That's a real good imagination you've got there—"

"I *saw* you. I saw it all." Jonathan's fingers stopped tapping. "And I've kept your secret all this time. So cut the crap, man, and start dealing straight with me." The engine revved. "We both know the hell that's hiding in this town. I can help you, but you gotta start trusting me."

Then Jonathan was gone. Racing away with a flash of his taillights and a roar of his engine.

Tanner waited until he was sure that the guy was good and gone; then he headed back for the house. He'd have to deal with his partner later, no getting around that, but for now, he had something more important waiting.

Someone.

Once inside, he strode up the stairs. "Marna!" The house was tomb quiet. Her scent hung lightly in the air.

Too lightly.

Inhaling, Tanner swore and raced up the rest of the stairs. He shouted, "Marna!" once more, but he already knew the truth.

He shouldn't have worried so much about Jonathan getting in the house and finding Marna. Shouldn't have worried about that at all.

His angel was gone.

Chapter Six

Monsters and men liked to walk the streets of New Orleans at night. Both would look for prey—sex, blood, willing victims—and both would find it under the cover of darkness.

Marna hunched her shoulders as she stared up at the entrance to Hell. Extra bouncers were on duty tonight. Probably in response to her and Tanner's little visit last night. She guessed the management didn't want any more dead demons being ditched in the alley.

Slowly, Marna inched her way toward that alley. She ignored the rancid scents and the piles of garbage. The body had been removed and only a dark stain remained to mark the woman's passing.

"Out alone tonight?"

The vampire's voice drifted to her.

Marna didn't stiffen, but she did hold tighter to the weapon she'd brought with her. "No. I'm not alone." She'd planned this. Tanner would never have agreed to any blood exchange from her. She glanced over her shoulder as she carefully kept her hands hidden. "You're here."

Riley leaned against the alley wall, his arms crossed over his chest. "So I am." He inhaled and frowned. "I can smell that shifter all over you." A pause as he shook his head in what looked like confusion. "You mean to tell me that after he had you, the guy just let you walk away?"

After he had you.

Well, Tanner hadn't exactly let her walk away. He'd been too busy running from her to pay much attention to anything.

Humans would have said he was a jerk. Marna would have agreed.

"This isn't about him." It never had been. Tanner wasn't being set up for murder. She was.

Time for her to handle her own problems. No more relying on the big, bad shifter.

"Tell me what you know," Marna told him, "then we'll see about getting what you want."

He laughed. "Do I look like I was turned yesterday?"

Since vamps didn't age, she had no idea how old the guy was—or when he'd been turned.

"It's been two hundred years." He sauntered forward. "Long enough for me to know better than to listen to an angel twist the truth in order to get what *she* wants."

Marna turned toward him but kept her hands behind her back. The pose probably made her look nervous. That was good. He'd never expect her attack if he thought she was weak.

He held up his hand. "Come with me."

She lifted a brow. "Where?"

"You don't expect me to dine in the garbage, now do you?" His gaze was on her throat. "Not when I'm going to be sampling some fine wine." He shook his head. "Those two just don't go well together."

Her right hand slid down so that her weapon was concealed by the jeans she wore. She'd snuck into her apartment earlier. Gotten clothes. Planned her attack.

Her left hand took his. "Lead the way. You tell me what you know, and I'll give you what you've got coming." *A stake to the heart*. Because the weapon she concealed so carefully was a stake designed to end this vampire.

More laughter. His hand closed over hers. Warmer than she'd expected. Vamps were usually cool to the touch. The few she'd taken over the centuries had been. "What's the rush, love? We've got all night."

"No, you fucking don't." Tanner appeared at the mouth of the alley. His hands were loose at his sides, his legs braced apart. "Let her go."

Her heart slammed into her ribs. She'd known he'd come after her. That was just the way he was. The cop in him, trying to save the day.

Only she didn't need saving. From now on, Marna was determined to save herself. "Leave us alone, Tanner."

She didn't know who was more surprised—the shifter or the vampire.

"Well, well . . ." Riley murmured. "Guess that's how it's going."

"No, it's not." Tanner stalked toward them, but his eyes were just on her. "You've got a death wish, is that it?"

Death wouldn't come so easily to her, but when he did, she knew she'd recognize her friend.

"I'm just making a bargain." Her voice sounded careless. Mostly. Maybe he didn't notice the slight tremble at the end of her words. "Now you need to get out of our way."

The vamp's fangs flashed. "Yes, shifter, *get out of the way.* The lady's made her choice."

And it isn't you.

The words hung in the air.

Tanner glanced down. Marna's palm was growing slick with sweat and the slickness made it hard for her to hold on to her weapon. If Tanner would just move . . .

Tanner cocked his head and met her gaze once more. "So you are gonna be a killer now?"

He knew what she had planned. And she'd tried so hard

to hide her stake. "I always was." She'd never asked to be—death had been all she'd ever known.

"Baby . . ." He sighed and angled closer to her. "Why don't you let me do the dirty work for you?" Then he grabbed Riley and ripped the vamp away from her. "I don't mind getting my hands bloody."

And his claws were out.

So was her stake. She'd leapt forward at the same instant. Tanner's claws were at the vamp's throat, but her stake was at Riley Kane's heart.

"Fuck me," Riley snarled. "Can't anyone just donate a little angel blood anymore?"

"Tell us who killed those shifters," Tanner demanded. "And you can walk out of here with your body mostly intact."

Mostly?

But then Tanner stiffened and swore.

When Riley's smile flashed, Marna knew they were in trouble. The vampire's stare cut her way. "I never expected you to come alone. Not when you've got that possessive shifter who guards you so closely."

Tanner's nostrils flared. "Five . . . six . . ."

Marna heard the soft footsteps behind her and knew that he was counting the number of vamps heading their way.

"Six," Riley agreed with a slow nod. "You see, I didn't come alone either."

"Like backup is gonna make a difference for you," Tanner muttered; then he slammed Riley's head back into the brick wall and whirled to grab Marna's hand. "Stay behind me!"

The vamps were racing toward them now. Fangs bared, their own claws out and ready to rip and tear.

Marna heard the sound of popping bones. Snapping. Breaking. Tanner was shifting, but while he shifted—

He was vulnerable.

His kind was always at their most vulnerable mid-shift. And the vamps knew that. They attacked. Their claws raked across his skin. His blood splashed onto the walls of the alley and dripped onto the ground.

"No!" Marna screamed and lunged for Tanner. But Riley caught her and jerked her back.

His arms locked around her as he shouted to his men, "Make sure he doesn't follow us!"

The stake was still in her hand. Clenched tight. Had Riley forgotten about her weapon? If so, *dumb mistake.*

The vamps were swarming around Tanner now. She could barely see him. "Let him go!"

Riley lowered his head toward her throat. Inhaled deeply. "Maybe I'll go ahead and take that bite."

Marna spun around and shoved her stake into his chest. Not into his heart—he'd moved to deflect her blow, but she still drove that stake into him as hard as she could.

His eyes widened, and he began to yank at the stake.

Marna leapt away from him. *Tanner.* She had to save Tanner. There was so much blood on the ground. Too much. And she could hear the panther now, grunting in pain.

"Get away from him!" Marna yelled again as she raised her hands. *"Get. Away."* A blast of fire shot out from her fingertips and flew at the pack of vamps.

Two caught on fire instantly. They screamed and fell to the ground, rolling desperately as they tried to put out the flames. Smoke drifted in the air around them.

The panther slashed out with his claws and cut the throat of another vamp.

More blood.

The scent of death hung heavily in that alley.

Marna stared at her fingers. Powerful angels could control fire, only she hadn't been able to raise the flames. Not since she fell, anyway.

But now . . .

A vamp raced toward her. A redhead with hate twisting his face. "I'm gonna drain you—"

"No, you're not." She raised her hands again. "But you will burn."

The flames slammed into him. Directed. Intense. The scent of burning flesh had her stomach churning.

The other vamps were struggling with Tanner. The panther had left them bloody and weak, and they were trying desperately to hold him off.

It looked like he was going in for the kill.

She caught a light floral scent in the air. Marna knew what that telling scent meant. A death angel was close. One who'd come to ferry souls.

So who would be dying in that alley?

Not me. The vamps were the ones biting the dust.

She rushed to Tanner's side. A charred vamp tried to slash out at her with his claws. She didn't move fast enough, and he ripped into her skin, tearing a bloody path down her side. Even as Marna cried out, the black panther attacked. He sank his razor-sharp teeth into the vampire's throat.

She looked away, not wanting to see the rest. But she knew that particular vampire wouldn't be rising again.

The others fled the alley. They left behind only blood and death.

The panther bumped into her side. Marna trembled. His head came nearly to her shoulders. Fully beast, so primal, but when she looked into his eyes, she saw a man's gaze staring back at her.

And she saw a dead vampire at her feet. No, not dead, not yet.

The shadows around the vampire thickened. She lifted a hand, holding her bleeding side, and watched as the large, black wings of a death angel appeared from the darkness.

Angels marked by despair always had black wings. Death

angels. Punishers. The most powerful of the angels, they were the ones that humans should fear.

The ones that could make even paranormals shudder.

The vampire stared up at the angel. Since the moment of his final death was at hand, he'd be able to see those broad, dark wings now. And he'd see the hard, carved features of the angel that she knew as—

Bastion?

Her breath froze in her lungs. *It was him*. Tall, strong, one of the few angels gifted with golden eyes—eyes the same color as the burnished gold that adorned the home in heaven she'd never see again.

She hadn't seen Bastion in weeks. After she'd lost her wings, he'd tried to help her at first.

Then vanished when he realized there wasn't any help to give.

He bent his dark head and gazed down at the vampire. Bastion hadn't said anything to her. Hadn't even looked her way.

It hurt. He knew she was there. Because of what she was, he also knew she'd be able to see him.

And he didn't look at her. In heaven, he'd been her closest confidant. Now he couldn't stand the sight of her?

"How the hell did you do that?" Tanner demanded as he reached for her. His arms caught her shoulders and he spun her around to face him. He'd shifted back to human form, and her gaze darted down the muscled expanse of his chest to—

She yanked her eyes right back up. *Clothes.* The guy seriously needed clothes.

And with just that thought, they appeared. A black T-shirt. Jeans. Even boots. A complete outfit to cover him.

Tanner's eyes widened. "Nice trick."

Angels were always able to conjure clothes. Since they had wings sprouting from their backs, they had to be able to use their powers to make articles that would fit around them. Except she hadn't been able to use that particular talent since she'd fallen.

Until now.

First the fire, now conjuring. It looked like her powers were flooding back. Finally. *No more weakness.*

Marna glanced over her shoulder. Bastion was still there. With both Azrael and Sammael walking the earth, he'd be the ruler of the death angels now, but once, he'd been her only friend. "Bastion."

His head lifted.

There was no emotion in his eyes or on the face that appeared to have been carved from stone. He looked at her as if he didn't even know her. Why? Didn't he understand?

"I miss you," she said.

Did he flinch?

"Who the hell are you talking to?" Tanner pulled her closer to him.

Bastion bent and placed his hand over the vampire's chest. Just that simply, another soul was taken.

The air seemed to chill, and goose bumps rose on Marna's flesh. Tanner swore, and then he scooped her into his arms. "Screw this."

Holding her tightly, he rushed toward the alley entrance. Her arms wrapped around him, but she said, "Tanner, no, I can—"

Bastion was in front of them. Staring at her with eyes that seemed to blaze.

"Stop," she told Tanner.

He froze.

He wouldn't see the angel. *Couldn't.* Fallen angels could always see their winged brethren, but most others couldn't. Not unless he had the blood of celestial beings in him. Since demons were descended from the Fallen, some of them could see the angels who walked among the humans—as long as their bloodline was strong enough.

But vampires? Shifters? No, they wouldn't see angels even though they sometimes strolled right beside them.

"I'm . . . sorry," Bastion told her, voice stilted.

Her arms were around Tanner's neck. She could feel the tension coursing through him. Tanner stared at the alley, glanced at her, stared again at the alley's entrance. "All right, who the fuck is there?"

She licked her lips. "An angel."

"I *know* that. Which winged ass am I dealing with?"

A muscle jerked in Bastion's jaw. His gaze dropped, then hardened when he saw the way Tanner's hands held her so tightly. "Be careful with him," Bastion warned her. "He's not someone you can trust."

Her stare turned back to Tanner. Right then, he was the only one she could trust.

"Who is it?" Tanner gritted.

"Bastion." She sighed the name. "He's—"

Tanner ran right at the angel. In a flash, Bastion vanished.

"No!" Marna leapt from his arms and almost fell flat on her face. She managed to stumble and barely stay upright. "I need to ask him—"

"Baby, this alley is a bloodbath. That smell will have every predator in a ten-mile radius coming out."

The predators were already out. She glanced over her shoulder and saw the eyes in the darkness. The flash of fangs.

Tanner's hand wrapped around her wrist. "Come on."

Bastion was gone.

Only the monsters remained.

And they were closing in.

Tanner pushed her behind his body. "Stay the hell back," he ordered those who waited in the darkness. He lifted his claws. "Or I'll start slicing you apart."

Silence.

But maybe that silence wasn't enough. Marna's shoulders straightened. Time to send a message. She glanced down at her hands. "I've got this," she whispered to Tanner.

He frowned over his shoulder at her.

Her chin rose. She *could* do this.

He stepped away.

Marna sent a ball of fire racing into the alley. The fire caught the vampire's dead body. Incinerated him, and sent the others fleeing back—back to whatever hole they'd crawled from.

The rush of power was amazing. Using fire . . . when she'd been an angel, it had never felt this way. Like the energy was pouring from within her, surging inside her.

Not as good as the pleasure that Tanner had given her, but still *good*.

Marna smiled. "Now you know to stay away," she said into the flames.

The warning wasn't just for the monsters. It was for the angel who lurked nearby. She wasn't the same woman she'd been. Every day, she was changing. Becoming more. It was time for the rest of the world to realize that fact.

And to stay out of my way.

He watched the action from his perch on the rooftop. The little lost Fallen enjoyed her fire. He could see the thrill on her face.

Angels didn't enjoy the rush of power. Angels didn't enjoy anything.

She wasn't an angel anymore. She liked the crackle of the blaze. Liked the heat of the licking flames.

She'd used her fire on the vampires. Finally, that power had broken free for her.

He watched as the shifter took her from the alley. Bundled her into an SUV and shot down the street.

He would be a problem. The panther watched Marna too closely. Touched her too much.

Do you think she'll be yours?

That wasn't the fate that waited for Marna. She deserved to have her vengeance. Deserved all the power that would come her way.

The panther? He'd get what he deserved, too. Death.

Because Tanner Chance was the key that he needed. In order to unlock all the power and magic inside of Marna, she would have to break. Chance could be used to break her.

When she broke, it would be brutal, and it would be beautiful. *Just like her.*

He leapt off the rooftop.

There was still plenty of time in the night, and there were some vamps that needed killing. Did they truly think they were just going to get away after attacking her?

No. Not likely. He'd make them pay.

And he'd enjoy the sound of their screams.

But first he'd follow his little angel. Just in case the shifter planned to stash her someplace else.

He liked to know where she was—all the time. That way, she'd never escape him.

Never.

Tanner raced through the streets. A fast left. A hard right. His blood seemed to burn in his veins, and he clutched the steering wheel so tightly, he could feel it starting to bend beneath his fingers.

Control.

He was losing more of it by the second.

He spun the SUV to the left. They were out of the Quarter and heading down a lonely, oak-lined street that would have to do for now. He slammed on the brakes and turned on her. "What the hell was that?"

Moonlight spilled through the windows. Onto her face. Made her look as if she were glowing. *Beautiful*. "I-I don't know, the fire came back to me and—" Her voice was all but humming with excitement.

She'd saved his ass back in that alley. No getting around it. But she'd also scared a good ten years off his life when she sent that fire blazing out, missing his body by, oh, about two inches as she aimed it into the alley and at all the pricks who'd waited in the darkness.

"A little warning next time would be good," he managed to snap. Enough of a warning that he could jump out of the way and not get singed.

Her head tilted back. More moonlight fell on her. *Damn*. "I'm sorry," she said, "but don't worry. There isn't going to be a next time." Then she shoved open the passenger side door and jumped outside.

What the hell?

He pushed open his own door and followed right after her. Tanner caught her almost instantly, and pushed her back against the side of the SUV. "You walked right into that vamp's trap." Yeah, he was pissed over that, and would be for the next year or so. *The bastard could have drained her and tossed away her broken body*.

"I could have handled him!"

With her fire? With her stake? Didn't she get it? "Baby, when there are enough of them . . ." Six to one odds. It still had his stomach clenching. "They can take you out." Especially if they sank their fangs into her and drained her until she was too weak to fight back.

But then Marna drew in a ragged breath and said, "I don't want you getting hurt because of me."

He wouldn't have been more shocked if she'd stripped right then. Tanner forced his back teeth to unlock as he said, "And I don't want you dying when I can keep you safe."

Their eyes held. The night seemed so still. And she . . .

fuck, she was even prettier by moonlight. How the hell had he managed to walk away from her before? Had he really left her alone in bed? Some days, he could be such a damn idiot.

I knew playing the gentleman wasn't my bit. But he'd still tried. For her.

"There are times"—Marna paused and her tongue swiped nervously over her lower lip—"when we have to fight our own battles."

She wasn't doing this alone. The angel needed to think again. "You forget, this isn't just about you." And if that tongue of hers swiped out again, he'd pounce. Simple fact.

A furrow appeared between her brows. "But I thought—"

The murders were being pinned on her, but this thing stretched far wider than that. "If there's some rogue Fallen in the city, I need to know." Because he had to be ready to deal with the bastard. Fallen weren't easy to kill, but luckily he had the particular skill set—*claws and fangs*—to get the job done.

Marna shook her head. "A Fallen didn't kill the demon in the alley."

Maybe. Maybe not. The knife attack sure hadn't fit a Fallen's usual MO, but maybe their killer was just trying to throw them off the scent.

It wouldn't work. If there was one being who could track a scent better than any other, it was a shifter.

He caught her hand, lifted it up. Her palm was soft, small, and her eyes seemed to reflect the moonlight. "You been holding out on me?" he asked as his fingers rubbed lightly over her palm.

She swallowed and seemed to shiver. The night wasn't cold. "N-no. It just happened. Wh-when I saw them go after you . . ." Her breath whispered out. "I wasn't going to let them hurt you."

He could take down six vamps, any day of the week.

Sure, they'd gotten their claws into him, but he'd been well on his way to kicking ass by the time her flames erupted.

Still, she'd saved him. Other than his brother, Cody, he'd never had someone try to look out for him before.

Back when he'd been a kid, he'd had to learn early how to take care of himself. In those days, everyone had tried to pound the shit out of him.

So he'd started beating back.

He bought her hand to his lips. Pressed a kiss to her palm. "Thank you." Because he couldn't help it, he tasted her skin with a slow lick of his tongue.

Marna sucked in a sharp breath. "You . . . you said . . ."

Take.

The panther clawed inside of him. Tanner growled out, "I said I wouldn't fuck you." No, he hadn't said that. He'd said if he did, there'd be no escape for her.

Already, he needed her too much. He could smell her scent, sweet, but rich . . . with arousal.

She wanted him just as much as he wanted her. That didn't make things easier. It made him just want to fuck her all the more.

Tanner grabbed the reins of his control and pulled back. Turned away. "We need to get the hell out of here." Before some dumbass came driving up, offering to help because he thought they were broken down or—

Marna grabbed his shoulder and spun him back around with surprising strength.

"Marna, look—"

She rose onto her toes and yanked his head down toward her. Her lips pressed against his, and the lady sure didn't kiss like an angel.

More like a woman too used to sin. The sensual press of her lips and the silken glide of her tongue had his whole body burning with lust.

Her taste . . .

He pulled her closer. Two steps, and he had her pinned against the vehicle. She'd been warned. She knew the risk.

He kissed her harder. Deeper. Took in her sweet taste. And realized he was starving for more.

Her breasts—nipples tight—pressed into his chest. He wanted them in his mouth again. More, he wanted his mouth on the heat between her legs. Nothing had ever tasted so good to him.

Marna.

He began to kiss his way down her neck. Her head tipped back, and he scored the flesh with his teeth in a light bite. *Mine.*

"You're . . ." Her voice was husky, heavy with desire that made his cock swell bigger. "You're better . . . than the fire."

He wasn't sure what that meant, but Tanner wasn't gonna argue. His hands went to the snap of her jeans. The zipper eased down with a hiss. Then he slid his hand inside, pushing his fingers under her panties.

"Tanner!"

The snarl of an approaching engine grated in his ears.

Fuck. Fuck. Fuck!

He stared down at Marna. The smooth curve of her stomach. The silken edge of her panties.

The snarling engine grew louder.

His hands were shaking when he snapped her jeans. As he hurriedly pulled her clothing back into place, they didn't speak. Right then, he wasn't sure he could speak. The panther roared too loudly inside of him.

Marna's cheeks were flushed, but her head had jerked toward the approaching car so she knew what was happening.

Wrong place.

He opened the passenger side door. Pushed her inside. He'd just slammed the door when the car slowed beside them.

Not just some friendly dumbass looking to help them out.

A patrol car.

This was so not his night. Hadn't the vamps been bad enough?

The patrol car, of course, pulled to a full stop and its blue lights flashed on. The cop climbed out, shining his flashlight. "There a problem here?"

"No problem." Tanner exhaled, cleared his throat and tried to sound less like a snarling animal. "I'm a cop."

"Are you now." Not a question, just a statement of doubt. The cop tried to shine his lights toward the passenger seat.

Tanner moved his body and blocked that light before it could fall on Marna. "My badge is in the vehicle, but you can go ahead and call my ID number in on your radio. 5-2-7. Detective Tanner Chance."

The cop, a fresh-faced newbie if Tanner had ever seen one, immediately pulled out his radio and called in the badge number. Tanner began to head toward the driver's side.

"Hold on there!" The flashlight hit him right in the face when he glanced back. "You move nice and slow, got me?"

Smothering a sigh, Tanner tried to play it cool. The last thing he wanted was for this kid to get a look at Marna. If he'd heard the talk at the station . . .

But Marna hunched into the shadows when Tanner opened the door. He grabbed his badge from the glove box and held it up for the kid. "Are we good now?"

The guy swiped the badge. Brought his light up real close to it as he peered down at the badge. Hell. This uniform was so green. If he'd wanted, Tanner could have jumped the kid five times by now.

Amateur hour.

"You need to be more careful," he snapped to the kid, not able to hold back. "Never get within striking distance of a suspect, no matter what shit he says."

The guy gulped and jumped back. "S-sorry." The flashlight bobbed.

"Keep your weapon ready, and don't ever give any perp an advantage." The kid needed backup. He shouldn't be out riding alone.

The boy's fingers were shaking when he gave Tanner back the badge. "Why—" The word cracked so the kid cleared his throat and tried again. "*Why* did you stop here, Detective Chance?"

Because I had to taste her. "Lust." Tanner turned away and climbed into the car. "It'll get you every time, kid."

When he drove away, the patrolman was still standing in the middle of the road, staring after him.

Officer Paul Hodges exhaled on a long sigh as he watched the SUV's tail-lights vanish. He'd screwed up. And in front of a detective no less. How was he supposed to live this down? When word spread at the precinct . . .

Shouldn't have let down my guard. Rookie mistake. He'd been patrolling for five months now. He knew better.

But . . . when the guy had said he was a cop . . .

"People freakin' lie." He headed back to his car. He grabbed his radio and spoke into the mike, "Affirmative on the ID. Verified it was Detective Tanner—"

Headlights flashed on the dark street. Bright lights that pinned him in their glare. "What the hell?"

A vehicle was coming toward him. Too fast. Paul waved his arms. His cruiser was *right there.* The guy had to see it. Him.

The ground seemed to shake beneath him. *Not stopping.* He dove for the side of the road.

But those bright lights—that big vehicle— followed him. The front fender slammed into him, and Paul went flying. When he hit the ground, he heard the snap and crunch of his bones.

And the vehicle stopped. Reversed.

Paul tried to drag himself farther across the road. He tried to call out because someone might still be on the radio. "Officer down! *Officer*—"

The vehicle—an SUV—hit him again. The tires rolled right over his legs, and Paul screamed. Everything went black and all he knew was agony. So much pain.

Too much.

Someone hit him. Punched him in the face. His eyes had been closed—*had he passed out?*—but Paul's eyes flew open at that impact.

"You're not dying, kid." That voice. He knew that voice. Detective Chance had come back to help him. He must have seen the accident! He must have—

"I'll let you live a few more hours." Tanner Chance smiled down at him, and Paul's blood iced. "But you won't escape me for too long." Then Chance drove his foot into Paul's side. "That'll fucking teach you," the detective snarled, "to ever question me!"

Paul spat up blood.

Chance kept smiling. And kicking. And Paul realized Tanner wasn't there to save him.

He's the one. Only one vehicle was at the scene. An SUV. Tanner had come back all right.

The detective had come back to kill him.

CHAPTER SEVEN

"So what happens now?" Marna asked. It was still dark, and she still wanted Tanner.

Wanting him was becoming natural for her. She didn't think about it. Didn't question it. She just . . . did.

"Now it's our turn to hunt."

She glanced at him. Saw the hard line of his jaw. "What do you mean?"

He was driving fast, his eyes on the road, not her. "It means we both know that vamp has info on what's happening in this town."

That vamp. Riley Kane. "You want me to give him my blood." She hadn't expected that. Marna swallowed. She didn't know if she could do it. The guy's teeth, in her flesh? "Tanner, I—"

"Hell, *no.*" He tossed her a fast glance that called her crazy. "We're gonna track that vamp down to his hole, and we're gonna make him tell us everything he knows."

Oh, yes, she liked that plan much better.

His stare slid back to the road. "It'll be daylight soon. We'll wait for the sun to rise, then we'll find him."

Because vamps were always weaker during the day. So weak, they were almost human.

But weren't they overlooking kind of an obvious point? "How do we find him?"

He laughed, and the deep rumble had her tensing. Had she ever heard him laugh before? Marna couldn't remember him laughing. She liked his laugh. It made her almost want to smile.

"Easy, baby. All I have to do is follow my nose." Shifter senses. She realized that he was taking them back to the Quarter. He'd circled down some narrow streets and was returning to the city. "I've got his scent. I won't be forgetting it anytime soon." Anger roughened the words. A promise of retaliation. "All we have to do is follow the smell of blood and death all the way back to that vamp's hiding spot."

Then they'd find out what secrets the vampire held.

Two police cars raced past them, lights flashing.

Tanner frowned, but kept driving.

And Marna wondered just what they'd have to do in order to make Riley talk.

She'd seen plenty of tortures in her time, and they'd always made her . . . *sick.*

The other angels hadn't seemed to care what they saw. They'd witnessed carnage. Hell on earth. Heard screams and pleas.

They'd been unaffected.

She hadn't.

"Bastion, please, I don't want to do this." Her broken confession from so long ago. He'd been the only one she told. She'd turned to him because she'd thought he could help her. He'd been higher in the angel rankings. So powerful.

But there'd been nothing he could do.

"What, Marna? Do you want to fall?" He'd shaken his dark head. *"Life down there, for us, it's agony. You would never survive being earthbound."*

Her hands fisted.

They were snaking through the back streets now. Tanner had lowered his window.

The better to catch the vamp's scent?

Shifters and their noses.

"What was Bastion to you?"

Marna blinked, surprised by the question—and the deadly intensity that had entered Tanner's voice.

"He meant something, I could tell." He wasn't looking at her. "I couldn't see the bastard, but I smelled him." A muscle jerked in his jaw. "And I recognized that scent. That one, he came to Cody's when you were hurt."

Yes, Bastion had come to her during those terrible days. He'd promised to help her.

But what could he do? He still had heaven.

She had hell.

"Bastion." She sighed when she said his name. Was she sad about what she'd lost? Or sad that her friend had seemed pained just to look at her?

"You . . . care for him."

"Yes." Another fault. Angels didn't form attachments, but she had. Humans could love. *Why couldn't angels?* "He tried to watch out for me." How many times had he covered for her? When she'd been afraid? Weak?

"And now he's following you."

That had her shaking her head, then realizing he couldn't see the move. "No, he was just there—" *Because you killed a vampire. Ripped his throat wide open.* Um, better not to think too long about that particular visual. Her stomach was already clenching. "He was just there to ferry a soul."

"And the other times?"

Now she was lost. "What other times?"

"I've caught his scent before. At my house. In that bar last night. He's been watching you."

Tanner was wrong. "I didn't see him." And she would have. She could always see her own kind, even without her wings.

"Maybe he didn't want you to see him." He parked the SUV on the side of the road, near a line of broken down buildings that hadn't recovered after the storm. "Maybe he just wants to see *you*." There was an edge in Tanner's voice that had her tensing. Then he glanced at her, cutting her with his bright stare, and said, "The same way I did."

"Wh-what are you talking about?" The sun was rising, sending streaks of pink and gray across the sky.

"I had to watch you, too. You didn't know. You never know when danger is close."

He'd been watching her? "Why?" Her nails dug into the leather seat.

"Someone had to make sure you were safe." He turned away. Climbed from the vehicle.

She hurried out and rushed to confront him. "Making sure I was safe?" Marna shook her head and stabbed her finger into his chest. "Or making sure I wasn't killing?" She knew how the guy's mind worked. He was a shifter, a paranormal, but a cop, too. He'd been staking her out, just like he did the other criminals he hunted.

One shoulder lifted in a shrug as Tanner admitted, "Maybe a little of both."

Right. Figured. She turned away and rubbed her arms. Her gaze raked over the dark lines of buildings that rose into the sky. So many boarded-up windows and doors. Giant KEEP OUT signs. Yes, this place was a vampire paradise if she'd ever seen one.

"Or maybe," Tanner's voice drawled, "maybe I just wanted to make sure you weren't fucking anyone."

Her jaw dropped. She snapped it closed and whirled on him. "What I do isn't—"

He put a finger to his lips. "He's close."

Her eyes narrowed. He was just trying to—

"There." He pointed to the second building. Tanner's nostrils flared. "I can smell him."

She could only smell the scent of decay and garbage. Not exactly pleasant.

Tanner marched toward the building. He grabbed the heavy wood in front of the door and yanked.

It broke away like a twig snapping. Sometimes, she forgot just how strong the panther was.

He shoved open the door with a push of his hand, splintering any lock that might have been there. "So much for going in quietly," she muttered.

But Tanner was already lunging forward, racing into the dark interior, and she scrambled to keep up with him.

Hurry. Hurry.

Tanner didn't waste time. Just ran straight for a door on the left side of the building. He kicked it open, and when Riley lunged for him with a silver blade, Tanner just laughed.

Marna lifted her hands, ready to send fire racing toward the vamp, only . . . *nothing happened.*

What? Where were the flames?

Riley sliced out with his blade. Tanner kicked it aside. "That the best you got?" Tanner wanted to know.

Marna's head jerked back toward them. They were in an apartment, of sorts. Big bed. Heavy oak desk. No other vamps that she saw, but wasn't Riley enough of a threat?

The blond's brows rose. "I was wondering when you'd get here."

"Yeah." Tanner's claws tore from his fingers. "And I bet you were hoping we'd be dumb enough to arrive *before* dawn."

The vamp's mouth kicked up on the right. "I was."

Tanner inhaled. "You've got no backup in this place. No other vamps for you to throw in my way this time."

Marna dropped her hands and stepped forward. "You'll tell us what we want to know—"

Tanner lifted his claws. "Or you'll be losing that head of yours."

The vamp's half-smile didn't fade. "You think death is going to scare me?" He laughed then. "I watched my whole family get slaughtered by vampires. My father, mother, my wife. Everyone died, and guess what? I got to turn into one of the murdering bastards. For two hundred years, they led me around on a puppet string, had me killing . . . torturing."

He grabbed his head between his hands and closed his eyes. "I got as fucking far away from the Born as I could, but I *can still hear him in my head!*"

Marna's breath caught. *Born.* She knew the term. Most vampires were humans who became infected with the vampire virus. That's all it was, too—a virus. One that had been transmitted through a very, very bad mistake millennia ago.

Those humans who were transformed, they were called the Taken. But every Taken was linked to the vampire who'd made him or her. All Taken could be traced back to the Born.

A rare few were actually born as vampires. They aged like any other human, until about their twenty-fifth year. Then the change came. The virus in their bodies activated, and they became immortal.

"They were supposed to be guardians." She'd heard this whispered story once, from Bastion. Stronger than most of the other paranormals, the Borns should have kept the others in check. They hadn't.

Power and bloodlust had driven most of them insane.

Now those unlucky enough to be Taken were bound to their Borns. Linked through the blood. They had to follow every command given by their Born. Do every task, no matter how dark.

The only way to break that bond? Kill the Born.

Not so easy.

That had been where everything went wrong.

"I'm *tired* of killing," Riley muttered. "I'm ready to just . . . stop." His head had sagged forward, and she couldn't see his face. His shoulders hunched. "But *he* won't let me." Then he lunged forward, fangs bared, and tried to sink his teeth into Tanner's throat.

Tanner sighed. "Sad fucking story." He punched Riley in the face.

The vampire staggered back.

"Now let's hear another story. One that involves two dead shifters in an alley."

Riley swiped the blood off his chin. "Make me a deal first."

He watched his family die. A whisper of memory teased at Marna. Two hundred years ago? And the vampire . . . with his slanting cheekbones and that sharp nose. He'd seemed so familiar to her.

Two hundred years. A bloody night. A man's screams.

And she remembered.

A man on the ground. Begging. Screaming. Shaking the bloody body of a woman. That woman, with her blond hair stained red, had been so still.

Victoria! Don't leave me.

But Marna had already taken her away. She'd taken her as quickly as she could, so the woman wouldn't suffer any more.

Victoria had suffered too much during those last moments of life. She hadn't needed the agony to continue in death.

"There's no deal. You talk or die." Tanner's brutal words pulled her from the past.

Riley nodded. "That's what I want." A rough sigh expelled from him. "Kill me, so I can finally be free."

She'd taken Victoria and left the shattered man behind. There'd been nothing that Marna could do for him.

She'd wanted to help him, but that had been forbidden. A different fate waited for the man who'd mourned so brokenly on the bloody field.

This? This is what waited?

Riley lowered himself to the edge of the bed. "Cadence

was in the alley that night when the two shifters were killed. She told me that she saw a blond, just like you"—he motioned to Marna—"heading after those shifters."

It wasn't me.

"Cadence said she'd never seen an angel, not until that day. But when the blond touched and killed, she knew just what she had to be seeing."

How many times would she have to say it? "*I didn't kill them.*"

"Cadence just wondered . . ." He kept talking as if she hadn't spoken. ". . . why the angel didn't have any wings. She'd heard that even if angels fall, demons can still see the shadow of their wings behind them."

Marna frowned and glanced over her shoulder. When she'd met Cadence in Hell, the demon had said she'd seen her wings.

"Whoever that was killing those shifters, she didn't have wings." Riley rubbed his chin. "If you don't have wings, then I guess you aren't really an angel."

No, you weren't.

"Maybe she just couldn't see the wings," Tanner said, frowning as he glanced back at Marna. "Not all demons—"

But Riley shook his head. "Cadence was a pureblood. She had enormous power. Hell, that's why she was so screwed up in the head. She couldn't control the voices that whispered to her. Voices that always told her what was coming." Riley pointed at Marna. "She saw your wings the instant you walked into Hell. I was at the bar with her. How did you think I realized that you were so fast?"

Marna rolled her shoulders and felt the phantom pull of wings that were gone. She couldn't see any shadows when she looked over her shoulder. You weren't allowed to see what you'd lost. That was one of the rules.

Punishments.

But she'd seen the shadowy images on other Fallen. On Sammael.

So if a Fallen wasn't doing the killing, then who was? And how?

"That's all I know." Riley tipped back his head and offered his throat. "So, now, do it. Put me out of this sick-ass misery of an existence."

Marna tensed. "Tanner . . ."

But he shook his head and turned away from the vamp. "Despite what you think, I'm a cop, not just a killer. And I'm not executing an unarmed man, vamp or not." He offered his hand to Marna. "Let's go."

She couldn't walk away.

And Riley didn't give her the chance.

"I'm not unarmed." His hand had disappeared under the mattress, and, in a blink, he yanked out a gun. Only he didn't aim it at Tanner.

At me.

"Dumbass move," Tanner snapped as he spun back to face the vampire. "Bullets won't kill her."

"Brimstone bullets will." Now the vampire's smile was just sad. Tired. "I've done my research. I heard about the shit that went down in this city, just a few months back."

When Azrael had battled Brandt. Because Brandt had been a hybrid—the product of a rare mating between a shifter and an angel—it had taken a lot to kill him.

Bullets made of brimstone, bullets formed from a hellhound's claws, could kill any angel, no matter how old or strong. Brandt had learned that lesson. He'd tried to use those bullets against others of his kind, but in the end, he'd been the one to die.

She stared at the barrel of the gun. "I'm sorry."

"Fuck this—" Tanner began.

"I was the one who took your wife," she said, cutting

through Tanner's words and taking a step toward the vampire. He deserved to hear the truth. "That night, so long ago, it was me."

The gun barrel shook. His hand tightened. "You *bitch.*"

"Once I took her, Victoria didn't hurt anymore."

"My Victoria—"

"But I had to leave you behind." The words were hollow. No, she was hollow. Why hadn't she rebelled then? Tried to save this man, before he'd become a monster?

What he was . . . all the things he'd done . . . could she have stopped this?

"They *fed* on me, for hours—"

This part hurt to confess. "I was gone by then." The memory of his screams had chased her as she flew away. No wonder the vampire had looked familiar to her. But there'd been so many deaths over the years. So many souls. Sometimes, their memories dimmed in her mind.

He leapt from the bed and fired the gun.

Tanner took the bullet. Marna never even had a chance to scream. Tanner jumped in front of her, and the bullet thudded into his chest.

He barely staggered. One step, then he lunged forward and ripped the gun from Riley's hand before the vamp could fire again.

"Now you'll kill me," Riley whispered, and he sounded so grateful. "Now."

No. "Tanner!"

His claws were at the vamp's throat. Blood soaked Tanner's shirt. The bullet had sunk in near his shoulder.

"I knew . . ." Riley wasn't fighting. "If I shot at her, you'd kill me."

Tanner's claws shoved into his own shoulder, and he yanked out the bullet from his flesh. "Nine caliber." He tossed it aside. "Brimstone, my ass."

Why did everyone get to lie but her?

Tanner shook his head and glared at the vamp. "You think you're the first suicide junkie I've gotten? Death by cop isn't in the cards for you. Why don't you just try fighting for life instead of clawing your way to hell so fast?"

The knife that Riley had dropped lay just steps away from Marna's feet. She bent and picked it up.

"I can't fight!" Riley's teeth flashed. "I'm not strong enough! The Born is in my head every single—" He stopped and his head snapped to the right.

His eyes locked on Marna.

And on the blood that dripped down her arm. She'd sliced into the flesh just below her elbow, and she lifted her arm, offering it to the vampire. "Maybe my blood will be strong enough to help you."

Didn't she owe him that much?

He'd been a good man, once. He would have been a good father. Had he even known that his Victoria was pregnant?

Everything had been ripped away from him.

While I watched.

He surged to his feet.

Tanner blocked him. "Hell, no, you aren't—"

"Tanner, make sure he doesn't take too much." She didn't even know if this would work. Angel blood was supposed to contain power, she knew that. But would it be enough power to help him break free of his Born? As far as she knew, no one had ever used angel's blood to sever a link like that.

I have to try.

Tanner's hands had locked around the vamp's shoulders as he held Riley back. "Are you sure about this?" he asked Marna.

Atonement. She had to do her part. "Yes." But she needed the shifter to help her because she didn't trust the vamp to stop once he started drinking. She only trusted—

Tanner.

When had that happened? Maybe the "when" didn't matter. Marna pulled in a deep breath. "Just stop him when I say so."

Jaw clenching, Tanner nodded. "But let me just say," he muttered as he jerked the vamp closer, "I really don't like this shit."

Riley stared at her blood with wide eyes. "Wh-why?"

"Because you are more than a killer." *And I'm more than just a lost angel.*

Time to start showing it. She lifted her arm to his mouth.

Tanner shoved the vamp to his knees and kept the guy's hands locked behind his back. "Don't even *think* of hurting her," her shifter ordered.

Riley nodded. His head lowered to her arm, and Marna closed her eyes. She didn't want to see this. She could feel his mouth on her skin, tasting her blood, and goose bumps rose on her flesh.

The other angels she knew would never have allowed themselves to be used this way. They would have found it degrading. Shameful.

She'd never been like the others. She found this to be . . .

Atonement. The word slipped through her mind again.

The edge of his teeth pressed into her skin, and her eyelids flew open as she gasped at the sting.

"Easy," Tanner shouted.

Her gaze flew to Tanner. His own fangs were out. His eyes glowing. There was a fury on his face, a dark and savage rage. One that she'd never seen there before.

He stared down at Riley like he'd take joy in killing the vamp. But, before, he'd wanted to spare him.

Tanner's gaze met hers. *"Enough."*

But Riley was still drinking. Marna tried to slide her arm back.

Riley followed.

He didn't get very far. Tanner ripped him away from her and sent the vampire hurtling into the wall. "I said *enough.*"

Her breath heaved out. Tanner caught her arm. Stared down at the wound. A muscle jerked in his jaw. "Never again." A lethal promise from him. But for all of his rage, his touch on her flesh was incredibly gentle. His body surrounded hers. "Whatever the hell this was about, whatever debt you think you owed him, consider it paid in full."

She managed a slow nod. Her arm throbbed where she had cut herself, but the wound was already starting to close.

Angel healing. She loved that perk.

"And you . . ." Tanner glanced back over his shoulder. "Stay away from her. 'Cause if you don't, I'll decide to give you that death you seemed to want so freaking badly."

Marna turned away from Riley. Tanner's body moved with her, in perfect time, shadowing her, as she headed for the door.

"The call . . ." Riley's voice stopped her. She didn't look back. "I-I . . . the Born's voice is already getting dimmer. Can barely hear him."

Something hit the floor with a thud. Helpless, Marna turned back. Riley had shoved the nightstand to the ground. He was on his feet, staring at her with wide eyes.

"He's gone. He's gone from my mind."

Then maybe Riley could be the man he used to be.

The man he should have been?

"Come on." Tanner pushed open the door. Led her out. His hand was wrapped around her arm. Did he even realize that he kept caressing the now-healed wound with his fingers?

And why did his touch push away the cold she'd felt? How could he do that to her, so easily?

They didn't speak again. Just marched out of that dark house. The sunlight seemed far too bright when they hurried back toward the street and the SUV that waited.

So bright.

Marna reached for the passenger door. Before she could grab the handle, Tanner spun her around. "What—"

His mouth took hers. Not easy. Not gentle. Hard. Deep. Burning with lust and need, and she opened her mouth wider. Kissed him back just as hard.

"Never again," he growled against her lips. "I never want him touching you again."

Her fingers sank into his hair, and she pressed her body closer to his. Marna rose onto her tiptoes so that she could reach his mouth better. The hunger inside her, the hard lust, was driving her, and she *wanted.*

Tanner caught her hips. Lifted her higher. Her legs wrapped around him, and the erect length of his cock pushed against her sensitive sex.

A gasp slipped from her.

Tanner's head rose. "Not . . . here."

He managed to get her into the SUV; then he rushed around to the driver's side. Tanner gunned the engine and spared her one more glance.

The heat from his stare singed her skin. "I tried to do what was right," he said.

Her body ached for him. How did humans stand it? How did they live with the lust?

And now that she knew what pleasure waited . . .

She wanted to feel that rush of release again.

"Remember that, would you?" His voice roughened as the SUV leapt away from the curb. "I tried, but I was too weak."

Weak? Not Tanner. He was the strongest man she'd ever met.

And it looked like the shifter would also soon be her first lover.

★ ★ ★

"What the hell happened to you?"

Paul tried to open his eyes. Couldn't. He heard sirens and voices, and he wanted to talk, but it was just too hard.

Someone lifted him up. Put him on something soft. The world started to move. Or maybe that was just him. A sharp pain jabbed in his arm. Needle?

"Just hold on. We'll be at the hospital in five minutes." Another jab. Somewhere, machines started beeping.

An ambulance. Understanding sank in slowly.

Help had finally come. He tried to open his eyes once more, but he still just couldn't do it.

"Someone did a real number on him. Poor SOB."

Paul fought to swallow. He had to tell them what had happened.

"He's a fighter. I can't believe he's still holding on. Jesus, look at his legs!"

Paul coughed, choked, but managed to say, "T-Tan . . . ner . . ."

A hand grabbed his arm. The fingers curled tight around him. "What is it? What are you saying?"

"Ch-Chance . . ." A whisper was all he could manage. "T-Tanner . . . Ch-Ch—"

"You want us to call someone for you? That a friend?"

No. Not a friend.

The machines began to beep louder. Wilder.

"He's seizing!"

The sirens were screaming.

Something pounded against his chest.

And Paul managed to whisper, "He . . . k-killed . . . me."

Then he couldn't talk at all.

Chapter Eight

He couldn't make it back to his house. Too far. Tanner needed her, naked and beneath him, needed to be *in* her, so badly that his whole body shook.

But her first time wouldn't be in a vehicle. Or up against some dirty alley wall. She deserved better.

He'd give her everything that he could.

He parked the SUV near the river. She followed him out of the vehicle, asking no questions. Just staring at him with eyes that reflected his own hunger. Tanner caught her hand and led her inside the old building and up the winding stairs. Up higher, higher, to the small apartment that he kept as an escape in the city.

He'd never taken anyone else here. Before, he'd wanted to be alone. To be able to stand above the city. To look out at the river.

Freedom.

"Tanner?"

He led her into the bedroom. Threw open the balcony doors and let the sunlight pour in.

She was beautiful with the sunlight on her. As beautiful as she was in the moonlight.

Always so perfect to him.

Don't fuck this up.

The panther was snarling inside of him. As desperate for his mate as any predator could be.

He took a breath. Tasted her. "Get on the bed." He had to give her pleasure first. Had to make sure that she enjoyed what was to come.

But his angel wasn't looking shy and innocent. Her cheeks were flushed. Her eyes bright. As she headed for the bed, her perfect ass doing a little roll that he hadn't even realized she could do, Marna stripped.

She kicked her shoes away. Tossed her T-shirt to the floor. Slid out of her jeans in a move that had his cock twitching.

Clad in her underwear and bra, she slid onto the bed. Big, king-sized, the bed was positioned to face the river.

The view of the river was amazing. It was nothing compared to the view he had of her right then. Damn, she looked good enough to *eat*.

And he did like to bite.

Tanner yanked off his own T-shirt and began to stalk toward her.

"Do I get to . . . taste this time?" she asked him, her voice a mix of sin and innocence.

The beast inside snarled.

If she put her mouth on him—*fuck, yes*—he was done. "Me first." Then he caught her ankle. Pulled her legs apart. His nostrils flared as he inhaled her scent.

Nothing had ever smelled as good. Sex and flowers. Sin and temptation.

Paradise.

He climbed onto the bed. Settled between those long, silken legs, and put his mouth right between her thighs.

She whispered his name, and he kissed her through the thin silk of her underwear.

The panties were getting wet. Good. He wanted her wetter. He needed her wetter.

Marna had to be ready for him. She had to want this as much as he did.

Want me more than your next breath.

The way he wanted her.

His fingers slid under the panties. Found the tight entrance to her body. Thrust inside. She squirmed beneath him. Not trying to get away.

Closer.

He tore away her panties. Put his mouth against the flesh he wanted to taste. And he tasted. His tongue slid over her. Into her. Her hips arched and her breath panted out.

He licked. Learned every curve of her body.

She whispered his name.

He kept tasting. More. *More.*

She came against his tongue.

The first time.

The second time, he'd make sure she came when he was buried deep in her.

The climax had her stiffening beneath him. Arching her body. Closing her eyes.

He loved the taste of her pleasure. Rich, but sweet.

He jerked open his jeans. Pulled out his cock. Her body waited, open, *perfect.*

With one hand, Tanner guided his cock to the entrance of her body. Her eyes were on him. Wide. Eager. No hesitation. No fear.

Jaw clenched, he began to thrust inside her. *So hot.* Hot and tight. He pushed slowly, yanking back on the beast and fighting for control as hard as he could.

"It's okay." Marna's whisper. "I want you."

But for her first time, he had to use care. Later, he'd let the beast break free. This time . . .

Has to be for her.

His mouth took hers as he pushed deeper into her. His tongue slid over hers. Her legs wrapped around his hips.

Nothing had ever felt so good. So damn perfect. Her sex wrapped around him, the best dream he'd ever had. Wet. Warm. Tight.

His muscles clenched as he fought the urge to plunge balls-deep into her. He wouldn't hurt her.

Her nails dug into his shoulders. Her mouth broke from his. Her hips lifted up against his, demanding, even as she said, "More!"

Tanner gave her more. He pushed into her, one long, deep glide, and they both gasped.

So good. But . . . "Am I hurting you?"

Her nails dug deeper into him. "Give me the pleasure . . . *again*."

What his angel wanted, he'd make sure she got.

He withdrew, thrust, again and again. Sweat slickened his back, and he kept the beast inside chained up tight. Not too hard. Not too wild.

Not this time.

He caressed her breast. Sucked her nipple. Enjoyed the way her moans filled the air, and the lush scent of sex deepened in the air around them.

He took her hips and positioned her so that he could thrust deeper—and slide right over her clit with each move of his body.

She gasped his name again. Her sex tightened more around him. Her climax was close. He could see it in the blindness of her eyes, hear it in her gasps.

Close.

The panther snarled inside.

Tanner put his mouth on the curve of her shoulder. Licked her flesh. Scored her with his teeth.

Bite.

Beasts liked to mark what was theirs. After this, there'd be no denying what she was anymore.

Angel.

Fallen.

Mine.

He thrust. Withdrew. Thrust—

Marna came. Her sex clenched around him as pleasure flashed across her face.

That was what he'd wanted. Her climax milked his cock, silken strokes that shredded his control.

Mine.

Deeper. Harder. He drove into her. Again and again. He pushed her legs over his shoulders. Opened her to him completely.

Fast. Frantic. He plunged. The base of his spine tightened. He took her mouth. Tasted her—

And came harder than he ever had in his life. Tanner held tight to her, shuddering, as the pleasure pounded through him in a powerful wave that left him hollowed out.

But wanting more.

Of her, *always,* more.

His head lowered. He licked the small wound he'd made on her shoulder. She wouldn't know the mark for what it was.

Claiming.

But he did.

"I understand." Her voice was soft and satisfied.

Tanner forced his head to lift. His cock was already getting hard inside of her again.

Her gaze found his and a smile lifted her face.

Fucking trouble. His chest began to ache.

"Now I know why." She licked her lips, a fast swipe of her pink tongue. She'd offered to use that tongue on him before.

He thrust into her again.

Her eyes widened.

But he asked, "Why . . . ?" Not sure what she'd meant.

Marna's smile widened. The sight took his breath away

even as she said, "I know why humans are so interested in sex."

Ah, getting that part, was she?

He pushed up onto his elbows and stared down at her.

"They fight, lie, even kill . . ." Her breath whispered out as he pushed into her. "For the pleasure."

A pleasure that could make a strong man break.

Or drive him to destroy anyone or anything that came between him and the woman he wanted.

"I-I didn't know . . ." Marna's voice stuttered a bit as her hands curled around him.

He almost slid out of her, then pushed back.

"I didn't know how good it would be," she told him in a rush.

Tanner stilled and stared down at her. "Baby, it's only gonna get better." Time to show her that he was a man who could keep his promises.

Always.

Her sex was still slick from their releases. Pushing deep, he had her arching toward him. He rolled them, sliding so that she was on top, giving him one phenomenal view.

Her hands flattened on his chest. "Tanner, I—"

He locked his hands around her hips. Lifted her. He saw the flare of her pupils. *She liked that.*

Her knees pushed into the mattress as she pressed back down. Up. Down.

The second time should have been easier. Softer.

It wasn't.

It was rougher. Harder.

She moved quickly on him, rising and falling, and he thrust into her wet heat. His hips pushed off the bed, and she gasped when he went deep inside of her.

Then Marna tried to take him even deeper.

Did she know her nails drew blood on his chest?

The panther growled.

His own claws wanted to break free—*were* breaking free. He yanked his hands up and away from her. The claws would be too sharp.

Not. Her.

He lifted his arms over his head and drove his claws into the wooden headboard. She stilled for an instant, and her gaze tracked up to his hands.

"Won't . . . hurt you," he grated. It was pretty phenomenal that he'd managed speech right then. All he could think was *fuck her.*

Her gaze came back to his. Held. "I know."

Then she started moving again. Faster. Stronger. This time, she didn't come with a whisper.

Marna shouted his name.

Only fair, since he roared hers when he exploded. His orgasm barreled through him. White-hot. The pleasure was so intense that he shuddered.

Fucking an angel had given him a taste of heaven. No, it had been better than paradise. Much better.

Her gasps filled his ears as she fell forward. Her blond hair covered them. He yanked his claws from the wood. Carefully, he put his arms around her.

Held her close.

One taste wasn't gonna be enough.

Not nearly enough to satisfy him—or the beast he carried.

Bastion turned away from the scene of the lovers, his hands clenched.

Marna was lost to him.

It shouldn't have been this way.

Not for her. Not for him.

His wings beat against the air as he soared higher, higher into the sky. His heart raced, and his guts seemed to twist. And he wanted to destroy the shifter.

Rage.

Angels weren't supposed to care about others. They did their jobs. They did their duty. There was nothing else.

Rip. Him. Apart.

How could she let the animal touch her? Tanner's own brother had been the one to slice away Marna's beautiful wings. Why would she allow the beast to defile her now?

Humans lusted. They fucked. They took their pleasure when they wanted.

Angels were better than that. Marna had been better. Until the shifter came to her.

His wings beat faster against the air. Tanner would pay for what he'd done.

Defiling an angel? Did the fool truly think there would be no consequences? There always were.

Punishment would come.

The fury deepened as he flew higher.

The shifter would suffer.

Just as Marna had suffered. And . . . *just as I do.*

Tanner's phone rang, a loud peal of sound that had him swearing. He didn't want to move. He wanted to stay buried inside of Marna and go for another round of lovemaking.

Maybe six more rounds?

Never get enough.

But the phone kept pealing at him. Swearing, he fumbled around the bed and found the jeans he didn't remember ditching. Tanner fished out the phone—good thing he'd managed to snag it after his shift; then he tensed when he saw the number revealed on the screen.

Jonathan.

He glanced at Marna. Her eyes, so wide, were on him. Slowly, carefully, he withdrew from her body.

A light gasp left her, and he caught the faintest scent of blood.

Virgin.

He'd just had sex with a virgin angel. There had to be some kind of special place in hell for a guy like him.

If she only knew all the things I've done.

Marna never would have let him touch her. Funny, because he would've traded the last remaining scrap of his soul for another chance to take her.

The phone rang again, vibrating in his hand. Turning away from her, he lifted it to his ear. "Chance."

"You've got a real big problem," Jonathan told him, voice low. There were shouts behind him. The sound of sirens.

Frowning, Tanner headed toward the balcony. "And that's new . . . how?"

"A rookie cop was just rushed to St. Mary's. The guy was left for dead in the street, and guess just who the hell was the last person he radioed in about?"

"I didn't—"

"He was still conscious when the EMTs pulled up, and the guy ID'd you." A low hiss of breath whispered over the line, followed by the scream of more sirens. "Man, you need to come in to the station, freaking *now,* and clear this mess up."

Tanner's hand tightened around the phone.

"Otherwise," Jonathan said, "you're going to find your ass on the Most Wanted list, and every cop in the area will come gunning for you."

The line went dead.

Sonofa—

"Tanner?" Marna's voice. Soft. Worried. "What's going on?"

He turned away from the balcony. "Looks like I'm wanted for an assault on an officer." Assault? Attempted murder?

What. The. Hell?

"That kid who pulled us over . . ." He yanked on his clothes. Checked for his badge. He'd kept it shoved in his back pocket after flashing it to the other cop. "He's on the way to the hospital."

"What?" She jumped from the bed, giving him an eyeful that was enough to make his cock jerk up.

Down, dumbass. Now wasn't the time for wanting. Though she could sure make him want more than any other.

"What happened to him?" she demanded as, with a wave of her hand, she had her clothes magically back on her body. Handy talent, only he liked it better in reverse, when those clothes hit the floor.

"What happened?" Tanner repeated, gut clenching as he thought about the possibilities of just what could have gone wrong on that dark stretch of road. "According to the cop, me."

Marna blinked. "I don't—"

"He said I was the one who hurt him. And if I don't get my ass down to the station and figure out what's going on, then, baby, we could be in for a whole world of trouble." Because Jonathan had been right. The cops *would* come looking for him.

And they might find her. He'd rather not explain a dead woman right then. Or a not-so-dead woman. It looked like he had enough shit hitting the fan without adding that to the menu.

Let the kid be all right. The thought whispered through his mind. The rookie had seemed like a decent sort. Naïve, but—*but he didn't deserve death.*

Tanner stalked toward Marna. He buried his hand in her hair—like silk—and tipped her head back. "Stay in the apartment. I'll come back as soon as I can."

"I can help—"

"You can stay out of sight." The whole damn thing had to be a setup. One designed to make him a target. "Someone is trying to pin this attack on me, so that means someone wants me out of the way." Why?

To get at Marna.

"I was there," she said, eyes searching his. "I know you didn't do anything to that officer."

No, he hadn't done anything. This time.

She was staring up at him with those big, blue eyes, looking at him like he was some kind of hero.

What will you do when she realizes just how like your brother you really are?

He swallowed back the fury that wanted to build and brought his lips to hers. One taste. Fast. That was all he allowed himself.

For now.

"I'll come back," he promised. "I'll figure out what happened, and I'll be back for you."

Then, because there wasn't anything left to say, he headed for the door.

He'd taken only a few steps when . . .

"Thank you."

Her words stopped him cold. His hand was reaching for the doorknob. "For what?"

"Teaching me about pleasure."

She was gonna break him.

"After all the pain . . ." She stopped, and he heard the faint inhalation of her breath. "I didn't know that much pleasure was possible."

Helpless, Tanner glanced over his shoulder. "Baby, we're just gettin' started."

Her smile lit up her face. "Yes, we are."

And he realized that there had been something left to say, after all.

The police station was swarming with activity when Tanner marched inside. But all that activity sure stopped dead when folks got a look at him.

Every eye in the place turned to him. Every conversation—ended.

Great. He'd managed to piss off too many people in the PD over the years—folks who were now only too eager to watch him burn. Just a few months back, he'd managed to anger even more cops when he'd donned a uniform and jumped into an investigation—one that had been headed by other officers. But that case had involved another angel and Brandt's ex-lover. He'd had to get involved, or else those other cops would have wound up dead.

He stepped on toes. He made enemies. But the humans just didn't get it—he did it all to keep them safe.

Now they were lining up to burn his ass. Too bad for them. He wasn't in the mood for a bonfire.

"What the hell are you looking at?" Tanner snapped. He'd brought in his weapon and still had it holstered on his hip.

Two uniformed cops headed for him with eyes narrowed and we'll-kick-the-shit-out-of-you expressions on their faces.

"Tanner Chance." The captain's bellowing voice stopped them all. Tanner glanced to the left and saw that Captain Jillian Pope had left her office. She stood with her arms crossed over her chest, glaring holes in every officer in the room.

After a moment, that glare of hers turned to him. "In my office," she ordered.

Tanner began to cross toward her.

"Your ass is gonna fry," one of the uniforms muttered as he passed. A guy named Lawson Phillips. They'd clashed before. "You think you can turn on one of your own?"

"I haven't turned on anyone." Tanner kept his voice flat. "It wasn't me." The fact that he was echoing words Marna had once said to him—well, yeah, that was damn fitting.

"Unlike people, video cameras don't lie."

That stopped him. He frowned at Lawson. "What are you talking about?" What video camera?

Lawson's smile was evil. "The next time you play a game of hit the cop, make sure his car video isn't turned on, dumbass."

Oh, someone was begging for a beating. He could oblige.

"Chance."

His head whipped back toward the captain. Her cheeks were flushed. "Inside. Now," she demanded.

This was gonna be ugly. If his face was on that video, how the hell was he supposed to talk his way out of this mess?

"We'll talk later," he promised Lawson. The guy backed up a step.

With one last glare at the uniform, Tanner headed into her office. She slammed the door closed behind him. Held up her hand. "I want your weapon, Detective."

With those words, Tanner knew he was screwed.

When she heard the pounding on the apartment door, Marna tensed. Was that Tanner? Back already?

But why would he be knocking at his own place? The guy had a key.

Not Tanner.

She crept toward the door.

The pounding shook the wooden frame. "I know you're in there!" A man's voice shouted through that wood. "Now open the door!"

Definitely not Tanner. Her hands flattened on the door. She glanced through the small peephole. Saw a tall, blond man. Her heart began to race. Like she'd forget him anytime soon. It was pretty hard to forget the face of the cop who'd shot you.

Jonathan something. She couldn't recall his last name, but she sure recognized Tanner's partner.

As she stared at him in growing horror, he held up his

gun and pointed it at the door. "Open up," he said, "or I'll just start shooting my way inside."

She believed him.

Captain Pope marched back and forth in front of Tanner, anger tightening her small body. She'd been promoted just six months back, but she'd already gained a reputation for being one of the hardest ass-kickers in the New Orleans PD.

"You wanna tell me what the hell you were thinkin'?" she demanded, the South rolling hard in her words.

"I didn't do it." His conscience was clear on this one. "I didn't hurt that kid cop."

She scoffed. "You're on the video. Big and bold as life."

His jaw clenched. "How is he?" Because he was worried about the kid. The guy had just been trying to do his job. And for that, some SOB had tried to kill him.

No, not that. Tanner knew the killer had gone after the other cop deliberately. *To pin the crime on me.*

"Officer Paul Hodges is in intensive care," the captain told him, and her voice was grim. As grim as her eyes. "Too many internal injuries to count. He's spitting blood. Barely breathing."

Hell.

"I don't even know how he's alive." She turned away. Headed toward her small window and stared down at the street. "But he *is* alive. And he was able to ID you."

"It's a setup. I didn't—"

"Do I look like a moron to you?" She tossed a glare over her shoulder. "Even on video, I can tell one of my own kind." And as he watched, the captain's green eyes faded to black.

Demon black.

Tanner didn't move. But he did sure wish that his gun wasn't locked in her desk drawer.

Not that he needed the gun to kill but . . .

"Whoever that asshole was, he didn't count on another

demon watching that video." She ran a tired hand over the back of her neck and paced back toward him. "Hell, that's even *if* he knew that he was being recorded at all. My guess is he just used the glamour to fool that poor SOB he sent to the ICU."

Even more careful now, because Tanner wasn't sure just how much he could trust his captain—if at all—he said in a disbelieving tone, "Demons?"

Her eyes were still pitch black. Every part of 'em. Sclera. Lens. A demon's true eyes were always black—some said to match their souls.

Though Tanner didn't believe that bullshit. His brother, Cody, was half-demon, and the guy wasn't evil. Not even close.

Cody had been the only one to escape that particular family curse.

"Do I look like a freaking idiot to you, shifter?" the captain snapped.

He almost smiled. Would have, if he hadn't been knee-deep in paranormal hell. "No, ma'am, you don't."

"Then let's start shooting straight with each other, because if we don't, there's a roomful of cops out there I can toss your ass back to. Wanna see how fast they lock you up and throw away the key?"

Like any cage could hold him.

"Lady, don't make me shoot you," Jonathan told her, then paused and said, "again."

Her eyes narrowed. Jerk.

"I watched the surveillance video from the patrol car. The techs on scene played it back, and I saw *you*. You were with Tanner when that cop questioned him."

She'd worried that the officer might have seen her, but she'd never even thought about a camera in the squad car.

"I don't have time for this crap." The cop glanced over his

shoulder, then back toward the door. Marna still had her eye pressed to the peephole. "I'm giving you to three, then I'm going to start firing. Once folks realize who you are, do you really think they'll care that I emptied a few bullets into a killer?"

Wasn't he a charmer?

"One."

Marna whirled away from the door. If she let him in, wouldn't he just shoot her then? Probably, so letting him in didn't exactly make sense to her. The fire escape was right outside the balcony. She could get out that way.

"Two!" he shouted..

She shoved open the balcony doors. Hurried outside.

"Three!" He fired.

Fired?

So much for waiting.

Marna glanced back and saw him kick in the door. His bullet had taken out the lock, making it easier for him to bust inside. His gaze met hers. He had his gun up.

"It doesn't have to be this way," he called out to her. The faint lines on his face had tightened. *"It doesn't."*

There was no other way for it to be.

Marna grabbed for the fire escape.

And the thunder of another bullet chased after her.

"Some demons are so strong when it comes to glamour magic"—the captain sat on the edge of her desk and lifted one brow-—"that they can change every aspect of their bodies. When humans look at them, the fools see only what the demon *wants* them to see."

Yeah, he knew this bit. So Tanner finished, "And in this case, some demon wanted that kid to see me?"

She nodded. "Looks like you've got yourself one powerful demon for an enemy." Her head cocked to the right. "Know someone like that? Someone strong enough with glamour magic that he could copy your face and body? That he could be your twin?"

Tanner made sure to keep his expression blank. "No. I don't know many demons." He offered her a tight smile. "Demons and shifters aren't exactly close."

"Really?" One dark brow rose. Her nails tapped on her desk. "That's odd, especially since the gossip I heard said that your own brother was a demon."

Someone had been talking too much.

"A demon gifted with a high level of glamour power." She gave a low whistle. "Now, that same gossip also told me that you had *two* brothers."

"Brandt is dead." She would know about him. In the paranormal world, everyone had known about his panther-shifter brother. Hard to ignore a sadistic alpha bent on raising hell.

And slaughtering everyone in his path.

"So the stories go." Captain Pope rolled her shoulders. "But the stories also say that your family has a history of being some twisted fucks."

True. So much for sugar coating. Tanner rose. "You shouldn't listen to so many stories." Time to leave. Either she could throw his ass in jail or—

"And maybe you're trusting the wrong person. Maybe fate didn't just screw you with one sadistic killer of a brother. Maybe you've got two who want you dead."

Tanner kept walking. "You're wrong. I know Cody." He'd protected his brother over the years. Taken punishments meant for his younger brother, over and over.

So much pain.

Cody wouldn't turn on him.

And he sure wouldn't turn on the only family he had left.

"We never know people nearly as well as we think." Now a note of sadness had entered her voice. "We usually find out the truth far too late."

He already knew the truth about Cody.

"We could clear this up quickly enough," the captain offered. "Let me talk to Cody. Let me find out just what he's capable of."

Not a good idea. "My brother isn't in the city." He'd gone back to his place in the swamp. The guy craved his solitude. Being in the city just drove him crazy.

"So where is he?"

He could hear the rumble of voices on the other side of the door. "He's got a makeshift clinic in the swamp. He helps out there." Did she catch his not-so-subtle emphasis on *help*? Because Cody wasn't a killer. He was a doctor. Tanner exhaled. Time to make a move. "What happens now?" If he walked out of that door, was he gonna have to beat off the uniforms who came gunning for him? He'd just like to know, so he could be ready for the fight.

"Three responders on scene saw that video."

Tanner glanced back over his shoulder.

"Me," she said with a shrug and lifted her hand. "Your partner, and a loud-mouthed uniform named Lawson. I think you know him."

Yeah, he knew the dick.

"Now we just have to convince those two that the footage was fake."

"And you think that's gonna be easy?" Lawson had already picked out his cell.

"Easier than letting 'em know that demons are running wild on the streets, yeah." Her eyes flashed black again. "Because some demons aren't ready for the truth to be spilled to humans."

He was guessing that she was one of those demons. Tanner cleared his throat. "Jonathan already knows about the supernaturals."

Her gaze seemed to chill. "Is that why he was so eager to run off with his gun?"

Tanner hesitated. He didn't like where this might be going.

"Humans who know the truth can be very, very dangerous," she said.

Like he had to be told that. "Where is Jonathan?" A chill had settled in his gut.

"He left the crime scene. Raced away right after we rewound the footage some more, and he caught sight of the woman you had with you."

Oh, hell, *no.*

The captain shook her head. "I'm not sure where the guy is now, he could be—"

Tanner yanked open the door before she could finish. He rushed out into the bullpen. Slammed right into Lawson.

Lawson grabbed his arms. "Where the hell do you think—"

Tanner tossed him aside. "Not now, asshole. *Not now.*" He'd been tricked. Jonathan had lured him out, lured him away—

So the guy could go after Marna.

Sonofabitch.

Jonathan was one of the few people in this town who knew about Tanner's apartment in the city. Since he was Tanner's partner, he'd needed a list of all Tanner's residences, in case of an emergency. *Does this count as an emergency?*

"Stand down, Lawson!" he heard the captain shout behind him.

Then there were gasps. The faintest snick of a safety being released.

Humans wouldn't have heard that sound.

A shifter wouldn't have missed it.

"Stand down!" the captain screamed.

Tanner spun and saw that Lawson had taken aim at him. The guy's gun was shaking, but he said, "A killer's not just walking away."

The other cops had frozen. What? Were they just gonna stand there and watch?

Then let's give them a show.

Tanner leapt forward and yanked the gun right out of Lawson's hand. He moved so fast, Lawson couldn't even squeeze the trigger.

Then he turned the weapon right back on the human. "The captain cleared me." He made sure his voice carried. He wanted everyone in the bullpen to hear this.

"No damn way!" Lawson's whole body was shaking now. Staring down the barrel of a gun could do that to a guy. "I was there, I saw—"

"What the killer wanted you to see." The captain's footsteps rushed toward them. "I had my techs take another look at the video. The video had been altered. One minute—one damn minute—and they knew it wasn't Detective Chance."

Tanner slapped the gun down on the nearest desk.

"He's clear," the captain's voice thundered out, "and our job is to find out who the hell is trying to set up one of our own."

Lawson's breath heaved out. Tanner saw the fury—*the hate*—gleaming in his dark eyes. Another day, another time, and he would give the guy the fight he wanted.

Today . . .

I have to get to her.

"Go," the captain told him with a jerk of her head toward the door. "You have your orders."

No, he didn't. But then, he didn't need orders. He knew how to kill on his own.

He'd learned to kill when he was nine years old. Too young?

Hell, yes.

And the blood was still on his hands.

He rushed for the precinct's exit. Everyone made sure to get out of his way.

* * *

"You can't run from me!"

The bullet had missed her and slammed into the metal of the fire escape.

She couldn't run? What did it look like she was doing? Hanging around, waiting to have tea with the trigger-happy idiot?

Marna's legs raced down the metal stairs.

And he followed right behind her. Fast, so fast for a human.

"I know what you are!"

She jumped to the ground. Staggered. Righted herself and—

He grabbed her.

Very fast for a human.

And to touch her? No, he had no idea of what she was. "You shouldn't do that," she whispered.

His breath heaved out. His face had reddened as he gave chase. "I've got . . . to know."

She stared at him with wide eyes while her heart raced. "I don't want to hurt you." But she would. Pain was a part of life that she'd grown accustomed to since her fall.

His face—maybe some would have found it handsome, but she thought it looked too soft, too weak, not like Tanner's fierce features—tightened. "And I don't want to hurt you. If I had . . ." He lifted the gun in his hand. "I would have aimed better."

But he'd already shot her once. Was she supposed to forget that? What was a little matter of blood and bullets between not-friends?

His gaze swept over her. "I knew you weren't dead."

She didn't like the way his eyes dipped down her body.

"I thought you'd have wings."

Her breath seemed to burn in her lungs. Maybe he *did* know what she was.

He whirled her around. "Shouldn't you have wings?"

Not if they'd been cut away.

"Doesn't matter." He locked a cuff around her wrist. Snapped another around his own.

The human was asking for so much pain.

"There's someone who wants to see you. You have to come with me."

No, she didn't. Marna yanked on her cuff and broke the chain linking it to his. One tug, that was all it took.

She was getting stronger, too.

Time to show the human just how dangerous she could be.

The darkness inside of her, a darkness that she'd always sensed and fought to suppress, seemed to stretch. Filled her.

She smiled at the human and knew he'd never see what was coming for him—not until it was too late.

A fire built inside of her, burning brighter, hotter.

No more.

Time for her to stop being afraid. Time for others to fear *her.*

CHAPTER NINE

Tanner saw the flames before he saw her. Red, gold, twisting and crackling, the flames rose up around his apartment building.

Humans were out, running, screaming for help.

But Marna just stood in the middle of the flames. What the hell?

"Marna!" He yelled her name but wondered if she could even hear his call over the crackle of the fire. In the distance, he heard the wail of a fire truck's siren, but this wasn't a fire that humans could handle.

They couldn't fight magic.

Marna's arms were up in the air, and her face—even through the flames he could see the light of power that bathed her features.

"Marna, pull it back!"

The flames flared higher.

Tanner knew he had to go into the fire, for her. Jaw locked, he raced forward and bellowed her name once more.

Just before the flames would have licked over his skin—*like it would be the first time he felt that agony*—Marna's head turned and her eyes—dazed, wild—found his.

The fire died away, vanishing in mere seconds and leaving behind only wisps of smoke that drifted into the air.

"T-Tanner?"

The humans had hauled ass, so, luckily, no one was left to see his angel just extinguish those flames with a stray thought. No one was—

His nostrils flared as he pulled in the scents. The fire had been so strong that he hadn't even noticed . . .

Jonathan.

His partner lay on the ground near Marna's feet. Not moving.

Tanner rushed forward. "What did you do?"

She shook her head. Glanced down. Her hands lowered and a loose handcuff banged against her wrist. "He was trying to make me leave with him."

The sirens were coming closer.

"I wasn't going to let him hurt me." A different note had entered her voice now. Harder. Colder. "No one's going to hurt me again."

Tanner crouched next to Jonathan. He rolled his partner over and sucked in a breath at the guy's ashen features.

"He's still alive," Marna said. Did she sound disappointed? His angel?

What was going on?

"Yeah, he's still alive." Tanner grabbed Jonathan and tossed the guy over his shoulder. He wasn't leaving him. Not when he had so many questions for the man. "And we all need to go, *now.*"

"You're helping him?" Marna backed up a step. "He—he wanted to hurt me. He tried to take me away."

"And we'll find out what the hell he was thinking once we get away from here." Once they'd gotten out of sight and didn't have trucks full of firefighters racing toward them.

She drew in a ragged breath. "He wants me dead."

Not gonna happen.

Tanner stared down at her, willing Marna to trust him. They all needed to leave, but he had to make sure she wasn't about to unleash hell on them all again.

As he stared at her, Marna's eyes seemed to darken. The blue deepened. Seemed to almost flash . . . black?

What?

The sirens screamed.

"He said—he said someone was waiting for me."

Tanner had Jonathan flung over his shoulder. With his other hand, he caught Marna's hand. Locked his with hers. "Then we're gonna find that someone." The same SOB who'd set him up? Who'd set her up?

Time to end this nightmare.

Marna nodded, and her gaze flickered back to blue. He felt the punch in his gut. Angels weren't supposed to have eyes that looked like a demon's, were they?

But he didn't have time to worry about her eyes then. They rushed away from the smoke-filled area. Rounded the corner. Marna climbed into his SUV. Tanner dumped Jonathan into the back.

When he leapt into the front seat, Tanner spared Marna one more glance. Her hands were fisted in front of her. She wasn't looking at him.

He gunned the engine.

"Something's wrong." He almost didn't catch her whisper. Even with his shifter hearing, it had been hard to hear her. She breathed the words more than said them. "Something's wrong with me."

"Nothing's wrong." *Her eyes had been black.* "Everything's fine." They'd find the demon who was setting them both up, and Tanner would end that bastard.

The tires squealed as he raced down the narrow streets.

"I like it too much."

Another confession that was little more than a breath.

"I'm not supposed to like the fire," she said softly.

His hands clenched around the wheel.

"I'm not supposed to lust, not supposed to want so badly."

His gaze cut to her and found her stare on him.

"I'm not supposed to want so badly," she said again, louder now, "the way I want you." She swallowed. "The things I want, the things I want to *do* . . . this isn't me."

No, it wasn't who she'd been, but Tanner realized that Marna was becoming someone else.

Someone stronger.

Someone . . . someone who could be very, very dangerous.

"Tanner, what happens . . ." Now she looked away, staring out at the blur of buildings, and finished. ". . . when an angel goes bad?"

Hell came calling. Tanner knew because he'd seen it happen before. He didn't want to face that nightmare again.

Tanner dropped his partner in an old chair, then bent to quickly cuff the guy. Tanner made sure that Jonathan was locked up tight in the cuffs, and then he gave the man a good, hard slap.

Jonathan groaned, and his eyes slowly opened. He focused first on Tanner, then on Marna, then his gaze swept around him—and Tanner knew his partner took in every aspect of the old, abandoned warehouse with that sweeping glance.

If you needed a private place to torture or dump a body, Tanner knew this was a perfect spot. No one was around for miles. That meant there was no one to hear the screams.

Not that he expected Jonathan to scream. At least, not right away.

Jonathan jerked at his cuffs. "You really think these are necessary, *partner*?"

"Was it necessary to cuff me?" Marna demanded, stepping forward.

Tanner wrapped his arm around her shoulders. "Easy." Who would have thought that he'd be the one playing good cop?

Jonathan's gaze slid over them both. Lingered on the hand Tanner had around Marna. "I thought it would be . . . like that."

"Watch it," Tanner advised, voice still mild.

"I mean, why risk everything? Why put your job on the line? Why lie to me? Unless . . . unless you were screwing her."

Tanner kicked out, sending the wooden chair slamming to the ground. It hit on the side, and Jonathan groaned when his arm rammed into the cement.

"Told you," Tanner said, "to watch it." That jerk wasn't going to slam Marna.

Jonathan looked up at him and his lips tightened. "You think you can keep her? You think there aren't a dozen paranormals in this town desperate for a chance to get at her?"

"Is that why *you* were trying to get her?" Tanner demanded as the fury rose inside him. "Were you planning to sell her off to the highest bidder?" *Over my cold and dead body.*

Marna's hands pressed against Tanner's side. "I told you, he said there was someone waiting for me."

Jonathan shrugged and tried to lever himself off the ground. "What can I say? Angels are in demand."

Growling, Tanner surged forward and yanked the bastard to his feet. Tanner's boots kicked away the shattered remains of the chair. "I thought you wanted me to trust you," Tanner said. Right, he'd known that was bull. Mocking now, he continued, "I thought you wanted to *help.*"

"I did! Then I realized you weren't exactly playing on the side of the good guys anymore." Jonathan didn't fight Tanner's hold, but his eyes blazed. "Turning on your own, leaving that poor kid to—"

"That wasn't me!" Tanner shoved him back. He had to. His claws wanted to break free, and he didn't want to accidentally behead the guy.

Maybe not so accidentally.

"I *saw* the video."

"What you saw . . ." Tanner glanced back at Marna. She watched the human with narrowed eyes. "What you saw was a demon using one hell of a lot of glamour magic. My face, not me."

Jonathan blinked, and his shoulders seemed to slump. "What? They can . . . they can do that?"

Marna laughed. The sound was bitter, not like her. "If they're strong enough, they can do almost anything."

Since Cody was a demon, Tanner had learned early on about the power levels among those beings. Some demons were on the low end of the demon power scale, ranked as ones or twos—pretty much humans with a few extra skills. But, while the majority of the demons running loose on the earth were low-levels, there *were* some badass demons out there.

Demons who tipped the scales by hitting a power level of nine, or even . . . in the *worst* case situation, ten.

Level-tens were supposed to be able to bring hell to earth. Literally. To be able to control the minds of humans with barely a thought.

He'd heard rumors of one level-ten in Atlanta. A guy named Niol who could destroy a city block with a wave of his hand.

Just another reason why Tanner made it a point not to visit that area.

Was he dealing with a level-ten in New Orleans? If so, they could all be screwed.

"I'm supposed to just believe you, right?" Jonathan blasted, face reddening as he pulled against the cuffs again. "You've been lying to me for days. You're hiding a killer and screwing her—"

Tanner punched him. Jonathan slammed back down to the ground once more.

Marna's breath whispered out in a soft exhale. Tanner

caught her hand and rubbed his fingers over the back of her knuckles. He wasn't just . . . screwing her. If Jonathan said that again, he'd taste some more cement.

Groaning, Jonathan managed to crawl back to his knees.

"I'm not a killer," Marna said quietly. Then she added, "Not anymore."

Jonathan's head lifted, and he stared at her. Tanner didn't like that look. Too intense. Too dark.

It's the way I look at her.

Tanner put his body in front of hers. "I lied to you." Fine, time to clear the air. "But what the hell was I supposed to do? Tell you that the suspect we were bringing in was an angel of death? That you couldn't touch her, because she might kill you?" Jonathan didn't need to know that her touch didn't work anymore.

No one needed to know that fact. If he could keep her safe by making everyone else think that she was too dangerous to be around . . .

I'll lie my ass off. And he wouldn't be sorry about it. Hell, he wasn't ever sorry. Just another line. Another lie.

Cops weren't supposed to lie.

Killers were.

Some days, it was so hard to be both.

"She can kill with a touch?" Jonathan managed to stand on his feet with only a slight stagger.

"I told you not to touch me," Marna said as she stepped around Tanner. "You should have listened."

The lady still wasn't lying. Maybe he should learn to twist the truth the way she did. Would that make his conscience any cleaner?

"So you *did* kill those men in that alley." Jonathan shook his head. "And you did it with just a touch? No drugs. I thought for—"

"I didn't kill them." Marna's voice was fierce.

"You were seen—" Jonathan began.

"Just the way I was seen on the video," Tanner cut in. "It wasn't me. It wasn't her." How many times would they have to say it before it sank in for the guy? "A demon is behind the attacks. He took her face, and he took mine, and he was trying to set us both up."

"Why?" Jonathan demanded. "Why the hell would he do all that?"

"As soon as I find him, you can be sure I'll make him tell me that." But Tanner already had suspicions. Why set up Marna? Maybe because the killer had wanted to draw her out. To cut away the safety of her secrecy and push her into the spotlight. The cops had yanked her from her solitude. Left her out in the open.

What would have happened to Marna at the police station if Tanner hadn't gotten her free?

The suspicion gnawed deeper at his gut. Had getting Marna to the station been the plan all along?

Get her there. Make her vulnerable.

Only maybe the demon hadn't counted on Tanner getting Marna out so quickly. Getting her out and running with her.

When I ran, you had to set me up, too, didn't you?

Because the killer had wanted to separate Marna and Tanner.

"There was no evidence left behind," Jonathan muttered. "The scene in that alley was so clean. Everything pointed back to *her*."

"Cops know," Tanner began as that gnawing suspicion dug deeper, "how to clean up scenes." And even how to stage them.

He mentally flipped back through the possibilities.

You'd need a high-level demon to pull off a glamour trick like that.

A demon who knows his way around crime scenes.

One who had access to all the case files.

Another piece of the puzzle slid into place. "The patrol

unit . . . that kid called in our location. He read out my badge number." By doing so, he'd painted a giant bull's-eye on his back. Someone with access to that radio line had known exactly where Tanner was.

And exactly how to set him up.

"A cop?" Jonathan whispered, eyes wide, and Tanner knew his partner had reached the same conclusion he had.

He and Marna were being set up, all right, and the demon had probably been working right beside him, and he hadn't even noticed the guy.

Or the woman.

Jonathan yanked at the cuffs. *"Unlock me!"*

Tanner dug the key out of his pocket. But he didn't free Jonathan, not yet. "Who were you selling her to?"

Jonathan's jaw clenched. "I wasn't selling her, man. Get that part straight. I'm a good cop, okay? The captain . . . shit, she told me to find her. Pope saw her in the video, and she *knew* that you'd been hiding her. Hell, she's the one who told me what your lady was."

An angel.

"Captain Pope isn't human." Did the guy realize that?

Marna just watched them as she rocked forward on the balls of her feet. He could feel the tension rolling off her.

Jonathan swallowed. "I was beginning to suspect that was—"

"She's a demon." Tanner just didn't know how strong she was.

"Sonofabitch." Jonathan's gaze darted to the boarded-up warehouse windows. "She probably followed you. Probably set the whole department after you."

She'd said that she was gonna clear his name. She'd told him to go.

Don't trust a demon.

There was only one demon he'd ever trusted in this

world. His brother. The captain had been desperate to find out where Cody was.

And I told her.

Fuck.

What in the hell was going on?

"Let me out of these cuffs!" Jonathan demanded, lurching forward. "Let me help!"

Tanner stepped toward his partner. Marna stopped him. "When Jonathan came to your apartment, he shot his way inside." Her hand felt silken soft against his skin. "When I ran, he followed me, shooting."

The panther snarled and tried to push past the man's control.

Eyes wide, Jonathan scurried back. "Warning shots! I wasn't aiming at her, I swear. If I had been, I would've hit her!"

Was that supposed to lessen his rage? The bastard had shot at her.

"Yes, he would have hit me," Marna said, sending a hard glance his way, "just like he did before." She shook her head. "I don't trust him, and I don't want that human free."

Yeah, well, after a bullet, who could blame her?

"Tanner, man, *listen* to me." Jonathan's voice was desperate now. "Don't do anything crazy, okay? Don't do anything like—"

"Like let my animal side out?" Perhaps it was time the guy saw just what he could do. Tanner let his claws break free.

Razor sharp. Ready to kill.

Jonathan scrambled back some more. His back almost brushed the wall. "*Please,* man, I—"

"Come near her again," Tanner told him, "and you'll see just how dangerous my beast can be." Jonathan's bullets wouldn't have killed her, but Tanner couldn't stand the thought of Marna in pain.

She took his hand, not even seeming to see the claws. She'd been so afraid of them before. But now . . .

"Let's get out of here," she told him.

They needed to haul ass. Needed to find Cody and make sure the captain wasn't going after him next.

How many more dead bodies? Blood was starting to fill the streets in the Big Easy.

"I *can* help you!" Jonathan's stare was fierce as he gazed at Marna. "Just give me a chance to make things right."

But she wasn't looking at him. She'd already turned away and headed for the door, giving them both a view of her slim back.

"Why doesn't she have wings?" Jonathan's voice. Quieter now. Curious.

Afraid?

Tanner stared down at his claws. Long. Lethal.

Monster.

"Because they were sliced away." He tossed the key to the cuffs, threw it toward the far wall. By the time Jonathan freed himself, they'd be long gone. He marched toward his partner. Kept his claws out. "A shifter's claws can slice through just about anything."

He could smell Jonathan's fear. The panther liked that scent.

Tanner brought his claws up to Jonathan's throat. "You ever shoot at her again, and you'll see just how sharp they truly are."

A fast nod. "I-I swear, I—"

"Stay the hell away from her." Because he wouldn't play so nicely the next time.

Then, because Jonathan had *shot* at her, Tanner punched him once more. The guy hit the floor, and Tanner knew he'd be out for a while.

That would give Tanner plenty of time to disappear with his angel.

"Sorry, *partner,* but I just don't trust your ass." Right then, there were only two people he trusted.

His brother—and his angel.

Bastion stared down at the male human. Paul Hodges. Weak. Helpless. His body was bruised and battered, and connected to a dozen different beeping machines.

Doctors and nurses rushed around him. Some barked orders. Others grabbed for needles. Tubes.

They were trying to save the cop.

They weren't going to succeed.

Bastion stepped closer. The male's eyes were closed. Drugs poured through his system, but . . .

The cop's body twitched.

You know I'm here.

The dying always knew when an angel was close. Paul's eyelids began to jerk.

The cop would die young. Leave behind no family. A few friends. He'd drift right away.

But his life had served a purpose. Did he realize that? He'd been useful.

A tool.

A broken tool, one that had been cast away now.

Bastion eased closer to the bed. No one else there could see him. Only humans were in the room.

They could only see his kind when their time was at hand.

"We're losing him!" one of the nurses shouted.

No, they'd already lost him. They just didn't realize it yet. He'd been lost from the moment his patrol car had stopped on that dark road. He should have stayed away from the shifter and the lost angel.

Should have kept driving.

But . . . really, there was no changing fate.

Paul's eyelids flew open. His stare locked right on Bastion. He tried to scream.

Impossible, of course, especially since he had a tube shoved down his throat.

"Time to go," Bastion told him and lifted his hand.

But Paul began to thrash violently. His head shook, back and forth, and his right arm flew out.

His fingers clenched round a scalpel. Someone screamed.

The cop tried to use his weapon on Bastion.

Strange. He hadn't expected the human to fight so fiercely.

Paul's eyes were stretched wide, and fear rolled from him in waves.

A doctor wrestled the scalpel away from him. "We're trying to help you!" the man shouted.

Trying, failing.

Paul kept fighting. Tears slid from his eyes and a mewling sound broke from his throat.

Bastion's hand lowered over the man's chest.

Paul shrank back. The fear in his eyes deepened.

Paul looked at Bastion, saw him for exactly what he was, and the cop was terrified by that sight. Why? Paul hadn't led a bad life. No agonies waited on the other side for this man.

Yet the human feared.

He fears me.

Bastion's wings stretched behind him. The human stared at them with . . . recognition?

A low, long humming filled the operating room.

"He's flat-lining!"

And the human's eyes stayed open. Terrified.

Another soul to take.

Bastion's wings spread more as he rose. He wondered . . . when had he begun to dread his duty?

To resent the souls?

I want more.

An image of Marna flashed before his eyes. Not the Marna he'd known before. Quiet. Innocent.

Perfect.

The Marna he'd seen just a little while ago. Moaning. Eager. Flushed with pleasure.

I want more.

The doctors and the nurses gasped when a long, thick crack ripped across the ceiling.

I'll have more.

And he left, without taking the soul of Paul Hodges.

Chapter Ten

"Where are we going?" Marna asked as she hunched down into her seat. They'd headed away from the city, and the only light that she saw now came from the heavy, thick moon that hung low in the sky.

Twisting trees surrounded the narrow road. To the left, dark water glinted in the moonlight.

"We need to find Cody."

The demon doctor. Her fingers pressed against her legs. When she'd been so afraid and angry earlier, she'd been able to start the fire once more. She'd felt the hot rush of power, and it had left her feeling . . . restless.

Tense.

Edgy.

Her gaze returned to the window once more. Past those trees, she saw only the lines of the swamp.

I lost my life in a swamp like this. No, not *like*—this place *was* where she'd lost her life.

The exact spot waited just a few miles away.

A girl didn't forget the worst moment of her life. Not when she got to re-live it over and over again most nights.

"I hate the swamp." The words slipped from her as she glanced back at him. She did hate it. The musky smell. The dampness. The death. Maybe some looked at the savagery of the swamp and saw beauty, but she'd never see it. Because she could never forget.

"Don't worry. We're not staying long." She saw his nostrils flare and his body seemed to tense. "We'll find Cody, make sure his ass is safe, and then we—"

They'd rounded a corner. Driven down deeper into the swamp. And now they could see the blaze. Had that been what he'd scented moments before?

A fire, only one that was burning far brighter than the flames Marna had created back in New Orleans.

Tanner slammed his foot down on the accelerator.

Marna's breath ached in her lungs. The fire was coming from Cody's cabin.

Memories rushed through her mind. Inside that cabin was Cody's makeshift clinic.

I woke up there. Tied down.

Tanner and Cody had been afraid to let her loose because they'd been worried that she'd touch them.

And kill them.

Only she hadn't been able to kill anyone.

The vehicle lurched forward as Tanner pushed the SUV to drive even faster. She grabbed for the door and held on tight as they raced toward the flames.

Was Cody inside that cabin? Demons were supposed to be able to control fire, so few ever died in flames. Unless . . .

Unless someone was there to make *sure* a demon died.

Cody . . . he wasn't a bad demon.

Smoke drifted into the sky, and Marna could have sworn that, even in the vehicle, she felt the heat from that fire on her skin.

Cody had saved her. Stitched her up. Protected her.

And now the one haven she'd ever had burned before her.

Tanner slammed on the brakes, and the SUV screeched to

a jarring stop. He leapt from the vehicle and ran toward the blaze. Hands shaking, she followed him.

"Cody!" Tanner yelled his brother's name.

Marna didn't speak. She knew Tanner would be able to smell his brother, hoped he could, anyway, even over the harsh scent of fire and smoke. He had those great shifter ears, so he should be able to hear if Cody—

Tanner's head whipped to the left. Toward the thick line of vegetation bordering the swamp. His nostrils flared, and he took off running.

At first, Marna didn't move. She'd never wanted to go back into a swamp again. But if Tanner needed her . . .

Her shoulders straightened. She could do this. No, she *would* do this.

She followed her panther shifter into her own hell. The trees were gnarled, hunched, and insects chirped all around her as she followed the pounding thud of Tanner's racing feet. He was shouting his brother's name again, so she knew he must have caught Cody's scent.

Not in the fire.

Cody had escaped. He'd gotten out. He'd—

Tanner's footsteps stopped. They just seemed to disappear. Marna frowned and slowed. He'd been up to the right. She'd heard his shout from that area moments before.

Marna hurried forward. Raced to the right.

But saw only more thick trees. More heavy vegetation. *He'd been there.* Hadn't he?

Only now he was gone.

The insects chirped louder.

Try to fucking fly now.

The voice from her nightmares whispered through Marna's head. She looked up, across the water, and saw the spot that had marked the end for her.

Fall.

The ground wasn't blood-soaked anymore. The remains

of her wings didn't litter the earth, but the area was black. Everything in a ten-foot radius had died, marking the place where an angel had lost her wings.

She turned away, not wanting to see that place. "Tanner!" He had to be close by. He was—

"Marna . . ." A whisper. One that came from behind her.

Not Tanner's voice. Her blood chilled.

Tanner lunged forward and flew through the air. His body slammed into his prey's, and they fell to the ground, twisting and hitting the earth with a heavy thud.

"What the hell?" Cody demanded. "Get the fuck off—wait, Tanner?"

His brother was alive. If he weren't so happy about that fact, Tanner would be kicking the jerk's ass for scaring him so much.

Tanner climbed to his feet. "Who did it?"

Cody pushed off the ground and glanced around with a heaving chest. He'd been running, and the guy hadn't even seemed to hear Tanner's shouts. Tackling him had been the only option available. "What are you talking about?" Cody asked, giving him a fast, sideways glance.

Huh. Now why was his voice so cautious?

Tanner shook his head. "Don't play dumb. You were never good at that bit." He jerked his thumb over his shoulder. "Your place is torched. Flames are shooting up into the sky, and you're running like the devil's chasing you. *What. Happened*."

Cody didn't meet his gaze. "Someone was coming after me. I needed to throw 'em off. To make 'em think—"

Hold up. "*You* set the fire?"

"You know I've always been good with flames." Cody carefully looked over Tanner's shoulder.

Tanner glanced back and expected to see Marna rushing up behind him.

Only she wasn't there. That sick rush of fear began to fill him again. "Who was after you?" *Come on, Marna. Get over here.* She'd been right behind him.

"You don't want to know." Now Cody was backing away. "You've got enough shit on your hands, bro. This time, I can clean up my own mess. You don't have to play hero."

But he'd always taken care of Cody. That had been the—

"Story of my life," Cody muttered, taking another step back. "I screw up, but you're the one who suffers for it. Not *this* time."

"Tanner!"

Marna's voice. She was . . . scared. Tanner inhaled. Caught her scent. Only, she wasn't alone. "Marna!" He didn't even spare another glance for his brother as he took off through the swamp.

"I'm sorry." Cody's voice followed him. "I'll make it right. I swear I will."

But Tanner didn't turn back to him. The brother he'd nearly died for—he left him alone in the woods.

She tried to calm her racing heart as she stared at the angel who'd confronted her. Bastion. Why was he there? What did he want?

Bastion's gaze wasn't on her. He stared at the blackened ground. "I thought you'd died." His voice was hushed.

She didn't move.

"I found the blood and your wings, and I thought you'd been killed." His hands were clenched.

Anger? Fury? From him? There was no denying the rage vibrating in his words, but—but he still had his wings. He *shouldn't* feel emotions like that.

Bastion glanced up at her, and his eyes seemed to burn. "I wanted to kill then."

Death angels carried out their duties. They didn't *want* to take souls.

She swallowed. "Bastion, this isn't . . ." *You.*

He glided closer to her with a powerful movement of the black wings that sprouted from his back. "Everything is changing. Up there and down here." He stood just a foot away from her now.

Marna found that she was backing away from him.

His eyes narrowed at her movement. "Are you afraid of me?"

She shouldn't be. He'd been her confidant for centuries. The closest thing to a friend that she had. But the way he looked at her—*yes.* "Have you been watching me?" Marna whispered the words and was afraid of the answer that she knew would be coming.

Bastion had always been far more powerful than she was. If he hadn't wanted her to see him—

Then I wouldn't have seen him.

But she'd still caught his scent in the air a few times. Felt eyes upon her.

"The shifter is the one who watched you. Who followed you when you didn't know."

His words made her hesitate. But how would he know that about Tanner? *Unless he'd been there, too.*

"He's hunted you." Bastion was even closer now. Close enough for his wings to stretch out. To block the light. To surround her. "And yet you let him fuck you."

She flinched away as a cold horror filled her. Bastion had watched *that?* Why? Why would he—

"Marna!"

Bastion's eyes narrowed at Tanner's shout. "He's not going to save you. He'll betray you. Destroy you. Just as he's destroyed so many others."

But Bastion stepped back, and Tanner ran to her. Her

shifter grabbed her hand, pulling her close. His heart pounded, and she felt the fast rhythm beneath his chest. "I heard you scream," he growled the words. "I heard and—" He stopped, breaking off abruptly.

Marna tilted her head back as she stared up at his face. His eyes had narrowed, and they drifted around the small clearing. Drifted, and seemed to stop directly on Bastion.

Because the angel was still there. Watching them with a gaze gone hard and cold. Not burning any longer.

Ice.

"We aren't alone," Tanner said with absolute certainty.

Yet he couldn't see Bastion, she knew that.

His nostrils widened even as his head inclined to the left.

Shifters didn't have to rely on just what they could see. Not when their other senses were in overdrive 24-7.

Tanner wrapped his arm around her shoulders and pulled her against his side. "What does he want?"

He. *Bastion.* Tanner's senses were definitely on target. "I'm not completely sure," she said as she stared straight at Bastion. Truth, but . . .

Part of her was afraid that maybe, just maybe, Bastion wanted—

Me.

The whisper slid through her. An uncomfortable suspicion because, now that she'd been with Tanner, she could understand what she'd seen in Bastion's stare.

Need. Desire.

Lust.

Angels don't lust.

Or did they?

Bastion had retreated and she thought he would leave, but suddenly, he marched right toward them.

No. Marna shoved Tanner back. She put her body between his and Bastion's. "Don't even think about it." Her voice came out as a low, furious order.

Bastion stilled.

"Think about what?" Tanner demanded from behind her.

Marna kept her eyes on Bastion. She wouldn't look over the angel's shoulder, at that burned ground that marked her change. She stared into his eyes, saw all that she'd lost, and knew that she wasn't losing anything else. "You won't touch him."

Bastion's eyes widened. "You'd protect the animal?"

Marna nodded. Tanner *wasn't* an animal.

"What the hell is happening?" Tanner demanded. "I can smell him. I just can't see the bastard."

Most folks wouldn't describe angels as bastards. Then again, Tanner wasn't in that "most" category.

"I just want you to be safe," Bastion said, and a muscle flexed along the length of his jaw. Another sign of emotion. Did he even realize how close he was to the edge?

"Don't worry about me," Marna told him. "Take care of yourself." She wanted to touch him. To grab him and hold tight and *shake* him. This wasn't the Bastion she'd known. "You have too much to lose."

Bastion glared at Tanner. "I've already lost."

Wind seemed to whip around them. Tanner swore. "If that asshole wants to play . . ."

Tanner couldn't *play* with a death angel. Not and come out still living. No one could win that particular game.

"I'm trying to help you," Bastion snapped as the wind beat harder. He was losing control. Breaking apart right in front of her. His wings stretched. Flapped. "He's nothing but a danger to you. If he's not stopped, he'll destroy you."

Marna lifted her chin. *Angels don't lie.* Yet she trusted Tanner. So where did that leave her? "You aren't touching him." Bastion was now the leader of the death angels. Refusing his order would be unheard of among their kind. Turning against him? An unforgiveable act.

But . . .

But she wasn't in heaven anymore. And so far, only one person had been there for her since her fall. There to keep her safe. To fight for her.

Maybe it was time for her to start fighting for him.

"You can't stop Death." Bastion began to rise into the air. A faint smile twisted his lips. "You know that better than most."

Damn him.

He vanished.

And Marna finally took a deep breath.

"He's gone." Tanner's voice. Growling. Tense.

She managed a nod.

He turned her toward him. Glared down at her. "What the hell is going on?"

You've got a death angel who wants you cold in the ground. She couldn't lie, but that didn't mean that she had to tell the truth. "It was just a visit from an old friend." A warning visit. "Someone who's worried about me."

His hands were on her arms. His warm fingers curled around her flesh. "An old friend makes you scream in fear?"

"Yes." Truth. "When you have old friends like I do." She should tell him more. "Tanner, I—"

His mouth took hers. His tongue slid past her lips and thrust into her mouth.

After a moment's hesitation, she kissed him back. She wanted the rush of passion that he could give her. She wanted to forget Bastion and the nightmare memories that waited on that far bank. Marna kissed Tanner with all her passion and felt the wild surge of desire inside her. The lust she felt for him could banish any chill.

His hands slid over her body. Found her ass. Curled and pulled her up against him. There was no mistaking the hard bulge of his arousal. "You're not going back to the angels." He whispered the words near her lips. "That's not your life anymore."

No. She couldn't go back. Without her wings, there'd be no way for her to ever get to heaven.

Lost.

His head lifted and his gaze blazed at her. "You're mine now."

Marna shook her head. No, she wasn't. She belonged only to herself, not to—

Tanner kissed her again. She opened her lips and her tongue met his because she liked his taste and loved the heat that spilled through her at his touch. But . . .

Not his.

She wouldn't belong to another. Not even to someone like Tanner. She'd watched too many humans over the centuries. Belonging led to pain. Betrayal.

If he's not stopped, he'll destroy you.

She wouldn't forget Bastion's words.

One more hard press of his mouth, and Tanner pulled back. "We have to go." His gaze darted behind her. To the blackened ground. His stare hardened. "Cody's out there, and he's running from who the hell knows what." His fingers twined with hers. "We have to hurry, we—" Tanner stiffened and spun around.

They weren't alone any longer—and this time, their visitor wasn't an angel. Marna didn't know the woman who stalked so slowly from the woods, but she had two men beside her. Marna recognized those men—*shifters.* They'd been in this swamp before.

That long ago night, when her wings had been ripped away, they'd been there.

Laughing.

Panther shifters.

"Captain?" Tanner faced the new threat. His claws were out. "What are you doing here?"

The woman, petite, with dark brown hair, offered them a smile. As she came closer, the shifters behind her began to change into beasts with snarls and cracks and snaps of their bones.

"I'm here to apprehend an angel." The woman pointed at Marna. "A wanted killer."

Tanner shook his head. "Jillian, we've been over this—"

She laughed. The sound was cold and bitter and sliced through the night. "I don't give a damn if she's innocent or not, Chance. Angels are worth too much money to walk away from, especially weak little things like her who can't get up enough power to hurt anyone."

There was a badge clipped to the woman's belt. This Jillian, she was a cop? Like Chance?

"Everyone wants angel blood," Marna muttered, disgusted and sick of being on the menu. "Can't you all just leave me alone?"

"It might not matter upstairs." The woman's voice was still as cool as you please. "But down here, money talks. As much as I'll get for you . . . hell, I can buy forgiveness for anything I do."

"You're a cop!" Tanner shouted.

The others had completely shifted. Transformed into big, hulking panthers with yellowed, razor-sharp teeth.

"I'm a demon first." She pulled out her gun. Aimed it at him. "In all the time that I've watched you at the PD, you just never seemed to get that. We're paranormals first, not cops. The humans . . . they're second to what we need."

The panthers began to creep forward. Their heads were low to the ground. Their big bodies tense. Two panthers, and one demon with a gun.

They could handle this, right? They'd taken out those vampires, and these odds had to be better.

"You might as well give her over to us," the woman—Jillian—said. "She's worth so much, the supernaturals won't stop coming until she's dead. A helpless angel." She laughed again. That high-pitched laugh was getting on Marna's last nerve. "That's like throwing a child into a pool of sharks."

Marna felt the now familiar pulse of fire push through her body. She lifted her hands and hoped the flames wouldn't desert her again. Only one way to find out.

But who was the bigger threat? The demon? Or the shifters?

"You've been misinformed." Marna's voice came out a little shaky. Okay, a lot. Whatever. *Do this.* "I'm not helpless."

"Not when you're standing behind the big, bad shifter." Jillian smirked. "But what will you do when he's not there to protect your ass? Can't fly away." Her lips pursed in a smirk. "Not anymore."

One of the panthers growled and swiped out at Marna. Tanner lunged and pulled her back, and his own claws flashed.

He'd need to shift in order to fight the other two panthers. He'd be weak while he shifted.

But not if she was covering his back.

"Run," Marna told the demon. The woman's green eyes had faded to black. "This is your only chance." She was trying to give her a fair warning.

Instead of heeding that warning, Jillian fired on her.

The bullet never hit.

Because in that same instant, Marna lifted her hands and sent out a wall of fire. The fire circled her and Tanner, closing them in—but keeping the others out. The fire raged so hot that the bullet melted, vanishing in the inferno.

Power, pulsing heat, poured from Marna. *"I'm not weak!"* she screamed. Too many thought of her that way. All the supernaturals who wanted to cut her open and drain her dry. Even all the angels upstairs, the ones who used to whisper about her. The ones who'd thought she wasn't strong enough to do the job of a death angel.

The panthers jumped back, hissing as they cringed away from the fire.

The demon didn't move. She would move, though. Marna would make her move.

With a wave of her hand, Marna sent the fire flying toward that demon. But the cop laughed again. The woman tossed her left hand up toward the blaze. "I've been playing with fire since I was five years old."

The flames died before they touched the cop's skin.

Marna sucked in a deep breath. Okay, so the fire wouldn't work on the demon. But the shifters couldn't control the flames.

She lifted her hands toward them, palms out. These two jerks had been in her nightmares because they'd been there that night with Brandt. "The next time a woman is bleeding on the ground"—fury pumped inside of her—"don't just stand there and laugh." Fire exploded in two streams. One from her right hand. One from her left. The blazing trails ripped right toward the two shifters.

They jumped back, but the fire singed their fur. Oh, she could do a lot more than just singe them, she could—

"Give her to me," Jillian yelled. "Stop the bitch's fire and give her to me, or your brother is dead."

Wait—what?

She felt Tanner's start of surprise. The circle of fire around them had vanished, courtesy of that demon.

And now she was talking about Cody? Threatening him?

"Bullshit," Tanner called as he lunged forward with his claws out. "And you're a disgrace to the PD."

The cop scrambled away a few feet. The panthers had retreated to stand at her side. "I'm in the PD to protect my own kind. Same as you *should* be. You think I'm just gonna stand there and let the humans lock up demons?" Her hair slid over her shoulders as she shook her head. "Not on my watch."

Marna's flames had scorched the earth. The pulsing fire—

that feeling of power that surged beneath her skin—it was starting to die away.

No, no, she couldn't lose that power again!

Can't be weak.

"You think these are the only two I brought with me?" Jillian put her hand on the head of one of the panthers. "I was hunting your brother. I knew he'd be the key to breaking you."

Tanner's only blood relative. The man he'd always protected. Yes, Marna knew he'd do anything for Cody.

Even trade me?

It was Marna's turn to back up a step.

Tanner didn't move. "I don't know why you teamed up with these assholes, but it was a bad move."

Jillian shrugged. "They needed an alpha. I needed some fangs and claws to get the job done."

Marna's gaze searched the trees. She didn't see anyone—anything—else out there. Was the cop bluffing?

"My men caught Cody's scent, just the same as you did." Jillian's hand was still on the panther's head. What? Did the lady think they were some kind of pets? Didn't she know shifters would just as soon bite the hand that fed them? That they *liked* to bite that hand? But, calm as you please, Jillian continued, "Except they didn't give up the chase once they heard an angel scream. My men kept going. They've got him now, and unless you want to be trying to sew the pieces of him back together, then you'll step away from the angel."

A bluff. Tanner wasn't stepping away from her, and Marna knew that he had to realize—

He stiffened. *"You bitch."* There was a dark mix of fury and hate in his voice. "I can smell his blood."

Oh, no. That meant—no bluff.

Then Marna heard it. The sound of thrashing in the bushes. Grunts. Three men burst from the darkness. She recognized Cody's bloody form instantly. But the others? She'd never seen them before, but with one look, she knew they were shifters. It was rather hard to miss those fangs and claws.

Cody was barely on his feet. Stumbling. Slashes covered most of body. "I didn't . . . scream," he managed to say.

No, he hadn't screamed. *She* had. She'd screamed, and Tanner had come running to her side. And he'd left Cody alone in the dark.

"My kind have a weakness," Jillian said with a *tsk*. "Some of us can't handle our drugs, and some can't handle the alcohol. One drunken night, your brother just had to run his mouth in Hell about the pretty little angel his brother was keeping so close."

That pulse of power began to build within Marna once more. She could feel it, like a surge growing inside of her. If that surge got strong enough, she could blast at the shifters holding Cody. Free him.

One of the shifters sank his claws into Cody's throat. "One move," the shifter warned and his eyes were on Marna, "just one, and I rip his throat open."

Cody moaned, trying to speak.

He couldn't.

"You know I will, man," the shifter continued with a grim smile. "Because you fuckin' know me."

Marna hadn't seen this shifter before, but was he also a part of Brandt's old pack?

"I know you don't want to screw with me right now," Tanner said. "Because if you do, Russell, I'll make you beg for death."

Russell's face tightened. "You always thought you were such a badass." His claws drew more blood from Cody's throat. "Who's the fuckin' badass now?"

"You've made the wrong move here," Tanner snarled.

Marna caught the sweet scent of flowers, and her shoulders stiffened. An angel was there. She hadn't seen him—or her—yet, but a death angel was on the scene.

Some of them wouldn't be leaving alive.

What would Tanner do if Cody was the one to die?

The one called Russell could kill Cody long before her fire reached the guy's flesh.

"Step away from her, Chance. Give us the angel, and you"—Jillian pointed to Cody—"and your brother can both walk away."

"I'm supposed to buy that?" His voice mocked her. Called her an idiot.

Jillian's face tensed. "If you don't, I'm killing him in five . . ." She held up her hand and continued counting. "Four . . ."

Tanner raced forward, but the two shifted panthers at Jillian's side jumped for him. They met in a tangle of claws and teeth and fury and blood.

"Three . . ."

Jillian's gaze wasn't on Tanner. It was on Marna. "Wanna try some of that fire again?" Jillian asked. "Maybe you'll have better luck this time. Then again, maybe you won't."

One of the panthers screamed in pain.

"Two . . ." Jillian inclined her head toward Russell and the guy smiled with sick glee.

Tanner couldn't save Cody. He was trying. Fighting and clawing, and he had one panther dead on the ground. The beast's body shifted back to the form of a man, a man whose head was gone from his body. The scent of flowers deepened around Marna.

Death angel. A soul had been claimed. Who'd be next?

Only a second left. Just . . .

"One," Jillian whispered, and Cody's eyes fell closed.

"No!" Marna screamed even as Tanner roared his fury.

Tanner lunged forward and sank his claws into the panther's side.

"Don't kill him!" Marna yelled.

Jillian smirked. "Why? You gonna trade yourself, angel?"

Marna nodded. She would. Cody had saved her life once. Twice if you counted his deception at the hospital. Tanner had fought for her, over and over. Now it was her turn.

She took a slow step toward Jillian. Then another. Faster now. But she found Tanner in her way. Bleeding. Bruised. With his claws out and his eyes glowing.

"No." The word was barely human. "You aren't going with her."

"Go ahead and rip his throat open, Russell," Jillian called out. "I can—"

Marna tried to lunge for her, but Tanner yanked her back.

"Kill my brother," Tanner said to the shifter, "and I'll make you beg for death. By the time hell gets you, there'll be nothing left, I promise you that."

One thing she'd learned about Tanner, he always kept his promises.

Chapter Eleven

Tanner kept his hand wrapped around Marna's wrist. She was straining against him as she fought to break free.

Like that was gonna happen.

His brother's eyes were on him. Blood soaked Cody's shirt, and the captain that he'd actually been close to respecting was standing there . . . *laughing*.

The beast inside roared. His claws had already ripped free, his fangs were out, and Tanner was barely—*barely*—holding back the change.

There was too much fury within him. If the beast broke free now, there'd be no controlling the panther.

Betrayal. Cody's blood. Death.

"The angel or your brother, it's your choice." Jillian crossed her arms over her chest. Looked smug and satisfied. "But you aren't keeping both tonight."

Yeah, he was.

"Let me go," Marna whispered. "I'll be okay, but he—he doesn't have much time left."

Because Cody was already swaying. His face had gone white, and the glamour had fallen away from him, revealing his demon black eyes. His brother always held his glamour. *Always.* Cody hated what he was, so he tried to pretend he was nothing more than a human.

He wasn't.

Neither am I.

Why wasn't Jillian just trying to take him out? She'd gone for his brother, but she hadn't come at him directly. *Why?*

His gaze tracked back to her. For an instant, he saw the flicker of emotion on her face. *Sonofabitch.* She wasn't scared of a death angel or another demon, but even though she had panthers as her bitches, she was afraid of—

Me.

Good. His eyes narrowed in anticipation. She should be afraid. He was about to show her just how deadly he could be.

The captain had set him up. Gotten him to draw Marna out into the open. What better place for an attack than the swamp? Had the captain even lied about seeing a demon in that patrol-car video? Just another part of her plan?

She'd regret trying to play a deadly game with him. This would be her last mistake.

Tanner turned his head toward Marna. Locked his eyes on her. She didn't need to see this. "Run."

Marna started to shake her head. Tanner dropped his hold on her. *"Run!"* More a roar than anything else, and that was the only word he could manage. He fell to the ground as his bones snapped and broke. Reshaped. His claws grew even longer, even sharper.

His beast was so dangerous. Far more dangerous than he'd revealed to Marna. Because when Tanner's panther truly took over, when the rage was too strong . . .

The beast loved the blood and the kills. He hungered for the screams. Tanner had always fought against his instincts, but the truth was, deep inside, where the animal lurked, he was just like his father.

And, despite what he'd told Marna, his beast was just like his brother Brandt's—their panthers had always been linked.

Just like the sadistic bastard who'd hurt Marna. Just like his father. Just like his brother.

Just. Like. Them.

Don't watch. The man couldn't tell Marna that now. The man was gone. The panther was taking the lead with a fierce rush of fury. *Don't see what I become. Don't fear me.*

Because she would. By the time he was finished, she'd have to.

"No!" Jillian's scream. Then she had her gun up, and she fired at him. Once. Twice. "Stop him before he shifts!"

Too late.

Tanner turned his head and saw with the intense sharpness of the panther. The fool shifter who'd thought to take his brother, the one who'd been a part of Brandt's pack for so long . . .

Russell dropped his hold on Cody, leapt away, and raced for the woods. *Coward.* Tanner would get him, but—

But the others were braver. One shifter came at Tanner with a roar.

Tanner's panther ripped his enemy's chest right open. His razor-sharp teeth sank into the guy. Blood filled his mouth. The panther snarled and wanted more.

"Tanner!" He didn't turn at the yell. He finished his kill. Tossed back his head and screamed his victory.

But there was more prey waiting. More to kill. *Kill.*

His hind legs pushed against the earth, and he leapt into the air, heading for the prey he wanted the most. Prey that was still trying to shoot at him, only her gun was out of bullets.

His front paws slammed into her chest, and he took the captain down.

"Tanner!" The scream again, but he didn't look back. His gaze was on his prey. On the demon who stared up at him as the scent of fear poured off her.

"Your life's ending," Jillian told him even as she trembled beneath him. "You think I cleared you at the station? Think again."

Kill. His claws sank into her shoulders and she shrieked as she bled.

"You're . . . gonna be . . . hunted. Not a cop anymore . . . *hunted!*"

Panthers weren't the prey. They were the predators. He brought his mouth to her throat. Suffocation. That was the way the panther liked to take his prey. One bite to the throat. That was all he needed.

"She's never gonna . . . be safe . . . not 'til she's dead."

The panther's rough tongue flashed out. Licked away flesh. Jillian screamed beneath him.

Don't watch. The man inside the beast still didn't want Marna to see what he was doing, but she hadn't run. She'd been the one screaming his name. Why hadn't she run?

Pain, white-hot, burning, lanced through him, and Tanner realized—*too late*—that Jillian hadn't been armed with just a gun.

She smiled up at him as she twisted the knife she'd slid into his chest. A knife that she'd plunged into the panther's heart. "I just had to . . . " she whispered softly as his blood soaked her shirt, "get killing close."

And she had.

But so had he. The panther's teeth closed over her throat. He bit down, sinking his fangs into her, suffocating her, even as that knife still twisted in his heart.

She was killing him, but he'd make sure he took her life, too. Marna would be safe. His brother would be safe.

And Tanner knew he'd finally get just what he had coming to him.

Hell.

Right then, he could have sworn that he heard the sound

of his father laughing. Tanner's head lifted, and he got ready to tear into the SOB that had ruined his life but . . .

But the ghost of his shifter father wasn't standing over him. An angel was. An angel with big, black wings, and gold, ice-cold eyes. Eyes that stared at Tanner with hate.

Then the angel reached down to touch him.

Bastion. The whisper slid from man to beast. He knew, *knew,* that he was staring at the angel who'd followed Marna.

You aren't taking me away from her.

Just as the angel's fingers came close to the panther's fur, Tanner lunged back, rolled, and the knife broke off in his chest. He howled in pain, but kept rolling, determined to get away from that angel.

Only Bastion wasn't following him. The panther shuddered to a stop, and Tanner saw that the angel had bent over Jillian's body. His hand feathered over her brow. Her eyes opened, stared up at him, and then her whole body jerked. *Like a puppet on a string.* The pain and the fury vanished from her face until nothing was left.

Nothing.

"Tanner."

His head turned at Marna's voice. She stared at him with wide eyes. Her hands were fisted at her sides. *Afraid.* Her fear smelled different from Jillian's. It didn't make him hungry for more blood and fury. It . . . pissed him off.

But then she ran to him. Marna wrapped her hands around the panther's body and pulled him close. "Don't ever scare me like that again!"

He kept his claws and fangs away from her and let the change sweep over him. Slower now, because he was weak. But the shift was still brutal. Painful.

Fur faded. Bones reshaped. Her arms soon touched his naked flesh, and it was his blood that stained her fingers.

"No," she whispered and pushed him back. The hilt of

the knife had broken off, and the blade was still in him. *In my heart.*

The heart that he'd never thought too much about, until he'd found a lost angel.

"Help me!" Marna screamed and footsteps shuffled toward them. Cody weaved, stumbled, then stared down at Tanner as horror slowly swept across his face.

Tanner tried to tell him that everything was gonna be okay. He'd take care of this. Just like he'd always taken care of everything.

But he couldn't speak.

And he was starting to feel so . . . cold.

Except where Marna touched him. Her hand was against his chest, and her fingers seemed to burn his flesh.

Cody dropped to his knees beside him. Claw marks lined his throat, and his blood still spilled down his shirt.

So much blood. They always seemed to be bathing in the shit. Story of their lives.

And deaths?

His hand lifted toward Marna. Air rustled against his skin. Wind?

No, air stirred by the rushing of an angel's wings because that bastard Bastion was back. Staring at him with a faint smile curling his lips. The guy still thought that he'd take him? No, not when Marna was so close.

"Fuck . . . off," Tanner muttered and his hand sank into the thick fullness of Marna's hair. He pulled her close and pressed his mouth against hers. If he was dying, she'd be the last thing he tasted.

"Not now, man," Cody snapped at him and his brother tried to pull Marna away.

Only Tanner wasn't letting her go.

The panther inside him, injured, weak, stirred at the thought. Why should he have to let her go? He'd just found her.

Something sliced into his chest. He barely felt the pain.

"Just got to get it . . . out." Cody's voice. Worried. Desperate.

But Tanner kept kissing Marna. He needed her to understand. In this world, she was the one thing he wanted.

The one thing that he'd kill to keep.

His claws began to stretch even more. The slicing in his chest dug deeper. Marna pulled back as she broke the kiss.

Tanner's eyes opened. Bastion stood just beyond Marna's shoulder. Watching. Waiting. Did this asshole really have to be the one to come for him? Figured.

"Got it!" And what was Cody sounding so freaking happy about?

But then the fierce pressure in his chest eased. He glanced at Cody and saw the bloody knife blade in his brother's hand. "Now just stay alive," Cody told him, voice grim and haggard—probably because his throat was still damaged, "until I can get you stitched back up."

He wished he could but . . .

Death is coming for me. No, Death was right there waiting. Tanner's gaze returned to Marna. Her cheeks were wet. Crying? Over him? He wasn't worth an angel's tears. Never had been. She should know that. She should also know . . .

"You were the best . . . thing . . . I ever had." The only thing, other than his brother, that had ever mattered.

So it seemed only right that she'd be the last vision he saw on this earth. The flames in hell would never burn her memory from him.

Let 'em fucking try.

"Time to go," Bastion said, his voice rumbling like thunder.

Tanner's eyelids began to sag.

Kill to keep her . . .

The man might be fading, but the beast was still struggling

inside of him. Fighting. Clawing. Desperate to reach out to the one woman he'd wanted to claim as—

Mate.

Jonathan Pardue raced into the swamp, his legs running as fast as they could. Behind him, a fire crew battled the blaze, a blaze that had destroyed the house of Tanner's brother, Cody.

It had taken him too long to track Tanner to this place. Too long to break free of those cuffs and haul ass out of the city.

Now, he just might be too late.

All of his plans. All his work.

Too late?

Hell, no. Things couldn't end like this. "Tanner!" Jonathan shouted his partner's name, but heard nothing. What he wouldn't give to have a shifter's sense of hearing or smell right then.

Where are you?

Tanner had taken the angel with him. She had to hate the swamp. If the stories about her fall were true—stories he'd forced supernaturals to tell him in the last few days—then she would have good cause to avoid the swamp.

Only she was out there now. With Tanner. With Cody?

More cops would be coming soon. They'd bring dogs. They'd search every inch of the area. Jonathan had to find Tanner before the others did.

But . . . where? *"Tanner!"* Darkness was coming, sweeping over the area in shades of muted red as the sun began to sink into the sky. It looked like damn blood in the sky.

He rushed ahead. Turned to the left. The right. Saw only more twisting trees with heavy moss hanging from their branches.

Swearing, he spun around. He'd go back. He could retrace his footsteps, check to the left, and—

And his gaze fell on footprints on the ground. He yanked out his flashlight. Shone the faint glow on those small impressions.

Hell, yes.

His left hand clamped tight around the flashlight, and his right hand reached for his gun.

Time to go. The words seemed to freeze Marna's blood. She grabbed for Tanner, pulling him close even as she turned on Bastion with a fury she'd never felt before. *"No!"*

But Bastion just stood there, face cold and hard and stoic, with his wings pulled low near his body. "Your shifter's time is up. His body's dying."

She shook her head, frantic. He couldn't leave her yet.

"Didn't you see what he did?" Bastion took a step closer.

Cody kept working on his brother's chest. Swearing and muttering, apparently oblivious to the angel who waited just steps away. An angel who, unlike her, could truly kill with a touch.

"He protected me," Marna said, lifting her chin. He was always protecting her.

Cody glanced up at her, brows pulling together. "Yeah, that's just great. My brother's a hero, but right now we need to—"

"You can't take him!" Now she sounded desperate, like others before her—so many others over the centuries. She'd never understood their rage and helplessness.

She did now.

Cody blinked. Then his eyes widened, and he followed her gaze over his shoulder. "One of 'em . . . one of the angels is here?"

She barely nodded. "Work faster," she whispered to him. Could Cody really not see the angel? He wasn't a pureblood demon, so maybe he couldn't see Bastion.

Or maybe he could.

Bastion's lips tightened. "There is no delaying, no deals, no borrowing. There is only death. You know this."

His eyes were too bright. His words too strong. He seemed satisfied. Almost eager. Did Bastion *want* to take Tanner's soul?

Yes.

"Come on, Tanner, *fight*. Shift again for me." Cody's desperate voice.

Because a shift would give Tanner strength. That was the way it worked for the shifters. That was how they got their power. Their strength came from the beast.

She'd already seen just how strong and dangerous Tanner's beast could be.

Bastion sighed softly. His wings moved with a faint rustle of sound. "He's too weak to shift. He'll die soon, and I'll take him."

And she'd be alone again. Marna glanced back down at Tanner. She held him cradled in her arms. So big. So powerful. So . . . still.

"What can I do?" Her own voice came out sounding broken.

"Nothing," was Bastion's answer.

But Cody, his hands bloody and still pushing against Tanner's chest to apply pressure to the terrible wound, looked up at her. "What *would* you do?"

To save him? "Anything."

Bastion lunged at her. He caught her chin in his hand and made her look up at him. "He's a killer."

He was also the only man who'd ever made her feel like she was more than an instrument of death.

Cody grabbed the knife blade that had been in Tanner's chest. He wiped off the weapon on his pants, smearing red. "Bleed for him."

Marna jerked her chin from Bastion's hold and looked at Cody. "What?"

He reached for her wrist. Did he realize how close he was to touching Bastion? No, you never knew the danger of a death angel. Not until it was too late.

"There's nothing more powerful than angel blood. It has magic in it. So much magic." He licked his lips and gripped the knife blade with a tight fist. "I've seen it even bring a woman back from the dead."

Her heart slammed into her chest. Could it be possible?

"No." Bastion's order. "I won't allow you to—"

He'd been her friend once. Her confidant. But now . . . "Sorry, Bastion, but I don't take orders from you anymore."

"We had to do a transfusion on her, she was human." Cody was talking fast. Rushing out his words in a jumble. "But Tanner . . . he can just drink the blood. The panther drinks blood and it gives him power."

Okay, the drinking blood part definitely had her stomach clenching, but she'd done that bit with the vampire. She could do it for Tanner.

No, she *would* do it for Tanner. "Cut me," she told Cody.

But a blast of powerful wind slammed into the demon and tossed him a good ten feet. The knife fell from his fingers.

"This isn't the way—" Bastion began.

"Screw the way," Marna snapped back at him and dove for the knife. She grabbed it, sliced open her lower arm, and forced the blood to Tanner's lips.

"Wh-what?" Bastion's stunned voice. "You can't do this!"

Watch me.

Tanner tried to turn away from her. "N-no, won't . . . take—"

"You'll take everything I want to give." Her voice hardened. "And you will live." She didn't want to stare down at his chest. She'd glimpsed the twisted mess before, and she wouldn't look again.

Too much pain.

"Make him take it!" Cody yelled.

She was. Tanner's mouth slowly opened beneath the pressure of her hand. She felt the lick of his tongue on her flesh.

Don't think about what he's doing. She'd forced herself not to feel, not to move, when Riley had fed from her. She could do the same now.

Only . . .

Not Riley.

Tanner's mouth felt different. His eyes opened as he took her blood and his gaze seemed to burn right through her. She could actually see him getting stronger with every second that passed.

It was working. Cody had been right. Tanner would survive. This was all he needed. He'd—

Bastion grabbed her and yanked her back. His hold was fierce, punishing.

Painful. But Bastion had never hurt her before. He'd—

"You dare to give your blood to him? To try and save *him?*" Disgust tightened his tone. He lifted her up as his hands clenched around her upper arms with bruising strength. "First you fuck him, and now you feed him?"

Horror filling her, Marna tried to break free, but there was no give in his arms. He shook her, and her head snapped back.

"You let him *touch* you—"

"She did a lot more than that." Tanner's voice. Only it wasn't weak or trembling. Strong. Determined. Furious.

He was back.

Bastion's eyes widened, and he glanced to the left just in time to get a hard punch to the face. Bones crunched, and Bastion fell back, freeing her.

Tanner reached for her instantly. His chest was still bloody. The flesh and muscles were torn, but he was on his feet—naked, muscled—and lines of fury marked his face. Fury that was directed at Bastion.

Tanner's fingers slid over Marna's arms and rubbed lightly over the marks that Bastion had left on her.

And Bastion—he was raising his hand to his nose and touching the blood that dripped down his face. "Wh-what—"

"What you're feeling?" Tanner said, and a growl built in his throat. "That's pain. Better get used to it. 'Cause there's a whole lot more coming."

Bastion's hand dropped. Clenched into a fist. His wings spread out behind him. "You aren't the first to teach me of pain."

Tanner's claws flashed out. "I can see you now, bastard."

And how could he?

Tanner lifted his claws. Pointed right at Bastion. "If you don't haul your winged ass out of here, I'll be the *last* one to teach you."

Angels didn't fear much in the mortal world. Why should they? Weapons forged from mortal men couldn't kill an angel. But a shifter's claws weren't a mortal weapon.

Claws like Tanner's had taken her wings away. Those same claws could easily kill Bastion.

"This isn't over." Bastion's vow. His gaze wasn't on Tanner, but on Marna. "Not even close." Then his wings swept back, and he flew high up into the air.

Marna spun back to Tanner. "How—"

"Nothing's stronger than angel blood," Cody said and winced as he hobbled toward them. "Hell, I could use some of it right now." His wounds had started to close—enhanced demon healing—but he was still dripping blood.

"No." Tanner's instant snarl.

Cody held up his hands. "Easy there, bro. You need to rein in that beast."

Tanner's eyes were blazing. She'd never seen them so bright. "I . . . can't."

As he stepped closer to her, his face a heavy mask of fury and need, Marna realized that the danger wasn't over.

Russell Marchand raced through the woods with his claws still out and his fangs bared.

That fuckin' well hadn't gone according to plan.

The pretty little police captain had told them that it would be an easy grab. A helpless angel. One lone shifter. They should have been able to take them out, no problem.

Then they could have cashed in on all that sweet angel blood. Drained her dry until nearly nothing was left and tossed the remains of her body to the highest bidder.

No one had said anything about the angel fighting back. Or about Tanner Chance getting so crazy when she was threatened.

Tanner. The captain hadn't told him they were going after *Tanner.*

He remembered that guy. Back in the day, they'd run in the same pack together. Tanner had been wild. Always ready for the hunt. Now he was gonna act like some white knight?

Fuckin' traitor. That's all Tanner was. He'd turned his back on the pack. Fought 'em all. Why?

Because one night they'd decided to have some fun with that demon half-brother of his. Even though he had panther blood, the demon couldn't shift. So what good had he been to the pack?

Stripping off some of Cody's flesh while he screamed had seemed like a good way to pass the night.

Then Tanner had found them. And gone *wild.* Just like he had tonight. Just like the guy's old man used to do. Nothing like the fury of the panther. Nothing like it in the whole world. The panther would strike down everyone and everything in his path until that bloodlust was gone.

Russell glanced over his shoulder once more, just to make sure he wasn't being hunted.

Fuckin' bastard.

Well, he was done with this town. Done with the captain. She thought that she had him by the balls because she knew about all the bodies he had buried? Screw her. He wasn't gonna be her attack dog anymore.

Not a damn dog. He was a panther. He was strong. He was—

"Going somewhere?" the captain's voice asked.

Russell froze. The captain sauntered from the trees, not a trace of blood on her. Her eyes were glassy, her smile too big.

But— "You were still back there . . ." Wait, no way could she run as fast as he could. Demons *couldn't* run that fast.

The captain kept heading toward him. Nice and slow. He knew her, would recognize her anywhere. Hell, he'd fucked her enough times to recognize her body and yet—

Russell inhaled. His claws flashed out. In an instant, he lunged forward and shoved them deep into her chest. *"You aren't her."* Because whoever the hell this was . . . she didn't smell like Jillian. Not like ashes and sex.

Her head slammed into his, and he stumbled back at the power of the blow as he yanked his claws free.

"Wrong move," she whispered.

He kept his claws up. Claws were a shifter's best weapon. Claws could take out anyone—or anything. Even those fuckin' angels. "Who the hell are you?" Wearing Jillian's face but . . .

Scents never lied.

Jillian's features faded away, and Russell realized he was staring at Death.

"I'm the one who's taking you to hell."

Russell opened his mouth to scream, but it was too late. Death leapt forward and touched him.

He expected the end to come instantly. It was supposed to happen with a touch. Just a touch.

But he screamed in agony as his claws and hands were slashed away. Screamed and fought . . .

Death didn't come instantly.

And soon he was begging—begging until his heart finally stopped.

Chapter Twelve

He couldn't stop the fury.

Tanner paced the close confines of the cabin, an out-of-season spot that he'd known would be empty. Just waiting for them to use as a shelter—and safe house.

Going back to his place in the city sure wasn't an option. Not with every supernatural in the area jonesing for Marna's blood.

Blood I took.

Blood wasn't supposed to taste sweet. Hers had. Hers had poured into his mouth, rich with so much power and magic. He'd felt the surge in his own body as he began to heal, as his torn heart mended—all from just a few drops of her blood.

No wonder the others were after her. If that was what a few drops could do, what would happen with more?

Power.

He turned and raked his claws across the wall, leaving deep impressions in the wood.

"The owners are sure going to be angry once they get back and see the . . . ah . . . new decorations you've made." Marna's voice. Marna's scent. Too close. Driving him wild.

Want.

He didn't turn to face her. "You should go back downstairs." With Cody. Where it was safe. Where she wasn't in danger of getting seriously fucked in the next five seconds.

"I wanted to check on you."

Right. Because that was what she did. Because she was so *good.*

While he was the big, bad beast, too eager to gobble her up.

Maybe it was time she started to see him for what he really was, not just what he kept telling her he could be. *How many times have I lied to her?*

He'd promised he wasn't like his brother Brandt. Promised he wasn't evil.

'Cause if you said something enough, wasn't that supposed to make it true?

Not for him. Never for him.

Once she learned what he truly was like, then she wouldn't sacrifice for him anymore. Wouldn't offer up her blood and make him . . . *want so much more.*

She'd held tight to him while they ran through the swamp. They'd found the truck Cody had hidden, hightailed it out of there, and managed to get to this old place under the growing darkness. Good thing he and his brother knew all the secrets of the swamp.

They knew the best places to hide and lick their wounds.

I'd rather lick her.

The floor creaked beneath her feet. She was coming toward him. *"Stop."*

The creaking paused.

Tanner glanced down at his chest. He'd always been a fast healer, but this—this was crazy. He'd been stabbed in the chest. That knife had *hit* his heart. Yet he was still standing.

Not just because of his panther, though, hell yeah, the beast had been what kept him going when that knife first plunged into him. A human would have died instantly. Good thing shifters had more fight in 'em than that.

The skin over his heart was red now, still mending. He was alive—*because of her.*

So he figured he owed her a warning. "If you don't get out of here, I'll have you on that bed beneath me." Or against the wall. Or on the floor. Wherever he could get her.

His cock shoved against the front of his jeans. Since he was used to Tanner shifting and hunting, Cody kept backup clothes for him in the truck. His brother had given him these faded jeans, but the denim did little to hide his arousal from her.

I could fucking eat her alive.

Not safe. Not normal. The lust he felt for her was raging out of control.

A woman like her needed control. Gentleness. Sweet promises in the dark.

He couldn't give her anything but fire and fury right then.

The floor creaked, and his shoulders tensed. Another slow creak followed a few seconds later.

She wasn't walking toward the door. His eyes closed. The panther roared inside of him.

She was coming to Tanner.

Then he felt the light feather of her lips on his bare back. Pressing against his old scars. Kissing him with such gentleness.

He was too far gone for that. *Too. Far.*

Tanner spun around, lifted her up, and in two steps, he had her on the bed. "Told you. Warned you," he growled, and his mouth took hers. A red haze of lust seemed to surround him. His tongue pushed into her mouth, driving deep, even as his hands caught hers and locked them together over her head.

He'd given her gentleness before. Maybe, later, she'd remember that.

His kiss grew rougher, harder, more demanding.

He locked his left hand around her wrists, and his right hand pushed between their bodies. He yanked up her shirt and pushed his hand under her bra. Her nipple was tight, pebble hard, and he had to taste it, too.

Tanner tore his mouth from hers. He unhooked her bra and threw it to the floor. Then he took her breast. Tanner sucked it deep into his mouth and scored her flesh with his teeth.

"Tanner!" He liked it when she moaned his name. Liked it even more when she screamed it.

He'd make her scream.

He freed her hands and yanked down her jeans. She helped him, shoving away the denim and the delicate panties. Then her sex was open to him, pink, flushed, wet.

Taste.

He pushed her legs apart, and he put his mouth on her. When she tried to buck against him, telling him she couldn't take it—

Tanner just tightened his hold. His mouth pressed harder. He licked her. Sucked her clit.

And felt the tremble in her thighs. He kept licking. Sucking. He thrust his tongue inside of her—

She came with a scream.

He liked that. Would have more.

Tanner shoved down his jeans. He positioned his cock and drove balls-deep inside of her in one long thrust. The bed groaned. She gasped.

He withdrew.

Tanner thrust deep. Again. Again.

He caught her hands once more. Pushed them against the mattress. His claws dug into the bedding. Ripping and tearing it as he fucked her hard and long.

But . . .

It wasn't enough. The pleasure waited just out of his reach. He needed *more.*

"Tanner?" She licked her lips and looked up at him with wide eyes. With every heaving breath he took, he tasted her.

There was no taste like his angel.

And if anyone else ever thought they'd get a taste . . . he'd kill them. Every. Single. One.

The growl ripped from him. More beast than man because right then, the beast was taking his mate.

Tanner withdrew from Marna and rolled her over onto the bed. He lifted her up, positioning her just right so that he could push deep inside and—

"Stop."

He froze.

Marna glanced over her shoulder at him, blond hair a curtain around her face. Her eyes . . .

Fear.

Now she saw him for what he was.

"Slow down," she told him. "I can't . . ."

The panther clawed inside, but the man jerked him back on a chain. He sucked in a breath.

Then he saw her back. The scars. Heavy red lines that trailed over her shoulder blades. Her wings had been there, until a panther's claws had cut them away. He could almost see the dark shadows of wings that had once been.

He looked down at the bed. His own claws had cut into the mattress. He hadn't cut her—*never would*—but . . .

He hated his beast right then. She deserved so much more than he could give her.

His fingers brushed across the strange shadows of wings. A phantom image that couldn't really be touched. Tanner pressed his mouth to the scar that sliced across her left shoulder-blade. She tensed beneath his mouth, then shuddered.

He stilled, afraid that he'd hurt her, but then he heard the moan that slipped from her lips.

Pleasure.

Tanner pressed a kiss to the scar once more. Used his tongue to lick. Her hips arched back against him. "That feels . . ." Her whisper was the most sensual temptation he'd ever heard. "So good."

An angel's wings were rumored to be the most sensitive parts of their bodies. That was why the fall hurt them so much. Why losing her wings had nearly destroyed Marna. But if he could give her pleasure, *then I will.*

His mouth feathered over her flesh. He was choking the panther back on his leash, and he wasn't about to break her skin with his sharpened teeth. Tanner licked. Kissed. First one slashing scar, then the other.

Marna moaned and arched against him again as she rubbed her sweet ass against his cock. With one hand, he reached around and spread her legs wider. And he kept kissing her. She shivered against him and said the words that broke him: "Fuck me."

Dirty words from such an innocent mouth.

He guided his cock to her sex. Already slick but swollen from her orgasm, her delicate muscles resisted his thrust at first.

But not when he licked her again. Again.

She opened for him, and he drove deep.

The leash began to break. His hands caught her hips. Held tight as he plunged into her. Marna tossed her hair—and shoved back against him. Not gentle. Not easy. Her movements were as demanding as his own.

Good. He wanted her as wild as he was.

Their desperate breaths and moans filled the air even as the scent of sex filled his nostrils. The bed shuddered beneath them. Harder. More.

He wanted to feel her release around his cock. Wanted to hear the scream of his name once more. Would hear it.

He slid in and out, in—

Her inner muscles clenched tightly around him, contracting and squeezing all along the length of his cock. She came, and, hell yes, she screamed his name.

The leash tore in two. He exploded within her and erupted on a wave of pleasure so intense that the world around him seemed to fade away, and there was only her—Marna.

Her soft, silken flesh.

Her tight, wet sex.

The pleasure she gave him. Nothing like it. Definitely worth a trip or two down to hell.

Worth everything.

He poured into her, held her as tightly as he could and knew that even death wouldn't force him to let her go.

"I can see your wings."

Marna forced her body to lift, and slowly turned to meet Tanner's bright gaze. His words caused a pang in her heart, and she shook her head. "I don't have wings anymore." It seemed so cruel that he would say that now, after all that had happened between them.

If only she did have wings.

He was on his side, watching her as they lay on the bed. His hand reached around her and stroked lightly from the scar on her right shoulder up into the air just a few inches above her skin.

As before, his touch sent a bolt of pure pleasure arching through her. *So sensitive.* She could almost feel his touch on the wings that weren't there.

"I see them. Like shadows, rising lightly from your back." His voice was a deep rumble of sound. He stroked her for an instant longer, and her whole body tightened at the caress.

How?

But then his hand fell away. His gaze came back to hers. "You shouldn't have given me your blood."

Her throat was dry. Probably from all the screaming and panting and moaning. How was she supposed to face Cody again? He would've heard everything.

Shame was a new emotion for her, too.

But she didn't feel *that* shameful. Actually, she couldn't wait to scream again.

"Marna."

Oh, right. He was talking about her blood. "It seems like everyone else wants my blood." Everyone but him. "Everywhere we turn, people are hunting us." Not *us,* really, more her. And she'd dragged him into her battles.

"No one else gets so much as a drop." His gaze held hers with its stark intensity. "No vamps. No demons. No one."

It wasn't exactly like she enjoyed being a walking, talking blood bank. But somehow, the supernaturals knew that she wasn't like the other angels of death. She couldn't kill them with a touch, not like Sammael could. No one ever went after him looking for a blood donation. They were too smart for that move.

They knew that if they went after Sammael, he'd destroy them.

Why couldn't she get a badass reputation like that?

Maybe because you aren't badass. A whisper from her mind. But she was trying to be. She *would* be. Getting picked off and drained wasn't an option for her. She wanted more. She'd fight for her life.

And for Tanner.

"Your blood's addictive. Nothing should taste so sweet."

Okay, now that was scary. No one had ever told her that an angel's blood was sweet.

"Like candy and power. And you can't let anyone have it again. If you do . . ." He exhaled on a rough sigh. "I'll have to kill them."

So, what, there was no in-between land? Just straight up go for the kill? Wasn't the shifter missing a big point there?

"You know, you could try saying thank you. In case you didn't notice, my 'candy and power' blood saved your hide back there." Then she rolled away from him, pulling the sheets with her and wrapping them around her body.

Oh, wait. *Angel.* Maybe she couldn't kill, but she could still conjure clothes. She dropped the sheet, waved her hand and had jeans and a T-shirt back on in an instant. Then Marna headed for the door.

Before she could yank it open and continue what was really a rather nice stalking-out scene, Tanner's hand slammed against the wood. His grip kept the door shut while caging her between the escape and his body. His naked body. If only shifters could conjure, too.

"Thank you." He whispered the words against her ear and a shiver worked over her body.

"You're . . . ah . . . welcome."

His voice hadn't been arrogant or cocky. Just soft. Sincere.

Slowly, carefully, Tanner turned her to face him. "Power is addictive."

So she'd always been told.

"My father . . . that bastard wanted to take as much power as he could get. He didn't care who he hurt. He took and he took until nothing was left."

Marna didn't speak.

"That's what he did to my mother." He exhaled heavily and moved away from her. She watched in silence as he found his jeans, jerked them on, then paced to the small window that overlooked the swamp. "She was just part of his collection."

"Collection?" She didn't understand. People weren't collections. They were . . . people.

His shoulders tensed. "He wanted to create the perfect son. One who'd be near indestructible, all powerful, and able to rule for as far as that dead old bastard could see."

Marna wanted to go to him because she could hear the thread of pain in his voice, but she didn't move.

"You already know about Brandt."

Like she could forget the shifter who'd sliced her and left her screaming in pain. Tanner's brother Brandt had been a dangerous hybrid. Half shifter, half angel.

"Brandt's mother was a guardian, and some dumbass upstairs gave her the job of watching after my father."

Many of her kind thought the guardians were the lucky ones. They never had to ferry souls. Just watch. Protect.

But guardians were the ones most likely to choose falling. They were so close to humans, day in and day out. Proximity led to temptation. That temptation had been too much for many.

Like Brandt's mom.

"He got her pregnant because he thought a child with an angel's strength would be his perfect weapon. But after he had Brandt, he didn't need her anymore."

She already knew how this story ended. "He killed her."

"Just like he killed my mom. Only . . ." His hand lifted, pressed against the pane of glass, then clenched into a fist. "He killed my mom because she was *'a disappointment,'* " he said, his voice deepening to a growl. " 'A waste of time.' Those were his fucking words to me when I found her body. He kept her around longer than he did Brandt's mother, but after a while, he said her powers were useless to him. That meant she was useless."

An ache lodged in her chest. "Humans don't have powers."

Tanner glanced back at her. "Some do. My mom, Katherine, she was . . . special."

Special. Psychic. Yes, she'd seen a handful of humans with those gifts. The other angels had said those mortals were touched. Favored.

To her, it had seemed as if they were cursed.

"My father destroyed things. My mother saved them. She was always trying to help everyone. Trying to *save* those jerks in the pack when they got injured. When they were hurt, she'd use her power, and she'd heal them. She could heal, just by touching someone. That was her special gift." His lips tightened. "She never should have been with him. She was just part of his *collection*."

A collection of women designed to create super children? Marna shook her head, still not fully understanding, then realized he couldn't see the movement. "I thought it was supposed to be hard for shifters to have children." Otherwise, the world would be overrun with them because their genetics made them far superior to average mortals. Survival of the fittest would kick into overdrive, and the human population would be nearly erased.

His hand slowly unclenched. "Some women are . . . better matches than others."

Mates. Not some heart link, no matter what tales she'd heard whispered over the centuries. For shifters, mating was a biological link. The beasts recognized the women who would be compatible enough to create offspring with them.

Tanner turned to face her. "Trust me, there were plenty of women who couldn't conceive. He got rid of them fast enough."

Marna flinched. *Evil.* There was no other word for Tanner's father. She'd seen some beings like him in her time. No good inside. Hollow. Rancid. Rotting with their greed and dark fury.

"Three women were matches for him," Tanner said. "An angel. A psychic. And a demon."

Marna stepped toward him. She wanted to touch him. To offer comfort in some way because he seemed to be in pain. Not physically, but . . .

I can still feel his pain.

"Then once my father had his hybrids, he set to work making sure we wouldn't be a damn bit like our mothers. He wanted any power boost his kids could get from such different mothers, but when it came to actions, hell, he only wanted us to be *just like him.*"

Now she did go to him. Marna crossed to his side, and her hands curled around his arms. "But you're not like him."

"Brandt was. My brother was exactly like him. He enjoyed the pain and the rage as much as my old man ever did."

She wanted to shake him. So she did. Hard. He barely moved. "You're not like them!"

His head sagged forward. She needed to see his eyes.

"Tanner!" Marna snapped out his name. "You're not like them!" He'd protected her. Helped her. How could he think that he'd ever be like his father or Brandt?

"Didn't you see me in the swamp?" he demanded. "I *enjoyed* those kills."

Her skin seemed to ice.

His head lifted. His eyes finally met hers, and there was a chill in his stare. "Baby, I'm my father's son."

No.

"I didn't want to be. I tried so hard not to be, but deep down, I have the same rage. The same violence. I'm—" He stopped, but she knew what he'd been about to say.

I'm like him.

She leaned onto her toes in an attempt to get as close to him as she could. She wanted the shifter to understand this. "What you are . . ." Her gaze searched his. "You're *better* than him."

And she thought his father had known that. He'd beaten his boys, attacked them from the time they were only children. He'd tried to force them to become like him.

Tanner wasn't.

Neither was Cody.

As for Brandt, the bastard who'd hurt her . . . were monsters born the way they were? Or were they made?

Voice dark, Tanner said, "You shouldn't touch me. And you damn well shouldn't let me touch you."

He was trying to be all noble. Fine. The guy was always trying to pull the noble knight card. She'd be the lusty one for a change. Marna caught his face in her hands, gripping that strong, square jaw she loved, and she pulled him down for a kiss. Her tongue licked over his lips, then darted inside to rub against his. "I know," she said against his mouth, "exactly what I should do."

She was done letting others tell her what was right, wrong, and everything in between.

Tanner's eyes seemed dazed, but he gave a slight shake of his head and said, "Don't you know how dangerous it is . . . to make me want you so much?"

No, but then, Marna was learning that she liked a bit of danger. Danger had pretty much become her life, and the adrenaline rush had her body on a taut edge.

Tanner sucked in a deep breath. "I can always taste you now."

She licked her lips and tasted him.

His gaze seemed to burn her. "I won't let anyone hurt you," he promised.

She smiled at him, but knew the curve of her lips was sad. "Every supernatural in this town is after me. They think I'm weak." How did they know? How had they realized the truth?

Then it hit her.

The bar. The panther shifters. She'd gone there that night and she'd tried to kill them. Her touch hadn't worked. "Someone was there," she whispered as understanding settled heavily in her chest like a cold knot of dread. "Another supernatural." Her eyes widened. The man who'd been setting her up, he could have been right there that night!

Only when she'd failed, he'd finished what she'd started. He'd taken out the two panthers.

Frowning, Tanner asked, "What are you talking about?"

But she knew now, and her heart was starting to race. "All of the paranormals coming after me . . . they all know I can't kill with a touch."

A grim nod. "They think you're an easy target."

She wasn't going to be. "One of them must have been in that bar when I went after Michael and Beau that night. Someone saw me try to kill them—and fail." She shoved back her hair. "That someone could be the same person setting me up for these kills."

His eyes narrowed. "Or he could just be the prick who's setting you up to get eaten by the supernaturals in town." He headed for the door. "Either way, we're finding him."

Yes, yes, they were. Marna hurried after him. They rushed down the stairs and entered the small den just in time to see Cody stroll into the room, a bloody cloth held to his throat. He looked first at Tanner, then her, then back to Tanner. One dark brow rose. "Done are we? No more screaming and shouting? Gotta say, I'm impressed, but for a minute there, I was afraid the ceiling would fall on—"

Tanner sprang at him. He leapt across the room and shoved his brother against the wall. "Only living family or not, you *don't* talk about her that way."

Cody didn't look particularly intimidated. He knocked his brother back. "I wasn't talking about her. I was . . . just talking about how . . . enthusiastic *you* seemed."

Tanner slugged him while Marna felt her cheeks burn.

But Cody just laughed.

We like the pain and the violence.

She crept down the last few stairs and rubbed her arms. Tanner was wrong. Yes, she'd been the one to originally think he was just like Brandt, but that had been before. Everything was different now.

No, not everything. *Me.*

Tanner eased away from his brother. "Now that we aren't fighting for our lives, you wanna tell me just what that hell in the swamp was all about? Why'd you burn your own place down?"

Cody rubbed his jaw. "I knew Jillian was coming after me."

"How?" Tanner asked. "And why the hell didn't you tell me? If you knew I was working for a dirty cop, you should have passed that critical intel along."

Marna's fingers pressed against the wooden banister as she waited for Cody's response.

"Jillian knew I'd helped you to make her"—a quick finger jab toward Marna—"disappear. The word I got was that Jillian was gonna force me to tell her where Marna had gone."

Interesting. It seemed the captain had learned a lot about her, very, very fast.

But Tanner shook his head. "You're lying," Tanner said, sounding surprised. "To *me*."

Cody swallowed, and his Adam's apple bobbed. Had he flinched? Yes, it looked like he had. Now his eyes were darting nervously around the room. *Liar, liar.*

Marna cocked her head to the side and wondered how Tanner had known. Lies. What would it be like to tell them? Some people could lie so easily, but for others, you could always read the lies on their faces.

At that moment, Cody's lie was clear to see.

"Are you using again?" Tanner demanded.

Using? Suspicion snaked through her, and that suspicion was confirmed when Cody started to sweat.

He told Tanner, "No. I don't do that. Haven't in *years.*"

She realized he was talking about drugs. After all, she knew all about the addictive mix that was demons and drugs. Many demons used the drugs to dampen their darker impulses but only learned, too late, that the drugs made them worse.

And no one could grow addicted as fast as a demon.

"You're keeping secrets," Tanner said, with a sad shake of his head. "Those will come back to bite you in the ass."

Cody stalked a few feet away from him. The bloody cloth had fallen to the floor. His throat had healed, mostly. Jaw clenched, he met Tanner's gaze. "I . . . sold angel blood."

Now Marna was the one to leap forward. "You did what?"

He wet his lips and stared at the floor before seeming to force his stare to rise. "A few months ago, when I had to run that transfusion from Azrael . . ."

Marna's knees locked at the name. Azrael was one of the most powerful angels of death she'd ever met. Well, he had been that way, until his fall. Then he'd become something even more dangerous.

Not like me. Everyone knew to stay away from Azrael, or he'd obliterate them.

Why couldn't she just have some of that power? The torching was nice, but she needed more magic in order to keep breathing.

"Azrael gave his blood in order to save his human." Tanner's voice was flat. "I was there, it was a fast transfusion. There was no choice."

Azrael's human. The female that Brandt had claimed as his mate. Only Az had taken her from him, and Az had been the one to send Brandt to hell.

She owed the powerful Fallen for that. *It should have been my kill.*

Az had just beaten her to the punch.

"There was some . . . extra blood." Now shame coated Cody's words. "I knew how powerful it was, and I couldn't just destroy it."

So he'd started selling the blood of her kind? "Do you know what Azrael will do to you," Marna asked quietly, "when he realizes what you've done?"

A faint nod. Then a laugh that was desperate before he said, "Why do you think I was burning my place and trying to run? I want out of this town before he comes gunning for me."

"There's nowhere to hide from him." Marna voiced the simple truth that he should have already known. "Az can find you wherever you go."

Tanner's fist slammed into the wall. "Dammit, you're the one who has all the supernaturals in this town so hot for angel blood! *You* turned them on to its power!"

Cody's shoulders couldn't hunch much more. "I—I was just trying to help. There was a demon. She was *dying,* and she was only eighteen. Just a kid. The drugs had eaten her up, and she couldn't even move. I had to try something. Hell, I didn't even mean to sell the blood!" His words tumbled out. "I swear, I was just trying to help. I wasn't even sure it would work until . . ." He glanced at Marna from the corner of his eye.

"Until?" she pushed. Anger had heated her blood. *Selling the blood of my kind.* And she'd thought she owed this guy?

He exhaled heavily. "I gave her a small transfusion. Within the hour, all of her withdrawal symptoms from the drugs were gone. She was normal, closer to normal than she'd ever been before in her whole life. She didn't hear voices. Didn't want to hurt herself. It was like she was glowing on the inside."

His gaze rose to catch Tanner's stare. "Her father's a human. A rich one. You know the half-breeds are always hit worse by the darkness."

Tanner didn't speak.

Cody's shoulders straightened, and his chin lifted. "He

forced me to take the money. Said I'd saved her life, that I had to take it. And I—I thought I could use the cash to help someone else. To buy more equipment."

But Marna could guess what happened next. "Word spread about how you'd helped her."

A grim nod. "Soon everyone wanted angel blood. It . . . healed the demons, but it also did more."

"Sonofabitch." Tanner turned from him and stalked toward Marna. "No wonder you wanted me to take her blood. You knew just what it could do."

"It could *save* you!"

It had. Marna lifted her hands. Turned them over and stared at the thin veins beneath her skin. All the hunting and all the death, just for her blood?

Marna took a deep breath and asked the question she feared, "What *more* does it do?" To make so many desperate . . .

"It ramps up a supernatural's power. One dose can make a level-three demon closer to a level six. It's like a shot of pure—"

"Magic," Tanner finished as his hand caught hers. His fingers traced over the veins inside her wrist. Marna shivered.

Cody kept talking, saying, "But then my supply ran out, and folks out there started getting desperate. They wanted *more.*"

"Because it's addictive," Marna said as Tanner's words from before echoed in her mind. He'd warned her upstairs. But wasn't power always addictive? Especially to the supernaturals.

"No wonder there are so many folks coming after me," Marna muttered. "I'm a freaking walking buffet for them." Because she was the weak angel in town.

It sucked having that tagline attached to her. *I've got to do something.* She had to amp up her own power, just like—

Her chin rose. "I need to see Sammael."

Tanner blinked, but it was Cody who gave a low whistle and said, "Ah, Sammael? Are you sure about that? He killed two vamps just last week for—"

"For what?" Marna snapped at him, because she could guess their crime. "For trying to take his special blood?"

Cody's lips clamped together.

"Maybe he didn't feel like bleeding," Marna said. And neither did she. "Sammael and Az are the most powerful Fallen I know. They can show me how to protect myself."

"You mean they can teach you to kill." Why was Cody suddenly so chatty with her? He'd been the quiet one, before.

Tanner's gaze just searched her face. "Is that what you really want? To be like them?"

To be able to kill with a touch. No, she'd never wanted that. She liked touching Tanner and finding pleasure, but if she wanted to stay alive, there wasn't a choice. "It's what I have to do."

He gave a grudging nod. "Then I'll take you to him." His head swung back to Cody. "But first, I want you to give me a list of every demon in this town with high-level glamour power."

"Glamour?" Cody rubbed a hand over his bruised throat. "All demons can work glamour." His gaze flashed to black. "Even me."

"You can do a whole lot more than just work it," Tanner murmured and there was a curious lack of emotion in those words. "Can't you, *bro*?"

"Yeah, I can."

Then, as Marna watched, stunned, Cody's features began to shift. To harden. His shoulders stretched. He grew taller. More muscled. The line of his jaw flared, and he became—

Tanner.

Her heart slammed into her chest.

"I can definitely do a lot more," the new Tanner said, and

it was only then that Marna finally realized just how dangerous Cody truly was. She'd thought he was fairly harmless. She'd never seen any power flares from him. He'd worked as a doctor. Patched her up, but—

But his power had just been lurking inside. And, too late, she saw him for what he was.

One very, very dangerous demon.

Chapter Thirteen

For as long as Tanner could remember, Cody had been able to steal faces.

Stealing faces. That's what they'd called it when they were kids. Cody had learned the trick by accident. He'd been trying to shift into a panther. How many times had he tried? Over and over, only the shift had never worked. He'd been so angry. So tired.

Their father had been yelling at him. Getting ready to swipe out with his claws because Cody was such a "fucking failure!"

Then the change happened.

Cody had taken their father's face. Become him in an instant.

Cody couldn't shift into an animal. Couldn't become the panther. But he could borrow the face and body of any person he saw.

Their father had been pissed when he'd seen the change. Pissed—and far from impressed. Turning into another person didn't amp up Cody's powers.

Animals were what mattered to him. Panthers had the power.

Cody's little trick had been useless to the old bastard.

Tanner had taken the attack that his father launched. He'd

been the one to scream when his father's claws had sunk into his back while Cody shifted back to his own form.

Tanner took a breath and stared at Cody. The guy was an exact copy of him. Even had his voice. *"Enough."*

With a shrug, Cody's own face and form slowly appeared again.

Most demons could manage basic glamour. Cloaking their eye color was second nature to them. Had to be—the eye trick was an adaptation necessary for their survival. But with Cody, that adaptation went up to a whole different level.

"How many others in New Orleans can do what you do?" Tanner wanted to know.

Cody's lips tightened, and Tanner realized he wasn't gonna like the answer even before his brother said, "None. You're looking at a one-hit wonder, bro. No way can the others manage what I do."

"There has to be another!" Marna said at once. "There *has* to be."

Damn right there did. Tanner kept his stare on Cody. "You find out who the other demon is."

"I'm telling you, there *is* no other—"

"Because he took *my* form," Tanner said. "He took my face, my body, and he tried to kill a cop."

Cody's mouth hung open in surprise.

"And he took my form," Marna said, voice tight. "He went into an alley, and he killed two shifters, all while he was using my face."

But Cody was shaking his head. "Th-there's no other! Just me!" His hands trembled at his sides. "Don't you think I've looked for others? Do you think I want to be the only freak out there? It's not just about demon power. It's about the shifter blood in me. I can shift, but only into other people. No one else can do that!"

"Someone else has to be doing it." Tanner was adamant.

Because if there wasn't someone else. Fuck, *no . . . it's not him.*

Cody couldn't be setting him up.

But . . .

But he could be after Marna's blood, a sly voice whispered in his mind.

Now that Cody knew just how powerful it was, just how much people would be willing to pay for it, had he been tempted?

Money had driven plenty of people to murder.

Not him. Tanner wouldn't believe it. Not yet.

"Find him," Tanner said again, and he knew by the tense expression on Cody's face that his brother understood what he was saying—and what he wasn't.

"It's not me," Cody whispered.

Tanner nodded, but he saw the flash of fear on Marna's face. He might be willing to trust his brother, but why would she? Why *should* she?

He brought her hand to his lips and pressed a kiss to her palm. "Trust me." She didn't have to trust Cody.

She nodded, and for just a second, time seemed to slow for him. Did she realize what she was doing?

"But what's gonna happen with you?" Cody wanted to know then as he rocked forward nervously on the balls of his feet. "Your captain is dead. You can't just go waltzing back to the station now."

No, he couldn't. He wouldn't be heading back, not until he was sure the other cops weren't about to turn on him, too. "We're staying low." He hunted better in the dark anyway.

"I hope you make that damn low," Cody told him. "Because as long as you keep staying with her . . ." An incline of his head toward Marna. "You're at the top of the supernatural hit list."

Bring it.

"I'm getting off that list," Marna said as her fingers tightened around Tanner's. "I'm going to see Sammael right now, and I'm *getting off that list.*"

Easier said than done.

And the truth was . . . he didn't want her to get that deadly power back. If she killed when she touched, would she pull away from him? Be afraid to touch him?

But if she wanted to see Sammael, he'd take her to the Fallen. Hell, there probably wasn't anything that he wouldn't do for her.

"Twenty-four hours," he told Cody with a hard stare. Because it was time to move. "We each do our hunting, then we meet back here." Plenty of time to kill.

And killing was exactly what he had planned.

Cody nodded.

Twenty-four hours.

His brother turned away. Tanner kept his gaze on him, and knew that while they were apart, he'd be doing more of his own digging. And if he found out that Cody was stealing his face again . . .

Could he put his brother in the ground?

Tanner glanced back at Marna.

He just might have to.

He'd lost their scent. *Dammit.* The angel had disappeared, running too fast with her shifter.

After all of his plans, his careful schemes, they'd vanished into the swamp.

Why couldn't he find them? He could always find anyone, at any time. That was part of his power.

But . . .

He couldn't find her.

Was something happening? He stared down at his hands. He'd washed the blood away in the water. His new trinkets were stowed in the bag near his hip. New weapons, courtesy of his last victim, that would come in handy soon.

Over the years, he'd learned to be creative with his kills. Sometimes, simple bullets did the trick. Other times, more exotic methods were needed.

Especially when he wanted to make his prey scream and beg for mercy.

Not that he was the merciful sort. No, he was far more into retribution and pain.

He glanced up and his gaze swept the thick vegetation once more.

Where was she?

And why the hell wasn't she appreciating all that he was doing for her? He'd taken care of the two shifters in that shit-forsaken alley. Gotten rid of the cop who could ID her. He *knew* the kid must have seen her in that SUV.

Well, he'd *almost* gotten rid of the young cop. A quick trip to the hospital would finish the job now. He'd be making that trip, after he disposed of Cody and Tanner.

He'd even taken out that asshole tonight, *for her.* He hadn't wanted the panther to decide to try for Marna again. So he'd eliminated Russell. Made the bastard suffer for his crimes.

He was doing *everything* for her, but she—

She just kept running from him.

Didn't she realize what was happening? She was getting weaker, but he kept getting stronger. He could show her the way. He'd teach her everything she needed to know.

If she would just stop hiding from him.

He slipped back through the swamp and headed for his car. The fire trucks had finally cleared out. The firefighters and uniforms on scene had been so clueless. They hadn't even found the bodies in the swamp. Not that there had been much to find, not after he'd taken care of things.

Captain Jillian Pope had already disappeared. Unless Tanner talked, no one would ever know what had happened to her.

She wasn't the first he'd let disappear into this swamp. It was such a good dumping ground. The gators that liked to come out at sunset were always so hungry.

Not the first. Jillian wouldn't be the last, either. With his power growing, why stop? There were so many in this world who deserved what he would give them.

But not his angel.

She deserved to be at his side. Fighting with him.

Soon, she'd see that. He'd *make* her see it. Once Tanner Chance was dead at her feet, she'd finally understand, and she'd be grateful for all that he was giving her.

Normally, Marna knew, it wasn't easy to get an audience with Sammael. Though he was a Fallen, the guy kept an army-load of demons at his beck and call. Those demons spent most of their time guarding the big boss.

Hoping to cut through that demon line, Tanner took her to the back door of Sammael's club, Sunrise, and he flashed his badge.

She thought the badge bit might work, but the demons just laughed.

When Tanner pulled out his claws, they stopped laughing.

"Sammael," Tanner snapped. "We want to see him, *now.*"

His body was partially blocking hers, but Marna felt the eyes of the demons as they raked her.

"You don't *demand* to see anyone—"

Tanner grabbed the demon by the throat and lifted him a good foot off the floor. "Yeah, I do. *Sammael.*"

Marna's breath rushed out. The demon he was lifting had to weigh about three hundred pounds—and it looked like that weight was all muscle.

Tanner held him with one hand. With his other, he pointed to the demon still blocking the back door. "You." A smaller demon—though not by much—with tattoos that circled his arms and neck. "Let your boss know we're here."

The heavy metal door behind the guy slid open. "He already knows." Sammael sauntered out. He raised a brow when he saw the demon squirming in Tanner's grasp. "Want to let Tommy go?"

Tanner dropped him. Tommy surged right back up with a wild yell, coming at Tanner with his hands fisted.

Tanner punched him in the chest, and the guy toppled back down. Before the demon could get back on his feet, Sammael lifted one hand. *"Enough."* Lethally soft, but packed with power. "As fun as watching a beat down is, I don't have the time for it now."

The demon froze. Marna hurried forward and made sure to move into the thin stream of light that spilled out from a nearby window. "I need to talk with you."

"And you brought your guard . . . cat with you." Sammael smiled, a chilling sight. "How charming."

"Listen, Sam," Tanner began, surging forward.

"No, *you* listen. I'm not one of your dumb criminals that you can chase down." He shrugged, then lifted his hands in front of him. "I'm Sammael. All-fucking-powerful Fallen. And I can kill you as soon as look at you."

Marna's heart stopped.

But then a woman's hand, fingers tipped with a blood-red polish, slid over Sammael's shoulder. "Easy. You know you wanted to visit with her again."

And Marna's heart started racing in a double-time beat. Sammael's face softened as he turned to stare at the woman behind him. Marna knew who she was, of course; every angel knew.

Seline O'Shaw.

Seline O'Shaw had been in heaven, for a very brief time. Half succubus, half angel, Seline was now a legend in heavenly circles.

It had taken a little matter of dying for Seline's angel side to come out and take over. Only once she'd entered heaven, Sammael hadn't been ready to let her go. He'd fought everyone in his path, been willing to sacrifice his life—just to get back to her.

After that, everyone had known that the mighty Sammael had a weakness.

Her.

Seline stared at Marna with sad eyes. "I'm sorry about your wings."

Marna rolled her shoulders. After weeks of numbness, the scarring was actually starting to itch a bit. Weird. "And I'm sorry about . . ." What? The fact that Seline had chosen to come back to earth? To stay with a man who most angels thought was becoming a true devil? She cleared her throat and decided not to say anything.

Seline's slightly wicked smile told Marna that she understood. "Let's go inside," Seline said, "so we can talk in private."

"Beats standing around with our asses out in the open," Tanner muttered, but he tossed Marna one more glance. His expression seemed to say, *You okay with this?*

She nodded and then followed him inside. The door closed behind them with a bang that made her jump. She glanced up and found that Sammael had moved to look at her.

Frowning, he said, "My dear lost angel, we aren't the ones who jump. We're the ones who make everyone else want to shit their pants."

If only.

They walked down a long corridor. Music beat. Pulsed. They didn't head out into the main section of the bar, but instead followed a twisting staircase upstairs. Marna glanced down. Saw all the bodies. The couples making out. Heat and lust seemed to pour from the people on the dance floor.

No wonder a succubus had been hiding there. It would have been the perfect place for Seline, before she'd changed.

Marna's gaze tracked up a bit as she climbed the stairs. Wait . . . was that a golden cage, hanging from the ceiling?

"Want to give it a try?" Seline murmured.

Tanner growled. Marna didn't speak because . . . *maybe.* There were two women in that suspended cage right then. Dancing. Gyrating their hips.

She bumped into Tanner's back. He caught her hand and steadied her. His gaze searched hers. So bright. "Marna?"

She realized that he'd barely glanced at the dancing women or the throng below. And . . . his attention always seemed to be on her. On what she was doing and feeling. She wasn't wildly sexy like the others there, certainly not like Seline who seemed to ooze sex appeal. When it came to sexy, no one beat an ex-succubus. They were made for sin.

But Tanner always looked at Marna like he could eat her alive.

It was nice. *Hot.*

They climbed the rest of the stairs in silence, then entered a room on the right. Tinted windows let them look down onto the dance floor, but Sammael assured them, "No one out there can see or hear anything that goes on in here."

Good, and a little scary.

"I was wondering when you'd be coming by." Sammael lowered his body onto a leather couch. Seline perched on the arm rest near him. "Especially since it looks like I'll be having to kill your brother."

Tanner lunged toward him, but Marna grabbed his arm as she fought to pull him back.

Sammael smiled.

"You *won't,*" Tanner growled.

"If he keeps selling angel blood, I will." One dark brow rose. "Do you know how many vamps I've killed in the last few weeks, all because those fools thought that they'd get a taste of my blood?" Then his eyes hardened. His hand came up, and his fingers curved around Seline's leg. "Or hers?" Real rage burned in his eyes, and Marna realized she and Tanner were very lucky Sammael hadn't already attacked.

Nothing could stop him when he went on a rampage. She'd seen his handiwork before. Had to clean up the bodies and collect the souls that had been left behind.

"He's not selling any more blood." Tanner's hands had fisted. Were his claws coming out? The last thing she wanted was for him to battle Sammael.

"He'd better not." A deadly promise. "I owe you and Cody because you helped Az."

Just the mention of Az's name stirred so many memories for Marna. She'd once been tasked with taking the soul of Az's human mate. Like Sammael, he hadn't been willing to give up the woman he loved. And when he'd refused . . .

That was when Marna had been attacked.

"Az and I both owe you," Sammael said, only he was looking at her now.

Marna's chin rose. "Cody won't sell the blood again. And you're right, you do owe us." Her shoulders were straight, her muscles tense. She wouldn't show him any more fear. "So I want you to pay that debt."

"How?"

Seline watched in silence.

Marna hesitated. Tanner's body was still locked in battle-ready mode. "I want you to teach me to kill." She lifted her hands and held them, palms out, toward Sammael. "With a touch."

A faint line appeared between his brows, but it was Seline who asked, "You mean you can't?"

Marna shook her head.

"Power comes back in different ways, for different angels." Sammael didn't seem particularly concerned. Since it wasn't his life, why would he be? "Give it time," he said with a shrug. "You've only been walking the earth a few months. You'll get stronger—"

"Time is what I don't have." She pulled in a ragged breath. "If I'm going to keep living, then I need to know how to kill."

Waves of tension seemed to roll off Tanner.

"Can you stir the fire?" Seline asked.

Marna nodded. "But fire isn't much good against a demon."

"And that's what we're facing," Tanner said as he stood with his legs braced apart. "The vamps want her blood, yeah, we know that, but there's a demon out there, pulling puppet strings and stealing faces."

Seline blinked her perfect eyes. "Stealing what?"

"He changed himself," Marna said, and her gaze darted to the window. To the mass of bodies below. Was anyone ever truly who you thought? "He took my body, my face, and he killed two shifters."

"Interesting." From Sammael.

"It's not *interesting,*" Tanner fired back. "It's dangerous."

The right side of Sammael's mouth kicked up into a half-smile. "Let me guess . . . he took your form, too?"

"And nearly killed a cop. This SOB is gunning for us, and we *will* take him out." Tanner's vow.

But Marna said, "Fire won't stop him. That means *I* can't stop him." She didn't have Tanner's certainty that they were gonna win the day.

"Hmmm." Sammael's fingers stroked Seline's leg in an absent caress. "But your shifter's claws should do the trick. Unless, of course, he's too squeamish to kill his own brother."

"Like you were too squeamish to kill yours?" Tanner fired back.

The air in the room got very, very thick.

Sammael's fingers stopped their stroking. "You should be careful, shifter."

"No, you should be." Tanner lifted up his claws. "I know how to kill you, too."

Had anyone else ever stood up to Sammael before? Marna didn't think so. If they had, those folks hadn't exactly lived to tell the story.

Sammael threw back his head and laughed. Wait, laughed?

Tanner wasn't laughing with him.

"I like you, shifter," Sammael said once he'd gained control of himself. It looked like Seline might have pinched him. "You're not afraid to piss off Death."

No, he wasn't.

Marna cleared her throat. "Can we get back to the Touch?" Or did they just want to fill the room with more supernatural testosterone? From where she stood, there was already plenty of that in the place. Enough to choke her and Seline.

Sammael gave a slow nod. "So you want to be able to kill demons."

"But what if a demon isn't the one . . . ah . . ." Seline cleared her throat and finished, ". . . stealing faces?"

"Demons can work glamour like no one else," Tanner said. "It has to be one of them. No one else can—"

But Sammael had turned to glance first at Seline, then at Marna. His brows lowered as he studied her. "Why haven't you told him?"

She stared back at him, lost. There was nothing to tell.

"Marna . . ." Sammael sighed her name as if she were a naughty child. To one as ancient as he, maybe she was. "You and I both know that demons aren't the only ones who can change their forms." Then his gaze turned back to Tanner. "Surely you've heard the legends about demons, about how they first came to be."

Tanner's back was to the tinted glass and the throng of dancers. "They were descended from the Fallen."

"Um . . . yes, and so where do you think that handy glamour magic first came from, huh?" He waited a beat, then said, "Angels. They're the ones who mastered glamour long before any demons walked the earth. Angels can steal faces, too."

Cody hurried down the darkened street. His neck had healed, but his gut twisted with every step he took. Another demon in New Orleans who could steal faces? How the hell had he missed that?

He'd always thought he was alone. A freak, even among demons. Others of his kind could stir powerful magic. Control the minds of humans. Not him.

His father had once said that he was a curse. Unable to shift into the powerful form of a panther, what good had he been? His father had laughed and mocked him for only being able to shift his physical appearance so that he looked like humans.

"Fucking useless. Should have killed you the first day I realized the panther didn't live inside of you." His father's words rang in his ears.

And the bastard *had* tried to kill him. He would have succeeded, if Tanner hadn't been there. Jumping in, taking those blows and the slices from their father's claws.

Tanner had saved him more times than Cody could count. And Cody would not fail him now.

He could do this. He could find the other freak and—

A footstep shuffled lightly behind him. Cody spun around. He didn't have senses as strong as a regular shifter.

Another fucking failure. He'd been caught unaware too many times before.

But no one was there.

His gaze swept the alley. Left to right. In the distance, he could hear the sound of laughter. Catcalls. Drunken voices. He wasn't headed to Bourbon Street. The crowd he looked for would be hiding in the deeper parts of the city. The darker parts that humans always stayed away from, as if sensing the danger.

Some animal instincts existed even within pureblood humans. Smart humans didn't ignore those instincts.

He turned around, hunched his shoulders, and picked up his pace. He'd search as many demon bars as he could. Money talked in this town, and thanks to that angel blood, he had plenty of cash.

If there was another freak out there, he'd find him.

Cody rounded the corner. He had to cross through another dark, tight stretch of alley space. Then he'd be at the first bar. Maybe he'd get lucky, maybe—

The whisper of a footstep behind him had Cody tensing. He whirled around.

Not alone this time.

A figure stepped from the shadows. A figure with hulking shoulders. Matted, dark hair, and a face that still chased Cody in his nightmares.

"Hello, son," his father said, as he raised a claw-tipped hand. "It's been too long."

Tanner stared at Sammael, body tensed. The Fallen looked too confident. Far too cocky. He'd never trusted this guy—because Tanner wasn't an idiot.

And now Sammael—Sam—was smiling at Marna.

"Her blue eyes are so pretty, aren't they? It would seem that most angels have blue eyes." Sam tapped his chin. "That's a lie of course."

"Angels can't lie—" Marna began.

But Sam just laughed. "When the emotions get strong enough, when you lose that last thread of control inside yourself, the glamour that's been in place since the moment you were created will falter. Your shifter . . ." Sam waved toward Tanner. "He'll look into your eyes and see the darkness that all angels try so hard to hide."

But Tanner wasn't looking into Marna's eyes. He was staring at Sam, and as he stared, Sam's eyes began to darken. Dark. *Darker.* Until . . .

They were as black as a demon's eyes.

"The apple really doesn't fall so far from the poisoned tree," Sam murmured.

Seline frowned at him. "Sam, we've been over this. You aren't evil."

He brought her hand to his lips. "Right. I'm just not good, either." He entwined his fingers with hers. "Most angels are like me, a mix of the two. So much power, bottled up inside, waiting to explode."

The more Tanner learned about angels, the less he liked. Weren't there already enough monsters in the world? *Monsters like me.*

Couldn't the angels have just been the good guys, for once? He had to kick vampire ass. Demon ass. Now angel ass? There were so many jerks to get in line to meet his claws.

"Different demons have different powers," Tanner said, trying to puzzle this mess out. "My brother . . ."

Sam leaned forward. "Yes, let's hear more about him. I've been so curious." A dangerous edge had entered his voice. "Three brothers. One half angel. One half demon. And then there's . . . you."

Tanner straightened his shoulders. "You stay the hell away from my brother, understand?"

Sam didn't appear intimidated. He would be—once Tanner had his claws at the guy's neck.

It was Seline who delicately cleared her throat. "Ah, Marna, perhaps you should stop thinking so much about demons. They're really not all bad, you know."

Since she was half-demon, Tanner figured the lady was speaking from experience.

"Just as angels aren't all good," Marna said, *speaking from her experience*. "I know that . . . now."

"Fast learner," Sam acknowledged with a sly half-grin.

Marna shook her head. "No. If I was, I'd be able to kill by now." Her hands had clenched into fists. "Instead, I'm helpless when demons attack."

Sam rose slowly and stalked toward her. Tanner tensed, ready to go at him—

"Keep those claws away from me, panther." Sam's flat order. "I'm not going to hurt her."

"You damn well aren't."

Sam reached for Marna's clenched hands. He lifted them. Held them cradled within his palms.

The panther began to growl.

"We don't lose the power of the Death Touch when we fall. The power is still there. It comes back to each angel of death. It just comes back at different times."

"And I'm supposed to do what?" Marna asked. "Wait? Hide?"

He shook his head. "*Fight*. It's only when you pull forth the fury inside that you can ignite the Touch." His fingers tightened around hers. "It's simple, little angel. You just have to want to kill badly enough. When you want death more than you want life, that Touch will be there for you again."

Marna looked . . . lost.

He dropped her hands. "You just have to want it badly enough." He turned his back to her.

Marna grabbed his shoulder and jerked him around to face her. "I *do*." Her cheeks flushed. "When Tanner was on the ground, when that bitch stabbed him in the heart, I wanted to kill more than I wanted my next breath." Shame and fury darkened her words.

Tanner watched her in surprise. So much emotion, boiling from within her.

"I wanted to kill all those who were hunting us. I wanted to destroy them." Her nails dug into Sam's shoulder. "But I couldn't. I can stir fire, but can't do much else. And while I do nothing, those hunting me just keep killing, using *my face*."

Silence.

Marna pulled in a deep breath and let her hand fall away from him. "Angels of death don't . . . steal faces," she said. Tanner noticed that her fingers were trembling. "Neither do guardian angels. Guardians watch over their charges. They help, they guide unnoticed. They don't change into something—*someone*—else and kill." Marna turned away from Sam. Now her fingers reached for Tanner. "Coming here was a mistake." She pulled him toward the door. "Sammael doesn't want to help. He just wants to blame all the angels who still do their jobs. The ones who didn't go on a murdering rampage and *fall* like he did."

He had to be staring at a ghost. Shock had held him immobile as he faced his worst nightmare, a nightmare that couldn't be there.

The moments ticked past as he faced the monster he'd never be able to forget. "You're dead," Cody whispered.

But the bastard just smiled, flashing his growing fangs. "Am I?"

Cody shoved him away and turned to run.

Then his father tackled him. Cody's face slammed into the pavement.

"You always were a shit-poor runner."

Cody tasted blood in his mouth. He rolled and tried to punch at the bastard.

His father just laughed and easily dodged the blow, but when he dodged, he had to back up. Cody sprang to his feet and his hands clenched into fists at his sides. "You aren't my father. Who the hell are you?"

Stealing faces. This prick might look like the bastard who'd tormented him, but he wasn't. No way.

His father was rotting away in the ground. Not walking the streets of New Orleans, laughing.

His father had never laughed. Not even when he tortured his prey. Cody had never heard laughter come from the bastard's thin lips.

"It's your fault I'm dead," the guy said, raising his claws. Familiar claws. Tanner had claws just like them now. *Not me.* Cody would never belong with the other shifters. He couldn't so much as flash a fang when he got pissed. "If you'd been better, stronger, I never would have died."

No. Cody's chin lifted. Sure, he'd once thought . . .

If I'd been better, stronger . . . then my father wouldn't be such a twisted freak. He wouldn't be so angry all the time. He wouldn't hurt us so much.

"It's your fault," the bastard said. "I can feel your guilt. I've always felt it."

"You don't feel anything." *It's not my fault the bastard was screwed up.* He'd been that way before Cody was born. He'd been a sadistic freak until he took his last, blood-filled breath. "And I don't know what the fuck you are, but you should stay away from me."

The guy wearing his father's face smiled. "I'm not going to stay away." He lunged forward and drove his claws into Cody's stomach before he had the chance to scream. "I'm here to kill you."

Oh, damn, his Marna was showing some bite. And if she wanted to get away from the jerk Fallen, he was happy to oblige her. Tanner made sure to cover her back as they headed for the door. *Ladies first.*

"Angels of death and guardians aren't the only angels out there," Seline called out. "I'm sure not one of them."

Marna hesitated.

"If someone is killing, hurting others, then you need to look toward the darker angels." Seline's voice held no emotion.

"Angels aren't goodness and light," Sam muttered. No, that guy sure as shit wasn't.

Marna glanced back over her shoulder. "P-punishment angels."

"Now you're understanding." Sam seemed satisfied.

Fine. So she was understanding. Tanner wasn't. He whirled to face Sam. "For the angel-fucking-impaired here, just tell me what the hell is goin' on."

But it was Marna who spoke. Marna who'd known this all along? "Punishment angels can take different . . . guises . . . when they deliver their justice."

Dammit. He wasn't liking the sound of this.

"They can take the appearance of any person that you've wronged. When you see them coming for you . . . guilt . . ." Marna swallowed. "Guilt can freeze you."

"And while you freeze, while you are too freaked to fight," Seline continued quietly as she walked slowly toward the bar and poured herself a drink, "that's when a punishment angel strikes." Her smile was sad. "It was one of the first lessons they taught me." She pointed to the ceiling. "You know, before I decided the view down here was so much better."

"I do make for an awesome view," Sam said with a flash of his teeth.

Seriously—what the hell did that woman see in him?

But at least they'd given him some ideas. And at least now

his brother wasn't the only guy in town who could be listed as a suspect.

Except . . . a punishment angel?

"They're one of the few types of angels who can walk right among the humans," Sam said, eyes hardening.

"They walk with them," Marna said. "The better to punish." Her voice had lowered.

"Know your enemy." Sam's advice. "From the sound of things, you need to get to know him pretty fucking fast."

Tanner cast a searching glance at Marna. The guy out there killing hadn't come at either one of them directly. Not yet, anyway. He'd gone after the shifters. That cop, and—

"An angel couldn't kill so freely. Only death angels are supposed to take lives. This guy isn't a death angel"—Marna was definite—"so you're wrong, Sammael. This isn't one of ours."

Ours.

"It's someone else," she insisted. "A demon, a—"

"Punishment angels can become corrupted, too, you know. All angels can be tempted."

Marna's gaze found Tanner's.

"And we can all fall," Sam finished softly. "I think that's a truth you're beginning to understand."

Too late though. They'd sent Cody out to hunt for the killer, but how was he supposed to fight an angel? Tanner yanked open the door. He spared one glare for Sam. "Spread the word. Make sure the twisted freaks in this town who fear you know that she's off-limits. They're not getting her blood."

Marna slipped through the doorway.

Sam inclined his head. "I'm already spreading that word. I think the dead demons and vamps I've left will make the fools think twice before any other attacks."

Sam's emotionless voice as he talked about killing reminded Tanner of the guy's words from just moments before.

Not evil. Not good.

Clenching his teeth, Cody hurried after Marna. He didn't like talking to Sam. Didn't like it at all because—

He's too much like me.

Not good.

And with more evil growing inside each day.

Chapter Fourteen

Tanner knew the bars that his brother would visit. You didn't live in this town as long as he had without discovering the darkest of demon hells.

Once upon a time, Tanner had pulled Cody from one of those hells. Dragged his unconscious body out even as he raged at his brother.

The guy had been a screwed-up seventeen-year-old. So sure his dad was a twisted fuck because *he'd* had the colossal bad luck of being born. Tanner had tried shoving some sense down the guy's throat. He'd had to break Cody's addiction first and get him off the drugs that just confused his mind and made him even more desperate.

But I got him clean. And Cody had stayed clean.

"Tanner, slow down!" Marna called sharply, and Tanner realized he'd been running.

They were at the mouth of a narrow alley. Just a few more turns and they'd be—

He froze.

Marna bumped into his back. "I didn't say stop," she muttered, pushing back. "I just said—"

Tanner's nostrils flared. "Blood." Not just any blood either. Demon blood had a stronger scent than others. Almost like ash.

And shifter blood . . . it smelled of animal.

Only one guy in town had that mixed scent of beast and demon.

Fuck.

Tanner raced down the alley, shouting Cody's name, but his brother wasn't there. There was just a too-big pool of blood, looking black in the darkness.

Tanner bent next to the blood and his claws scraped the pavement.

"It's . . . his?" Marna asked as she pressed closer.

Tanner's gaze followed the trail of blood as it snaked around the corner. "Like bread crumbs." A trail of blood splatter to follow.

And he could follow it. He had Cody's scent. He could follow that blood trail all the way back to his brother—and to the fool who'd hurt him.

Was it one of the angel-blood-addicted paranormals? Or the actual punishment angel that Sam had suggested? Either way, no one was getting away with hurting his brother.

No one.

Tanner rose in a fast ripple of power. He caught Marna's shoulders, pulled her close, and stared in her eyes. "When I shift, the panther's gonna hunt."

She nodded. "It's Cody's blood, isn't it?" Marna didn't give him time to answer. "I understand. We'll find him. He'll be okay."

She didn't understand. It wasn't about *finding* Cody.

Tanner kissed her. Deep. Fast. Hard.

It was about *destroying* the one who'd attacked his brother.

Tanner spun away. He started to run, and with every movement, the beast inside stretched and growled. Bones popped. Snapped. When he bounded past the corner, he hit down on all fours.

And he kept running as the beast took over fully.

He'd find Cody, and he'd tear apart the bastard who had thought to hurt him. Angels weren't immortal. They could bleed. They could die. You just had to use the right weapon against them.

His claws were the perfect weapon.

Marna ran behind him. The thud of her footsteps followed him. The blood trail led away from the lights of the bars and back into the darkness. Past the Square, deeper and—

Marna's footsteps stopped. Even with the rage pumping through him, he heard that telling sound. He'd been so focused on the blood trail, he hadn't let any other scents hit him, but now—

The panther's head swung back around. Marna had frozen. She stared at him with wide eyes. And then she looked down at her chest. A blooming circle of red appeared right in the middle of her breasts. Her mouth opened as if she would scream.

But Tanner's roar drowned out the sound.

Marna fell to her knees. The knife that had been plunged into her, from back to front, slid out with a slosh of sound that enraged the beast and had the man inside screaming.

Then he saw the bastard who'd hurt her. Saw his face—and everything stopped for him.

Standing there, smiling, holding the bloody knife—no, lifting that fucking knife to his mouth and licking the blood away—that asshole was Cody.

Cody smiled, and his teeth were stained with her blood. "You were right. It is so easy to get addicted. Especially when the blood is so sweet."

Tanner roared his fury. Marna was trying to rise. Her hands pushed against the dirty brick wall, and her body shook.

Tanner leapt forward. Brother or no brother, Cody had just signed his own death warrant. *I didn't want to believe it.*

He should have believed it.

Tanner knew just how much evil was in their bloodline. *I should have believed it.*

Not a punishment angel. Their killer was just a twisted prick of a demon.

My brother.

Cody turned and raced away. He laughed as he fled into the cracks that passed for alleyways. The panther rushed to Marna's side. His head pushed against her shoulder. He couldn't comfort her like this. Couldn't hold her. *Dammit.*

Her hand lifted. Rubbed against his head. "It's . . . okay. " Her voice was weak, but her gaze was strong. "This won't . . . stop me for long."

A knife wound to the heart couldn't kill her, but it could hurt her. It had.

I'll make him pay.

Cody had set him up. Left a trail of blood for him to follow and all the while, Cody had been hunting them. Waiting for his moment to attack.

Now it's my moment.

He rubbed his head against her shoulder once more. His brother's laughter drifted on the wind. So close. He couldn't let him get away. *Wouldn't.*

Time to make sure Cody never hurt Marna again.

He spun away from her and leapt into the air. He'd have Cody on the ground before his brother ever had a chance to scream.

My only family. He'd always thought Cody had escaped the curse that seemed to mark them.

Why hadn't he seen the evil before? *Why?*

Marna rose slowly and kept the heel of her palm pressed against her chest. That knife wound had *hurt*. Burned her with a white-hot agony.

And Tanner had roared with such fury. She hadn't seen her attacker, but she'd recognized that voice.

Cody.

She sucked in a breath. The hot ache in her chest had begun to ease. Now she just needed to force her legs to move so that she could follow Tanner. She wouldn't let him face this nightmare alone.

She wouldn't let him be the one to kill Cody.

Her hands fisted. The demon had come after her. Taken her blood. Laughed while she'd fallen into the dirt and grime.

Power began to lick through her. That power gave her the strength to stand upright. To put one foot in front of the other and run.

Rage could fuel her so well, but would it be enough power to kill? Maybe.

She was about to find out.

Tanner tracked the bastard. He followed that scent of ash and animal, and he rounded the last tight turn in the dark, knowing that his brother's death was at hand.

He flew through the air, his jaws open, ready to rip and tear.

His brother was on the ground. Blood surrounded him. Cody saw him coming toward him and hope lit his eyes.

Hope? He'd give the guy hope. Tanner attacked. In one lunge, he had his teeth over Cody's throat. Death would be fast. He could give his brother that much.

Cody took her blood. Stabbed her. Hurt her.

"Wh-what are you doin', bro?" Cody whispered. Tanner hadn't bitten him yet. Not yet. "H-help me . . ."

The scent of blood was so strong. Tanner pulled back and stared down at his brother. A knife was in Cody's hand. And his brother . . . aw, fuck, his brother's stomach looked like it had been hacked open.

Had he done that to himself? Was Cody really that far gone?

The panther inhaled deeply.

The blood on that knife . . .

It wasn't Marna's blood. It was only Cody's. And his brother was on the ground, barely moving because his wounds were so severe. But he'd been laughing just moments before, hadn't he?

"I . . . f-found . . . th-the other . . . f-freak," Cody whispered and blood dripped from his mouth.

As the panther, Tanner's sense of smell was far more acute than it was in his human form. As he inhaled again, he realized there was no trace of Marna's blood on Cody. There should have been. He'd watched Cody stab her with his own eyes.

Now he was supposed to kill him.

Footsteps thundered toward them. Tanner looked up and saw Marna stumble around the corner. Her hair flew out around her. Her eyes—had they ever looked so dark before?

She saw him, saw Cody, and her face hardened with fury even as she put a hand to her chest.

He could see the blood on her shirt.

"F-found him," Cody whispered again. "G-got to me . . . wearing b-bastard's face."

What bastard? Tanner couldn't ask right then. Sometimes, being in the panther's body sucked. He leapt off his brother and tried to catch another scent in the air. Someone else had to be there, someone else—

But the only other scents were older.

Ash and blood.

Marna began to stalk toward Cody. Tanner leapt between them, positioning his body.

Marna froze, and her lips parted in surprise. "Tanner, what are you doing?" She'd sure healed fast. The attack would have killed most folks. All humans—and most supernaturals he knew wouldn't be walking around so soon after taking a knife to the heart.

He hadn't even known she *could* heal this fast.

Her eyes were almost pure black, he could see that, even

in the darkness. Sam hadn't been lying. The rage was building inside of her. Hell, if someone had just shoved a knife into him, maybe he'd be feeling the rage, too.

But it wasn't Cody.

The panther snarled, trying to tell her that.

Marna's eyes widened. "You're protecting him? After what he did to me?"

Not Cody.

Screw this. He had to shift back. Had to change so he could make her understand. He let the burning transformation sweep over him. Barely heard the crunch and pop of his bones. He needed to speak. The man had to take over. He had to—

Mid-shift, when he was most vulnerable, that was when the bullet hit. It came hurtling toward him and thudded into his chest. One hit. Then another.

Silver. He could feel the hot scorching inside of his flesh.

Another thud. A lancing pain hit his knee and Tanner fell.

The shift kept burning through him, but it had slowed now, thanks to that silver. The one firing on him knew exactly what he was doing. *He knows all my weaknesses.*

Tanner's hands slammed onto the ground. He still had his claws out, but they were no good against bullets. Tanner tilted back his head and saw Marna rushing toward him. Her mouth was open and she was screaming—

"Stop!"

A tremble seemed to shake the ground beneath him. He blinked, then looked up again.

A bullet had frozen in the air. A bullet that was just inches from his forehead. As he stared, the bullet dropped to the ground.

Marna reached him, but she didn't help him up. She positioned her body in front of his. Her hand lifted. Pointed to a nearby rooftop. "I see you." Her voice was darker. Far harder than he'd ever heard before. And from her hand, a blast of fire erupted, rushing right up to that building.

A scream sounded.

She'd made a hit. Good for her.

Tanner used his claws and dug the bullets out of his body. He ignored the pain. What did it matter? He needed to get Marna and Cody out of that alley. Needed to sew up his brother before Cody bled to death right there.

And Marna—Marna was walking away from him. Stalking toward that now burning building. An empty warehouse, its roof blazed in the night and lit the sky. Firefighters would be called to the blaze. There was no freaking missing the way that fire was churning. Before the rescue squad arrived, they'd have to be long gone.

"No more," Marna said as her steps quickened, and, at her back, he could see those strange, shadowy wings once more as they stretched out behind her.

He tossed the bloody bullets to the ground. Pushed to his feet. She wasn't going in alone—

"T-Tan . . . ner . . ."

His brother's voice. So weak. He glanced back. Cody's face was ashen. The scent of blood was so thick around him. Blood and . . . flowers.

Death angel.

"Stay the hell away from my brother!" Dammit. He spun back around, torn. "Marna!"

She didn't stop. She was almost at the blazing building now.

"Marna!" If he left Cody, Tanner knew that his brother was dead. The angel of death would take him. And if he didn't go after Marna . . .

What would happen to her?

He had to choose. He couldn't save both. There wasn't a way. He couldn't—

I can sure as shit try. He grabbed Cody. Slung him over his shoulder. Tried to rush after Marna, but his wounds slowed him down. *Can never heal fast enough from silver. Never—*

Marna disappeared into the smoke. She'd gone into that damn inferno. He tried to move faster. He yelled her name again.

And the windows of the building exploded out as the flames flared even higher.

Marna was beautiful by firelight. He watched her through the flames, loving the way they licked around her form. She'd pushed out with her power and blocked the fire from touching her body.

Could fire ever hurt something so beautiful?

Her eyes were black now, and they burned with a dark fury. She couldn't come up to him. The ceiling would collapse on her before she ever got there. So he could sit back, watch, and wait.

The fire wouldn't hurt him, either. His scream had just been to lure her closer to him. To make her see . . .

She couldn't count on the shifter. When the chips were down, he wouldn't choose her. He'd choose his brother, even when it looked like his brother was nothing more than a killer.

For the shifter, blood was all that mattered.

Marna needed to see, *he* was more than that. He'd done everything for her. Would keep doing everything.

"I want you at my side," the words slipped from him.

Her head jerked up. She could hear him over the flames. Good.

She tried to step toward him—toward the stairs—but a chunk of burning ceiling fell down and crashed near her feet. He'd planned this blaze so well. He'd gotten very good at controlling the fire. From the outside, it had looked as if a giant explosion had rocked the building, sending glass and debris flying. The cops, when they finally came, would think a detonation of some sort had gone off.

They'd never realize the blaze had been the result of a supernatural just playing with some fire. Oh, how he did enjoy the burn.

"Who are you?" she shouted.

His smile dimmed. Why hadn't she realized who he was yet? "I'm the one who's giving you justice." What she deserved.

He was giving them all what they deserved.

His hand lifted. He'd touched her before. Did she remember? He wanted to touch her again.

"Marna!"

But that shifter just kept getting in the way.

She turned at the roar of her name, but she didn't leave the flames. Maybe she liked the heat as much as he did.

A wall crashed down. Not because of the flames, but because Tanner Chance had kicked it down. *"Marna!"*

He'd left his brother behind. Left him to die, and now he was coming after Marna.

Unexpected.

Annoying.

Tanner leapt across the flames and didn't even gasp when they licked against his skin. But by now, that shifter should be used to pain. He had enough scars on his body to prove it.

Maybe he even liked the pain.

Tanner caught Marna's hand. "We have to get out of here!" The crackling fire tried to drown out his words.

She shook her head and pointed up.

To me.

But Tanner pulled her close, wrapped his arms around her, and started carrying her out.

Fool. Playing the hero. Marna didn't need rescuing. The fire would never hurt her.

But Tanner would. He'd destroy her. Unless the shifter was destroyed first.

Turning away from the flames, the watcher eased back out onto the building's high ledge. The scent of the fire filled his nose. He spread his arms—

And fell.

Marna was fighting him. Kicking. Punching. Scratching. Tanner tightened his hold on her. Didn't the woman realize when she was walking right into a burning hell of a trap? That asshole was jerking them around. Moving them like freaking pieces on a chess set.

Tanner had always hated that game.

No more.

He heard the wail of sirens the instant he burst outside that hellhole of a building. The cavalry would be coming in fast, and he was stuck being on foot, with no wheels worth stealing anywhere around.

Screwed.

But at least they were all alive. For the moment.

"Let go!" Marna shoved harder and broke free of his grasp—because he let her—but when she whirled to race into the inferno again, Tanner roped an arm around her waist and pulled her back against him.

"Do you want to die that badly?" The words were ripped from him. "Is being here, on earth, really such a hell to you?"

She stilled. Then, panting, Marna glanced over her shoulder at him. "He . . . he was there. I heard him. Talking to me." Her gaze returned to the fire. "I could have killed him tonight."

"Or he could have killed you." *Then what would I have done?*

The flames and ash and smoke were clogging his nose. Choking him. Those scents were so strong that he couldn't smell the SOB who'd been in that building. Right then, he couldn't smell anything but the fire.

Maybe the guy in that building would do them all a favor and burn.

"Need a hand?" a cold, mocking voice asked. A voice that Tanner recognized instantly.

Though he hadn't smelled the man's approach, Tanner didn't start in surprise. It seemed only fitting that the last vamp he wanted to see would be the one to come crashing this nightmare.

"Riley?" Marna asked and he heard her surprise.

Tanner turned slowly. Riley stood next to Cody's prone body. Just the sight of Cody caused his gut to clench. How the hell was he still fighting to live?

"Don't run again," Tanner growled at Marna and rushed back to his brother. He lifted him, and Cody's eyes didn't open, but his chest still rose and fell in a ragged pattern.

"Instead of running, why don't we drive?" Riley suggested. He lifted a pair of keys and dangled them from his fingertips. "I've got wheels close by." He glanced at the fire. "From the look of things, you could all use a fast ride out of here."

"Why are you trying to help us??" Tanner demanded as his hold tightened on Cody. His brother's blood was on him. "You're being a good Samaritan?" 'Cause that's the kind of guy he was? Bull. More likely he was just looking for another chance to get Marna's blood.

"I'm paying a debt." The vampire was staring at Marna. Looking like he could freaking eat her. *No chance, dick. No chance.* "But if you don't want my help . . ." Riley began to back away.

Dammit. "Just get us out of here." Tanner's eyes met Marna's for the briefest of moments. "Then get the hell away." Because if that fanged parasite came at Marna for a bite, Tanner would make sure he lost all of his sharp and pointy teeth.

Still carrying Cody's unconscious form, Tanner followed them as Riley and Marna snaked through the alley turns and climbed into Riley's ride. They hurried away, making sure to avoid the fire trucks and patrol cars that were racing to the scene.

Tanner tried to put pressure on his brother's wounds. Cody could usually heal better than this.

But he wasn't. He didn't seem to be healing at all. "Don't do this to me," he muttered, pressing harder against the gaping wound. "You snap out of this and *wake up.*"

"What makes you so sure . . ." Marna's quiet voice came from the front seat. "That he wasn't the one who attacked me?"

"Because he didn't have your blood on him." Tanner didn't look away from Cody. Blisters and deep burns covered Tanner's body, and every move *hurt,* but that pain meant he was alive.

Did Cody feel the pain, too? Did he understand just what it meant?

Use the pain, boy. His father's voice echoed through his mind. Another beating. Another day when his bones had snapped. *If you give in to it, you just become weak. My son won't be weak.*

"Are you sure that's even your brother?" she asked as the SUV hurtled to the right. They were heading away from the city and back toward the swamp.

Tanner gazed down at Cody. His brother's face had bleached a stark white.

"I mean, if the killer can take any face, then how do you know it's really Cody?" Marna's voice was quiet and totally devoid of emotion.

While Tanner felt as if emotions were about to rip him apart.

Cody stirred. His lashes fluttered just a bit. A groan slipped from his lips. He swallowed. Groaned again.

Tanner leaned closer.

His brother was trying to whisper something to him. Tanner could just make out . . .

"When I . . . was . . . five . . . you . . . took first . . ." A rustling breath, and Cody rasped, *"Beating . . . meant for . . ."*

Cody didn't finish. He didn't have to. Tanner remembered that day, and the beating. Hell yeah, he'd taken his younger brother's beating. Had he been supposed to just stand there and watch the kid suffer?

Tanner's jaw clenched. "I damn well know he's my *real* brother." Slowly, Tanner turned his head to meet Marna's stare. Her eyes weren't black anymore. They were back to that blue that seemed to look right through him. "It's him, Marna. Trust me."

"Trust ain't easy," Riley said. Like he'd asked for the vamp's input. His ride, yeah. His two fucking cents? *No.* But the vampire continued, "Now look, if I'm chauffeuring around a killer—"

"It's not like it would be the first time you've done that." And speaking of killers . . . Tanner leaned forward and slashed out with his claws, letting them come to rest right against Riley's throat. He didn't slice that throat open, though, not while the guy was driving them. But the warning was there. "If you're trying to screw us over and take us to a den of vampires, you'd better think again. I'm not in any mood to play tonight."

Riley's hands tightened around the steering wheel. "I told you, I'm just trying to pay back a debt."

"There isn't a debt," Marna said. "We're even now."

Even? How? She'd bled for the guy. What had he done for her?

Riley cast her a quick glance. Marna was sitting in the

front passenger seat. "Then let's just say I like the idea of an angel and her shifter owing me."

Figured. And that story he actually bought.

Tanner pulled back his claws. He didn't trust the guy. Perhaps he should just kick the vamp out on the side of the road.

"I know a safe place," Riley said quickly. Maybe he realized Tanner was seriously considering the idea of throwing him through the windshield. "There are bandages there, drugs, whatever you need for him. And *no questions asked* is the only policy they follow."

Okay. So he wouldn't toss the guy through the windshield. Yet.

"Then haul ass," Tanner told him because Cody wasn't talking anymore. "And get us there before my brother dies."

He knew an angel of death was chasing them. He'd caught a glimpse of Bastion. *Still seeing angels.* But that prick wasn't taking his brother.

Not without one hell of a fight.

Chapter Fifteen

The vampire took them to the edge of the swamp. A cabin waited, one that looked abandoned from the outside, but inside, the place was stocked with bandages, antibiotics, and . . . bags of blood.

Marna turned away when Riley pulled one of those bags from the extra-large refrigerator and began to drink.

Cody was in the back of the cabin. A woman had rushed out to meet them as soon as they'd arrived. A doctor? A nurse? Marna wasn't sure, but the woman with warm brown eyes and coffee cream skin sure seemed to know what she was doing. Tanner was back there with the woman, trying to force his brother to live.

And Marna was grappling with her own desire—*to kill.*

"You gave me freedom." Riley tossed away the empty bag. A little bit of blood stained his lips.

Marna shrugged. "I gave a blood donation." The least she could do.

"Is my family . . . are they safe?" Riley's question was halting, and it seemed to be pulled from him.

She nodded. This much, she did know. "The instant they left you, they didn't know any more pain."

His breath eased out as he crossed toward her. His steps were slow. His eyes watchful. "Do they know what I became?" There was no missing the pain in his eyes.

She could give him this release, as well. "They only remember what you were." *Not what you are.*

Monster.

Wasn't that what she was now, too?

His hands came up and curled around her shoulders. "We can both be more." His head lowered toward hers.

"And you can get your fucking fangs and hands away from her," Tanner said, his lethal voice cutting through the room better than any knife ever could.

Riley's hands didn't drop, but his head didn't lower toward her any more, either.

"Want to lose them?" Tanner asked. " 'Cause I can accommodate you."

Marna glanced toward Tanner. Sure enough, his claws were out.

Riley's hands dropped. "I wasn't—" he began.

"No, you weren't." Blood stained Tanner's shirt and hands. He looked tired—and pissed. "With her, you're not doing anything."

Marna's eyes narrowed on him. "That's not your call to make."

Tanner's head turned slowly toward her. "It's not?" How could a man's voice be so cold and yet so furious at the same time? What an interesting blend, and very chilling. "I thought when you gave yourself to me, it sure made things like this jerk coming on to you my *call.*"

Men—humans or paranormals—could all be idiots. Marna exhaled. There was a room upstairs for her. Riley had showed it to her earlier. Right then, she just wanted to crash. The men could attack each other if they wanted. More bruises, scrapes, and busted ribs would serve them right.

She headed up the stairs. "He wasn't coming on to me. He was *talking.* Maybe that's something you should try more of."

But all she got in response to that was silence. She was

learning that Tanner could say more with his silence than most men could with their words.

She pulled at her shirt as she climbed the stairs. She was tired of smelling like blood. Tired of feeling like hell. And tired of her shoulders *itching.* Because on top of everything else, her scars had been bugging her for hours.

This day really did just . . . suck.

A knife to the heart—okay, from the back *to* the heart—could sure put a girl in what she knew Tanner would call a *piss-poor* mood.

But, jeez, at this rate, what else could happen?

The scent of flowers teased her nose. Her eyes squeezed closed. "Bastion, if that's you . . ." She exhaled. "Stay away from me right now."

Because she was in the mood to fight. Anyone. Anything. Even an angel.

Or a shifter.

Tanner watched Marna head up the stairs. Her shoulders were slumped. Her steps slow. He could feel the tiredness pouring off her, and it infuriated him.

Attacked. Stabbed with that knife.

While he just watched.

"You need to do a better job of keeping her safe," Riley's cold, drawling voice told him.

What? Advice from the vamp? *Sonofabitch.* Tanner tossed the guy against the nearest wall. "What I *don't* need is some undead jerk telling me how to handle my angel." He bared his own fangs. "And what you need to do . . . you *need* to learn to keep those hands off her."

Riley smirked. Smirked? Really? Could he have begged any more for an ass beating? Apparently, he could because the vamp said, "What if she likes my hands? Maybe she's in the mood for some . . . variety. Not every woman likes to lie with an animal."

Tanner slammed his forehead into the guy's nose. Bones crunched. Riley howled. Ah, that was one of his favorite moves. Why didn't more people ever see that hit coming?

Tanner smiled, then said, "Trust me, she likes my animal side." He'd been worried that he might scare her, but he hadn't. Marna had been just as wild and fierce when they came together.

His gaze lifted to the stairs. He heard the roar of water and knew that she'd turned on the shower. She'd be up there now, naked.

Wet.

He dropped his hold on Riley and walked straight for the stairs.

"You really think she's just gonna turn and greet you with open arms?" Riley's voice mocked him. "That was one very angry angel who stalked up those stairs."

Tanner tossed a glare over his shoulder. "Don't worry about what happens between us."

Riley laughed. "You are one clueless asshole. Go on up there. She'll toss you right back down."

Jaw clenching, Tanner grabbed for the thin stair railing. The day he needed romantic advice from a vamp—

I'll be cold in the ground.

He took the steps three at a time. There was no lock on the door to Marna's room, so he pushed it open and hurried inside. Steam came from the small room near the bed. She'd left the bathroom door ajar.

But Tanner didn't rush inside. He stopped. Shut the bedroom door behind him, and took a deep breath.

I could have lost her.

He understood the game that the killer was playing now. The sick prick. The guy had set things up perfectly, and Tanner had been the one forced to choose.

Save the angel or save the demon.

Bastard.

Tanner had managed, just barely, to save them both. But what would happen next time? He couldn't just let his own brother die.

He *wouldn't* let Marna slip away from him.

So next time . . . he reached for the edge of his bloody shirt and tossed the garment aside. Next time, Tanner would make sure he was the one hunting—and the one killing.

He'd keep both Marna and Cody safe. He had to. There just wasn't any other option for him.

He kicked off his shoes. Finished stripping. The water continued to pour from inside the shower. The steam rose, and drifted into the room like smoke.

Tanner glanced down at his arms. He'd shifted a few more times, trying to push his body's natural healing powers into overdrive. The burns and blisters had all but faded. Now there were just faint lines, scars, left to remind him of how close he'd come to death.

More scars. More pain. At this point, his body was a mess of memories. Most days, he just wanted to forget them. But these new marks . . . the ones that reminded him that he'd gotten Marna out of that blaze, that she was safe . . .

He wouldn't be forgetting them anytime soon.

Tanner stalked toward the bathroom. The old hardwood creaked beneath his feet. A few more steps, and his hand pushed the faded bathroom door open all the way. Marna stood behind a thin, clear shower curtain. He could see a perfect outline of her body. Water dripped down her curves. Such a gorgeous body. He'd touched and kissed every part of her.

I want to do it again.

"I was wondering if you would come in." Her voice drifted to him, but Marna didn't turn to face Tanner. "You sure took your time about it."

He swallowed and realized he could already taste her.

"How's your brother?" she asked. Still under the water. Still so perfect she made him ache. His cock couldn't swell any bigger.

In her. That's where he wanted to be.

He was almost drooling. Right. Way to be in control. Tanner cleared his throat. "He's stable." For now. The doc, a lady who'd barely looked twenty—but then paranormals were good at hiding their real ages—had patched Cody up the best she could. He was resting, and as for surviving, he'd better.

Marna faced him. *Finally.* She pushed the curtain aside and stared at him through the steam and pouring water. Her gaze dropped to his chest. Lingered. "You've got blood on you."

He'd always had blood on his hands. It would never wash off. He took another step toward her.

She lifted a hand. "You were an ass."

His angel and her dirty mouth. He rather liked that. When she cursed at him, he always got turned on. How screwed up was that? "I was . . ." He cleared his throat and managed to drag his gaze off her breasts. *Want them in my mouth.* "Jealous."

Her brows rose.

Did she really think they were just gonna stand there, naked, and *talk?* If so, Marna didn't understand a whole lot about shifters.

He was managing to keep his claws in and the beast on a leash, and that was pretty much all he could handle.

Tanner climbed into the too-small shower with her. Deliberately, he let his body brush against hers. "Yeah, jealous." The water crashed over him. "As in . . . if that vamp touches you again . . ." He'd been able to all but smell the vamp's lust, and it hadn't just been lust for her blood. "He'll lose those fingers." Not an idle threat.

And, unlike a few other paranormals that Tanner knew, the vamp wouldn't regrow those appendages.

"I don't want him to touch me." Her gaze met his. "I don't want him."

His hands rose. Sank into the heavy weight of her damp hair. "You want me." Not a question.

Her chin lifted. "As much as you want me."

Enough talking. He couldn't handle any more. Tanner's mouth took hers. The kiss was deep and hot, and just made the shower steam more. He'd never be able to get enough of her taste. Sweet but rich. Flowing right on his tongue. Making him insane with need.

Her body, so slick and warm, pressed against his. His fingers skimmed down her back, over the scars that he'd learned could bring her pleasure and not just more pain.

He only wanted her pleasure. Always.

She moaned into his mouth, and his fingers trailed lightly over the marks on her back. Raised ridges and the ghosts of wings that were gone. Only . . . he could almost feel those wings. So soft and silken beneath his touch.

But her hands rose and pushed against his chest. She shook her head at him, and Tanner's gut clenched.

That damn vamp was right. And Tanner had been wrong. Marna didn't want to have sex with him. She was still angry.

Some women don't want animals.

His breath seemed cold in his chest. Strange, when the water was so warm.

"This time," Marna told him, and her voice had become a husky rumble that skated right over his flesh, "it's my way."

Uh, her way? He'd take her any way.

The water poured over them, and she gave him a smile of pure sin. *Not an angel.*

Then she stepped out of the shower. Naked, body glistening, she was the sexiest thing he'd ever seen.

Compared to her, he was big, rough, and scarred.

But her eyes were hot as they tracked over him, and Marna licked her lips as she stared at his erection. "If you want me," she said, "come and get me."

Just the kind of game that the beast inside liked. Nothing was better than a hunt for your mate.

Mate.

The word had slipped through his mind again, but as she disappeared through the open doorway, he knew that was exactly what she was.

Did she realize it?

Tanner yanked the shower knob and turned off the blasting water. The drip, drip, drip of the water followed him as he followed her, nice and slow. No need to rush. He'd get her in his bed.

Sooner, not later.

Tanner didn't bother drying off. What was the point? She had him so hot steam was rising from his own skin.

The bedroom was dark. The bed was empty. His gaze scanned to the left. The right—

"Get in bed," Marna told him.

His eyebrows rose. Since when was Marna into giving orders?

But he'd keep playing, for now.

He climbed into the bed. Still naked, she crept from the shadows. Did she know how well he could see in the dark? She should. The lady seemed to know all the secrets that shifters carried.

Marna stared down at him; then she climbed onto the bed. The mattress dipped beneath her weight.

Her hands pressed against his legs. "I've been wondering . . ." Her breath blew lightly over his aroused flesh. "Just how you'd taste."

Then she put her mouth on him, and Tanner couldn't think about anything else.

Hot. Wet.

She kissed him. Sucked his flesh. Took him deep into her mouth.

Too damn good.

His flesh stretched even more. His balls tightened. Her mouth and tongue were hesitant at first, as if she was unsure, but she was so sensual and her mouth felt *fucking great.*

His hips arched toward her. He wanted to bury his hands in her hair and push her to a faster, harder rhythm. Instead, his claws sank into the mattress on either side of him. He wouldn't push her.

Pleasure.

He'd take what she gave him—and they'd both burn with pleasure.

His claws dug deeper. Her tongue licked over him.

Tanner's eyes squeezed closed. Her mouth . . . Marna was one *fast* learner. But he didn't want this to be just about him. "Stop," he growled out, "before I come."

Another lick. Another silken caress of lips and tongue, but then she pulled back. His eyes opened.

"I like the way you taste," she whispered.

He lunged off the bed. Tumbled her back onto the mattress. In one move, Tanner parted her legs and drove into her in a thrust so deep they both shuddered.

Not enough.

He withdrew. Thrust again. Her legs wrapped around him, and her hips arched. Harder. Faster. Their pants filled the air. His orgasm pushed down on him. So close.

Her first. The thought that he was the first man to know her sweet flesh still staggered him. The first, the only.

He pushed into her again. *Again.* She was wet and hot, and he took her breast into his mouth. Licked. Sucked.

She gasped his name. Her sex clenched around him. Almost there. Almost.

He drove into her once more. Felt the climax that shook

her whole body. When she opened her mouth to cry out, he caught the sound with his own lips.

Then he came. So long and hard that his body felt hollowed out and empty when he was done. Pleasure. So intense that it left him wondering . . .

How the hell did I go without her for so long?

Nothing had ever been this good. No one else ever would be.

He was so fucked.

His claws had retracted. He lifted his hand and brushed back the hair from her cheek. Her lashes rose as she stared at him. Hell, he had to be crushing her. Tanner eased his cock from her silken sheath, hating to take his body from hers, and it was right then that he realized—

No protection.

His heart stopped. Shifters didn't generally have to worry about condoms. They couldn't catch the diseases humans spread and as for pregnancy—well, most shifters *wanted* to be able to have kids. Only they couldn't have a child with just anyone. Their partner had to be a perfect genetic match-up. One strong enough to carry a shifter child.

One strong enough to be a . . . *mate.*

Like Marna was.

"I'm sorry." He couldn't look at her eyes. He pulled her back up to the head of the bed. Arranged her on the pillows and made sure to tuck the covers around her.

But she laughed. "You don't have anything to be sorry about. Trust me, Tanner, I think I was the rough one, not you." Her little nails had dug into his back, and her legs had squeezed so perfectly.

He liked it rough.

He shook his head. She didn't understand. "I didn't . . . use anything." Not *any* of the times he'd been with her.

Fucking blind. That's what he'd been. Desperate. Crazy or—

His jaw clenched. Or maybe he'd been trying to hedge his bets. Had he done that? Unconsciously? Had the beast wanted a chance to take her—*all of her?*

"Use anything?" she repeated and Tanner forced himself to meet her stare. Her eyes widened. "You mean—"

"I mean you could be pregnant right now." Angels could get pregnant, just like any other fertile being. Since his mother had been an angel, Brandt had certainly been proof of that.

It didn't happen often, so maybe they'd have luck on their side, but it *could* happen. "I'll get condoms," he said. "We'll be safe from now on." He wouldn't make this mistake again.

She simply stared back at him. Uh, yeah, why wasn't she freaking out on him? He'd just told her she could have a shifter hybrid in her belly right then. And she was just . . . staring at him.

"A child?" She bit her lower lip and tilted her head to the right. "I've never thought about having someone of my own like that."

Well, it wasn't like the hypothetical kid would *just* be hers. He'd never walk away from his child. "I wouldn't be like my father." His voice came out rough, gravelly. Tanner cleared his throat and tried again. "I promise, if something . . . if we have . . ." Could he screw this up more? Probably not. He exhaled. "I would never hurt him." She had to believe that. He would *never* hurt any child he had.

Voice soft, she said, "I never thought you would."

What?

"You've never hurt me. Why would you hurt your baby?"

Because he was the product of one screwed-up family tree. Because he was violent inside. Dangerous. "I *wouldn't.*" He'd sooner cut off his own hands than ever lay one on a child. No matter what else happened in this world, he'd never hurt an innocent.

He could still hear his own cries in his nightmares. It had

taken the child he'd been a while to learn that the tears only made his father hit more. Hit harder.

He took another deep breath and just pulled in more of her scent. Marna would never hurt a kid. She'd love the child. Protect him. Always keep him safe.

What the hell? Was he starting to picture her carrying his kid now? "It might not happen." He rolled away from her. Headed to the desk of drawers near the wall and found an extra pair of jeans inside. Kali, that doctor with the dark brown eyes and sad smile, had told him that she kept extra clothes upstairs for her patients.

He'd count himself as a patient then.

He glanced back at Marna. "I'll be careful from here on out." Shouldn't she be yelling at him? Telling him how he'd messed things up for her? It wasn't like she could actually want to be saddled with his kid.

Hybrids weren't exactly the easiest of the supernaturals to raise. They both knew how the last shifter and angel mix had turned out. Brandt had been more devil than savior. "You can yell if you want," he offered cautiously.

Her brows rose. "Why?"

Because I fucked up. Because I didn't take good enough care of you. "Because I put you at risk! I could have gotten you pregnant."

She shrugged. *Shrugged.*

She might just make him lose his mind.

Then she said, "I think I'd like to have a baby." Her words almost broke him.

Careful now, he asked, "A baby . . . or *my* baby?" Because if any other dumbass came around her . . .

She might want a child with another angel. A pureblood. And Bastion had sure been sniffing around her.

Bastion could screw off.

Tanner took a nice, long count to five. The red faded

from his vision. He could actually stay sane. He could. "I didn't mean—"

"Yours."

The panther roared inside, pride filling him. Tanner advanced toward her. "Marna, I—"

Footsteps raced up the stairs. Heavy. Hard. Tanner's head whipped up and around to the door just as a fist pounded on the wood. "Kali needs you downstairs, shifter!" Riley yelled. *"Now!"*

Marna jumped from the bed. Her back was to Tanner, and he glimpsed her wounds. He frowned a moment. The red scars looked like they'd risen higher, and when he'd touched them before, the ridges had actually felt more solid, too. He hadn't really thought much about it then because he'd been too lost in the best orgasm of his life, but—

They look different. They felt different.

"Your brother's dying!" Riley shouted.

He forgot about her scars and leapt for the door.

Chapter Sixteen

Marna raced behind Tanner as he hurried down the stairs. When he'd yanked open the bedroom door, she'd immediately conjured her clothes. Being naked in front of Riley wasn't an option she was in the mood to consider.

She only wanted to be naked with Tanner. For Tanner.

He leapt over the last few stairs and darted toward the back room. Marna wasn't sure what she expected—maybe a makeshift operating room like Cody had once had at his place in the swamp—but inside the tiny room, she only saw a bed. A wall of surgical instruments. And a line of refrigerators that hummed.

She took a breath and caught the heavy scent of blood.

"Usually vamps are the only ones who come to see Kali." Riley was at her side. "We figured out fast that we needed one of our own to help us when things got desperate."

The small woman with the dark eyes and fragile beauty—she was a vamp? The lady's hands were currently covered in blood because she had her fingers shoved over Cody's bleeding wounds.

"The sutures didn't hold. The bleeding's too intense!" The woman—Kali—glanced up, and Marna clearly saw the fear on her face.

Cody's eyes were open. They looked faded, tired, but his

gaze found Tanner's. "I-it's . . . okay." His words were a bare whisper.

"The hell it is!" Tanner was at his side instantly. "We can fix you, Cody. *We can fix you.* Just hold on and—"

Cody's body started to shake.

Marna stepped forward. "Give him my blood." It had worked before, with Tanner. It would work again.

Kali looked at her. "I tried giving him a transfusion already. It didn't—"

"You didn't try my blood." Marna held out her arm. "Take my blood. Give it to him."

Kali frowned at her. The woman managed to look angry, desperate, and hopeful all at once. "And your blood's special because—"

"It just fuckin' is," was Riley's response as he took what actually looked like a protective stride toward Marna. "Now stop asking questions. Take the blood, and give it to the demon."

"N-no," Cody's whisper.

Marna looked over at him. Tanner had put his hands on his brother's chest, and she knew he was trying to stop the blood. Trying, but it wasn't going to work. His fingers were just getting soaked in blood.

Kali reached for a needle and syringe. "You the right type?"

Humans had types. Angels didn't. "I'm the only type you need."

Kali's brow rose, but she didn't ask any more questions. She just said, "Then I'm gonna rig this thing because we don't have time to waste. Your veins to his, and if he dies . . ." Her breath rushed out. "Then at least we tried."

Marna wondered if the others could smell the light scent of flowers that had drifted into the room. Death was close.

"N-no." Cody began to thrash on the narrow bed. "Don't w-want . . ."

"You want to live, don't you?" Tanner snapped at him. "Then you let us help you."

Cody shook his head. "W-won't take her . . . bl-blood. "

Kali hesitated.

Tanner swallowed and stared down at his brother. Just looking at Tanner's face hurt Marna then, and she rubbed at the ache in her chest. An ache that seemed centered right over her heart.

Voice quiet, Tanner said, "If you don't take her blood, you'll die. Are you really gonna make me watch you die?"

Lines of pain bracketed Cody's mouth. "If . . . t-take it . . ." Every word seemed to bring him more agony, but he kept struggling to speak. "Go back to . . . wh-what I was . . . l-like . . ."

"You'll never be that way again! I promise. I can help you. I can—"

"A-addic . . . ted . . ." was Cody's hushed whisper. "L-lost."

Marna lifted her hands and stared down at the faint, blue outline of the veins at her wrists. Someone who didn't want her blood? Now that was a change.

"I'm not letting you die." Tanner was adamant. Fierce. The way she liked him.

Blood dripped from Cody's lips. "Pl . . . please . . ." His whisper was almost painful to hear. "One t-time . . . let m-me . . . do . . ." His body jerked. "S-something . . . right."

"You've always done the right thing!" Tanner yelled back. Yells and whispers. So opposite, but both so desperate. So sad. "You were the good one. The one who had a chance. We both know I'm screwed up. That I've got the bastard's darkness in me."

Marna frowned. Tanner didn't have darkness inside of him. He was good. Kind.

Kali and Riley just watched the brothers and didn't speak, and Marna found she had no words to say, either.

Another tremor shook Cody. *"Please . . ."*

Tanner's hands were still on his chest. "What the hell am I supposed to do without you?"

"L-love . . . her."

The words were so garbled Marna wasn't sure if she'd heard correctly. Her gaze dropped to Cody's body. His stomach . . . how much pain he must feel. How much suffering. Why hadn't a death angel come for him yet? If Cody wasn't going to take her blood, why did he have to suffer?

"Why?" The whisper was hers, but then she noticed . . .

Something was happening to Tanner's hands. A faint glow appeared around his fingers. Frowning, she stepped closer. She'd never seen anything like that before, and in her very long lifetime, she thought for sure that she'd seen everything. "Tanner?"

"What the hell?" Riley's voice. He'd seen it, too.

Kali's gaze flew back to her patient. "What are you doing?"

"Trying to make this bastard live! If he doesn't take the blood, he'll—"

"No." Marna cut through his words. She was almost close enough to touch Tanner now. Only she was afraid to touch Tanner. That light . . . "What are you doing with your hands?"

Tanner stared at her, face tense; then he looked down at his hands, resting on Cody's wounds. At the fingers with their faint white light.

"You're a healer." Kali's voice was relieved. "Jeez, man, you should have said that right away. I thought you were a shifter—"

"I am." He was still staring at his glowing fingertips.

Cody wasn't jerking any longer. His eyes had closed. Were his wounds trying to close, too? It looked like less blood was pouring from him, but maybe she was just hoping too much.

Kali leaned in closer and stared at Cody's wounds. "Then how the hell are you doing this?"

"I don't know." The light began to dim.

Cody's body trembled.

"Don't stop!" Marna realized she'd yelled and cleared her throat. "Your mother, Tanner . . . your mother was a healer."

His hands weren't glowing any longer. He stared at his fingers and clenched his fists. "But I'm just a killer."

No, he was so much more.

He sucked in a deep breath. "I told you, I didn't get any of her power. I've never been able to—"

Marna grabbed him and yanked him back around to face her. "Just because you haven't before, it doesn't mean that you aren't using that power now." Who knew what had happened. Maybe he'd just gotten desperate enough to unlock a magic buried deep inside himself. She'd sure heard of wilder things in her time. His mother *had* been a healer, and maybe Tanner hadn't realized it, but she'd passed on her gift to him. "You've got your father's beast inside, but you've also got part of her in there, too."

He stared back at her. She could see that he wanted to hope but he was holding back. Too many years of facing the darkness alone?

He wasn't alone anymore. "You can do this," Marna told him. "Just *try,* Tanner. Try for me. Try for Cody." If it didn't work, she'd shove her blood down that demon's throat. Marna wouldn't stand by helplessly while Tanner suffered.

Losing his brother would make her shifter suffer. She wouldn't allow that. No one was hurting him any longer. Not while she was there.

It was time someone started to protect Tanner.

The ridges on her shoulder blades seemed to burn and itch again, but Marna ignored them. Right then, Tanner was all that she could think about.

"Put your hands back on him." Kali's voice. Sharp.

Tanner stared at Marna a moment longer; then he put his

hands over Cody's wounds. "Nothing's happening." Fury ripped through his words.

"Because you're not making it happen." Kali's eyes were blazing with dark heat. "I've seen a healer work before. I've been walking this earth for three hundred years and been patching up the wounded for most of that time. You really think you're the first to come my way?"

She barely looked twenty-one. Vampires . . . so tricky. And . . . Marna would have once thought . . . *evil.*

Once. But Riley was different. This Kali, she was different, too. Not mistakes as some of the angels claimed. There was far, far more to them.

Hope. Passion. Life.

"You've got to pull the power up from inside." Kali put her hands on top of Tanner's. "You have to want him to live more than you want anything else. You have to take your power . . ." Her gaze dropped back to Cody. "And give it to him."

Jaw clenching, Tanner stared down at his brother. Cody wasn't moving now. Barely breathing. "I'm . . . trying," Tanner gritted. "Nothing's happening."

Fighting to keep her voice calm, Marna told him, "You can do this." But if he didn't do it in about the next thirty seconds, she'd make—

A faint glow appeared around Tanner's fingers.

"Sonofabitch." Riley's stunned voice.

But Tanner didn't look his way. He stared at his hands, so did Marna, and she watched as, very slowly, Cody's wounds began to heal. What had been slashed now slipped back together, mending, bonding, and it was one of the most amazing things she'd ever seen.

Then she felt Tanner's body tremble against hers. Her gaze flew to his face. He was pale—no, *white* and sweat had beaded his upper lip. "Tanner?"

He didn't answer her.

Then she understood, too late.

You have to take your power. That's what Kali had said. Take it—

And give it to him.

But if he gave Cody everything, then what would be left?

Cody's breath was coming easily now, the wounds almost closed. He could survive them now.

"Stop," Marna told Tanner. But he didn't. He just kept pouring his power right into his brother.

"Stop!" This time, Marna didn't wait for Tanner to obey. She shoved him away from that bed, and he stumbled back a few feet. His sluggish movements told her just how weak he'd become.

She didn't like him this way. She wanted him strong. He fell to the floor. His eyes began to sag closed.

Cody was fine, but what about Tanner? Marna lifted her arm toward the vampire. "Get your needle ready." Because she was going to make sure Tanner was back to one hundred percent strength and power.

It was her turn to take care of him.

"It's the blood."

Tanner heard the words, muffled at first, but they pushed through his consciousness, and his eyes opened.

He was on a bed. A bed that still carried Marna's scent, but she wasn't around.

His brother sat in a chair just a few feet away, watching him.

Tanner leapt up. "You're alive!" He ran to his brother and yanked him out of his chair. The bear hug he gave the guy could have crushed bones, but, hey, Cody was a demon, he could stand a little pain.

Especially since he was healed now.

I did that.

For once, he hadn't destroyed or killed. He'd saved someone. How the hell was that for a change?

"Thanks to you," Cody said. "I'm most definitely alive."

Tanner stepped back and studied his brother. There was no sign of an injury that he could see. Hell, the guy didn't even look pale. He'd been moments away from dying—*I felt the cold touch of Death, that bastard, coming too close*—but Cody was as good as new now.

Maybe even better than new.

"All my life . . ." Tanner gave a quick laugh. When was the last time he'd laughed? "I thought I was just a killer. I never knew I could—"

Cody's lips firmed. "It's the blood," he said again.

Tanner blinked. Then he rubbed a hand over his face. How had he gotten back up to the bedroom? He remembered the glow from his fingers. Marna's voice, telling him to *stop.*

He hadn't stopped. *She'd* stopped him.

Cody cleared his throat. "I told you, angel blood can amplify a demon's powers. It . . . looks like that same amplification is true for all supernaturals."

Tanner's gaze narrowed.

"Because you took Marna's blood, you tapped into the dormant genetics your mother passed to you."

Marna had helped him to become this way?

"I don't know how long the changes will last. Probably until the blood in you gets diluted, but since you just got a fresh supply—"

Tanner held up one hand. "Wait, I just got a what?"

"You've got to understand how dangerous this is. Why you *can't* heal again." Cody's voice and face were grim as he said, "When you heal, you give your own life force. If you give away too much, you'll be the one who dies. That's how . . ." He glanced away and rubbed a hand over his face.

His shoulders were tense as he muttered, "I never told you. I didn't want you to hate me."

Now what the hell was the guy rambling about? Cody was alive. Tanner was alive. He could freaking *heal*. Shouldn't they be doing some celebrating?

Cody lowered his hand. "You tried so hard to protect me, but there was one day you weren't there." Cody glanced back at him. "I *should* have told you. Years ago. I know. It's just that you were the only family that ever mattered to me. I couldn't . . ."

Tanner's heart began to beat faster. He didn't like this, and the punch in his gut told him that dislike was about to get one hell of a lot worse. "Told me what?"

Silence. Cody swallowed and his gaze kept holding Tanner's. When had those lines appeared on Cody's face? When had he stopped being the kid that Tanner protected and turned into the demon who stood before him?

Then Cody spoke. "One day, you were gone—off training with Brandt—and our father came at me." His hand lifted to his chest. "He drove his claws into my heart, and he left me to die."

"What?" And his brother had neglected to tell him this damn important fact? *"You almost died?"*

"But . . ." A rasp of breath, then, "Your mother was there. Katherine found me." Cody swallowed and still held Tanner's stare. "Her hands were glowing, and she put them right on my chest. My whole body seemed to pulse with power when she touched me, and Katherine kept telling me, 'It's gonna be all right.' "

Tanner could barely remember his mother. Only glimpses. Flashes. The impression of someone *good*.

She loved me. He'd held tight to that one truth. Always.

"But helping me made her weak." Cody's voice broke. "Just like helping me today made you weak."

"I don't feel weak." He felt stronger than ever before.

Cody shook his head. "That's only because your angel gave you blood. Without her, you'd still be in a coma."

He stiffened.

"There wasn't an angel around to help your mother. There was only our father. He found us. Saw what she'd done, and when he attacked, Katherine was too weak to fight back." Pain whispered beneath his words. "And I was too scared. I stood there, and I watched her die." A stark confession.

Tanner felt as if his own heart had been clawed out then. He remembered coming back in and seeing the shifters carrying his mother's body away. He'd screamed and punched at them.

But she'd already been gone.

"If Marna hadn't given you blood today, you would've been too damn weak to protect yourself. You have to understand what's going on." Now Cody's words came faster. "I know you think this new power is some kind of gift. That it makes you better because it came from *her*." Cody shook his head. "But it doesn't. It makes you weak. Vulnerable. Just like it made Katherine weak. And you've got to promise never to use it again."

"Did she . . ." Tanner stopped, cleared his throat. His mother had been gone so long. So why did he hurt so much? "Did my mother say anything . . . ?" Hell, why was he even asking?

The floor creaked behind him. Tanner looked over and found Marna standing in the doorway. She'd been there, of course, the whole time. Her scent had come to him like a soothing touch the minute she'd stepped into the doorway.

"She said your name." Cody brushed past him. "It was the last thing she said."

She loved me.

Cody was beside Marna now. He stood near her, but didn't touch her. "I'm sorry." Shame lurked in his words. "If I'd been stronger . . ."

Then his mother wouldn't have died? "He never kept his women around too long." Forever hadn't been a concept their father understood. Since he hadn't been the sharing sort, he viewed death as the only option for getting rid of his unwanted mates.

The bastard really had been born without a soul. And to think, most supernaturals believed shifters had *two* souls. Those of beasts and men.

Maybe he only got the soul of the beast. Maybe that was why his father had only known fury and violence.

Shoulders hunched and steps slow, Cody crept from the room. After a moment, Marna came inside and quietly closed the door. "You scared me," she said.

He didn't move toward her. Tanner felt raw inside. Dangerous.

My mother died for Cody.

"Do you blame him, for her death?"

Tanner shook his head. *She was always trying to save the pack.* "She died when I was seven. He was only four then." Just four, and he'd taken claws to the heart. "Saving others . . . that's who she was."

She'd never walked away from anyone in pain.

Marna studied him a moment, then said, "I think you're a lot like her."

No, I'm like him. Marna was close enough to touch now. Why did he feel that touching her would make her dirty? *She deserves better.* "You weren't supposed to give me your blood again."

"And you weren't supposed to start seizing right in front of me." She gave a little shrug. "I guess fate had other plans for us."

Fate could be a cruel bitch. He'd known that since his second birthday. "Did Kali see you?"

A nod. "Who do you think ran the transfusion?"

Shit. "Then I'll make sure she doesn't talk. She won't—"

"How are you going to make sure?" Her hand touched his arm. Her fingers were so light against his skin. "She's already gone. With you and Cody out of danger, she slipped away."

Fuck. His muscles tightened. "Then she could be selling you out right now. Telling everyone where to find angel blood." They had to find her. They had to—

Marna gave a slow nod. "She could be, or she could have just been going out to help someone else. That's what she does, you know. She helps. And she drinks her blood from a bag, not a live source."

Ah . . . that was his Marna, being too trusting again. "Is that the story she gave you? Baby, how many times do I have to tell you? A lie from a supernatural sounds like the sweet truth from an—"

"Angel?" she finished with raised brows.

He turned away from her. Headed to the window. Someone had opened it, letting in a spill of light from the stars and moon.

A rustle of sound teased his ears. Like wings . . .

A shadow moved closer to the cabin. "Your blood," he said slowly, staring out at that shadow, "makes me see things I shouldn't see."

The floor creaked beneath her feet. "Like what?"

Tanner glanced over his shoulder at her. So beautiful. "Like the shadows of wings that were cut from your back."

Her lips parted in surprise. Tanner stepped away from the window and headed closer to her. Moving to protect. "And like that asshole angel who's coming toward us right now."

"Someone's coming? But—"

But he was already there.

Tanner saw the angel fly right through the window opening, twisting his body easily, fluidly, and then landing on his feet. The angel's eyes were only on Marna. For a being that was supposed to be stone-cold when it came to emotions, that golden stare was sure burning hot.

Tanner stepped a foot to the left and blocked his view. "Hello, again, asshole."

Bastion's gaze snapped to his face. A muscle flexed in the angel's jaw. "Can you do nothing but take from her?"

Tanner's shoulders stretched. He hadn't intended to take her blood again. Not like that detail had been written down in his game plan. "Can you do nothing but be a prick?"

Bastion lunged forward. Because he'd wanted to attack since he'd first watched Bastion stare at Marna with lust in his eyes, Tanner swiped out with his fist. The punch slammed right into the side of the angel's face—

Even as Bastion shoved his hand against Tanner's chest.

"No!" Marna's scream.

The touch burned him, as if he'd been branded, cutting into skin and stealing his breath. In that burning instant, Tanner realized that the bastard had just given him the Death Touch.

Except he wasn't dying. Tanner glanced down at the hand that still rested against his chest, and when he looked up once more, he knew his smile held an evil edge. "My turn." Then he lifted his claws.

Fear flashed over Bastion's face. He stumbled back, his eyes wild as he looked for an escape. Fool. Didn't he know just how much the beast liked to hunt? Tanner stalked forward. His claws were now ripping from both hands. "This is gonna—"

"Tanner!" Marna's voice froze him. Then she was there, putting her body between him and the angel. "Don't." Her gaze dropped to his claws, and she shuddered. "*Don't.* Don't make him like me."

It pissed him off that she even said the words. But, with

care—*because it was her*—he lifted his hand and caught her chin. "Baby, I won't touch his wings."

She blinked and a faint furrow appeared between her brows.

"But I am gonna kick his ass. That angel needs to stop lusting after you, and I'll make sure he does." *Time for Bastion to realize that she's mine.* He wasn't giving her up to anyone or anything.

Even an angel who *might* be better for her.

Mine.

Because he did believe in forever.

"I'm not afraid of you, shifter," Bastion shouted. "You think because you're high on angel blood that you're some kind of threat?" A sneer twisted his face. "You're nothing, you're—"

Marna stepped to the side. "A *little* ass beating." Her gaze turned to Bastion. "Because no one calls Tanner 'nothing'."

Fuck but he could love her. *Could?*

The angel tried to fight. Tanner slammed his fist into Bastion's stomach. When the guy doubled over, Tanner kicked out. Punched. Tanner didn't use his claws though because, well, he didn't want to get any angel blood on Marna.

And you want to show her you can have control.

Bastion caught Tanner's fist in one hand. Froze the blow. *Ah, so he was gonna fight back.*

"I'm not as weak as you think," Bastion muttered. Then he hurtled Tanner across the room.

When he smashed into the wall, Tanner laughed at the impact. Now, things could get interesting. He leapt back to his feet and charged across the room. His right shoulder plowed into Bastion's stomach, and he took that angel down old-school, football-tackle style. He might have even heard a bone or two crunch. Sweet music.

Tanner rose easily and stared down at the groaning angel. "I think you're starting to—"

Bastion's legs swept out. Nice move, but predictable. Tanner dodged easily. Grunting, panting, Bastion climbed to his feet. Aw, was the angel's nose bleeding? Too bad.

"Okay." Marna grabbed Tanner's arm. "Enough fun."

Not really, but for her, he'd stop. He'd proved his point. *I can kick your ass, angel.* Any day of the week, and if the angel wanted, twice on Sunday.

Bastion swiped the blood away. "You're . . ." He grabbed his nose, cracked it, and put the bones back in place. "Messing with fate."

Tanner shrugged. "Then fate shouldn't mess with me."

Bastion's teeth ground together. His gaze, bright with anger, lit on Marna. "You've given a shifter resistance to the Touch. What do you think will—"

"Times are changing." While Bastion's voice had been heavy with emotion, Marna's was cold. Quiet. "Angel blood is being traded on the streets here in New Orleans, and I'm betting in other places, too. *We're* starting to be the ones who are hunted."

His eyes widened. "Wh-what?"

"Tanner isn't the only one that you'll find hard to kill. The secret's out," she said, her shoulders rising and falling in a sad shrug, "so that means angels are on hit lists." Her lips pressed into a tense line, and after a moment, she said, "So make sure you spread the word. We all need to stay on guard. It's not just about us taking them anymore."

It was about angels being the prey.

And angels being killers. Tanner's gaze swept the angry angel once more. "One of your kind is killing in New Orleans," Tanner said.

But Bastion's smile mocked him. "Death angels kill every day. That's not—"

"No." Marna's voice. With more heat. "We take souls. We follow the orders we're given. We take those who are meant to die." Her gaze held Bastion's. "This is different. We think—we think it's a punishment angel, and he's taking the forms of other people to kill."

Bastion's smile faded away.

"He took my form," Marna said, "and killed two shifters."

"And he used my face when he put a cop in the hospital," Tanner added.

Bastion's head shook. "A punishment angel wouldn't ever use another angel's face—"

"He almost killed my brother just hours ago." Tanner's hands clenched as he remembered the cold fear that had coursed through him. And this guy was trying to play innocent? *Not lying, but still twisting the truth.* "You fucking know. You were there when we were fighting to keep him alive."

Bastion's eyelashes flickered in the faintest of moves.

Tanner advanced toward him. "You were downstairs, waiting to take his soul, so don't pretend otherwise. I've got your scent. *I know.*" He was so in the mood to keep kicking ass. "What I want to know—*right now*—is did you come after that bastard left, or were you there when that angel attacked Cody and left him to die in that alley?"

CHAPTER SEVENTEEN

"Were you, Bastion?" Marna pressed. "Did you see the punishment angel who attacked him? *Were you there?*" Because if Bastion knew who was playing a deadly game with her life, and he didn't tell her . . .

Maybe she'd let Tanner keep up that ass-kicking. Or maybe she'd try a little ass-kicking herself.

"He wasn't on my list." The words were spoken quietly as Bastion's powerful wings folded behind his body.

"What damn list?" Tanner wanted to know.

But Marna already understood. "The death list." Because there really was a list of names, a list of those who would soon have their souls taken.

"Cody wasn't on the list. I had no warning about him, I just—" Bastion exhaled. "There was no foretelling for his case. When I got to him, he was already on the ground, with half of his stomach cut out."

Marna flinched.

Tanner didn't move. "And his killer?"

"There was *no* sign of another angel there." Bastion was adamant.

"No scent?" Tanner pressed. "No fucking flutter of wings? *Nothing?*"

"Just your brother and the blood. There were humans a

few streets over, I could hear them, but nothing else." Bastion turned away from them and headed back to the window. "The guy isn't an angel. You need to look closer to home for this killer." Then he leapt through the open window, wings soaring and breaking glass in the top windowpane as he flew high up into the dark sky.

Marna stared after him. Her old life had never been so far away. As if to remind her of what she'd lost, the scars on her back seemed to burn. Burning, itching—why wouldn't they just stop bothering her? *Reminding me of what's gone.*

She put her back to the window. "There's one person who can tell us what he saw." A guy who'd gotten a very up-close look at the killer.

And Cody was recovered enough now to tell them everything.

Tanner nodded. Marna pushed past him, ready to find Cody and—

He stopped her. "Do you still miss . . ." Tanner began, but then his words died away.

She knew what he'd been about to say. "Heaven? Sometimes." How could she not? "But I'm finding there are things here that I like very, very much."

His gaze lifted to meet hers.

She offered him a smile. "Now let's go find out who this guy is and let's stop him." Because she was ready to move on with her life. Humans knew joy—she'd seen it on their faces. Maybe, just maybe, she could know it, too.

A home. A family. Tanner . . . and a child? Perhaps all of that could be hers.

But not with the killer waiting out there. Not with him playing his games.

Finish him. Then she could really start living.

Only . . . as soon as they opened the bedroom door, Tanner swore. He rushed past her and barreled down the stairs.

Marna heard the faint sound then, too. A car's motor, speeding away.

Tanner yanked open the front door. Marna was steps behind him, and she saw the glow of fading taillights.

"Cody," she whispered.

The sagging front porch creaked as Riley stepped from the shadows. "The demon said he had hunting to do."

"Sonofabitch." Tanner stared after those red lights with his body tight.

"The guy was muttering about owing you, and making things right." Riley stopped at Marna's side, but his eyes were on Tanner.

Tanner threw a hard glance over his shoulder. "And you just let him drive away?"

"Why would I stop him?" Riley wanted to know. "I paid my debt." He gave a little salute to Marna. "I don't owe anyone now." He started walking back into the house.

Marna caught his arm. "We were even before this. Now I'm the one who owes you."

He sent her a quick smile, one that showed the edges of his fangs. "I like having an angel in my debt."

Why did everyone seem to keep forgetting? "I'm not an angel anymore."

His grin widened. "Even better."

A snarl came from Tanner.

But Riley just laughed. He reached into his pocket and pulled out a set of keys. "There's a motorcycle hidden about a hundred yards to the east, under an oak. Take it. Join the hunt." He tossed the keys to Tanner and gave him a little salute. "And now, that means you're in my debt, too."

Whistling, he headed into the cabin.

"Bastard," Tanner muttered.

Yes, but he was a bastard who'd helped them. She caught Tanner's hand. Laced her fingers with his. "Come on." If they hurried, they'd be able to catch Cody. Dawn would come soon, and this battle would best be fought under the cover of darkness.

It was easier to hide the truth from humans in the dark.

They raced through the brush, heading east quickly through the night. Marna had to double-time it in order to keep up with Tanner. Her shifter was so fast.

Then they were at the motorcycle. Tanner climbed on, and she jumped behind him, holding tight. The engine burst to life with a growl as great as Tanner's panther, and they leapt forward.

Her heart slammed into her ribs as they gave chase.

She couldn't see any sign of Cody's vehicle now, but he had to be close still. The motorcycle leapt off the old path and onto the twisting two-lane highway with a jarring thud that had her holding even tighter to Tanner. Faster, faster. Her hair whipped behind her as they drove.

Another corner.

Another tight turn.

Her thighs squeezed around his as the vibration from the bike shook her legs. When had she grown so used to the adrenaline rush of danger? When had it started to turn her on?

Not such an angel.

Maybe it was time for everyone to realize that.

Another turn. Her body was plastered against his. Another—

A siren screamed and a police cruiser seemed to leap right out of the darkness. Blue and red lights flashed in a blinding whir.

The cops had found them. Had tracked them.

Tanner didn't slow. Faster, faster . . .

Another turn. Another tight corner, another—

A car was blocking the road. No, not a car. An SUV. Riley's vehicle—the one Cody had taken. Tanner tried to stop the motorcycle. Brakes squealed and sparks flew into the air—

But there wasn't enough time to stop. They were going too fast. The SUV was too close. The motorcycle slammed into the side of the vehicle. Marna tried to hold on to Tanner, but she was ripped away from him. She flew through the air—*not like when I had wings.* This flight was terrifying, short, and her body slammed back into the pavement after only moments.

Her skin ripped away at the impact. Pain burned through her side and her arms.

Metal crunched and groaned. Those sirens were squealing, hurting her ears. Marna tried to rise—

"It's okay," a familiar voice told her, "I've got you." Then arms wrapped around her body. Too tight. Too hard. And she was flying again. Rising higher and higher into the sky. She tried to fight the hold on her but couldn't break free. When Marna glanced down, she saw the wreckage below. Tanner and Cody were both there, running toward her. Tanner was screaming her name.

But she couldn't break free and get back to him.

"No! *Marna!*" Tanner stared up, body shaking with fury, as the angel took Marna away from him. Fucking Bastion. He wasn't taking her. He—

"He flew right at me." Cody's words tumbled out. Blood dripped from the gash in his forehead. "I was trying to get back to town—and my windshield shattered. I couldn't even see him, not at first." Cody's breath shuddered out. "He forced me to stop."

And he'd taken Marna. Tanner had caught a glimpse of the angel's black wings. He'd moved too fast for Tanner to see his face, but he knew just which angel had come calling.

A door slammed behind him. Footsteps raced toward them. And those sirens kept screaming.

"Tanner!"

He couldn't see Marna anymore. But he would find her. The angel wouldn't take her.

"Tanner!" Hard hands slammed into him, and Tanner jerked his gaze away from the dark sky and found himself staring at his partner's tense face. Wait, what the hell was Jonathan doing there?

"Man, we are in one big-ass shit storm," Jonathan told him. The guy was sweating and shaking. "I've been searching this swamp for you all night."

Tanner shook his head. "I have to—"

"What? Go after the girl? Not right now. Right now, you have to avoid the damn manhunt that is coming your way. They found the captain's body, and now, they are looking for *you*."

Did everything really have to go to hell at the same exact time? He glanced around. The motorcycle was smashed and twisted into a heavy mass of undriveable metal. The SUV was totaled. Only one way out. "Then take me into custody." He headed for the patrol car. The same patrol car that he'd raced past moments before.

Jonathan grabbed his arm in a surprisingly strong grip. Huh. Maybe the human wasn't so weak after all. "Are you insane?" Jonathan demanded with narrowed eyes. "Why do you think I was hauling ass to find you first? I'm trying to keep you *out* of custody."

Tanner jerked free and kept marching toward the car. The guy wasn't *that* strong. "Maybe I wasn't clear enough." He didn't climb in the back of the car. He slid behind the wheel. "I'm taking this car." More sirens were screaming. Coming ever closer

"Shit." Jonathan jumped in beside him. "You're not leaving without me. I'll be damned if I have to keep chasing your ass."

"You're not goin' without me!" Cody, weaving a bit, stood in front of the vehicle. "I won't let you face him alone!"

Jonathan stared through the windshield at the bleeding demon. Then he shook his head. "I think it's time you brought me up to speed, *partner.*"

Tanner's hands clenched around the wheel. Being in the car was the perfect camouflage for him. While the other cops were out beating the streets in their search for a fugitive, a cop killer—*time for me to kiss that badge good-bye*—he'd be safely behind the wheel. Tracking an angel who was bent on hell.

You aren't walking away after this. He'd make sure Bastion didn't have a second chance to go after Marna. He'd seen the lust so clearly in the angel's eyes. He should have expected—

"Tell me," Jonathan insisted as he slammed his fist against the dash, making the radio shake.

Cody ran around to the back of the car. He climbed in, sending blood drops raining against the cage that kept suspects in check.

"Drive," Cody told him.

Like he needed to be told. Tanner kept the windows down. He pulled in the scents around them and got locked on the one that mattered most.

Sin and sweetness. Rich, lush woman. A lost angel.

And he followed her. He shoved the gas pedal to the floor, weaved around the wreckage, and asked his partner, "You know Marna's an angel of death . . ." She *had* been. "Well, one of those other death assholes just took her away." The patrol car raced through the darkness. "And we're getting her back."

They landed on a rooftop. The sun was rising, just cracking open the sky with streaks of red and gold. The instant Marna's feet touched down, Bastion let her go.

Marna whirled on him and drove her fist up into his jaw. He didn't flinch. *He's getting used to pain.*

His gaze, steady and intense, just held hers. "I don't care if I make you angry."

When had he gone crazy? How had she missed it? "What were you thinking? You can't just abduct—"

He gave a tight shake of his head. "I'm keeping you safe."

"No, you're marking yourself for death, that's what you're doing." She spun away from him and hurried to the edge of the roof. They were back in the Quarter. She knew these streets. Tanner would be searching for her. How long would it take before he turned his attention back to the city?

Doesn't matter. She wasn't going to wait around for Tanner to find her. She'd go back and find him.

Strong fingers closed around her arms. "If you go back to the shifter, you'll be the one dying."

Shocked, she turned and her gaze lifted to his. "Tanner would never hurt me." She believed that with complete certainty.

"It's not him I'm worried about."

Her heart raced faster in her chest. "You *did* see who was in that alley with Cody."

He shook his head. "You know angels can't lie."

She struggled to remember his exact words. Then—*dammit!* "Just tell me! Tell me so I can keep Tanner safe. I have to know—"

His hands tightened on her arms. "I *don't* know! If I knew, I would have killed him already."

His words shocked her into silence.

"All I know . . ." His voice dropped, and he exhaled on a long sigh. ". . . is that my list has changed."

The death list.

He swallowed, and Marna saw the flash of pain in his eyes. "And now, you're on the list."

* * *

"Death angels." Jonathan gave a slow nod that Tanner saw from the corner of his eye. "Okay, so there are different *types* of angels? I thought—I thought they were all the same."

"Hell, no. They're like anyone else—some good, some evil. The most dangerous ones…they have to be stopped." Which was what he'd do to Bastion once he caught the guy. Bastion had flown so fast, it was hard to trace the scent. As soon as he'd reached the Quarter, Tanner had lost that elusive smell. Now he circled around, gaze darting from the left to the right. *Where are you?*

"How can angels . . . be bad?" Now Jonathan sounded confused. Who could blame the guy? Humans were at a serious disadvantage in the paranormal game. The guy had already been jerked around once. No telling what bull the captain had fed him.

"The world is full of good and evil." This came from Cody. Had the guy stopped bleeding yet? "Even angels can sin."

Right. Tanner said, "And they can get their lily white asses tossed from heaven." Like Sammael. Like Az. Soon . . . like Bastion?

"Is that—is that what happened with your angel?" Jonathan asked as his fingers drummed against the dashboard. He'd dented it with his fist earlier. "Did your Marna get cast out?"

"No," he snapped. He needed to shift. The panther would be able to pick up Marna's scent so much better. But dawn was coming, and there were already too many humans out in the streets. There wasn't enough space to hide the beast in the daylight.

"Marna was different," Cody said softly as he leaned forward, and his fingers curled around the cage. "Our brother Brandt cut her wings away."

Jonathan gave a low whistle. "That's one sick family you have there," he muttered. "I hope you gave that bastard exactly what he deserved."

I didn't. But someone else sure did. "He's in hell."

Jonathan grunted. "Sounds like he's just where he needs to be."

"You're saying that I'm going to . . . die?" But she didn't want to die yet. She had just really started to live. She wanted to stay there, with Tanner, to have a child—

Bastion shook his head. "It's not going to happen. I won't let it. I'll keep you safe. You don't have to worry."

Then she realized what he was doing, and it broke her heart. "You can't . . . you can't change what's meant to be." An angel was supposed to follow orders. To take the souls in their care.

She knew of another angel who'd refused to take a soul. The angel had been right here, just blocks away in New Orleans. One dark night, the angel called Keenan had refused to take the soul of a human woman. He'd thought that Nicole St. James should have the chance to live.

For his sin, he'd been punished. He'd fallen.

A tear slipped down her cheek. Why did things have to be this way? Why did everything have to be so twisted? "You can't fall because of me."

His hand lifted. His fingers trembled as he brushed the tear away. "I'm not going to stand back and watch you suffer." His jaw clenched. "I'll do what I must in order to keep you safe. Others have changed fate. I can do it, too." A pause. "I've done it once already, and I didn't fall. I'm still here."

What? "You know you can't get away with that. It's only a matter of time until—until—" *Until his crimes caught up with him.* She shook her head. "I won't let you be punished for me!"

His hand was still against her cheek. "You never should have been a death angel. I know. I saw how much taking each soul hurt you."

She shouldn't have felt pain. He shouldn't be feeling pain now. They'd always been taught—

Angels don't feel.

It looked like they'd all been taught wrong. Was that why so many were falling? Because they couldn't hold the emotions in check any longer?

"I'm going to hunt the one who is after you. I will kill him." A vow from Bastion.

No. She couldn't let him sacrifice so much for her.

Marna drew in a deep breath. She didn't want to hurt Bastion, but sometimes, there wasn't a choice. Sometimes you had to hurt the ones you loved.

I won't let him be punished for me.

She caught his hand and curled her fingers around his flesh. "Did I ever tell you," she asked softly as her gaze met his, "how much I care for you?"

His eyes widened. "Marna . . ."

"So I hope you understand why I have to do this." She pulled up the power that had been growing within her. *Getting stronger each day.* And Marna blasted that energy right at Bastion. Not enough power to kill him, never that, but enough to send the angel flying away from her and crashing onto the rooftop. "I'm sorry," she whispered as she turned away. "But it's my battle, and I won't have you turned into—"

Me.

Broken. Lost.

"Marna—" Her name, gasped, weak.

She hurried to the edge of the roof. She'd never tried this without wings before. Hopefully, it wouldn't hurt her too much. Either way, she'd heal. Angels always did.

"Marna!"

She stepped off the roof and fell straight to the ground below.

"So where the hell are we heading?" Jonathan asked, voice rising. "If an angel took her, can't she be anyplace?"

Yes, she could be. Tanner shoved his foot down harder on that accelerator. When he caught up to Bastion, he was going to make that angel wish for a swift trip to hell.

You can't take her from me.

"He would have gotten her as far from Tanner as possible," Cody said. "Taken her someplace where he felt in control."

"And that's not the swamp." The swamp wasn't the place for that lily-white, pretty-boy angel. But the city, probably some spot up high so he could look down on everyone else, yeah, that was more the angel's style.

And that was why Tanner had driven back to the city as fast as the patrol car would go.

"We have to be careful," Jonathan told him as his gaze swept the tight streets. "If any other cops see you . . ."

Tanner nodded. "They won't be taking me in." His life as a cop was over. Gone. He knew that. Pity. Fucking shame. He'd always wanted to protect. To stop the criminals hunting in the streets.

To make up for my own past. But that was all gone now. He was hunted, because of the freak who'd targeted him and Marna.

"What—what kinds of angels are out there?" Jonathan asked. A fast glance showed him running a shaking hand through his hair. "When Captain told me . . . she never said there were so many."

"Maybe she didn't know," Cody said, still leaning forward and holding that cage. "I think Jillian was more interested in stealing angel blood than anything else."

"Bitch," Jonathan muttered. "She deserved the death you gave her."

Tanner didn't speak, just kept driving as fast as he could. *Hold on, Marna. I'm coming.*

"There are so many. Angels of death . . . guardians . . . punishers," Cody began, listing some of the angels that walked the earth.

"Punishers?" Jonathan asked as he turned to look at Cody. "What—like angels who actually punish humans?"

"Not just humans," Cody said. "Anyone. They've come after their share of supernaturals, too. You cross the line, and they'll come for you."

Tanner wished the two of them would just shut the hell up. He wanted to focus on Marna. If he could just pick up her scent again . . .

A sudden blast of music filled the car. Swearing, Jonathan yanked out his cell. "Detective Pardue. *What?* Where?"

Tanner raced through a yellow light. He'd go search by the Square. Maybe she was—

"Go to St. Louis Street," Jonathan told him, shoving his phone back into his pocket. "I've got an informant there, one who's paid to let me know when he sees anything unusual going on."

Because the human wanted to know everything about the supernaturals. Didn't he realize just how dangerous that was?

"That was him on the phone. He said—he said he just saw a woman jump off a three-story building, and then the woman just walked away without a scratch."

Marna.

The tires squealed as Tanner rounded the corner, and because, dammit, humans were coming out and cars were in his way, he flashed on his lights and let his siren scream.

The buildings rushed by him in a blur.

"Low profile, man," Jonathan snapped. *"Low freaking profile."*

Screw that. Another screeching turn. One more. Then . . .

He had her scent. It was the sweetest scent in the world. Tanner slammed the car to a stop and leapt out. He raced through the line of alleys. Jumped over fences. His body burned with the need to shift, but he held the beast back. Not here. Not now.

Not—

He saw her. She must have heard the thud of his footsteps because she turned around. Her eyes widened and she ran toward him with her arms out.

"He loves her," Cody said, voice tight. "If anything happens to Marna . . ."

Jonathan jumped from the car. Tanner had already taken off, running fast as he followed the angel's scent. He hadn't even looked back.

A mistake.

Cody was in the back. The demon was strong enough that he could probably kick the doors open, but, for the moment he was trapped. Vulnerable.

Jonathan pulled out his gun.

Cody's eyes widened. His fist slammed into the window.

And Jonathan's bullet shattered the glass between them. Because it wasn't a normal bullet—he knew better than to battle a monster with a bullet made by humans.

"She doesn't love him," Jonathan said and fired again. "And soon it won't matter how the fuck that animal feels—he'll be dead."

He'd make sure of it. He turned away from the car and began to stalk after his partner. The power pulsed just beneath his skin. Then, because he could, because it would be so fucking fitting, he let his form shift. The bones of his face twisted and reshaped. He grew taller. Leaner.

And became the demon that he'd left bleeding in the backseat of that patrol car.

Vengeance is mine.

It would be so sweet.

Chapter Eighteen

Marna ran to Tanner and threw her arms around him. He felt so good—solid, warm, strong. "I was coming to find you."

He lifted his head and gazed down into her face. "Like I was gonna let you go." Then he kissed her. Deep and hot and she met him with a hungry need. Only Tanner. He was the only one who could make her feel this way. Free. Wild.

You're on the list.

Marna pulled away from him. "We have to go." Go where? She didn't know. They just had to get out of the street. Get someplace safe. Away from the death that stalked her.

But Tanner wasn't moving. And . . . had she heard gunshots? Or had that just been a car backfiring in the distance?

"Where is he?" Tanner demanded. *"Where's Bastion?"*

He hadn't come after her. She hoped he stayed away. "Gone." She didn't want to tell Tanner about the list. What was the point? So he'd get desperate and risk his life for her? If she was on the list . . .

No escape.

Marna grabbed Tanner's hand and pulled him toward the building on the right. The big FOR SALE sign told her the place was empty, and with one kick, she sent the front door flying in. The house was dark inside, and all the furniture was gone. Hollow.

The way I feel without him.

"Marna—"

She pushed Tanner back against the wall. Kissed him. How much time did she have left? Couldn't be long. No one ever lasted long once their name came up on the list.

She wanted her last moments to be with him. Happiness, before whatever hell was waiting for her came calling.

His hands were on her waist. Rough fingertips, but with a touch so gentle. His claws were out, but they didn't so much as scratch her skin. They never did. He always treated her so carefully.

"Tanner!" She heard Cody's voice as if from a distance. Footsteps pounded outside. She didn't want to pull free from Tanner. Couldn't they just stay together a little longer? And let the rest of the world disappear?

But Tanner was gently pushing her back. "He's worried about you."

Marna swallowed. She needed to tell him this. Too many humans had passed—at her hand—with unsaid words in their hearts. She didn't want to go the same way. "I've been happy with you."

A faint furrow appeared between his brows.

"I don't want to leave you," she whispered. But sometimes it wasn't about what you wanted. It was about what fate had planned.

"Then don't." His eyes seemed to glow as his beast pushed ever closer. "Stay with me, forever."

She wanted to. Wished that she could. But Marna couldn't make a promise that she wouldn't be able to keep. Her hand traced the hard edge of his jaw. "I love you." She'd never said the words to another.

"Tanner!" Cody was shouting again. So close out in the street. He'd find them at any moment.

Why did that thought make her shiver?

"You what?" Tanner asked. Then a wide smile broke his face. "Baby, you know I'm fucking insane for you."

She started to smile.

The door flew open and banged against the wall with a thud. Marna's head turned, and she saw Cody standing in the doorway. His eyes found hers. Narrowed when he saw Tanner holding her so close.

And why was Cody holding a gun?

"I was worried, brother," Cody said, taking a step closer to them. "You didn't answer when I called."

Tanner inhaled, and in a flash, he had Marna behind him. "You're not my *brother.*"

Laughter from Cody. Had laughter ever been so cold?

"You're not soaked in his blood this time," Tanner snapped, "so I can smell *you.*"

"I'm not your brother." An evil grin. "And you're not the white knight who gets to live happily-fucking-ever-after with the lost angel."

A gunshot blasted. Marna screamed. Tanner flinched.

"You don't get to live at all," Cody told him. Then he fired again. But Tanner was already leaping forward. The bullet tore into him, and he knocked the gun from Cody's hands.

Tanner's claws went for the guy's throat. "You don't . . . steal my brother's . . . f-face."

Tanner's body slumped. Marna rushed toward the men and grabbed Tanner just before he hit the floor. Tanner looked up at her, and his pupils were pinpricks in his eyes. She'd never seen his skin look so ashen. "Tanner?"

Blood poured from his chest, and smoke drifted up from the wounds. But . . . silver wouldn't take her shifter out like this. He was too strong.

"I stole his life, so why not his face?" More laughter. Cold and grating.

Tanner was trying to claw at his wounds in order to get the bullets out.

"I learned from my mistakes," Cody said. No, not Cody. Who the hell was it? "Those bullets had enough tranq in them to take out an elephant. Much less a mangy shifter like him. Tranq and a dark witch's magic."

Marna surged to her feet. Her hands clenched at her sides. She stared at the man who thought he'd take Tanner away from her—and she let her fire rip right out at him.

He lifted his hand and waved the flames away. "You have to do better than that, angel—"

She grabbed for the gun that had dropped on the floor—and then she pointed the weapon right back at the jerk. In a flash, she had the barrel pressing against his chest. "I'm just getting started."

She pulled the trigger as he screamed. The bullet blasted through him even as blood splattered around her. He fell back. His body twitched on the floor, trembling, and Marna aimed down at him, then fired again.

He stopped twitching. And he stopped being Cody.

As she watched, his features slowly changed. In death, shifters always resumed their human forms. She didn't know what the hell this guy was—shifter, demon, angel—but he was changing back.

His shoulders narrowed. His body thinned. Bones snapped in his face. His cheeks became leaner.

Not a face of evil. Not a monster. A man she knew.

His eyes were closed, his body not moving—and he was Tanner's partner. Jonathan was the monster who'd been after them. *Jonathan.*

He was also the man she'd just killed.

The scent of flowers teased her nose. Grim satisfaction filled her. A death angel would be coming to collect his soul soon.

One less monster in the world.

She turned back around to find her shifter. Tanner was still on the floor. His eyes were closed, and his breathing was labored. She knelt next to him. His claws were buried in his chest. He'd been trying to take out the last bullet. Swallowing, she guided his hand and used his claws to dig deeper into his flesh. Then she reached inside the wound, biting her lip to stop the trembling, and she found the bullet with her own shaking fingertips.

She pulled the bullet out. Dropped it. Marna took his face in her hands and smeared blood on his cheeks where she touched him. "It's going to be okay," she promised him. "He's gone now. We're both going to be—"

Laughter.

The cruelest sound she'd ever heard. Marna kept her hold on Tanner, but she turned her head so that she could see Jonathan's body.

Only he wasn't dead. Not even close. He sat up. Blood streamed down his chest, but Jonathan didn't seem affected by the injuries. "You play dirty," he told her.

She reached out and grabbed for the gun. Fired again. More blood. *How many more bullets?* And shouldn't the tranqs knock him out, too? Why weren't they working?

He rose to his feet.

The gun clicked. No more bullets.

"Seems being a hybrid has more than its share of advantages. Drugs don't have an effect on me. They can't knock me out—can't even give me a damn buzz. And other wounds . . ." He touched his chest. Just that fast—*not bleeding anymore. Not good.* "They heal almost as fast as I get 'em."

She had to find a weapon. The guy was a hybrid. Okay . . . so half human, half angel? Or half angel and half something else that would be really, really hard to kill?

When it came to angels, mortal weapons just wouldn't do

the trick. So she needed something strong enough to kill the guy, something not made by mortal means. Marna glanced down at Tanner's hands. His claws hadn't retracted. Not yet.

Those will do the trick. She just had to get the guy killing close.

"I can see your wings, you know," Jonathan told her, his eyes at a point just over her shoulder. "The first time I saw you—and them—I knew just how perfect we'd be together."

So he'd taken her face, Tanner's face, Cody's face . . . and killed. "We're not going to be anything together." She kept her hold on Tanner. Had his breathing changed or was that her imagination? *Heal faster. Heal faster.*

"Do you know what it's like to be different?" Jonathan was just talking to her like they had all the time in the world to chat. Like he hadn't shot her lover and killed people all over the city. *Insane.* Yes, she could see the madness now. He wasn't bothering to hide it anymore. "To know that you're all alone, while the rest of the world is running around, blind?"

She licked her lips. Okay. If he wanted to talk, she'd keep him talking. That would give Tanner and his shifter self more time to push the drugs from his system. "You're earthbound."

Jonathan blinked. "I'm an angel, just like you."

Not even close. "You don't have wings. Not even shadows." Like the Fallen did. She took a deep breath and fought to keep her voice flat. She didn't want to give him her fear. "We call—we call those like you the earthbound." Because no matter what, they weren't supposed to make it up to heaven. Not while they were still alive, anyway.

The only earthbound who'd ever made it upstairs had been Seline. And Sammael hadn't been about to let his lady go without a fight.

Sammael. She could sure use some of his power right then.

You have to get angry enough. You have to want to kill. That's what he'd told her, but well, hell, *wanting* to kill wouldn't help her now. Even if she could summon up that power, the Death Touch never worked on those with angel blood.

Angels weren't supposed to kill their own kind.

But then again, there was a lot that angels weren't *supposed* to be doing.

"Earthbound." Jonathan seemed to be tasting the word. His smile flashed again, and he lifted his hand toward her. "Come. It's time to leave him behind."

She wasn't going anywhere.

"At first, I didn't realize why I needed to kill." Jonathan's voice was smooth, thoughtful. He still offered his hand to her. "I mean, I was only fifteen when I made my first kill. I thought something must be *wrong* with me. I just—I couldn't stop myself. I found my prey. Stalked him. Made sure he suffered."

She didn't want to hear this. But the stiffness of Tanner's body told her that he was definitely coming around. Now if he'd just use those fierce claws of his . . .

Jonathan's hand dropped to his side. "He was one of my old foster dads. I was always being bounced around. Fucking abandoned as a kid—why would an angel do that?"

Marna didn't answer. Not that she had time to talk. Jonathan's eyes were burning brighter, and his words came faster as he said, "He never should have touched me. I told him . . . *told* him I'd get him back. *Vengeance.* And I did. I found him. I hunted him. I killed him while he begged and screamed." His breath sighed out. "The first kill, but not the last."

The way he was talking about vengeance . . . "Your—your mother or father—one of them could have been a punishment angel." Only the way he'd been killing—that wasn't the way punishers worked. When they punished, it was never about emotion or payback. It was just . . . duty.

The punishment angels weren't supposed to enjoy their dark work.

"How many?" Marna asked quietly. The guy wasn't coming closer to her. She needed him closer. "How many more did you kill over the years?"

"Hundreds." Said with relish. "Criminals. Thieves. Whores. Murderers. They all needed to be punished, and I was the instrument of that punishment."

Her mouth was so dry that it hurt to swallow. "How did you know . . . what they'd done?"

He took a gliding step toward her. "I could see the sin on them. Almost smell it." His gaze dropped to Tanner. "Like I see it on him. Evil. He reeks of it. He's got blood on him, and it will never wash off."

Like the crazy jerk in front of her could talk.

"I'm going to kill him for you," Jonathan promised with a nod. "Just like I killed the others for you."

For you. Her heart lurched as she began to fully understand.

The two panther shifters in the alley . . .

"I knew you wanted those animals dead. You tried to do it. I *saw you.*"

A shiver slid over her at his words. She'd felt eyes on her, but she'd thought it had been Tanner watching over her. It had been Jonathan?

"I shot 'em full with one of my special mixes. A quick injection . . ."

Back in the interrogation room, he'd mentioned drugs. The cocky bastard, he'd been *telling* her what he'd done to them.

"They never even had the time to scream."

No, they'd just had time to die.

Jonathan's gaze dropped to Tanner's still body. "He's the one who led me to you. He was so focused on you, almost addicted. I wondered about the woman who was driving him crazy. Then I saw you. Your wings. And I knew."

"You knew nothing," she whispered. Tanner's body was completely still against her. Still—but tight and tensed for battle. He was ready to attack, she knew it. And when he made his move, those claws of his had better go deep. She stood up, determined to distract Jonathan. She needed to give Tanner the perfect moment to strike. "You don't know anything about me. I am *nothing* like you."

Jonathan's brows rose. "You wanted to kill. You wanted to punish." His eyes were bright with a feverish light. "I punished for you. I killed for you, and I'll do it again." He rushed for her.

Marna was ready. She pushed out with her fire. He batted it away with one hand, but that was what she wanted him to do. In that instant, while his focus was on the flames, she kicked him, then drove her fist into his jaw. He stumbled back.

And Tanner attacked. He jumped up from the ground and struck with his claws out. His claws sank into Jonathan's chest.

Jonathan screamed in fury and pain as he wrenched away from the attack. The hybrid stumbled back.

"I'm punishing now," Tanner snarled. "I'm—"

Jonathan sent a wave of fire blasting right at Tanner. Tanner's arms burned, and Marna leapt in front of him. *"Stop!"*

The flames froze. Not by Jonathan's will, but by hers. Fury pumped inside of her. So strong that her whole body seemed to ache. "You aren't killing him." Not when Tanner was the one thing on this earth that she cared about.

The flames disappeared into a wisp of smoke.

"You choose *him?*" Shock had slackened Jonathan's features.

What? Was the guy really that delusional? Did he think—

"I'm just like you!" His hands fell limply at his sides. "I've killed . . . *for you*." Now he sounded lost. "He's done nothing for you, while I've done everything."

Wrong. Tanner had done the one thing that mattered most. He'd given her a reason to live.

Jonathan shook his head. "We can put the world back to order. Punish the wicked. Send the monsters to hell."

Didn't he see? "You are one of those monsters." One of the worst she'd ever seen. And he didn't understand just how evil he truly was. "That cop you attacked, what was his crime?"

He'd left an innocent to die—why? The cop had never done anything to her.

But Jonathan shouted, "He *saw* you! I know he did! You were with Tanner, so he must have seen! And he would have told the others that you were still alive! That—"

"You almost killed him for that?" she broke in, stunned. Tanner was behind her, swearing, and . . . she could smell his burned flesh.

Jonathan's lips curved. "I've killed for less."

Monster. "That's not the way of our kind."

Jonathan glared back at her. "I thought you'd understand. I thought you'd appreciate all I've done." He shook his head and looked sad, but determined. "I see the truth now."

The truth? What? That she was standing between him and Tanner, determined to keep her lover safe?

"You don't see a fuckin' thing," Tanner growled, "but in a few minutes, I'll be makin' you see plenty."

Marna glanced back quickly. Tanner was on his feet. Burned. Bloody, but not out. Not by a long shot. The floor creaked as he stalked closer.

She focused back on Jonathan.

He smiled. "You still think this can end well for you?" His furious gaze was on Tanner.

"I know it will." Tanner pushed to her side and weaved a bit. He needed to shift, but if he did, he'd be vulnerable. Could she keep Jonathan busy long enough for Tanner to make that shift?

I'll have to.

"Your brother is bleeding out in the back of a patrol car." Jonathan spoke casually as he wiped his bloody hands on his shirt. "You're both dying today, shifter. The only question is . . . which one of you gets to hell first?"

"*You* do," Tanner promised him. "Then when we . . . get there . . . Cody and I will take turns kicking your . . . ass."

Jonathan laughed. "Want to taste that fire again?" A ball of flames rose above his hand. "I'll burn all your skin right off your body."

No, he wouldn't. She just had to get him away from Tanner long enough for her shifter to heal. To heal . . . and then kick ass. He did that so well.

"You're not killing us," she told him. "We're killing you." Not a lie. Promises weren't lies.

But he laughed and sent his blasts of fire all around the room. The fire licked its way up the walls.

Marna pushed out with her own energy, whirling around as she tried to fight the blaze. Why was he so strong?

While she was still so weak?

Every time she put out the fire, he started it again. Bones were snapping near her, popping, and Tanner was shifting. *Yes.* She just had to keep battling the flames and keep Jonathan fighting her long enough for Tanner to—

Something sharp pressed into her side. Pain stabbed through her—no, she'd been *stabbed*.

The flames rose higher. She turned, and found Jonathan inches from her. "You disappointed me," he said and sounded so sad. "So I have to punish you now."

No. She shook her head. The flames were so hot.

Bones were still popping. A panther was growling and . . .

"Your lover wasn't the first shifter I met," Jonathan told her. "So many beasts over the years. So fucking many. Those animals begged for their justice, and I gave them just what they deserved."

The pain twisted in her side. Marna glanced down. Her blood spilled down her clothing.

"At death, a shifter's body always goes back to its human form."

She knew this crap. Pain pulsed through her. The fire was rising again, and she couldn't seem to muster the energy to fight the flames.

"But if you can cut off a shifter's limbs before it dies, those pieces don't ever change back. They freeze, and you get a real nice souvenir."

He was a sick freak.

He yanked his hand back. Marna gasped at the agony. And she saw it wasn't a knife that had stabbed into her. Heavy claws had dug into her flesh and torn her muscles.

Claws?

Her gaze rose to meet his.

"I took these from that panther shifter in the swamp. Russell. The guy thought he was such a badass, but you should have heard him crying when I sliced off his hand. I took my time with him. I tore that animal apart with his own damn claws." He smiled. "Then I kept my souvenir, because I knew just how well a shifter's claws could work against the other supernaturals out there."

Other supernaturals . . . *me.* Angels could be killed by those claws. So could every other supernatural beast that walked the earth.

Her body trembled. The scent of flowers deepened. And . . . was that an angel she saw? Slipping into the room?

"I didn't want to use these on you. But you gave me no choice." He lifted his hand and drove the claws into her chest. "If you're not with me, angel, then you're dead to me."

Blood dripped from her lips. *"Bastion . . ."* She could see him now.

He'd come for her. Just like he'd said.

"You should have been more." Spittle flew from Jonathan's mouth. His face was right next to hers. Her body shook, and he snarled at her, "You were supposed to be mine. Supposed to be perfect! Forever!"

No one was perfect. Not even an angel. She hurt so much, but the pain wouldn't last. *Nothing lasts.* She tasted blood and death on her tongue. But she heard the fierce growl of her panther and the sound had a smile curving her lips. Jonathan wouldn't kill anyone else. Not after Tanner got hold of him.

"Go to hell," she whispered and fell back.

Even as the panther leapt into the air.

Cody crawled from the car. *That bastard* . . . Cody had always told his brother that he had to watch out for the humans. *I was right.*

Only he hadn't been watching well enough this time, either.

Pain ate at his insides and twisted his gut. The blasts from Jonathan's gun had knocked him out for a few moments, and he still couldn't see straight.

Drugs.

Yeah, he knew the feeling, but . . .

The bastard cop had made a mistake. Demons and drugs . . . when you mixed them, you never knew what you'd get.

Addiction. Hell.

He wouldn't listen to the whispers now. Couldn't. He had to find Tanner. Find the lost angel. And he had a cop to kill.

He pushed to his feet. Took a heavy breath. Then, he put one foot in front of the other. Again. Again. Blood fell in his wake. The drugs had started to numb the pain but the blood, nothing was stopping it. With every step, more flowed from him.

I won't be weak this time. He'd show Tanner. He could be strong. He could be there to save his brother.

It was his turn.

He just had to . . . get to Tanner.

Good thing it was turning daylight. Otherwise, his blood would be drawing the vamps in.

Good thing . . .

Then he heard the faint whisper of footsteps behind him. His eyes squeezed closed. He'd *never* had good luck.

"Um . . . look at that," a familiar voice drawled. "A walking blood buffet."

Cody turned and saw the vamp stalking him.

No, he'd *never* had good luck.

I'm sorry, Tanner.

Then he faced the creature that stalked him.

Chapter Nineteen

Kill. Destroy.

Tanner slammed his body into Jonathan's. The jerk just laughed as he crashed into the floor.

He wouldn't be laughing when Tanner ripped his throat out.

The scent of Marna's blood filled his nose and drove the panther into a frenzy. *Hurt. His mate was hurt.* He'd destroy the bastard who'd made her bleed.

And how had he missed the evil in Jonathan? How had he looked right at him and not seen it?

Because he was human.

No, Tanner had just thought the guy was human. He hadn't smelled like a shifter, like a vamp, or even a demon. And he hadn't possessed the telltale scent of an angel.

Just smelled human. Smelled human. Acted human. But that had been nothing but a lie.

Now Jonathan was on his feet and holding some kind of claws in his hands. The SOB thought he was a shifter now, too? Tanner would show him the damage real claws could do.

Tanner sliced out and let his claws rip across Jonathan's forearms. Jonathan screamed. Blood flowed.

More. Destroy.

Tanner slammed his paws into Tanner's chest. This time

when he took his partner down, the guy didn't get back up. Because he didn't want to make it easy on him, Tanner sank his claws into Jonathan's chest. This bastard was going to suffer before he went to hell.

For Cody. For the pain that he'd put his brother through.

For the young cop. That kid hadn't deserved to have his body mangled on a dark, lonely road.

For Marna. Jonathan *never* should have come for her. To make her bleed, to make her cry out in pain . . .

She wasn't crying anymore.

That knowledge slowly penetrated the rage of the beast. With his claws still buried in Jonathan's chest, the panther's head turned to the right. He saw Marna. Lying on the floor. Blood all around her.

Not moving.

Breathing?

Yes, yes, she was breathing. He could hear the faint rasp of her breath. And he could smell . . .

An angel.

The panther roared, and his head swung back to face Jonathan. The guy was grinning his sick, satisfied grin. Not screaming anymore.

He'd scream again. Tanner would make sure of it.

"F-fuckin' animal . . . you'll never . . . have her again."

He'd have her forever. Marna was his. This bastard was dead, and Marna was going to—

"I touched her . . . heart."

The panther's gaze flew to the claws that Jonathan still gripped in his hand.

Touched it? Or . . . *Took it?*

"She deserved . . ." Jonathan coughed up blood. "To be p-punished."

The beast snarled and his teeth sank into Jonathan's throat. Jonathan struggled, shoved, tried to break free, but the panther held tight to the prey that would never escape.

Death didn't come softly. He came hard. With a violent flash of fangs and fury. When Jonathan's breath choked back into his lungs, when his body stopped spasming, Tanner let him go—straight to hell.

And he saw the angel standing over them. Only Bastion wasn't reaching down to take the cop.

Bastion was staring over at Marna, and there was no missing the sorrow on his face. "I told her . . ."

No.

The panther leapt back to her side, but—but there was nothing the beast could do. Nothing but kill and destroy and he'd done that job well.

With her breath barely rasping out, Marna needed the man, not the panther. The shift hit him, brutal and swift, as the fur melted away and his bones reshaped.

Hold on. Marna just had to stay with him a few more moments. He'd shift, and then he could heal her. The same way he'd healed Cody. He could do this.

He reached for Marna with the hands of a man and not the claws of a beast. His fingers were shaking as he lifted her up against him. Her eyes were closed, but at his touch, her lashes slowly lifted.

"I was . . . waiting for you," she whispered.

He'd spent his whole life waiting for her.

"Is he . . . d-dead?"

Tanner didn't glance back. Bastion had done his job while he'd shifted. "He's rotting in hell." Jonathan had better be.

She swallowed. "You know . . . I . . . loved you."

Screw this. "Baby, you're gonna keep loving me." He put his hand over her chest. Her blood was warm against his fingers. "You're gonna love me for the next fifty years, at least." Power pulsed through him, familiar, as if he'd been using it all of his life.

When he'd just been killing and fighting like a beast.

But this time, he was healing. Saving her life. He'd used the power before, and he could use it now. He *would* use it.

He pulled the healing magic from deep inside of him and pumped it toward her. He could feel the death angel coming closer to him.

"Stand back," Tanner snarled at Bastion. "You aren't taking her." No one was.

"Another soul must be taken," Bastion said quietly.

"Well, it won't be her." Energy poured through him, and drove right into her. She gasped and arched beneath his touch, and a faint white light appeared where his hand touched her chest.

His hands had always been used for killing. His claws came out so quickly. But not now. Now was all about healing.

Tanner bent close to Marna. Did she even realize just how important she was to him? "I knew from the first moment I saw you." Covered in blood. Broken, on the ground. Broken, but still so beautiful. The most beautiful thing he'd ever seen. He'd taken one look at her, and realized his life would change. "I knew . . . you were mine."

He'd planned to kill Brandt for hurting her. Brother or not, he'd been a dead man. But Azrael had beaten him to the punch.

After that, he'd tried to give Marna space. Tried to let her go. He knew how dangerous he was.

Her breathing steadied. The flesh seemed to close beneath his fingers.

He'd tried, but he hadn't been able to stay away from her. He'd needed to see her, just to make sure she was safe.

Once he'd actually had her body against his, had his body buried *in* hers, there'd been no turning back.

Love? The word was too tame for the way he felt about her. And he'd never be tame. She consumed him. Made him wild, desperate.

For her. Always her.

There was another wound in her side. Deep, and bleeding too much. Lethargy pulled at him, but Tanner lifted his left hand and pressed it against her side. Bastion was still there, watching him, but not touching. The guy needed to leave. Just drag his winged ass away and go.

"She's not dying," Tanner growled. Not on his watch. The bad guy was dead. This was the point where they got to live happily ever freaking after.

He was getting his princess. She'd get her beast. The rest of the world could go and screw off.

"Tanner!" He didn't look up at his brother's shout. He couldn't take his attention off Marna. She needed his focus. His power. If that power broke, what would happen to her?

He dug deep, pulled more energy from within, and pushed it toward her wounds.

"No! You can't!" Now Cody was beside him. He could smell his brother's blood. So Jonathan hadn't been lying. The bastard had shot him and left him to die.

We're harder to kill than you thought.

"Help me!" Cody shouted to someone. Bastion? But then Riley's form appeared as the vamp crouched down next to Marna. He reached for her.

"Touch her," Tanner managed, voice barely human, "and die."

"A soul must be taken," Bastion said quietly.

Riley jerked and his gaze flew up. Had he heard Bastion? With Marna's blood in him, he just might have—

Cody's hands grabbed Tanner. "You're *killing* yourself! Let her go!"

Never.

She just needed a little more energy.

"You're shaking, dammit! Blood is coming out of your eyes!"

Was that what the moisture was? He'd thought it was tears.

"You're dying!"

Yeah, well, without her, he might as well be dead. What was he supposed to do? Go back to the life he'd had before her? Not when she'd shown him what he could be.

What he *would* be.

Cody tried to pull him away. Tanner didn't budge. He wouldn't move. Not until her eyes opened again. Not until he saw that she was going to be okay.

"You're all I've got, man! The only family who ever meant shit to me!" Cody was still jerking on his arms.

"And she's . . ." Tanner swallowed. Why was talking so hard? "She's . . . what matters to me."

Marna's eyes opened. Her eyes weren't filled with pain. They were so bright and blue that it almost hurt to look into them. Her gaze found his. Widened. Her lips curled in a smile. "Tanner."

The light vanished from beneath his fingertips. His heart raced in his chest. Far, far too fast, that drumming beat seemed to shake his whole body.

But then fear flashed over her delicate features. No, she should never be afraid of him. He'd never hurt her. He'd protect her, take care of her and—

"Tanner?" She sat up.

He slipped back and fell onto the floor.

Then her hands were on him, touching him lightly, but he couldn't seem to feel her touch. Why couldn't he feel her? Her skin was silken and soft, and he wanted to feel it one more time.

But he couldn't seem to feel anything.

Bastion looked down on him. "You traded yourself for her." He sounded . . . surprised?

Tanner couldn't speak, but, hell yes, he'd made the trade. He'd known the risks. Gladly accepted them. His death, her life?

Fucking fair.

Then Marna slapped him. "You aren't doing this to me!" Good thing he couldn't feel anything, or that hit might have hurt.

She caught his face between her hands. "You aren't dying for me."

"Yes." Cody's voice. Sad. Hopeless. "He is."

Bastion reached down for him.

Marna stiffened. "Bastion, you'd better yank that hand back, or you *will* lose it."

"So someone else does see him," Riley whispered and eased back a few feet. "Thought I was goin' crazy."

"Vampire . . ." Marna's voice held a lethal edge. "Don't even think of leaving."

Why was the vampire there? Tanner tried to push up but found his arms wouldn't move. No, *he* couldn't move.

Marna leaned over him again. "You save me, I save you." She bent and pressed a kiss to his lips. He tasted salt. Tears? "That's how it works," she whispered.

She pulled back. He didn't want her to pull back. Didn't want her to leave.

But Marna lifted her arm and bared her wrist. "Bite me, vamp."

A growl broke from Tanner's lips. Riley had better not—

"It's okay." Marna's eyes were on his. Bastion stood at her back. The angel was always too close to her. "He's not drinking from me."

"Uh, I'm not?" Riley asked. Then Tanner saw him, coming up on Marna's side. Taking her offered wrist. "Then what am I doing?"

"Opening a vein." Her eyes didn't leave Tanner. "And saving my shifter."

Her blood. He'd told her not to give him her blood again. It was too addictive. The blood connected him to her even deeper, so deep that if she ever left him, what would remain?

Nothing.

"I'm not leaving you." Did she know what he was thinking? A flash of pain crossed her face. "And you're not leaving me." She put her wrist to his mouth. Blood trickled past his lips. "There's no time for a fancy transfusion, but it worked when you drank my blood before."

Because the beast inside lived on blood and death.

Not her blood. It was the beast's denial, and the man's.

"If you want to stay with me, if you want to be sure all the vampires and the demons out there don't get my blood or me, then you'll drink."

No one would get her. No one would hurt her.

"Drink," Marna said again, and he did.

Her blood slid down his throat. The panther had taken blood from prey plenty of times, but the man hadn't. He choked, hating what he was doing to her. Hard hands held him down. His gaze flew to the left. To the right. Riley and Cody were pinning him down, making sure he couldn't move.

"Drink for me," Marna whispered, "because I don't want to lose you."

He closed his eyes and drank. At first, the blood didn't seem to do anything to him. Maybe he was already too far gone. He'd wanted to stay with her, wanted to be at her side forever, but maybe fate had other plans.

Fate had always screwed with him.

Marna pulled her hand away. Tanner licked his lips. He still tasted her, and now, he could almost feel her, inside his mind. A warmth spread within him and filled him with energy and strength.

Deep within him, the panther seemed to stretch and roar.

Alive.

Tanner opened his eyes. "I'm . . . not leaving you."

Her smile was the most beautiful thing he'd ever seen.

"No, you're damn well not." Then she bent toward him and her lips feathered over his cheek.

Cody and Riley eased their grips and pulled away from him. Over Marna's shoulder, Tanner saw Bastion. Waiting. Watching. His dark wings curled toward his body. His eyes flickered with emotion.

Was he going to have to fight the angel now? He'd killed one jerk-off already. What else was he gonna have to do?

Tanner rose, but kept a strong grip on Marna. He was naked because of his shift, but that was the least of his worries right then. They'd cheated death, for the moment, and *that* was what mattered.

"Nice trick, shifter," Bastion said.

Riley flinched. "I need to get the hell out of here."

"I didn't realize beasts were so adept at healing." Bastion's wings unfurled. "Guess there is more to you than killing."

"And there's more to you than death," Marna said, her voice strong and certain. "There always has been more, Bastion. You aren't like the others."

The angel's hands were clenched into fists. "I was supposed to . . ." He swallowed and said, "You should have died today."

And what would happen, Tanner wondered, once the angel went back upstairs without his charge?

But Bastion lifted his chin and smiled. "I've heard the fall is one wild bitch of a ride."

Wait . . . had the guy just said—?

"I didn't want you to fall for me," Marna told him. Yeah, well, Tanner sure as shit didn't want that either. Blondie, earthbound? Dogging their steps? Spilling over with emotion?

"Not for you." Bastion shook his head and straightened his shoulders. "For me. Because maybe I *want* to know just what it is that humans feel."

Lust. Fury. Need. Love.

"Find me when I fall," Bastion said. His gaze darted between Marna and Tanner. "Help me, and any debt you owe me is paid."

A debt for not taking a soul? Yeah, they'd find the guy all right.

And then Tanner would make sure the Fallen kept his hands *off* Marna.

A strong wind ripped through the room, sending them all stumbling back. All but Bastion. He rose up, tossed by the wind. The air around him grew dark.

"See you soon," Bastion whispered as the wind grew even stronger and howled with its own fury.

Then he vanished.

"Holy fuck," Riley whispered. "Is he really gonna fall?"

Marna's face tightened with sadness. "Yes."

Because he hadn't taken Marna's soul? *Or because he didn't take mine?*

Either way, Blondie would be earthbound soon.

Cody strode toward them. He glared at Tanner an instant, then hauled him close in a back-breaking hug. "Bastard. You weren't supposed to use that fancy-ass light trick anymore." Then he eased back and gazed steadily at Tanner. "But for her, you'd do any damn thing, wouldn't you?"

Fight. Lie. Kill.

Die.

Tanner nodded.

Cody released him and grabbed Marna. He hugged her just as tightly. "Welcome to the fucked-up family," he whispered against her ear, though Tanner's shifter hearing easily picked up his words. "I promise, from now on, things will be different. Better."

Could they be any worse?

Then Cody released her. "We're not just our father's sons."

No. Not even close. Tanner couldn't even feel the echo

of that old bastard anymore. He really was gone now. Rotting in the ground. Burning in hell. Either way, he was *gone.*

"We're more," Tanner said, nodding, but his gaze was on Marna. He'd prove to her that he could be more than a killer.

But first . . . first he was getting her out of that place. Away from the dead body on the floor. Away from the blood and the memories and the fear.

Someone must have heard all the gunshots and howling. The cops would be coming. And since he wasn't exactly on good terms with his brothers and sisters in blue . . .

Time to leave.

Tanner lifted his hand to Marna. Without any hesitation, she wound her fingers through his. Marna's gaze didn't drop to Jonathan's dead body as they left the trashed room. Tanner's did. In death, Jonathan didn't look so violent or twisted. But then, most of the time, he hadn't looked that way in life, either. Not until the end.

The end . . .

It could have been me dead on the floor.

"But it fucking wasn't," Tanner growled, and his hold tightened on Marna. They walked out together and left death exactly where he belonged—behind them.

Tanner wasn't sure what he'd find waiting back at his place. Half a dozen cop cars, maybe a SWAT team? All gunning for him. Because he was the hunted now, right? The cop who'd gone bad and taken out his captain.

But . . . the street was empty.

He parked the patrol car and turned to stare at Marna. "We're gonna need to leave town." Because the cops would come for him, sooner or later.

She just smiled and looked so beautiful she made his heart hurt. "I'd like to see the rest of the world. When you're out ferrying souls, there's not much time for sightseeing."

No. He, ah, bet there wasn't.

The door squeaked as she opened it and hurried toward the porch. Tanner pushed open his door, and when the wind blew toward him, he immediately caught the scent of the intruder. They weren't alone after all.

Not so empty.

"Marna!" She was on the steps now.

His warning had come too late. Sammael strolled out. He quirked a brow and put his hands on his hips. "Took you long enough to come home, shifter."

Tanner bounded up the steps. "What the hell are you doing in my house?"

"Waiting." Said so casually. "You didn't really expect me to sit outside, did you?"

What? Did the Fallen think he was some kind of damn celebrity? "Why. Are. You. Here?"

Sam lifted his brows. "So you can say thank you?"

Tanner lunged for the guy. Marna grabbed his arms and held him back. "Easy." Her breath whispered against him as she turned to face Sammael. "We found the killer on our own. So if that's what you were coming to tell us—"

"And where is Jonathan Pardue now?"

Tanner's whole body tightened. How long had the Fallen known Jonathan was the guy gunning for them? That hard stare of Sam's gave nothing away. *Probably the whole time.* "He's dead."

"Yes, well, I always say, a death job is always done best when it's done by your own hands." He offered a faint smile. A smug one. "Right, shifter? Don't you feel better knowing that *you* sent the guy to hell?"

Like he needed to be taught some kind of life lesson by Sam. "Marna could have been the one to die."

"I was on Bastion's list," she said, anger humming in her voice.

But Sam just shrugged. "He's always been half in love with you. He never would have taken your soul."

Tanner rushed away from Marna. He grabbed Sam around the neck and shoved him against the wall of the house. "Listen, you cold bastard—"

Sam shook his head. "This isn't the way to thank me."

"Thank you?" Marna repeated, coming closer. "You haven't done anything!"

Sam shoved back against Tanner. Because he was trying—*trying*—to hold on to his control, Tanner eased back a few feet. He caught Marna's hand. Rubbed his fingers over her knuckles and took a steadying breath.

Don't kick angel ass. Not yet.

"I've done plenty." Now Sam sounded, what? Insulted? Definitely. He glared at Marna and said, "I'm the one who made sure your pet wasn't locked in a cage. Shifters do hate those cages, don't they?" His knowing gaze drifted back to Tanner. "Something about the beasts they carry . . ."

Tanner growled at him.

Sam smiled. "Let's just say that I made all the trouble with the law vanish for you. You're now cleared of the attack on that boy wonder cop. Cleared of all the shit with the captain. Hell, when you go back to work, they might even give you a medal." He lifted his hands with an honest-to-God *voila*-type gesture. "What can I say? I am that good."

"You're full of shit," Tanner said. "I'm not—"

"The chief of police is a demon, and a guy who owes me more than just his soul." Sam dropped his hands. "All I had to do was explain a few facts to him. A little while ago, he took care of making all the evidence fit with the new version of the story."

The chief of—well, he'd suspected that after meeting the guy a few times. Tanner rubbed his chin. "And the new version is . . . ?"

"Your captain was killed in the line of duty. She was tracking the real killer, one who'd been killing all over the city. You tried to save her, the same way you tried to save that kid cop—Hodges—but sometimes, well, death can't be stopped."

Sometimes, he could be.

"You took out the killer today, one rogue cop who'd crossed the line by attacking others on the force and manipulating evidence." Sammael made a little *tsk, tsk* sound. "Sometimes, even the boys in blue can go bat-shit crazy like Jonathan."

"And the video?" The one showing someone with his face attacking the injured cop?

"What video?" Sam asked, voice mild, then firmer. "There *is* no video."

Right, he got the picture. Not anymore, there wasn't any video.

Sam brushed past them and headed down the steps. "You still haven't said thanks."

He was back on the force. Not wanted. Not hunted. He could stay in New Orleans with Marna. *After* he took her on those sightseeing trips she wanted. Things wouldn't always be perfect, and he was sure he'd have to smooth over more shit at the precinct to make sure all suspicion was gone, but . . . "Thank you."

"That's a start." Sam didn't look back. "It'll take more before we're even."

With that guy, there was always a price.

Sam headed down the sidewalk. Then he paused, and glanced back at Marna. "You still can't kill, can you?"

She stared back at him, then shook her head. "Not with the Touch."

His brow furrowed.

"It's not like the Touch would have worked on another

angel anyway," Marna said, her shoulders lifting and falling in a small roll, "but believe me, I *wanted* to kill."

Sam's gaze had become hooded. That gaze swept over Marna once, twice, and seemed to measure her.

Then his eyes widened. He glanced back at Tanner, and for an instant, Tanner thought the guy had pity in his stare. Now why the hell would Sam pity him? All was supposed to be freakin' sunshine now.

"Some aren't meant for death," Sam murmured. "Some are meant for something much different." His head cocked as he studied Marna again. "You never should have been a death angel. We all knew you hated carrying the souls. *Everybody* knew, but you did your duty for so long."

"Not anymore," Marna told him, and her fingers tightened around Tanner's. "Now I'm free."

Did Sam shake his head a little? Tanner's gut clenched. That Fallen knew something he wasn't saying. Something that already had Tanner's whole body locking up as if he was about to take a blow.

But Sam pointed at Tanner and said, "Stay close to her." His gaze drifted back to Marna. "Guard what you want the most." Then he turned away. "Oh . . . and, by the way, I made sure every damn supernatural in this city knows that angel blood is off the menu. Permanently." The words floated to them on a breeze. "And I only had to kill a few paranormals to get the point across."

Just a few?

"Don't worry, cop, they all had it coming." Sam was at the edge of the sidewalk. There one moment, gone the next. Vanished, as if he'd never been there.

Guard what you want the most.

Tanner pulled Marna close to him. She actually wanted him, loved him—scars, claws, beast, and all. She'd been willing to risk her life for him.

He'd guard her for as long as he had breath.

Tanner bent his head toward her and brushed his lips against hers. He didn't care about the rest of the world then. Right then, she was the only thing that mattered.

Not his job. Not the fears from the past.

Nothing but her.

Her tongue slid against his.

Only her.

By the time they made it inside, he was so hard for her that he ached. Tanner slammed the door closed behind them and lifted Marna into his arms. He rushed up the stairs with her, kissing her, loving her taste.

Nothing had ever tasted as good as her. Nothing ever would.

Sunlight drifted through the window, lighting up the room and the bed. He put her down gently and choked back his lust. This time, he wanted to show her care and control. Wanted to show her how much she meant to him.

He stepped away from her. Stripped. His shirt hit the floor. His boots and jeans vanished into a corner. Naked, he went back to her.

She smiled and stole his breath. Since when did an angel look so familiar with sin?

Marna pulled off her shirt. Tossed it to join his. "I want you so much, Tanner." Her voice was husky with desire.

She slid out of her jeans and underwear. So perfect. He swallowed and stood back, almost afraid to touch her. His hands were too big. His body too rough.

Then she crooked her finger at him. "Come and get me."

Death didn't matter. Life did. She mattered.

And he'd most definitely *get* her.

He pulled her to the edge of the bed. Knelt on the floor. Parted her thighs. And put his mouth on her. Her moans filled his ears and made his cock twitch. Her flesh was so silken and pink, and she was slick with her arousal. *Love her taste.*

He felt her first orgasm against his tongue. Heard the gasp of his name. A good start.

He pushed his fingers inside of her. Rose up so that he could stare down at her face. Her skin was flushed, and her eyes sparkled. Her breasts pointed toward him. Her nipples were tight peaks that seemed to beg for his mouth.

Another taste.

He took her breast into his mouth. Sucked. Licked. Let her feel the edge of his teeth.

The second time she came, her sex clenched around his fingers.

Good, but he wanted more.

His cock was heavy and hard when he positioned it between her legs. No protection, just flesh to flesh. His fingers twined with hers as he pushed her hands back against the mattress. Her hips arched up, and he leaned over the bed to better push his cock into her core.

He kissed her when he thrust inside. Kissed her and loved the tight, slick feel of her sex around him. He drove into her, deep and steady, then withdrew. Again and again.

Then his thrusts became faster.

His control started to fracture. Marna could always break his control.

Her legs locked around his hips. Her tongue slipped over his lips.

His thrusts became harder.

Her hips arched against him, eager, and he pushed into her.

Deeper. Harder.

His mouth tore from hers, and he kissed his way down her neck. Down, on down, as she called out his name. When he came to that sweet spot where neck met shoulder, he licked her skin.

Panthers claimed their mates with a mark on this spot. He'd bitten her once, but this time—this time he knew what he was doing.

Forever.

His teeth scored her flesh. Her body stiffened beneath him, and, fuck, yes, she came around his cock.

Tanner exploded inside of her as his control shattered. He didn't whisper her name. He roared it.

And he held on to her, thrusting deep as he climaxed into her body. The end hadn't come for them. This . . . this was their beginning.

His heart drummed wildly in his ears. So fast. But he wasn't sated. Not close. He wanted her again and again, and he'd have her.

But for now, he lifted his body off hers. He stared down into her eyes, and told her, "I love you."

More than life. More than enough to beat death.

She gave him a smile, one sweet and sexy at the same time, and she rolled away from him.

That was when his heart stopped. Her hair slid off her back and revealed the scars that crossed her shoulders.

But they weren't scars any longer.

When they'd made love before, back at that cabin in the swamp, the scars had felt rougher beneath his fingertips. Hell yes, he'd noticed that, but he hadn't thought much of it. He'd been too busy catching a killer. He'd forgotten the scars.

Until now.

Guard what you want the most.

Carefully, his fingers touched what *should* have been red scars. She gasped beneath his touch. The sound was filled with pleasure, not pain.

Wings are the most sensitive part of an angel's body.

But her wings had been cut away. She'd lost them. Become trapped on earth with him.

She couldn't go back to heaven because she didn't have her wings.

His fingers slid gently over her back.

Only he was touching silken wings that were growing from her shoulders. Her wings might have been cut away, but they were *growing back.*

If her wings were coming back, then that meant she'd be going back to heaven. Angels didn't stay on earth. Only the Fallen did, and Marna had never truly fallen.

It was time for her to go back home.

Chapter Twenty

When Marna woke, it was dark. No sunlight streamed through the windows anymore, and the room was lit only by the faint glow from the stars and the moon.

She was in Tanner's bed, with his arms around her. They'd made love twice—three times?—that day. She'd fallen asleep with his name on her lips and now she'd just awoken to—

The feel of his lips on her back. Pressing lightly against the blade of her left shoulder. The spot where her wings had once been. The touch of his mouth against that sensitive flesh had her whole body tensing. Her nipples were hard. Her legs restless. Just that touch . . .

Because the touch of his mouth sent pleasure streaking through her. Stronger than before. He'd kissed the scars another time, but it hadn't been like this.

Her breath heaved out. Marna didn't move. She wanted him to keep kissing her. Her sex was wet, her body tight.

He licked her flesh. She bit her lip to keep from crying out. *So good.* It had hurt so badly when she lost her wings, but this . . . *pleasure.*

Tanner had taught her so much about pleasure.

His lips whispered over her again. "I'm gonna fucking miss you."

He was going to—wait, what? Marna stiffened and tried to turn and face him, but he held her still in a grip far too strong. Shifter strong.

"When you go back, remember me, okay?"

She wasn't going anyplace.

"Should have known I couldn't keep you with me. Too good for me . . ." His breath rasped against her skin. His fingers skimmed over her flesh, and she shivered. *"Remember me."*

"I could never forget you." What was he even talking about? "And I'm not going anywhere."

"Yes." Sad. "You are."

Another kiss on her flesh. Another caress that sent a shudder of pleasure through her. Then he said, "Your wings are growing back."

Her world seemed to stop. No, maybe that was just her heart. "That's not funny, Tanner." The shifter should know better than to joke about something like that. Angry—no, furious—she ripped away from him and rolled from the bed. "I *lost* my wings. They won't ever grow back. They—"

"Would you go back to heaven, if you had the chance?" His face was tense, but his eyes were blank, showing no emotion.

Go back to heaven? Marna hesitated. *No fear. No pain.*

"Right." Tanner climbed from the bed. Jerked on his jeans. Turned so that she could only see his back and the scars that crisscrossed his flesh in a painful reminder of all that he'd suffered.

"Angels don't lie." He said the words without looking at her. "Shifters, though, we were born to deceive. Born to be beasts who hide beneath the guise of men." His shoulders were strong and straight. "But I never lied to you."

No, he hadn't. From the very beginning, he'd always told her the truth. Always been there, trying to help her.

Was it any wonder she loved him? *Love.* She finally knew what the humans talked about. No wonder it made them crazy. It was wonderful. Consuming. Addictive.

Terrifying.

"I'm not lying to you now." Tanner still wasn't looking at her. "Your wings are back. They're growing slowly, but they *are* growing. Small, silken, pure white and—"

And she was across the room in an instant. Marna grabbed his arms and yanked him around to face her. "Angels of death don't have white wings." Their wings were touched by the darkness and despair of their work, so death angels and punishment angels always had black wings.

He blinked at her. "But I saw them. You're growing white wings."

Marna whirled away from him and raced for the bathroom. She flipped on the light and twisted as she strained to see her body in the mirror. *He has to be wrong. He has to be wrong. He has to—*

But she had wings growing from her back. White wings. Her hands gripped the marble countertop so tightly she almost ripped it from the wall. "How?"

Tanner had followed her. He stared at her with eyes that seemed so empty. Cold. Not like Tanner. Not like him at all.

"Wings don't grow back." She shook her head. The words tumbled from her as she said, "Not after a fall. All the angels know—"

"You didn't fall." Said simply. Sadly. "A shifter tried to force you to earth. He hurt you. But now, you're healing."

Healing. The breath in her lungs seemed to burn. Her gaze lifted and locked on his. "You did this."

Tanner shook his head.

She grabbed his hands. She was still naked. So what? He'd seen her naked plenty of times and would do so again. "*You* did this," she said again as the puzzle pieces slipped into place. When her scars had been itching, she'd been healing.

Because *he'd* healed her. "When you brought me back . . ." Maybe even when he'd kissed her scars that first time? Was it possible? *It must be.* "You healed my wounds." All of them. He'd given her his power, and he'd healed the flesh that had been clawed open—and the wings that had been savaged.

He'd given an angel back her wings.

Marna laughed and threw her arms around Tanner.

But he didn't hug her back. Didn't so much as move. A chill skated down her spine. "Tanner?" She pulled back to look at him. "What's wrong?"

His smile was bittersweet. "I'll miss you."

But she wasn't—

A wind swept through the house, ripping through the bedroom and rushing into the bathroom. The wind grabbed at Marna and pulled at her body. She waved her hands as she conjured clothes and tried to fight the force of the wind.

It was pulling her away from Tanner.

The wind felt like hands on her skin. Not rough. But steady, strong.

Tanner watched her. The wind tossed his hair, but didn't move him.

Then Marna was back in the bedroom. The big window was wide open, letting in that rush of wind, and the angel that came in with wings of white.

Carmella.

Marna recognized the angel instantly. How could she not know her? Carmella—with her light brown skin and jet-black hair that trailed down her back—was the leader of the guardian angels. She'd been protecting mortals for as long as death angels like Sammael and Bastion had been taking their souls.

"It's time to come home with me," Carmella told her, the angel's voice soft, almost sweet. She lifted her hand. "We've been hoping you would join us."

Marna shook her head. "I'm . . . not a guardian."

"You are now." Carmella's gaze drifted over Marna's shoulder. To Tanner. "Your fate changed."

And she understood. *He'd* changed her fate. An angel's wings weren't supposed to grow back, but Tanner . . . he wasn't just a shifter.

Healer.

She turned away from Carmella and walked to stand right in front of Tanner. She could feel the small growth of wings now. Not itching so much anymore, not since the wings had broken through the skin. "You really did this." With that light of his. When he'd healed her other wounds, he'd given her back her wings, too.

But it was Carmella who spoke. "Your wings didn't burn away, Marna," the guardian told her. Carmella's voice was so easy and gentle, but without any emotion. "The burn is forever, but your injuries . . . even if your shifter hadn't sped up the healing process, your wings would have returned to you eventually."

Your shifter. "But would they have been black?" And would she have gone back to taking souls?

"You *earned* the title of guardian," Carmella told her. "Because of what you did here on earth. You guarded those closest to you."

Marna stared into Tanner's eyes, and realized, too late, the words that Sammael had spoken hadn't been for Tanner. They'd been for her.

Guard what you want the most.

He'd known that the Death Touch hadn't come back to her because she wasn't a death angel any longer.

She'd always wanted this. To be close to the humans. To be able to see them while they were happy, *alive,* and not on the brink of death. But . . .

But she wanted more now. Not just to see emotion. She reached for Tanner's hand. He was staring down at her, but his gaze was blank.

"It's time for us to go," Carmella said.

"Just like that?" Marna whispered. After all the months she'd been down here, *now* the angel appeared to whisk her away? "Why didn't you come sooner?" Marna didn't look away from Tanner. He'd been there the whole time. He'd been the one guarding her.

"Because the battle wasn't mine to fight." Carmella's sweet voice was starting to annoy her. It was that whole lack of emotion. Would a little bit of passion really kill an angel? "It was yours, and the end result—that result determined your fate."

Her fate? Marna's chest had begun to feel hollow. "I was supposed to die."

"Or become a guardian."

Why wasn't Tanner talking? *"Say something,"* she gritted, angry. "Talk to me!"

His eyelids flickered. "I'll miss you." Growled. He'd said that before. Each time he said those words, she felt as if he was ripping into her soul.

And, what? That was all he had to tell her? He'd *miss* her? How about . . . *"Baby, don't go. My heart will be torn out if you leave me"?* Couldn't he just growl those words instead?

Because if she left him, that's how she'd feel. The wings didn't matter. Nothing mattered but being with him.

Well, he could stand there, look all stoic and strong, and act like this was the big dramatic end for them, but she wasn't playing that game. "I'm not going anywhere."

Now *that* got his attention. His eyes widened and suddenly, his hands were gripping hers hard enough to bruise. Good thing she wasn't human. He might have just accidentally snapped some of her bones if she had been.

"You'd choose me?" He shook his head. Looked stunned and thrilled and hopeful all at once. "But . . . with your wings, you can have everything you ever wanted. You can have your life back."

"I don't want that life back." It had been so cold and

empty. And she didn't want to be a guardian—just watching life pass. She wanted to keep living and loving. "I want what I have with you." Didn't he understand? "Tanner, I meant what I said. I love you."

Love. Not just a human emotion. Shifters loved. Vampires loved.

So did angels.

Now only hope lit his face. His lips curved in a smile that took her breath.

"I'm sorry, Marna," Carmella said, voice still soft. "But that isn't how this works."

In a blink, Marna found herself across the room and at the angel's side. Tanner stared at them in confusion for an instant; then he lunged toward them. *"Marna!"*

Wind ripped through the room and tossed him back against the wall. The same wind seemed to grab Marna and lift her up. Up and toward the open window.

"Marna!" Tanner was fighting against the wind, roaring his fury and slashing out with his growing claws as he tried to reach her.

And Marna fought. She kicked and clawed with her own hands against the unseen force that lifted her higher and higher. She didn't want to leave. She belonged on earth, with Tanner. This was her life. She wouldn't go back to that cold, emotionless existence. Not now.

The wind beat faster. Tanner was fading from sight. She was losing him, and the last thing she heard him say was, *"Stay with me! I love you, Marna. Stay. With. Me!"*

But fate had other plans. Fate ripped her away and lifted her so high that she couldn't even hear his roar anymore.

The wind died away, slowly freeing him from its unbreakable grip. Tanner hit the floor when the last of that powerful blast faded, but he was on his feet a mere second later. He raced for the window. His claws sliced into the wall. *"Marna!"*

She wasn't outside. Not on the ground. Not above him where the angel had been.

She was just . . . gone.

The beast inside was snarling with fury. Wild and desperate, he seemed to be clawing Tanner apart from the inside out.

Marna hadn't wanted to leave him. *I love you.* Her words echoed in his head. She'd been so beautiful when she said them. Eyes clear. Face lit with happiness. She'd been choosing *him*.

And then she'd been taken away.

He leapt through that window and landed on the ground. His bones were already popping and snapping. The panther wasn't being held back on a leash this time. He was free, and he was pissed.

As pissed as the man.

No one took his mate. Marna had been afraid. She'd been fighting.

She wants me.

And he'd kill to get her back.

His feet raced over the earth. He had Marna's scent. He'd track her, find her, fucking break down the door to heaven if he had to, but he was getting her back.

Heaven couldn't take her, and if the angels thought they were finished with him, then they'd better think again.

The panther threw back his head and screamed his fury to the night.

Heaven was as perfect as the humans thought. The floors were lined with gold. The walls made of heavy, white marble. Everything was clean and glistening. No darkness. No evil.

The world below was full of that darkness. So much evil and hate.

"Why would you even want to go back?" Carmella asked, but her voice held no curiosity. Why would it?

"Because I love him." So simple. Why couldn't Carmella see that? Marna turned away from her and marched toward the elaborate doors that sealed the room. Those were made of gold, too. Heavy gold that wouldn't move beneath her touch.

Carmella followed her. "For him . . . for one doomed shifter, you'd trade all that heaven can offer?"

Now Marna stiffened. The doors weren't budging, and little Ms. Sunshine there needed to watch herself. Marna turned on her heel and eyed the angel. "Tanner isn't doomed."

But Carmella nodded. "I'm afraid he is. I've watched him. I know what he's done. All the lives he's taken." Carmella seemed to glide toward her. The angel's voice dropped as she said, "He's evil, you see."

"No," Marna snapped right back, "he's not."

Carmella blinked. Was that surprise on her face? "How can you not know? You were with him. You had to sense the darkness he carries."

"Yes, well . . ." She had. "There's more to life than a little darkness, okay? People can do some very, very bad things, but still be capable of good, too." That was the beauty of life. You could find goodness even in . . .

Well, even in hell on earth.

She squared her shoulders. "Tanner isn't doomed. He has me." And she'd watch out for him. Just not from a perch on some fluffy white cloud.

Guard what you want the most. "I'll guard him," she said, nodding because this was a duty she'd gladly accept, "but I'll do it from his side."

Carmella's eyes widened the smallest bit. "You know what you're saying . . . ?"

"I'm saying I want to go back to him."

The angel shook her head. "It doesn't work like that." Her white wings skimmed over the golden floor. "To go to earth, to *stay* down there with him, do you know what you have to do?"

Marna's gut was tight with fear and dread because, yes, she knew. All angels knew. If you wanted to live with the humans below—or even with a certain sexy shifter—then first you had to kiss your heavenly life good-bye.

You had to fall. "I lost my wings once." These white wings were so new, she'd barely grown used to the whispery feel of them. "I can lose them again." She'd survive. No, she'd do more than survive.

She'd be happy.

But first . . . Marna swallowed and realized Carmella was looking at her with emotion now. Finally. And in that stare, Marna saw pity.

"How can you give up so much for one man?"

"It's not just for him. It's for me." For the life she would have. A child. Memories. Laughter. Passion. Now she understood what Bastion had meant. The fall wasn't just about Tanner. *For me.*

"You'll burn for it," Carmella warned her.

Her chin lifted. "Yes, I will."

The heavy doors swept open. Her choice had been heard. The howl of the wind filled her ears. Marna closed her eyes as the wind lifted her body. She hoped she didn't scream. Hoped she could hold back the cries.

But then she started to fall and the fire came at her . . .

Tanner. It was his name that she screamed.

The panther leapt through the window, sending shards of glass flying into the interior of the antebellum home. Not a home in construction like his—one that blazed with glory and wealth. Snarls and roars escaped Tanner as he charged for the stairs—and for the man who was already racing toward him.

"Are you insane?" Sammael demanded, glaring at him and stopping short in the middle of the stairs. "Or do you just have a death wish?"

The panther roared again.

Sam's mate, the blonde with the eyes that saw too much, rushed up behind him.

Tanner had hunted through the city. Gone into the swamps. Searched every place he could think of, but he hadn't been able to find Marna. Her scent had faded. She'd just vanished from the face of the earth.

Gone to heaven.

"Shouldn't an angel be with him?" the blonde asked, peering over Sam's shoulder. "I mean, there's something missing from this picture, right?"

Tanner snarled.

Sam sent a bolt of fire at him and singed his fur. "You *don't* snarl at her."

Fine. He'd just take off the Fallen's head. The panther charged at Sam.

"He's hurting," the woman said, sounding sad.

Sam lifted his hands, not to attack Tanner, but to ward him off. "Easy, beast. I don't want a war with you."

The panther's claws dug into the gleaming hardwood.

Sam winced at the damage, then sighed. "She's gone, isn't she?"

And because he couldn't speak as a panther, Tanner let the shift sweep through him, fast, brutal. He didn't even feel a whisper of pain. Too much fury rode him. He kept his claws out even as his body became that of a man again, just in case he needed to behead a Fallen.

Tanner would *make* Sam help him. "Her wings grew back."

"Impossible." From Seline.

But Sam nodded. "I thought your healing magic might work on her."

And he hadn't bothered to pass along that little bit of info? Tanner jumped up and hit him in the jaw. The blow would have shattered a human's jaw, but Sam just lifted a brow. "Feel better?" the Fallen asked him.

Hell, no. He wouldn't feel better until he had Marna back.

"And, damn, man, put some clothes on." Sam waved his hand and conjured a pair of jeans on Tanner's body. "Or are you trying to make me go blind?"

The Fallen was an asshole. Tanner lifted his claws. "You knew I'd lose her."

Sam didn't back down. "I knew Marna would have a choice. She didn't fall, not technically, so she could go back, as long as she had her lovely black wings."

"Her wings were white," Tanner growled out. "The ones growing back were white."

"Interesting." A little shrug. "But then, I never thought she belonged to the death angels." He caught the woman's hand. *Seline, that was her name.* Sam pressed a kiss to her palm. "Maybe she'll get to guard you. It seems as if she's earned someone's favor, so perhaps your angel will be by your side."

Sam brushed by him and left Tanner standing on the staircase, just feet from Seline.

"If she's my guardian . . ." Tanner cleared his throat, almost afraid to hope. "Will I see her again?" *Get to touch her? Hold her?*

"Guardians aren't meant to be seen," Seline told him quietly, voice even sadder now.

"And never meant to be touched," Sam said, his voice rising from below them. He was staring out of the shattered window. His gaze was on the darkness that waited beyond the house.

Tanner's breath heaved out. So she could come back, but still be forever beyond his reach? That sucked.

"She could fall for you." Seline's voice again. Her words had him stiffening because, hell no, he didn't want her falling.

"If she falls"—Tanner knew his voice sounded too hard, too rough—"then she burns." He'd never want that agony for her. She wanted her wings.

"Yes." Seline stared at him.

"It's the only way," Sam said. "If you want her back here with you, then she has to fall. She has to choose to come back."

While he stayed there, helpless? She would have to suffer?

"Does she love you enough to burn for you?" Sam turned slowly to face him. Tanner could see the shadows of the Fallen's wings. As dark as the night behind him.

Sam's gaze drifted slowly to Seline, and Tanner knew the woman had suffered the fire for Sam. She'd burned for the Fallen she loved so much.

Did Marna love him that completely?

"I don't want to know," Tanner said, and he forced his feet to move. His chest ached, not from the shift, but from the giant freaking hole where his heart had been.

Gone. Marna was gone, and he didn't want her to suffer in order to come back to him.

He stopped, his bare feet crunching the glass beneath him, courtesy of the window he'd shattered on his way in. "How does a shifter make it to heaven?" He'd suffer. He'd take the pain, whatever it was.

"Even when you die, you won't see her." Was Sam just trying to piss him off? "The carried souls have a different paradise waiting. You won't be with the guardians."

So he was *never* going to see her again? *Never?*

That hole just burned hotter.

"Tanner!"

His head yanked up. That had been Marna's voice. She'd been scared, hurting, screaming.

Only . . . Sam looked like he hadn't heard a thing. The guy was just staring at him. Pity was in his eyes again.

Tanner shoved the Fallen out of his way and pushed through that broken window. "She's calling me!" Maybe no one else had heard it, but they didn't have the ears of a shifter. He *knew* that she was out there. Not in heaven. Not watching over him, but *out there,* on earth, needing him.

He'd find her.

Hope began to fill that hole in his chest.

"I'm guessing you just heard her scream. Huh, that happened fast," Sam muttered. "When we fall, the fire always makes us scream. A thousand times hotter than anything here on earth, no angel can stand that pain." Sam's words iced his blood.

A shard of glass cut into Tanner's arm as he looked over at the Fallen.

Sam shrugged. "I guess she does love you that much."

She was in pain because she was *burning* for him?

Sam's hand closed over his arm. "You should know . . . after the fall, things will be different."

He didn't care about different. Marna was falling. Her scream echoed in his ears, and he needed to *find* her.

"Most angels don't remember who they are right after they fall." Sam's voice was bleak.

"I didn't remember for months," Seline said as she came to the bottom of the stairs.

Sam stared straight at him. He was getting damn tired of the pity in the guy's eyes. "When you find her, you'll be a stranger to her. That's just the way the fall works."

Stranger or not, that didn't matter. The only thing that mattered was *getting* to her. Making sure that she was safe. That she wasn't alone.

He didn't want her to open her eyes and have no memory of her life—*of him*—and to be afraid.

Tanner shook off Sam's hold and rushed back into the night.

He *would* find her.

"Follow the scent of ash," Sam yelled after him. "You're already a lucky bastard, you *heard* her scream! You know she's close."

Tanner kept running.

"I didn't know." Sam's voice was lower now, fading in the distance. "I had to hunt for my angel."

And Tanner would hunt for his. Hunt until he found her and had her back in his arms.

Then he'd never let her go again.

He found her at dawn, just as the darkness was fading away. She was walking along a dirt road, near the edge of a swamp. She was naked, and long, angry burn marks crossed her back. Marna moved slowly, her head down, one foot in front of the other.

"Marna!" He yelled her name and rushed toward her. Most of his hunting had been done in panther form, but when he'd finally caught her scent—ash and innocence—he'd shifted back to the body of a man. He'd stolen some clothes, and raced after her.

He hadn't wanted her to see him as a beast. Not this first time. She'd be scared enough as it was.

Marna turned toward him. And just stared blankly. Not with fear or love. With no recognition.

Then she turned away and kept walking.

No. *No.* Tanner ran after her, grabbed her in his arms, and held her tight. "You aren't alone." She'd never be alone again.

Marna began to struggle in his arms. He held her tighter,

being careful not to touch the wounds on her back. "It's *me.*"

She kicked against him. Clawed with her small nails.

Tears trickled down her cheeks. She broke his heart.

"I can fix this," he promised her. She had to be hurting. Those wounds on her back . . . he'd heal them. Heal her.

Heal her.

That was it. Sam had said that the angels needed time to heal after their fall. He could heal Marna right now. She wouldn't need any time. He could take away all of her pain.

He *would* take it away.

His fingers hovered over her wounds. The power began to bleed through his skin and pulse through his body. He pushed that power at her, and Marna stopped struggling.

She gasped and her eyes—so blue—widened.

"My name's Tanner Chance." His voice was ragged as the healing energy drained from him and slid into her body. "And I'd die for you."

Her eyes held his.

"I love you," he told her as he gave her all the power he had, "and by some freaking miracle, you love me, too." Enough to fall.

Her breathing had steadied. The paleness in her cheeks wasn't so stark. He kept pushing his magic and energy into her. "Remember me."

She shook her head.

"Remember." And he pressed his lips against hers. His hands were on her back now, hovering over the slashes there. Carefully, he put his fingertips on her. As he touched her, the skin scarred over, the blisters and burns fading, as her flesh healed—as much as it could, anyway.

Her lips were closed, but so soft and silken beneath his. He kept kissing her. She had to remember him. Pain and pleasure. Fire and life. Hope.

Love.

"Please." He breathed the ragged rasp against her lips. He was as close to breaking as he'd ever been in his whole life. "Just remember . . . me."

Her lips parted. Her tongue snaked out. Touched his. Tentative. So uncertain. He forced himself to stay controlled. To kiss her gently when—

She pulled away from him. Marna's eyes searched his. "How many times . . . ?" Her voice was weak, as if she'd broken it. When she had been falling? And screaming for him?

I'm here.

"How many times . . . " she whispered again, "do I have to tell you . . . I want to stay . . . with you?"

His heart almost jumped right from his chest.

Marna smiled up at him. Stared at him with eyes that *knew* and said, "I . . . know you. I . . . love . . . you."

Tanner's control snapped, and he pulled her as close as he could get her. His mouth took hers, wild, hot, desperate.

He'd found the one woman in this world who could make him whole. Who could make him be more than just a monster.

She'd chosen him over heaven. Brought him out of hell.

And he'd spend the rest of his days making sure she never suffered again. No more fire. No more pain.

Only pleasure. Love.

Life.

"You gave it up," he whispered against her mouth as he lifted her into his arms. "You came back to me."

Her arms wound around his neck. "I wasn't letting you . . . get away." Her voice was weak, but growing stronger. Just as she was. "Someone told me . . . guard what I want . . . the most."

She was the only thing he wanted. He'd take her back to his home. Their home. He'd get her in bed, and he'd kiss every inch of her body and make absolutely sure this wasn't just some desperate dream.

"For the rest of my days, I'll be . . . guarding you," Marna told him, her lips curving in a faint smile. "I don't need to . . . have my wings . . . to be your guardian."

A killer shifter, with a guardian angel always by his side? Maybe fate was playing a game of makeup with him. Whatever was happening, that plan sure sounded fine to Tanner. Damn fine.

An angel and a shifter together forever. Hell, yes. He kissed her again. Curled his body over hers.

And knew that even heaven couldn't be any better than this.

Nothing could ever be better than holding his angel tight in his arms.

Together, forever.

He'd found his paradise.

Turn the page for a sneak peek at Cynthia Eden's BURN FOR ME, Book One in the new Phoenix Shifter series, coming in February 2014!

Subject Thirteen was staring right at her. A small shiver slid over Eve's body. His eyes were dark, they looked almost black—as black as the thick hair that hung a little too long as it brushed over his broad shoulders. Thirteen was a handsome man, strong, muscled—*definitely muscled*—and with the sculpted bone structure that had probably caught plenty of attention from the ladies.

High cheeks. Square jaw. Lips that were hard, a little thin, but still sexy. Sexy, though she could have sworn that mouth held a cruel curve.

Her heartbeat began to pound faster because Thirteen's eyes . . . they were sweeping over her body. A slow, deliberate glance. "Can he—can he see through the mirror?" His gaze felt like a hot touch on her skin.

"Of course not," was Dr. Wyatt's instant response. The doc sounded annoyed with her.

Her shoulders relaxed.

Subject Thirteen smiled.

Damn. Her shoulders tensed right back up again.

Wyatt checked his notes and then told her, "Go check his vitals before we begin the procedure for today."

Right. Vitals check. Her job. Eve nodded. She'd done two years of med school before realizing the gig wasn't for her, so she could pass muster with these guys, no problem. Only part of her resume was faked.

The good part.

Eve walked slowly toward the metal door that was the only entrance and exit to Thirteen's holding room. A guard opened the door for her. An armed guard. Which brought up the next question. *Why did volunteers have to be guarded?*

Oh, jeez, but this place was creeping her out. *Volunteers, my ass.*

Sure, she'd seen a couple of other subjects during her time at the Genesis facility. Not many, though. Her clearance wasn't high enough to get her past level one. Or it hadn't been . . . until today.

Until she'd been told that Dr. Wyatt needed her services for his latest experiment. Dr. Richard Wyatt *was* Genesis. A former kid genius, the guy had a couple of fists full of degrees, and, currently, Wyatt was the leading expert in the field of paranormal genetics.

He was also a hard-ass who gave her the creeps when his cold green eyes locked on her. Sure, maybe he was a fairly attractive guy, but something about him made her blood ice.

The guard waved his hand, indicating that it was clear for Eve to proceed. When she walked into Thirteen's holding room, Eve saw the slight flare of the man's nostrils. Then his head turned toward her, slowly, the move almost like a snake's as he sized her up.

He didn't speak, but his powerful hands clenched.

Eve opened her small, black bag. "Hello." Her voice came out too high-pitched. She drew in a steadying breath. The guy was chained. It wasn't like anything could happen to her right then. She needed to get a grip and do her job. "I'm just here to run a few quick checks on you." No machines were hooked up to him. No monitors. Wyatt wanted these checks done the old-fashioned way—hell if she knew why.

Eve pulled out her stethoscope and stopped just a foot away from Thirteen. "I-I'll need to listen to your heartbeat."

Still nothing. Okay. Eve swallowed and offered a weak smile. Obviously, she wasn't dealing with a chatty fellow.

Eve slid closer to him. Her gaze darted to the chains. They held his arms trapped at his sides. Even if he'd wanted to grab her—*don't grab me, don't!*—he couldn't move.

What if Wyatt was setting her up? The guy was chained and that had to mean he was dangerous, right? Those were some seriously thick chains. They looked like something right out of a medieval torture chamber.

"I won't hurt you."

She jumped at the sound of his voice, and what a dark, rumbling voice it was. If the big, bad wolf from that old fairy tale had been able to talk, Eve bet the beast would have sounded just like Subject Thirteen.

She exhaled and hoped she didn't look rattled. "I didn't think you would."

His lips twisted in the faintest of smiles that called her a liar.

Eve put the stethoscope over his heart. She adjusted the equipment, listened, and glanced up at him in surprise. "Is your heartbeat always this fast?" Grabbing his chart, she scanned through the notes. No, fast, but not *this* fast. Right then, his heart was galloping like a racehorse.

Eve put her hand against his forehead and hissed out a breath. The guy was hot. Not warm, not feverish, *hot.*

And she was now so close to him that her breasts brushed his arm.

Subject Thirteen's heartbeat grew even faster.

Oh . . . just . . . *oh.* Hell. She hurried back a bit.

"I need to draw a sample of your blood." She also wanted to take his temperature because the guy had to be scorching. Just what was he? Not a vampire, those guys could never heat up this much. A shifter? Maybe. She'd seen one of those subjects on her first day. But the shifter had been in a cozy dorm-type room.

He hadn't been shackled.

Eve put up the stethoscope and reached for a needle. She eased closer to Thirteen once more and rose onto her toes. The guy was big, at least six three, maybe six four, so she couldn't quite reach his ear as she whispered, "Are you here willingly?"

Eve began to draw his blood. Thirteen didn't even flinch as the needle slid into his arm.

But he did give a small, negative shake of his head.

Shit. She eased back down and tried to figure out just how she could help him.

"I'm Eve." She licked her lips. His gaze followed the movement. The darkness in his stare seemed to heat. Everything about the guy was hot. "I-I can help you."

He laughed then, and the sound chilled her. "No," he said in that deep rumble of a voice, "you can't."

Eve realized she was standing between his legs. His unsecured legs. His thighs brushed against hers, and Eve flinched.

The smile on his face was as cold as his laughter. She'd been correct before when she thought she saw a cruel edge to his lips. She could see that hardness right then. "You should be afraid," he told her.

Yes, she was definitely getting that clue.

Eve pulled out the needle. Swabbed some alcohol over a wound she couldn't even see.

Then she stepped back, as quickly as she could.

"Don't come back in here," he told her, eyes narrowing. A warning.

Or a threat?

Eve turned away.

"You smell like fucking candy..."

She stilled. Now her heartbeat was the one racing too fast.

"You make me . . ." His voice dropped, but she caught the ragged growl of "hungry."

And he made her afraid. Eve slammed her hand onto the metal door. "Guard!" Her own voice was too high. "We're done!"

The door opened and she all but fell out of the room. Even though she was afraid, Eve risked one last look back. Thirteen was staring after her, his jaw locked tight. He did look hungry. Only not for food.

For me.